Sweetgrass

New York Times bestselling author Mary Alice Monroe lives in South Carolina, where she is currently working on her next novel.

Also by **Mary Alice Monroe**

SWEETGRASS
(previously published in the UK as *The Secrets We Keep*)

THE BEACH HOUSE

SKYWARD

THE FOUR SEASONS

THE BOOK CLUB

GIRL IN THE MIRROR

Sweetgrass

MARY ALICE MONROE

MIRA

Published in Great Britain 2012
MIRA Books, an imprint of Harlequin (UK) Limited,
Eton House, 18-24 Paradise Road,
Richmond, Surrey, TW9 1SR

ISBN 978 1 848 45138 4

60-0812

MIRA's policy is to use papers that are natural, renewable and recyclable products and made from wood grown in sustainable forests. The logging and manufacturing processes conform to the legal environmental regulations of the country of origin.

Printed and bound by
CPI Group (UK) Ltd, Croydon, CR0 4YY

For my family—
Markus, Margaretta, Zachary,
Claire, John, and Jack.

And time has come now, child,
for you to learn the knot that ties us all together—
The circle unbroken,
And when your fingers talk just right
that circle will go out and out again—
past slavery and freedom, old ways and new,
and your basket will hold the past—
Just as surely and tightly
as my arms now hold and circle you.
                              —Margot Theis Raven,
                              Circle Unbroken

1

"Until fairly recently, the coastal region of islands, marshes, placid rivers and oak-shaded roads had seen relatively little change— but now change is widespread, often overwhelming and sometimes devastating."

—The National Trust for Historic Preservation

MARCH IS A MOODY TIME of year in the Lowcountry. On any given day, seemingly by whim, the weather is balmy and sweet-smelling and can lure reluctant smiles from the hopeful who dream of cool, tart drinks on steamy afternoons, creamy white magnolia blossoms and scented offshore breezes. Then overnight, everything can change. With a sudden gust of cold wind, winter will reach out with its icy grip to draw a foggy curtain over the gray marsh.

Mama June Blakely had hoped for an early spring, but she was well seasoned and had learned to keep an eye on the sky for dark clouds. A leaden mist hovered close to the water, so thick that Mama June could barely make out Blakely's Bluff, which stretched out into the gray-green Atlantic Ocean like a defiant fist. A bittersweet smile eased across her lips. She'd always thought it a fitting symbol of her family's turbulent history with the sea.

Perched high on the bluff was a weather-beaten house that had been in the Blakely family for generations. Bluff House had withstood countless hurricanes and storms to remain the bastion of family gatherings long after most of the old Charleston family's land holdings were sold off. Each time Mama June looked at the battered house, waves of memories crashed against her stony composure. And when the wind gusted across the marshes, as it did now, she thought the mist swirled like ghosts dancing on the tips of cordgrass.

Thunder rumbled, low and threatening. She tugged her sweater closer to her neck and shifted her gaze to the lowering skies. Weather moved quickly over the South Carolina coastline, and a front like that could bring a quick cloudburst and sudden winds. Worry tugged at her mouth as she turned on her heel and made her way across the polished floors of her home, through the large, airy kitchen, the stocked butler's pantry, the formal dining room with glistening crystal and mirrors, the front parlor appointed with ancestral furniture and straight out to the front veranda. Gripping the porch railing, she leaned far forward, squinting as she searched the length of ancient roadbed bordered by centuries-old oaks.

Her frown lifted when she spotted a broad, snowy-headed figure walking up the drive, a lanky black dog at his heels. Mama June leaned against the porch pillar, sighing in relief. At that pace, she figured Preston would beat the storm. How many years had she watched and waited for her husband to come in from the fields? Goodness, could it really be nearing fifty years?

Preston Blakely wasn't a large man physically, but his manner and personality made him imposing to anyone who knew him. People called him formidable in polite company, bull-headed in familiar—and she couldn't argue. He was walking with a single-minded purpose, heels digging in the soft road-bed and arms swinging. His square chin jutted out, cutting the wind like the mast of a ship.

Lord, what bee was in that man's britches this time? she thought with a sorry shake of her head.

On reaching the house, Preston sent the dog to the back with a jerk of his index finger. "Go on, now. Settle, Blackjack," he ordered. Then, raising his head, he caught Mama June's gaze.

"Hellfire," he grumbled louder than the thunder, raising his arm and shaking a fistful of crumpled papers in the air. "They've gone and done it this time."

Mama June's hands tightened on the railing as her husband came up the porch stairs. "Done what?"

"They done got me by the short hairs," he said on reaching the porch.

"Who got you, dear?"

"The banks!" he roared. "The taxes. The whole cussed economy, that's who!"

"Sit down a spell, Press, before you pop a valve. Look at you. You're sweating under that slicker. It's too hot for such a fuss and, I swanny—" she waved her small hand in the air "—I don't know what you're talking about. Taxes and banks and short hairs…"

"I'm talking about this place!"

"There's no need to shout. I'm old, not deaf."

"Then listen to what I'm tellin' you, woman. We're going to lose it."

"What? Lose the land?"

"Yes, ma'am, the land," he said. "And this house you're so fond of. We'll lose it all."

"Press," she replied, striving for calm. "I don't understand any of this. How can we lose everything?"

Preston leaned against the railing and looked out over his land. A cool wind rippled the wild grasses like waves upon the ocean.

"Remember when we were reassessed a few months past?" When she nodded, he continued. "Well, here's what they say this property is worth now. And here's how much they say we've got to pay. Go on," he said, waving the papers before her. "Read it and weep."

Mama June reached out to retrieve the crumpled papers and gingerly unfolded them. Her mouth slipped open in a soft gasp. "But...this can't be right. It's three times as much as before."

"Four times as much."

"We can't afford that. We'll appeal. They can't force us to accept this."

"They can and they will."

"There are lots of folks round here that won't stand for it," Mama June said, hearing aloud the indignation she felt stirring in her breast. "This can't just be happening to us."

"That's true enough. It's happening all over. And there's nothing any of us can do. Folks keep coming from the north in a steady stream." He shrugged. "And they all want to live along the water for the beautiful views. Trouble is, there's only so much property to go around. So property values just keep climbing and developers, like my own sweet, avaricious sister, are licking their chomps just biding their time. They'll wrestle away any and every acre of earth so they can turn around and plow it over with cement." He raked his thick, short white hair with his fingers. "Hell, I knew it was coming—we all did. I reckon I just didn't think it would be so quick."

He gave a rueful smile. "Kinda like a hurricane, eh? Well," he said with resignation, "looks like we miscalculated on this one. Just like we did with Hugo."

"We've always managed to hang on before. Through the war, the gas crisis, the bad economy, even Hurricane Hugo."

"I know it. I've done my best—God knows I've fought the good fight. But I'm old now. And I'm worn out. I don't have it in me to fight them anymore."

Mama June stepped forward to rest her hand on his drooping shoulder, alarmed to her core to see her usual bear of a husband so defeated. She was about to offer some platitude, to say "don't worry, we'll be fine," when she felt his shoulders cord up again beneath her palms. He exploded in renewed fury.

"Maybe if that no-good son of ours had stayed home we wouldn't be in this mess."

Mama June dropped her hand and wrapped her arms around herself. "Let's don't start in on Morgan…"

"Don't you go defending him," he said, whirling around to face her. "Not to me! He's my son, dammit. He should be here, helping his father run this plantation. It's too much for one man. I need his ideas, his energy. Is it too much to ask my only son to take his father's place?"

"He needs to take his own place in the world," she countered softly, even as she felt herself harden against her husband. This was an all-too-familiar argument.

"The hell with the world! It's Sweetgrass that needs him. It's his duty. His heritage! A Blakely has run Sweetgrass Plantation for eight generations, and though there may only be a few hundred acres left, by God, Sweetgrass is still in Blakely hands."

"He's got his own land," she reminded him.

"His own land?" Preston's eyes widened with incredulity. "You mean those few measly acres in the wilds of Montana that he hides out in when he's not out breaking some laws?"

"Oh, for pity's sake. He's not doing any such thing. He's protesting!"

"And for what? To protect some bison? Hell," he said with a snort. "*Bison*... He grew up calling them buffalo like the rest of us."

"He's trying to protect them."

"He's playing around. He's not working that land. He's not working, period."

"Stop, Press." His angry words were shredding her composure like razors.

"Worthless," he muttered, ignoring her.

She turned and began walking away. "I can't listen to this...."

"What did I bother working for all these years?" he called after her. "That's what I want to know. I have no one to pass this all down to."

She stopped and faced him with a cold stare. "You have your daughter."

Preston scoffed and brushed away the suggestion with a sweep of his hand.

"You can't keep brushing Nan aside."

"Didn't she do just that to us when she sold off her land?"

"Her husband..."

"That weasel! He only married her for her land."

"What a thing to say!" She'd thought as much herself but had never granted it voice. "Lest you forget, I sold my land when I married you."

"That wasn't the same thing at all, and you know it."

"I know no such thing."

"See, there you go. You always take their sides over mine."

"I do no—"

"I'm your husband! *I* should be your first concern. For once! I've worked all these years like a bull in the harness to keep this land intact, to keep hold of this house with all those antiques you love so much."

"Don't even..."

"All of this." His arm swept out in a grand gesture. "I've sweated from dawn to dusk. I've spilled blood. I've given my heart and soul to this place. My dreams. My youth. And now…" He stopped, clamping his lips tight and looking out at the land with desperation shining moistly in his eyes. "And now it's gone."

"Good!" she replied with heart.

Preston spun around to look at her. "What'd you say?"

"You heard me. I said *good*. Good riddance!" she cried out with a strained voice. She saw the pale blue of his eyes swimming with pain and shock at her outburst. But rather than take it back or soften the words, as she ordinarily might have done, she felt years of anguish burst forth with a volcanic gush.

"All you think about is the loss of this *land!*" she cried, thrusting the papers into the paunch of his belly. "What about your family? What about that loss? You haven't spoken with your son in years. Your daughter feels like a pariah. They don't come around anymore. You've *driven* our children away. But you don't care about that, do you? You didn't fight to keep the family, did you? All you care about is this piece of earth. Well, it won't be long before we'll die and be buried on this precious land. But who will mourn our passing? I ask you, Preston, will our children weep when we're gone?"

His face went still before he swung his head away, averting his gaze.

She took a breath to gather her strength and stepped closer to her husband, narrowing the distance. Pounding her breast with her fist, emphasizing each word, she said in a voice betrayed by a shaky timbre, "This land has stolen my children from me. And that is a far greater loss to me. Good riddance, I say. I despise this land!"

"You don't mean that." Preston's voice was low and husky.

She took a long, sweeping glance at the landscape she'd

called home for close to five decades. The roiling line of clouds rolled overhead like the closing of a curtain. Then she met his gaze and held it.

"I surely do. From the day I first stepped foot on it, all this land ever brought me was utter and complete heartbreak."

They stood face-to-face, silently recollecting the wide swath of years cut low by that statement.

Around them the storm broke. Fat drops of rain splattered loudly on the dry ground in gaining crescendo. With each gust of wind the grasses swayed and shook, rattling like castanets. Then the sky opened up and the heavens cried. The roof provided no shelter from the torrents of rain, and both felt the lash of water that whipped through the air.

Mama June doubted the rain hid from Preston the tears coursing a trail down her cheeks. Yet he did not move to console her or offer any word of either argument or comfort. Her shoulders slumped and she retreated inside the house.

Preston stood rock still and watched her go. He was unmoving as he listened to his wife's tread on the stairs, knowing she made her way to her bedroom. She would likely cloister herself for hours, perhaps for the rest of the evening, shutting him out.

Same as always.

He wouldn't go after her, wouldn't try to talk things through lest the words dredged up the past. She couldn't handle that, and he didn't know if *he* could anymore, either. Besides, it wasn't worth the risk of her retreating to a place far more inaccessible than her bedroom.

He sighed heavily, her name slipping through his lips. "Mary June…"

He'd spoken harshly and was sorry for it. She was delicate when it came to matters of the family. He'd always tried to shelter her from bad news. But this… He squeezed the papers once more in his fist. *This* had hit too hard. He couldn't bear this alone. Hellfire, he'd needed someone to share this burden with, and who better than his wife? She *was* his wife, wasn't she?

He cast a final glance up toward her room, where she was crying, and knew a sudden pain, as if the lightning in the sky just shot through his heart.

"To hell with it!" he cried, drawing back his hand and throwing the cursed papers into the storm.

The wind caught the papers, hurtling them toward the marsh faster than a Cooper's hawk. They landed, tangled in the tall grasses, beaten by the rain. Lightning flashed in the blackening sky, and by the time he heard the rumble of thunder, he was in the house, reaching for the snifter of brandy.

The storm passed quickly on its march from the mainland to the sea. Now the air was fresh and the pastel pinks of the sunset had deepened to a rich ocher. Preston sat on the porch, his clothes damp and his skin cold, staring out at the purpling sky while the brandy did its work. Usually Mama June sat rocking beside him in a companionable silence. He felt her absence deeply.

"At least you're here, aren't you, boy?" he said, reaching down to pat the black Labrador retriever curled at his feet. Blackjack, who had sneaked back onto the porch the moment Mama June left, raised his dark, melting eyes and gazed at Preston with devotion while his tail thumped with affection. "Good ol' dog."

With a heavy sigh he turned his gaze back to the westward slide of the sun. In the years past, he used to relish these waning hours of the day, just rocking and watching the sun set over Sweetgrass, knowing that, at least for one more day, he'd kept the Blakely heritage intact. The plantation once consisted of 1300 acres, yet over the span of three hundred years, one thousand of those acres were sold off. He'd always felt it was his duty as the last remaining Blakely male to try to hold on to what was left so that a Blakely would always have a place to call home. Thinking about this used to bring him a bone-deep satisfaction.

Tonight, he felt no satisfaction in anything. Tonight, he felt that all his efforts had been in vain.

Mama June's words had cut him to the quick. They'd extinguished the flicker of hope he'd harbored deep in his heart that someday, in the not-too-distant future, his prodigal son would return. Though he'd told no one, night after night he'd see that dream in the hallucinatory hues of the sunsets. In that dream he would be just like that father in the Bible he'd read about. He'd see his son coming up the road and go running out of the house to greet him with outstretched arms. He'd call for a feast to be held, for music to be played, for riches to be shared—all to celebrate his beloved son's return home after years of fruitless wandering. In his dream he would smile at Mama June and quote, "My son was lost but now is found."

Preston's frown deepened. Tonight he couldn't see his dream in the shadows of the sunset. His rays of hope had extinguished along with the sinking sun, and all that was left was this cold, dark silence. He felt as if he were already dead and put in the earth. Mama June's words came back to him: *Will our children weep when we're gone?*

They would not, he concluded bitterly. Then he downed his drink.

Gripping the sides of the chair, he pulled himself out, tottering as a wave of dizziness swept over him. Too much brandy, he thought as he plodded across the porch. Inside, the warmth of the house enveloped him. Glancing up at the tall clock, he realized with surprise that he'd been sitting out on the porch for several hours. It was no wonder he was chilled to the bone. He moved closer to the staircase and cocked his ear, straining to hear sounds from Mama June's bedroom. All was quiet. She must have fallen asleep, he thought, resigned to the fact that he would not likely be getting a hot meal for dinner this night.

Truth was, he wasn't hungry, anyway. All that fighting and drinking made his gut feel off. Besides, he was feeling too restless to eat. He never could settle down after a quarrel with Mama June. Couldn't rest until they'd made peace. That woman had his soul in her hands and he wondered if she even knew it. Some days, it seemed that she hardly even knew he was here.

He felt his aloneness acutely tonight. It was thrumming in his brain with a pulselike rhythm. He removed his slicker, letting it lie on the back of a chair, and wandered restlessly. His damp feet dragged and his blurry eyes barely took in the rooms as he meandered. His mind was fixed on Mama June's words.

I despise this land!

Could she have really meant that?

From the day I first stepped foot on it, all this land ever brought me was utter and complete heartbreak.

For him, the day Mary June Clark first stepped her tiny foot on Sweetgrass land was forever etched in his mind. His boyish heart had never known such infatuation, and later, much later, that youthful adoration had matured into a man's utter and complete devotion.

He'd never heard her speak so plainly. She usually kept strong opinions to herself, never wanting to make another person feel uncomfortable. But those words…it was as if they had all bubbled up from some deep, dank well. Very deep, he thought with a grimace. What was it that Faulkner had said? *The past is never dead. It isn't even past.* It nearly broke his heart to think that his life's efforts had been for naught. No man could bear that.

During one circuit of the house he poured himself another drink. After another, he headed toward the small mahogany desk in the foyer and dug out Mama June's blue address book. His eyes struggled with the letters and he fumbled for his reading glasses, an indignity of old age to which he'd never become reconciled. After a brief search through her feathery script, he picked up the phone and dialed the number in Montana.

His heart beat hard in his chest as he waited. Steadying himself against the wall, he listened to the phone ring once, twice, then two more times. At last he heard a click and the dreaded pause of a machine.

Hi. This is Morgan. I can't come to the phone right now. Leave a brief message and I'll call you back.

Preston was unprepared for the impact of his son's voice after so many years of silence. He fumbled with the phone cord a moment, his tongue feeling unusually thick in his mouth. When the beep sounded he skipped a beat, then blurted, "Uh, Morgan, it's your dad. I, uh…" Preston felt a sudden confusion and struggled to put his thoughts to words. He gripped the phone tight while his heart pounded. "I called to…to talk to you. Anyway, I—" This was going badly. He had to end it. "Well, goodbye, son."

Preston's hands shook as he hung up the phone. He leaned against the desk, panting as if he'd just plowed the back forty. Damn, he was even sweating! What bad luck that on his first call in years he got some damned answering machine.

The sadness in his heart weighed heavily in his chest. He couldn't catch his breath and he felt as weak as a woman, barely able to bear his own weight. He pushed back from the desk, straightening, then felt again a surge of light-headedness, as if he might pass out. He staggered out to the porch, determined to let a few deep breaths of the cool ocean air balance him.

At the creak of the door Blackjack leapt from the cushioned settee and came trotting to his side, tail wagging.

"Back, boy," he mumbled, stumbling past him.

The dog whined and pressed his muzzle persistently against his leg.

"Back!" he cried, swinging his arm. He lost his balance and reached out in a panic, searching for something—anything—to hold on to. His eyesight went blurry, and with frightening suddenness, he was teetering in the darkness. The thrumming in his head became a brutal pounding, building in crescendo, louder and louder. He was going down. His arms reached out toward the house as he hit the floor and it felt as if the lightning struck in his brain this time, jolting him, seizing his muscles. Everything went white with blinding pain.

"Mary Ju—"

The white faded to black. Then all was still.

2

Sweetgrass (Muhlenbergia filipes) is an indigenous, long stemmed plant that grows in tufts along the coastal dunes from North Carolina to Texas. This native plant is fast disappearing from the landscape due to urbanization and development of coastal islands and marshland.

THE ENGINE OF THE PICKUP truck churned loudly as it idled before the ornate black wrought-iron gates. Atop the gate, fashioned in the same elaborate scroll, a single word was forged: *Sweetgrass.* The truck vibrated with the idling engine, but that was not the cause of the quake in Morgan Blakely's heart.

The truck door squeaked on its hinges as he pushed it open. A breeze of sweet-smelling air rushed into the stale compartment, awakening him from the lethargy of travel. With another push, his feet landed on Lowcountry soil for the first time in more than a decade. He rolled his shoulders, stiff under his denim jacket. Then, lifting his face to the moist, early morning air, he yawned wide and rubbed his face with callused palms. Forty some hours of hard driving sure could make a man's muscles ache, he thought. He still felt the miles rolling beneath his feet. No wonder. It had taken him 850 miles on I-90 just to get out of Montana.

He hadn't thought the Road Buzzard would make the journey, but the old Chevy limped along the roads like a dog finding its way home. Nope, they didn't build them like they used to, he thought, giving the battleship-gray truck a pat of respect. He'd bought it when he was twenty-one and, being young and proud, had pumped serious money into it, adding a hitch, a winch, a toolbox and liner and, of course, a powerful sound system. Back then, he had money burning a hole in his pocket, dreams of adventure blurring his vision and enough anger and rebellion in his gut to fuel his own manifest destiny. He'd roared down this same road full throttle and never looked back.

It had been a long, hard journey. Now, years later, his tires were worn and his speakers were blown. Before leaving Montana, he'd stuffed what little extra money he had into his wallet, enough to get him home.

Home. Morgan surveyed the impenetrable wall of bush and pines that surrounded the family property from the prying eyes of folks zooming along busy Highway 17. A ragged culvert ran along the road—like a moat around a castle, he thought, mulishly kicking the gravel. He walked off to open the heavy gates. A moment later, he drove into his family's estate.

The sunlight dappled the road as the truck crawled along. In the surrounding trees, birds and squirrels chattered at the dawn, and from the ground, a quail fluttered, squawking, into the air. At every turn, sights brought back memories he'd kept pushed back for a long while. He saw the crumbling ruins of the old smokehouse where, in colonial time, meat was preserved. Not far from it, near an underground stream of water, was the foundation of what was once a dairy. Milk and cheese used to be kept cold in the frigid waters. The spot had been a favorite play fort for the Blakely children.

Farther on by the western border lay a large peach orchard. Morgan frowned with worry at the sorry condition of the once meticulously maintained grounds. Beyond that lay the family graveyard. A little farther up the road, the trees opened to reveal a vast, cleared and mowed space that was used by the parish for Sunday picnics, oyster roasts, turkey shoots and other church functions.

He rounded a final, wide curve in the road. What he saw made him bring the truck to a stop. As the engine rumbled beneath him, he leaned forward on the steering wheel. The wave of homesickness surprised him.

Before him in the misty air of early morning was the long, formal avenue to his family home. Massive live oaks dripping lacy moss lined the narrow dirt road, sweeping low, like ancient sentries from a graceful time long gone. If the road's culvert was the moat of this kingdom, he thought, then these noble oaks surely were her knights.

At the end of the long avenue, the Southern colonial house awaited him like a charming belle—petite, pretty and eager to welcome him into her warmth. His father loved the house like a woman—its slender white columns, the sweeping Dutch gambrel roof and the delicately arched dormers framed with quaint squares of glass. The low foundation was made of brick and oyster-shell lime, meant to last.

And it had. The house had survived two hundred years of storms, wars, tragedies and the vagaries of fortune. She was a survivor. His father had fondly referred to the house as having "pluck."

Suddenly the front door swung open and a petite woman with hair as white as the house appeared on the threshold, clutching a pale-blue night robe close around her neck. Morgan swallowed hard with recognition. Why had he never noticed before how very much like the house his mother was? It dawned on Morgan that his father must have made that comparison many times, as well.

Morgan slowly rounded the circle, then stopped before the house. Blackjack bounded from the porch and scurried down the front stairs, tail straight up and barking in warning. Morgan cut the engine and the truck shuddered to a halt.

When did her hair grow so white? he wondered. Or grow so frail a gust of wind could carry her away? The years seemed to stretch long between them as he stared out through the dark windshield and calculated that his mother was now sixty-six years old.

The black Lab had aged, too. Blackjack ran on stiff legs and his muzzle was completely white now, but he could still raise the dead with his barking. Morgan pushed open the door. Instantly, the large dog bounded forward, lowering his head, ears back, sniffing hard.

"Hey there, Blackjack," Morgan said as his feet hit the earth and he slowly extended his hand. "Remember me?"

At the sound of his voice the dog took a step closer, placing his gray muzzle right to the hand. Then recognition clicked in the dog's cloudy eyes, and with a sudden leap Blackjack began yelping and barking with unbridled joy.

"You're getting old, aren't you, Blackie, ol' boy?" Morgan said with a laugh, playfully petting the old dog and feeling a surge of affection for being welcomed with such devotion.

"Morgan!"

The sound of his mother's voice pierced Blackjack's clamor. Morgan closed his eyes for a moment, then slowly raised himself and looked over his shoulder toward her. His gaze locked with a pair of blue eyes that were shining bright through tears. It had been a long time since they'd seen each other. Mother and son stood staring for an intense moment, then she flung open her arms and took a faltering step forward.

Morgan wiped his hands on his thighs and then closed the distance to her side in a few long strides. Mama June reached up to wrap her arms around him in a trembling embrace and instantly Morgan was enveloped again in the scent of gardenias.

"Oh, my dear, dear boy!" she cried. "It's so good to see you. Shame on you for staying away so long. I've missed you!"

She felt his resistance in the stiffness of his arms and it pained her deeply, yet she clung a moment longer, as though her love would be strong enough to melt his iciness.

He felt awkward in the sudden emotion and drew back with shuffling steps, offering her a perfunctory kiss on the cheek.

"Hello, Mama June."

She held him at arm's length. "Darlin', let me get a good look at you. You're so thin! Aren't you getting enough to eat?"

"I eat fine."

"I'll just bet you do…. Don't you worry, we'll take care of that while you're here."

As her eyes devoured him, his did likewise. She was different somehow. Mama June had always been slender, but time had rounded her edges and softened her skin. Her face was sleep-worn and he figured Blackjack's barking had awakened her. Yet she didn't look tired—that wasn't the right word. *Older.* It shocked him to see it.

In his mind, his mother was always the same age as the last time he'd seen her. She was a wren of a woman, with bright eyes that shone with curiosity and quick movements that, while graceful, reflected the swift turns of her thoughts. Her hair, still long, was now a snowy white and loosely bound in a thin braid that fell over one shoulder. It was a style both old-fashioned and reminiscent of a young girl's.

He'd known she'd be older, of course. He'd not been home in years. But knowing it and seeing it were two different things. Yet her excitement colored her high cheekbones with a youthful flush, her joyous smile brought out deep dimples and her blue eyes sparkled like a light burning bright in a window.

Mama June grinned with elation. "I...I just can't believe you're here! It's a blessing! A true blessing. Oh, Morgan, what a surprise! Why didn't you call and let us know you were coming?"

"I didn't want to put anyone out. I figured y'all had your hands full with Daddy right now."

Her smile slipped. "You got my message?"

Morgan nodded. "And I talked to Nan."

Confusion flickered in Mama June's eyes. "Nan? Your sister didn't tell me she spoke with you."

"I asked her not to. I wasn't trying to be secretive, nothing like that. I just wasn't sure what I was going to do and, well, I didn't want to..."

"Get my hopes up?"

He laughed shortly and shuffled his feet. "Yeah, I guess."

Her brows furrowed. "What made you decide to come?"

He seemed surprised by the question. "I couldn't *not* come. I know it's been strained between us, but hell, he's still my father."

"Oh, Morgan, I'm sorry not to have been the one to tell you. I tried to call you right after your father was brought to the hospital, but there was no answer. I kept trying and finally just left the message. It wasn't an easy message to leave and I hated doing it. I'm glad Nan at least called you."

"She didn't call me. I called *her.* After I got Daddy's phone message."

She skipped a beat and her eyes widened. "His...his what? Preston called you? When?"

"A little over a week ago. Out of the blue. As luck would have it, I was on a hunting trip and didn't get the message till the following week." He paused, releasing a short laugh. "When I heard his voice on the machine, I sat hard in the chair, I can tell you. I listened to that message over and over again, just so I could believe it was the ol' coot. Then I got your message." He paused. "It hit me pretty hard. I just grabbed a map and every dollar in the house, got in the truck and drove south."

Mama June's jaw was slack with disbelief. "Preston called you…"

"You didn't know that he'd called?" Morgan asked, surprised.

She shook her head. "What did he want?"

"I was hoping you could tell me. He was vague, almost stumbling, like he didn't really know what to say. In the end, he muttered something about wanting to talk and then he hung up."

Morgan saw a multitude of emotions flutter through his mother's eyes as she stared off a moment and brought her fingertips to her lips. He remembered she was tenderhearted, and moved to comfort her. "Are you all right?"

"Me? Oh, yes, dear, I'm fine," she replied perfunctorily, but this was her pat answer and Morgan didn't believe her. She tilted her head and said with a tone of sadness, "Your father never fails to amaze me, that's all."

"Well, you could've knocked me over with a feather, that's for sure."

They shared a brief, commiserating laugh. The unpredictable nature of Preston Blakely was a family joke, and sharing it, Morgan felt one step closer to home.

"How is he?" he asked.

Her smile faltered as her tone grew troubled. "He's not good. It was a very severe stroke. The doctors don't know if he'll walk again. Maybe not even talk."

Morgan cursed under his breath. "I had no idea it was so bad."

"What's worse is knowing that beneath the still facade, he's just as mad as a wet hornet to be lying in bed, cooped up in that hospital. You know your daddy. He never spent more than a day in bed, no matter how sick he was."

"It's ironic."

"It's unfair, is what it is." Mama June tightened the sash around her waist and drew herself up. "There's a lot to be discussed, but it's getting chilly standing out here in my slippers and robe. And you have an empty stomach." She slipped her arm inside his and gave it a gentle squeeze. "Come inside where it's warm and let me feed you some breakfast. You must be famished."

"Sounds great." Morgan quickly grabbed a dusty black duffel bag from the back of the truck.

His vehicle, his clothes, even his luggage seemed coated with dust, like a caravan arriving from the desert. He'd traveled many miles. And now he was home, she thought, her heart near bursting. She led the way to the house, her critical eye taking in the shabby appearance of her usually pristine home. She'd been too preoccupied with Preston's stroke to notice. She flushed that the porch settee cushion was covered with Blackjack's hair, that dirt and cobwebs collected around the base of the empty porch planters. Here it was April, and she'd yet to fill them with pansies.

Blackjack paused at the foot of the stairs, eyes beseeching.

Mama June turned and pointed, directing the dog to his den under the porch. "I don't know why I bother. He'll likely sneak up soon as our backs are turned. Been doing that ever since your father took to the hospital. I expect Blackjack's looking for him. I can't recall when Preston has been away from the place for more than a day."

"Seems pretty quiet around here. Is Nona around?" asked Morgan.

"Goodness, no! Nona retired soon after you left. Keeps herself busy with her sweetgrass baskets. Our paths haven't crossed much since then, but I stop by her stand for a catch-up from time to time."

"House got too dull without me, I reckon."

"Oh, I'm sure that was the reason," Mama June replied as she opened wide the front door.

The sunlight filled the front hall and fresh air gusted in. Suddenly she felt full of joy, like a young mother again, calling her child into the house.

"Come in, Morgan. Welcome home!"

Mama June's heart skipped as, grinning, she ushered Morgan into the house. There was an awkward pause as they stopped in the high-ceilinged foyer and considered what to do first. It was finally decided that they'd freshen up before breakfast. Mama June led the way up the wide staircase, flicking on lights before her. Behind her, Morgan's head turned from left to right in a sweeping survey. His worried brow told her he'd noticed how the once-lustrous creamy walls had darkened to a dusky gray and how the silk on the antique chairs was as threadbare as the festoons of curtains that flowed to the frayed carpeting on the stairs, worn in spots to the wood.

"I gather Daddy still puts every penny into the farm?" he asked.

"And he owes another penny," she replied lightly. *"Plus ça change, plus c'est la même chose."*

"Well, it's nice to see ol' Beatrice never changes," he teased, pointing to a painting of a straight-backed, stern-faced woman in nineteenth-century clothes wearing a bright red cap. Beatrice Blakely was a founding member of the Blakely clan in the colonies, second wife of Oliphant, "Ol' Red," who had arrived on American soil earlier with a land grant.

"You ever figure out what she was scowling about?"

Mama June snorted. "Taxes, no doubt. Taxes have been

the bane of this family's existence since Beatrice's day. Morgan…" The sentence was left hanging for he'd moved on to the bedroom down the hall and opened the door.

Mama June paused but her gaze followed him. She saw him standing quietly, still holding on to his bag as he looked around his old room. She took a breath and hurried across the hall to the dimly lit room.

"I wish I'd had notice of your coming. I'd have opened things up for you."

She made a beeline for the window. With a couple of firm tugs, she pulled back the heavy blue drapes. A flotilla of dust motes danced in the sunshine. She waved them away, her cheeks coloring. She went to the other window to open the drapes and pry wide that window, as well.

"I don't come in these rooms much anymore," she said, looking around with a frown. She turned toward him again, slapping the dust from her hands.

He hadn't moved. He stood with a strange expression on his face as he took in the iron double bed covered in a navy crazy quilt and, over it, the ancient needlepoint rendition of the family crest. On the other walls hung paintings of the creeks, marsh and sailboats that he'd loved so much growing up. Under one dormer sat his pine schoolroom desk and chair, its soft yellow wood scarred with scratches. Opposite it, his tall bureau was missing the same two pulls. The only things she'd removed were his motley collection of dusty liquor bottles and posters of long-forgotten rock groups.

"It's like I've stepped back in time," he said.

I wish, she thought, but said nothing as she puttered about the room, absently moving a chair an inch, tugging at the bed-spread.

"Everything is pretty much as you left it. We knew you'd be back, sooner or later. I'll tidy it up this afternoon."

"It's a sight better than what I'm used to."

He dropped his bag, then stretched his arms wide, yawning as loud as a bear rousing from hibernation. The boyish gesture caught her by surprise, spiraling her back in time to when a young Morgan took great pleasure in yawning wide or belching loud, more to shock her than for anything else. She half smiled at the memory.

"I suppose you still know where everything is," she said, wringing hands that longed to reach out and touch him. Her heart ached just seeing him again—her son here in his old room! Yet she didn't dare embarrass him with maudlin shows of affection. He'd always been reticent to receive her hugs and backed off from kisses. Today, the invisible wall he'd built around himself was tangible.

"There should be fresh towels and soap in the bathroom. I'll go check to be sure. It's been so long since we've had an overnight guest." Then, realizing she'd just put her son into the category of guest, she stumbled on to say, "But you're not a guest, of course!" She clasped her hands tight. "Let me know if you need anything else."

"Yep. I'm fine. Thanks," he replied, scrubbing his face with his palms.

"You take a minute and rest, hear? You look exhausted."

"I just might do that. It was a long drive."

"Well…" She faltered again for words. "I best go see to breakfast."

He only nodded so she merely departed, closing the door quietly behind her.

She stood for a moment outside the room, gathering her wits. Was this really happening? Morgan was here? She glanced at her watch. Eight o'clock already. And she still in her nightgown! It was high time she made herself decent, she thought, hurrying to her own room at the other end of the hall.

Sweetgrass

With the swiftness of routine, she quickly dressed into her usual daytime attire of a long khaki skirt, a crisp cotton blouse and comfortable shoes. Her fingers deftly wound her braid into a bun and fastened it with a few bobby pins. Then she splashed her face with cool water and applied a swipe of color across her lips. She wasn't a vain woman and neither was she much interested in fashion. Her day clothes were comfortable, and for special occasions she relied on classic quality that stood the test of time. Though gravity had taken its toll, her dress size hadn't changed dramatically over the years, and some of the dresses in her closet dated back to the earlier days of her marriage when they'd entertained more frequently. It always amused her when her vintage gowns came back in style.

After a quick glance in the mirror, she felt much more together and ready to face her day. She wrapped her happiness around her like a shawl and went out to begin the myriad chores formulating in her mind.

A short while later, Mama June was standing at the stove stirring grits with one hand and, with her other, making a list of things she had to get done that day. First on the list was to announce Morgan's homecoming to the family and to invite them for Sunday dinner. At-Home Sunday Dinner had been a family tradition for generations, but like so many other traditions, this one had fallen by the wayside because of busy schedules, folks moving off and the altered priorities of modern-day living. Now the family dinners were relegated to holidays and reunions.

Certainly, Morgan's return was enough reason for a family celebration, she thought, her lips curving in anticipation. It'd been ages since she'd spread the white damask across the dining room table and lit the candles in the polished candelabra. She'd make sherried she-crab soup, Morgan's favorite.

Chicken fricassee might be nice, she thought, jotting down ingredients on her list.

Oh, how she'd love to have Nona's biscuits. Her smile broadened. Nona's biscuits… They were pure magic, like biting into air. She couldn't remember the last time they'd enjoyed them. From time to time she stopped by Nona's basket stand along Highway 17 to catch up, though it had been a while. Thoughts of Nona nagged as she added a few more items to her grocery list.

"Something smells good."

Mama June's head darted up to see Morgan enter the room. The sight of his bent head and lanky form in her kitchen once again filled her heart. His thick hair was spiky and damp from his shower, and his shirt of a pale blue that matched his eyes was wrinkled but fresh. He appeared a bit more relaxed, though his face still had the chalky sheen of deep fatigue.

"Coffee's hot, country ham is warming in the oven and the tasso gravy is thickening nicely," she said in a cheery voice. "Looks like you could use some of all of the above. Go on, darlin', sit down now. The table's all set. The *Post and Courier* is there, too. You might enjoy catching up on the local news."

"Thanks," he replied, moving with a preoccupied shuffle to the table.

She hummed softly as she fell into the old pattern of preparing breakfast for her son. Time was, every morning she'd fussed like a hen at her chick, urging him to eat a hearty meal before he dashed from the house, hurrying because he'd slept too late. Morgan had always been as slim as a beanpole, no matter how much or how often he ate. Her gaze drifted back to her son. He seemed so different, yet so much the same. The cut of his jaw was like her own. His blue eyes like his father's. His brown hair was still thick and in need of a good haircut, and he'd kept that lean, lanky physique, too, she thought, watching him stretch his long legs under the table. But the boy had filled out to a man in his chest and shoulders.

Her heart constricted as she began filling his plate with grits, country ham and eggs. "So, tell me," she said, opening the conversation. "What's going on up in the wilds of Montana?"

"Nothing much."

"I gather you still like it way out yonder?"

"It suits me fine."

"I don't know how you manage, living alone so far out. You're so isolated. I'd think you'd get pretty lonely."

"I do all right."

So he was not going to be forthcoming. Well, there was more than one way to eke out information. She cut the heat on the stove, then brought the plate over and set it down in front of him.

He stared at the food with eyes as wide as saucers. The food was piled high, overflowing the edges of the porcelain. A giant couldn't eat all of it and she felt a flush of embarrassment. It was obvious she was trying so hard to please.

"I'll try to do it justice," he said, picking up a fork.

"Perhaps I got a little carried away. Just eat what you can," she said, rubbing her palms on her apron. "I'll freshen up your coffee."

She hurried to add coffee to his cup, then poured a cup for herself. To keep from standing and staring at him, she began rinsing out the frying pan.

"Last time you wrote," she ventured, "you said you were finished with all that bison-protection activity you were so involved in."

"We got legislation passed. Things are better. It was time to move on. Besides, the politics were demoralizing."

"But I don't understand. Didn't you win?"

"It wasn't about winning or losing. It was about preserving a natural resource."

She was being inquisitive and he was cutting her off again. It was a familiar impasse. Their few phone calls over the years had always left her digging for clues and feeling frustrated by the time she lowered the telephone receiver.

Mama June's brows furrowed as she returned to her dishes. She was silent for a moment, but when she was drying the pan, she glanced to the table and noticed that he'd already set his fork back on the table after only a few bites.

"Too much salt?" she asked, concerned. "Preston always tells me I'm a heavy salter."

"No, it's fine." He picked up the fork again. "I was walking around upstairs, just looking around," he said, his eyes on the fork he was twiddling between his fingers. "I went into Ham's room." He set the fork down. "I noticed that Daddy's things are in there."

Mama June carefully folded the drying towel and set it on the counter. Morgan looked up at her with question burning in his eyes.

"Yes," she replied at length. "That's his room now."

"Since when have you had separate bedrooms?"

"I can't really remember for how long now." She could be evasive, too.

She hesitated, wondering how much to share with her son. He wasn't a boy, no matter how much she sometimes thought he was. He was a grown man and familiar with the ways of life. The trouble between her and Preston had been years in the making, a highly private, personal story between a husband and a wife.

She never had been one for speaking out and voicing her inner thoughts and troubles to others. The way some women went on about personal matters always made her feel as if she'd peeked through their windows. She'd always been one to close her curtains at night, and to her mind, what room was more personal than the bedroom? Son or no, this wasn't really any of Morgan's business.

"You needn't look so shocked. It's not all that uncommon after a certain age. And now with the stroke, of course, who knows what?" She carried more rolls to the table.

"Stop serving me, Mama June!"

She froze at his outburst.

Morgan looked at her sheepishly and pulled out a chair beside him. "Come on, sit, Mama. You don't need to cater. Please."

Mama June set the rolls on the table, then slid wordlessly into the chair.

Morgan placed his hand on her shoulder. "I'm sorry about the way I just showed up on your doorstep."

"Oh, that!" she said, recovering herself and brushing the awkwardness away. "This is your home. You're here. That's all that matters to me. It will mean so much to your father, too. You can't know."

She saw anguish flash in his eyes before he dropped his hand. "Yeah, well…"

"It *will*."

After a minute he said, "I should go see him. Do they allow visitors?"

She heard his declaration as duty rather than heartfelt worry. It defeated her.

"Of course they allow visitors," she replied. "The more the better. For the last ten days I've been reduced to begging folks to sign up and visit. I've received roomfuls of flowers and get well cards and more casseroles than I can freeze. Everyone's been very kind. And yet, no one seems to have the time or desire to go to the hospital and sit with him. It's so important that someone just be with him, you see. He's so helpless. Like a baby." She hesitated. "You… you'll be surprised when you see him. I hate to leave him there alone. You hear horror stories of mistakes being made in the hospital, or of things overlooked in the charts. I drive downtown every day and stay as long as I can, but it's not enough."

"I'll go."

She patted his hand fervently. "Thank you. It will mean so much to him."

"When will Daddy be getting out of the hospital?"

"That's undecided." She drew her hand back and leaned against the chair. She glanced over to the kitchen counter where she saw the cookbooks spread open and the shopping list—all preparations for Sunday dinner. For all the joy of Morgan's homecoming, she knew there would likely be another round of debate once the family gathered.

"What's the matter, Mama June?"

She looked at his long, thoughtful face and flashed to the boy who once sat at this table beside her wolfing down cold cereal, swinging his legs as he looked out the window, eager to get outdoors. He'd always been tenderhearted. Yet she'd rarely talked to him about things that plagued her, unlike with her daughter, Nan, with whom she used to talk freely.

"I'm so confused," she said with new honesty. "I don't know what to do."

He sat straighter in his chair, appreciating the confidence. "Are you worried about taking care of him? I'm sure the staff at the hospital will teach you what to do. And you can get help once you bring him home."

"That's just it. Your aunt Adele tells me I should *not* bring him home."

"Oh." He paused, his eyes shuttered. "Really?"

There had always been an odd tension between Preston's sister, Adele, and Morgan. His tone told her that time had not diminished the coolness.

"Adele is worried that he won't get the care he needs here. She thinks we are risking his recovery if we don't place him somewhere he can get professional treatment."

"Like a nursing home?" he asked, aghast.

"More a residential treatment facility. The costs of home care will be very high and..." She waved her hand. "Oh, it all makes sense when she explains it to me. She's done a lot of homework and went over the numbers with me. I can't remember half of what she told me—except that I should sell Sweetgrass."

"Sell Sweetgrass..." Morgan exhaled and leaned back in his chair. "Wow. I hadn't, I mean, I never considered that a possibility."

"Adele says that selling Sweetgrass would free me to provide for Preston and myself without worry of becoming a burden." She looked at her hands and fiddled with the plain gold band on her left hand. "We've never wanted that, you know. To be a burden."

"You're *not* a burden."

"No, not yet. But according to Adele, we could be. Quite quickly."

"Adele always deals in absolutes. You know that." He rubbed his jaw in consternation. "If the stroke doesn't kill Daddy, selling Sweetgrass will."

"My thought exactly!" she exclaimed. She took great heart that someone was finally understanding her point of view. And that the someone was her son.

"What do the doctors say? Can Daddy even be moved?"

"They feel he can come home, provided we get assistance,

of course, like an army of therapists, an aide and equipment." She could hear the hopefulness in her own voice.

"Hiring support will cost money."

"Yes."

"Can you afford it?"

"For a while. Maybe a very little while." Mama June sighed heavily. "I don't know why I keep fussing about the decision. Adele was pretty clear about what I should do. Sell Sweetgrass and move. Hank and Nan agree."

He considered this a moment, then asked, "What do *you* want to do?"

"I have to think about what's best for Preston."

"That's not what I'm asking you right now. I'm asking what *you* want to do."

She sat back against the ladder-back chair. It occurred to her that in all the many conversations with Adele, Nan and Hank, with the doctors, with the banks and lawyer, everyone had told her what he or she thought Mama June should do. No one had ever asked what *she* might want to do. No one, except Morgan.

"To be honest, I don't really know. When your father had his stroke, I was unprepared to make even small, everyday decisions concerning Sweetgrass. Now suddenly I'm thrust into the position of making all the decisions. Preston is going to need a great deal of care before he gets well—if he gets well. I've tried to think what's best for him, and for all of us and..."

"You're veering off again," he said gently.

"Oh, Morgan, I'm sixty-six years old. I'm too old to start over. I've lived in this house for nearly fifty years. This is where you were raised. This is our home. We've been happy here and..." She raised her eyes to his in mute appeal for understanding. "All my memories are here."

"Mama, what do *you* want to do?"

Mama June reached up to pat his cheek affectionately. Dropping her hand, she said, "I can't separate the decision of what I want to do for myself from what I must do for the family. To my mind—and to your father's—the Blakelys *are* Sweetgrass."

"You're beginning to sound like Daddy." He brought his face closer. "What do *you* want to do?" he persisted.

She found his pressure exhausting and lowered her forehead into her palm. "I don't know."

He leaned forward and this time kissed her cheek. "Don't fret, Mama. I'm not trying to annoy you. I was just hoping to hear what you wanted, for a change. Tell you what. You stay home today and mull it over. I'll go downtown to this hospital and check on Daddy."

3

During the days of slavery in the Old South, men made large work baskets from bull rush because this marsh grass was strong and durable. Women made functional baskets for the home using sweetgrass, which was softer and abundant. Today's baskets are made with sweetgrass, bull rush and long-leaf pine needles bound together by strips of the unopened center leaves of palmetto trees.

NAN'S HAND RESTED ON the telephone receiver as she gathered her wits.

"Close your mouth, Mama. You're catching flies." Harry jabbed his younger brother in the ribs as they laughed. They were gathered around the table, waiting on dinner.

Nan snapped her mouth shut only for as long as it took her to smile. She hurried over to the table.

"You won't believe it!" she announced, her voice rising. She was rewarded with the rarity of the complete attention of her teenage sons, Harry and Chas, as well as her husband, Hank.

Looking at the bunch, she thought there could be no doubt who the boys' father was. Not that she and Hank looked all that different from each other. The boys both had their parents' blond hair and bright blue eyes. Harry, at seventeen, had the Blakely height and slender build, while it looked as though Chas would be shorter and more muscular, like Hank. Though at fifteen, he might sprout another few inches and be taller than his father.

Hank's neatly cropped blond head emerged from behind the *Post and Courier.* "We won't believe what?"

"That was Mama June. You'll never guess who's home!"

"Morgan," answered Hank with little enthusiasm, returning his attention to the newspaper.

Nan felt a flutter of disappointment that his quick answer stole the thunder from her announcement. She rallied. "Yes! That doesn't surprise you?"

"Not really. Your father is in the hospital. It's only fitting he'd come home."

"What's the big deal?" Chas asked sullenly, disappointed in the news.

"Yeah, who cares?" added Harry. "We barely know who he is."

Her pale brows furrowed with displeasure at their lackluster reaction as she cut the heat on the stove with a quick twist of her wrist. "Well, it took me by surprise."

Sometimes it was just plain hard living with a bunch of males, she thought. They just didn't get it. Matters of *family* didn't register. She was sick to death of listening to their endless sports reports or excruciating details about cars. Sometimes she felt as though she were talking to herself throughout the meal, desperately trying to engage them in conversation while they ignored her and shoveled food.

Nan looked at her sons. Despite their outwardly good looks, they sometimes struck her as spiritless. She didn't detect the spark of drive or ambition or dreams that gave even ordinary-looking boys such appeal. She brushed aside her disappointment and told herself they were just going through a phase.

With practiced efficiency she gave the rice a final lift and poured the mass into a brightly colored serving bowl that co-ordinated with the dinner china. Then with a quick grab of serving spoons, she carried the rice and a bowl of buttered beans to the table of waiting men. She sat in her chair and they all bowed their heads and said the blessing.

"It's a sorry state of affairs that y'all feel so blasé about your only uncle being in town." Nan handed Harry the bowl of rice to pass.

"He's not our only uncle," corrected Harry, taking hold of the serving spoons and helping himself. "We've got Uncle Phillip and Uncle Joe living right close. We see them all the time."

"On *my* side, I meant. In the Blakely family, there's just me and Morgan."

Hank relinquished his newspaper to take his turn with the rice. "I don't know where you get this me and him stuff," he argued. "Seems to me your brother is a me only kind of guy. In all the years I've known him, Morgan's made it pretty clear how he feels about *family*. How long have we been married? We've seen him, what? Two or three times? It's his own fault that his nephews don't know who he is."

"I know, I know," Nan released in a moan, bringing the country-fried steak on a matching serving platter closer. Still, the criticism seemed to her unfair. "Morgan has a lot of history to deal with, don't forget."

Her hands rested on the platter as she paused and looked around the table. It was moments like this, seeing her family gathered together, that she treasured most. "I'm truly blessed to have you and the boys," she said, gifting each of them with a loving look. "Morgan has nothing or no one. It's just so sad, is all."

"Uh, Mama…" Harry lifted his brows, his gaze intent on the meat.

"Oh." The moment was gone. She reached out her hand with alacrity to pass the platter of meat around, followed by the beans. One by one the plates were topped with enormous mounds of rice, thick slices of fried steak and scoops of beans.

"Pass the gravy, Chas," Harry demanded.

Nan rose to carry the serving dishes to the sideboard. The boys were growing faster than cotton in July and she never seemed able to fill the bottomless pits they called their stomachs. She sighed as she watched them dive into their plates. The thought that it would be polite to wait for their mother to be seated at the table before eating never even crossed their minds. She looked at Hank for support, but he was ladling gravy on his rice, oblivious to the poor manners of his sons.

"Boys…" she muttered as she reached for her glass and poured herself a liberal glass of wine. When she took her seat at the opposite head of the table, no one so much as lifted a head. Nan sipped her wine, shoving her plate aside.

At least they were eating together as a family, she told herself, tamping down the disappointment she always felt at mealtime. Mama June had always maintained lively discussions at the dinner table, encouraging each of her children to join in. Nan remembered heated debates and merciless teasing and, always, laughter.

At least until Hamlin died. Her brother had been so alive! A natural storyteller with a joke or a quip always dangling at his tongue. Everything had changed after he was gone. To this day, she mourned.

When Nan married, she'd tried to restore the vitality in her own family that she'd felt was lost in the Blakelys after the trag-edy of her brother's death had torn the family apart. At the very least, she was keeping the family dinner tradition alive.

Suddenly, she remembered something else.

"Oh, yes! Mama June wants us all to come for Sunday din-ner."

This announcement was met with rolled eyes and groans from the boys.

"You just stop that, hear? You haven't been to see your grandmother in so long, she's taken to asking after you. Don't you realize how lonely she is with Granddaddy in the hospi-tal? You two boys are the apples of her eye and it's a scandal how seldom you pay her visits. I should take your car privi-leges away." It was a feeble threat and everyone knew it. Still, she felt compelled to assert some semblance of authority. "You are *going* to Sunday dinner."

"Yes, ma'am," they muttered, sullenly appealing to their fa-ther with their eyes.

Hank polished his glasses with his napkin, a habit she'd come to recognize as a preface to a lecture. "Morgan's being here will just complicate things, you realize."

"I don't see how. He's here to see Daddy. I don't expect he'll stay long."

"Not if he's true to form, he won't. But you know your mama's been real uneasy about leaving Sweetgrass, no matter how we've tried to reason with her."

"I don't expect his visit will make a difference one way or the other. More's the pity. Mama June could use the support of her family now. I wish he *would* take an interest."

"Are you so sure? We haven't seen the will and he is the only remaining Blakely."

She swirled her wine and replied dryly, "Last I looked, I'm still alive and I'm still a Blakely."

"You know what I mean," he said.

She tilted her head and drank. "I'm afraid I do."

"You're not a Blakely any more," Chas said, looking up with an obstinate glare. "You're a Leland."

Hank chuckled and raised his brows at his wife.

Nan's gaze swept the three sets of eyes that looked at her from across the table with a possessiveness she found oddly comforting. She thought back to the time her father had said those same words to her. Preston's tanned and deeply lined face, usually thoughtful, had been hard and his eyes were like blue chips of ice. She shivered at the memory. That day she'd told her father that she'd decided to follow her new husband's wishes and sell the fifty coastal acres deeded to her at her marriage. Hank had brokered a deal with a local development firm and it had been a major boost to his career in real estate.

She had been a young bride, behaving in the manner in which she'd been bred. *A woman's place was at her husband's side.* As the wife, she was the accommodator, the peacemaker, the right hand to her husband. She was doing what her culture—what the Bible—taught.

That deal had cost her. To her father's mind, selling the family land had severed her tie to the family. Her father cast her from the status of an "us" to a "them" in his polarized vision of the world. It wasn't something spoken; he was never one to confront her about it. He held his disappointment inside, simmering under the cool surface. The separation was felt indirectly, subtly, so that the relationship cooled not overnight, but over the course of months and years. Nan had always felt his silent treatment was undeserved. And it had hurt her, deeply.

"I surely am a Leland," she replied to Harry's assertion. "But you have Blakely blood running through your veins, too, don't forget."

"Forewarned is forearmed," her husband joked, jabbing at the meat with his fork.

"Now, that's not nice." Nan flushed as the boys barked out a laugh. She sat back in her chair, feeling as though a chasm had expanded between the two sides of the table, dividing them. She narrowed her eyes as she regarded her husband. For all his jokes, Hank had been plenty thrilled to be part of the historical Blakely clan when he'd married into it.

Though she couldn't blame him for his change of heart. Daddy's indifference toward him had been positively embarrassing.

She looked at her hands, tanned and slim. Beneath a thick diamond-and-gold wedding set, the skin was white, like a brand on her left ring finger. She was Nan Leland. For eighteen years, Hank and the boys had been the epicenter of her life. Wasn't a wife and mother supposed to be the heart of the home? Now, however, the boys were poised for leaving and her husband seemed more and more distant. Her father was near death, her mother was alone in that empty house… She took a ragged breath, then a thought brought a half smile.

But Morgan was home.

Her mind turned to the long, welcoming avenue of oaks at Sweetgrass. While the boys laughed between themselves, Nan was listening to the voice of the little girl still alive within her, fiercely whispering, "I'm a Blakely, too."

Across the churning, gray-green Ashley River in Charleston, Morgan was clenching his fists at his thighs, a nervous reaction to the strident ding of the hospital elevator. Seconds later, the metal doors swished open and he faced the mint-green walls of the medical center's third floor. He sucked in his breath and drew inward as he followed the yellow arrow painted onto the polished floors that would lead him to the

Sweetgrass

stroke rehabilitation center. As he walked, an elderly, pasty-faced inpatient clothed in the flimsy, dignity-depriving hospital gown limped past him with great effort, clutching a stainless-steel walker and supported on either side by some family member offering encouraging comments.

The nurse at the station looked up in a guarded greeting.

"I'm looking for Preston Blakely's room. I'm his son," he added. "Morgan Blakely."

"Your father is in room 321," she said after a quick check. Her voice seemed too loud for the hushed floor. "He's finished his therapy session and is resting."

"Will I disturb him?"

"Oh, no. He'll enjoy the company, though he might not show it." Her rigid face shifted suddenly to reveal concern. "This is your first visit, isn't it?" When he nodded she leaned forward and said kindly, "You *do* know that he can't speak? Or move much?"

"Yes."

"Just checking. Didn't want you to be shocked. It's never easy to see a loved one the first time in that condition." Her eyes remained dubious but she waved him on. "You let me know if you need my help for anything."

He clenched his fists again and swallowed hard. His feet moved as though on automatic pilot as he scanned the faux-wood doors for 321. When he found it, he paused outside the silent, dimly lit room.

Morgan rarely saw his father in bed. Preston Blakely was a man who prided himself on rising before the sun, the kind of man who liked to get a head start on his day. Morgan perceived his father as someone vertical, standing erect, upright and plumb. So to see him lying prone on the thin, hard, unforgiving surface of a hospital bed was unnatural, like coming across a buffalo down in the prairie. The first time

47

he'd witnessed that lifeless mountain of a beast, it had sent a numbing chill straight to his core. He felt the same helplessness now, unsure of what to expect or of what to do next.

It wasn't courage that compelled him to take the step into the dim, sterile room. Nor was it a son's sense of duty. Compassion brought him to his father's side. A thin blue cotton blanket covered his father, giving him a mummy-like appearance as he lay flat, toes pointed, one arm curled oddly against his chest, the other lying still by his side.

Preston seemed small. His usually tanned and ruddy complexion had turned pasty white, and skin sagged from his prominent cheekbones like putty. His mouth, which could deliver orders and a good story with equal authority, now hung slack and drooped to one side. It frightened Morgan to the core to see him this way. He was acutely aware that he was on his feet and his father was not.

Morgan pulled a chair closer to the bed and slumped into it. He folded his hands across his belly and sat quietly staring at his father while, inwardly, memories raged with an old, seething anger. After what seemed a long time, he checked his watch, then groaned, knowing he'd be here for hours more. Already he felt depleted. He got up to walk around the room, checking out the flower arrangements, recognizing the names of old family friends on the cards.

There was a chart posted on the door, a simple hand-drawn box with lines marking date and time of day. It was colored in red, blue and yellow, and he knew for certain that it was made by his mother, who had always made lists of the children's chores with little stars pasted on them. On the chart were the signatures of those who had volunteered to sit with Preston. The same few names appeared over and over, and as the days turned to weeks, even those names appeared less frequently. In the past few days, most of the slots were blank save for his mother's name.

Sweetgrass

Morgan was sorry to see how few times his sister's and nephews' names were listed. Today, his own name stood alone in his scrawling script. Writing it, he'd vowed it would appear on the chart every day until his father was released.

When he turned toward his father, he jerked back, stunned. His father's eyes were open in the cadaverous face, staring at him. Morgan's heart pounded as he looked into the vivid blue eyes so much like his own. The eyes that stared back at him widened, and Morgan could have sworn his father acknowledged him.

Morgan licked his lips, parched with nervousness. He moved the chair closer, the wood scraping loudly on the floor, and sat down. Yet there wasn't any reaction, not even a twitch, from his father. His stillness was eerie. Morgan thought of all the times in the past when his father had roared at him to do this or that, or berated him for what he'd done wrong. All those times, Morgan had wished his dad would just shut the hell up. But this mute, sad-eyed, terrified silence was far worse.

Morgan reached out and hesitatingly placed his hand over his father's. Touching his father like this was strange, even unprecedented. The bones of his large hand felt fragile and his skin felt dry and cool. Morgan leaned forward and in a hoarse voice choked with repressed emotion spoke his first words to his father in more than a decade.

"I'm here now, Daddy. You're not alone."

Later that evening, Morgan walked under the canopy of the avenue of oaks with a bottle of Jim Beam and Blackjack for company. The dog, delighted with the attention after weeks of neglect, shuffled at his side. The old dog's gait was stiff and labored, and his heavy paws dragged the dirt in the soft roadbed. Overhead, gnarled gray branches soared high into the sky to intertwine and form an arch that rivaled the flying buttresses of a European cathedral.

It was his father who had made that comparison, Morgan remembered. Preston used to walk this path daily, often with his head bent as though in prayer. Morgan flashed back to a time he and his older brother, Hamlin, were walking along the avenue with him. Preston had been in a rare mood of introspection and told his sons in a solemn voice that he felt closer to his Creator walking in this church of God's making than he ever did in one of man's.

His mother, in contrast, prayed in church. The Blakelys were long-standing, staunch members of the Christ Church Episcopal Parish, and his mother was no exception. When he was little, his mother used to settle him on her lap during service by whispering the names of all the Episcopal ministers that graced the family tree. Or she'd tell of how she, along with generations of Blakely women before her, had stitched the fine needlework that graced the altar. He remembered how he'd slowly relax in her arms, surrounded in her scent of gardenias, a fine sheen of sweat from the stifling heat across his brow, while the murmurs of the faithful droned on.

Morgan felt a sudden longing for the years lost. Each great oak that he passed seemed to him as one of his ancestors, erect and silent, watching with judgment as this last remaining Blakely heir slunk along the worn path, his pockets empty and his dreams unrealized.

Unworthy, he heard in the rustle of leaves.

"You're all dead!" he shouted, then swallowed hard, struck fresh with guilt at the sudden memory of his brother.

Morgan brought the bottle to his lips and drank thirstily. Why was he dredging up things he hadn't thought about in years? Families had a way of tossing one straight back to the nursery. He didn't have any intention of playing the role of angry young rebel again. He liked to think he'd traveled beyond that point in his life, at least.

Straight ahead, soft yellow light flowed from the mullioned windows of his family's house. When he reached the porch stairs, Blackjack paused, tail wagging, and looked up expectantly.

"You're like a ronin, aren't you, boy? Just an old, masterless hound, like me," he said, reaching over to pat the velvety fur. "No point in pretending any longer that you're staying in your den, huh? Mama June's wise to your tricks. Tell you what. She ain't going to chase you off the porch. Nope. Truth is, no one has the heart. So, come on, then." He grandly waved the dog up toward the house, tottering with the effort.

Blackjack's tail wagged and he bounded forward. Morgan took the stairs more slowly. Once on the porch, Blackjack brought his muzzle to Morgan's hand, demanding. Morgan patted his broad head. Comforted by the motion, Morgan obliged until Blackjack was at last satisfied and ambled at a soft, padded pace to the cushioned settee he'd claimed as his own. After climbing up, the old dog settled with a low grunt, worn out from the long walk.

Morgan eyed the curled-up dog and wished he could settle in as easily for the night. His joints were stiff from sitting all day in the hard hospital chair and, rolling his shoulders, he knew he'd ache tonight. Despite his fatigue and the bourbon running through his veins, however, his mind was still churning. He felt restless and wasn't ready to go in just yet, so he took a final swig from the bottle, leaned against one of the eight porch pillars and lit a cigarette.

What the hell was he doing here? he asked himself. He'd been away from Sweetgrass for more than a decade, yet even in the darkness he knew the land as well as the lines of his own body. Looking out, he could readily mark the Blakely borders along the shadowy, ragged outline of the marsh. It extended far out to where the cordgrass met sea and sky to form the horizon. The landscape seemed unchanged in all the years he'd been gone—at least within the gates of Sweetgrass.

He'd half expected his parents to remain the same, too. Yet, today he'd seen for himself the ravages that time wrought on the people he loved and had left behind.

He ran his hand in a sulky sweep through his hair. Time had not been kind to him, either. The years of wandering had not brought him the answers he'd hoped they would. The answers he sought were not on the open road, nor in the mountains of Montana. This he'd learned today while sitting at his father's side. As he searched those eyes that stared back at him with the intensity of an acetylene torch, the excuses had burned clean away and he'd realized that the answers he sought were here, at Sweetgrass, with his father.

"Aw, hell," he muttered, pulling a long drag from his cigarette and tossing the bottle into the darkness. It fell with a satisfying crash.

Behind him, the front door creaked open.

"Morgan? There you are! I thought I heard a noise." Mama June closed the door behind her and joined him on the porch.

"Just havin' a smoke."

"Thank you for smoking on the porch." Mama June pulled her sweater a little tighter around her neck and came closer.

He glanced to his side. His mother seemed small and slight beside him, more girl-like than he'd remembered. "Kind of chilly tonight."

"But it's so bright and clear. Look! Venus is flirting with the Carolina moon."

The moon was an upturned sliver of light cut in a swath of black velvet. Venus, piercingly bright, punctuated the curve like a beauty mark at the tip of a courtesan's smile.

"How is he today?" she asked. "It's the first day I haven't been in to see him."

"I expect he's much the same as when you last saw him." He flicked the ash and took another drag on his cigarette. "But he's sure as hell not at all the same as when I last saw him."

Her gaze searched his unkempt appearance with concern and he knew that she caught the scent of bourbon that clung to him.

"I was anxious about how you'd react," she replied at length. "Are you all right?"

"Sure."

"I see," she said.

And he knew that she did.

"It was damn hard seeing him like that."

"I tried to prepare you."

"How do you prepare someone for something like that?"

She sighed. "I suppose that's why Nan and the boys have such a hard time visiting."

Morgan swallowed his retort with the smoke, feeling the burn. He dropped the cigarette and ground it with his heel. "Have you given any thought to what we talked about this morning?"

Her face grew troubled. Turning, she gripped the porch railing. "I've thought of little else."

"Have you reached any conclusions?"

She looked out into the darkness for a moment. When she turned back, curiosity shone in her eyes. "Tell me, Morgan, you've looked into his eyes today. What did you see?"

He exhaled slowly. "I never thought I'd see fear in Daddy's eyes. But I saw it today."

"I've seen it, too!" she exclaimed, seizing the moment.

"Every day. He's trapped in there. He can't even tell us what he wants." She took a breath. "But *I* know what he wants. His eyes are speaking to me. They're screaming *bring me home!*"

"Then that's what you should do."

Her expression shifted from elation to worry. "I wish it were so easy. It's rife with problems. I know that bringing Preston home to Sweetgrass doesn't make a whit of sense in dollars and cents. But his recovery isn't just about money, is it?" she asked. "His recovery also depends on his spirit and his will. And I assure you, Preston's will and spirit are intricately connected with Sweetgrass." She looked up at him, her eyes entreating. "But I can't do it alone."

He knew where she was heading and placed his hands on the railing, leaning heavily. "Mama June…"

"Wait." She drew back her shoulders. "All right, I'm ready. Ask me your question. One more time."

A wry smile played at his lips upon seeing her rail-straight posture. He delivered his line sincerely. "Mama June, what do *you* want to do?"

She lifted her chin. "I want to bring Preston home to Sweetgrass. I want to care for him here, in his home, for as long as it takes him to get his voice back and let me know what he wants to do next." She paused to take a breath. "And, I want you to stay."

He barked out a laugh. "Well, ma'am, when you finally get around to answering a question, you sure deliver a mouthful."

"You *did* ask."

His jaw tightened, holding back the reply on his tongue. He'd been considering the option all day, wrestling with it with every bit as much desperation as Jacob with the Angel. He didn't want to stay. Every instinct told him to get in his truck and hightail it back to the quiet isolation of Montana. Then he looked at his mother, waiting expectantly, and his decision tumbled into place.

"All right, then, angel," he said with resignation. "It looks like you've won this one. I'll stay."

"Thank you, Morgan!"

He leaned back against the pillar. "Don't thank me yet, Mama June. I don't know how long we're going to be able to hang on here. It won't be easy. You may regret this."

"Regret you coming home to help your father? Regret bringing Preston home to heal? Never!"

He chuckled at the passion of her statement. "All right then," he said again. He ran both hands through his hair, scratching away the last of the bourbon from his head. "Now that that's settled, I'm starving." He patted his lean stomach. "Got anything to eat?"

Smiling at the age-old question, she stretched up to kiss his cheek. "Music to my ears. You go on and wash up and I'll fix you something. I'll be there directly."

She watched him go inside, heard the soft clap of the screen door close behind him. Alone, she turned toward the vast darkness beyond, then looked to the heavens. The stars sparkled with a brilliance nearly as bright as the hope shining in her eyes.

Later that night a storm barreled through the Lowcountry, bringing with it crackling lightning and rumbling thunder that shook the rafters. Mama June roused from her sleep, blinking her eyes slowly as she grew accustomed to the deep darkness. She could see nothing save for the intermittent flashes of light from the storm. She wasn't afraid. Ever since coming to live at Sweetgrass she'd thrilled to the fast-moving storms that swept from the mainland toward the ocean.

Restless, she turned over to her back and, placing her hands on her chest, played the game of counting the seconds between lightning and thunder. Rain tapped against the windows and the roof as she reviewed her decision to bring Preston home.

The tapping grew louder, interrupting her thoughts. Mama June glanced over to the window. Her breath hitched in her throat as she caught sight of a misty white mass hovering near the window. Squinting, she thought she saw a figure in the mist. The outline of a woman's form in a nightcap and a long period dress appeared, looking directly at her. Mama June felt the hairs on her body rise.

Then lightning flashed again, bold and bright, and thunder clapped so near and loud that Mama June clutched her gown and nearly jumped from her skin. When she looked again, the apparition was gone.

Mama June sat up in her bed and, with a trembling hand, flicked on the bedside lamp. Instantly, a soothing light filled the room, reassuring her that she was indeed alone. Only the curtains flapped at the window. She brought her hand to her heart, and as her breathing came back to normal, she tried to dredge up the memory of what she'd just seen. It had happened so quickly, she couldn't be sure if what she'd seen was real or a dream. Perhaps it was merely the strange light patterns from the lightning against the curtains.

"You old fool," she muttered to herself, lowering back into bed and turning off the bedside lamp. "You're just imagining things."

The storm quickly passed out to sea and only a gentle rain pattered on the rooftop. Mama June felt a heavy weariness droop her eyelids and weigh down her bones. She lay her head down on the pillow and brought her blanket close under her chin, telling herself for the thousandth time that her imagination had got the best of her on this emotional day.

Sweetgrass

And yet…a persistent voice in her mind told her that she'd not been imagining anything at all. She knew what she'd seen in the floating mist—or rather, who.

It was the ghost of the family's first matriarch, Beatrice. And she'd been smiling.

4

The art of basket making was brought to South Carolina by slaves who came from West Africa more than three hundred years ago. "For generations, the art has been passed from mother to daughter to granddaughter."

—Vera M. Manigault, basket maker

MAMA JUNE'S HANDS TIGHTENED on the steering wheel of her '95 Oldsmobile sedan as she leaned forward and squinted, focusing on the steady flow of traffic that whizzed past. Her heart beat like a wild bird in her chest.

The private road to Sweetgrass was accessed directly from Highway 17. In colonial days when Sweetgrass was a plantation, the roadbed was called Kings Highway and was a major artery for planters. In the twentieth century, it grew to become a sleepy highway for people traveling between Charleston and Myrtle Beach. As construction of housing developments, shopping malls and tourism burgeoned, however, the traffic roared by.

Mama June didn't care much for driving in the first place, and it was no time for daydreaming if she didn't want to get clobbered just trying to get out of her own driveway.

Sweetgrass

There was a break in the traffic and Mama June eased her great rumbling sedan onto the highway, earning a nasty honk from a speeding car that careened over to the left. As the car passed, the driver gestured rudely, yelling. Mama June smiled sweetly and returned the wave.

Most likely a tourist, she thought, her smile falling hard. She was smugly gratified to see the out-of-town license plate as it sped past. Mama June smoothed her hair, feeling both indignant and embarrassed. No one local would be so rude as to honk like that, or yell such things, she thought. Especially not to an elderly woman.

"What's becoming of this town?" she muttered as she gradually eased her Oldsmobile up to just below the speed limit. She didn't want to go so fast that she'd miss the stand. It ought to be coming up right soon.

The rickety wood stands that bordered both sides of the four-lane highway had been there for as long as she could remember. Beginning in Mount Pleasant and progressing clear up to Georgetown, African-American women could be found sitting in the shade beside their basket stands. They'd sit weaving the indigenous sweetgrass into baskets, patiently waiting for some local or tourist to stop alongside the road and purchase one of their works of art.

In bad weather, the lean-to stands stood stark and empty. In good weather, however, soft yellow-and-brown baskets by the dozens dangled from the wooden slats, some with bright red ribbons affixed during the holidays, some with paper price tags dangling gaily in the wind. All kinds of baskets were available: some with handles, some with tops, some large and flat and others with curves and twists. Mama June slowed down, her eyes peeled for one basket stand in particular.

Mama June remembered the day, so long ago, that her

mama drove this same road to Myrtle Beach. It was her eighth birthday and her mother was taking her on a special holiday—just the girls. There would be swimming on the long stretch of pearly beach, shopping and eating out at restaurants. Oftentimes, her parents went off to the Grand Strand, giggling like teenagers. So this time was very special. She'd packed her new yellow dress with the stiff pastel crinolines that made her feel like a princess and shiny patent leather shoes bought specially for the trip.

Her mother had to make a stop in Charleston, so afterward they drove north along Highway 17. It was the first time she'd seen the many rickety, wooden stands that lined the road. In her child's mind, she'd thought they were ramshackle houses and had felt sorry for the poor people who lived in those lean-tos. How her mother had laughed at that one!

Her mother had pulled over the big red Buick alongside one of the stands, Mama June recalled as if it were yesterday. Being young, she was nervous about approaching the two African-American women who sat in a companionable manner, weaving. They were kindly and took the time to show her how they wove the narrow strips of palmetto leaf through the sweetgrass to create a basket.

Mary June was mesmerized. As she watched the women's strong fingers twist the yellow, sweet-smelling grass into shape, her own fingers moved at her sides. Impulsively, she begged her mother for a basket, saying she'd rather have one than a trip to the Strand, a comment that made the weavers roll their eyes and chortle. Because it was her birthday, her mother let her choose any one she wanted. Mama June still had that basket in a place of honor on her dining room shelf. It was the first of many baskets she'd collected over the years.

Mama June smiled at the memory, then shook her head, focusing on the road. She didn't have to drive far before she spotted a basket stand that had a large number of more intricately designed baskets than most of the other stands held. Mama June pulled over to the side of the road and cut the engine just as an eighteen-wheeler pushed past her, causing even her large Olds to rock.

"Heaven, help us," she exclaimed, holding tight to the wheel. Coughing lightly from the dust, she peered over her shoulder before pushing open the car door and scurrying out from the sedan to safety. As she approached the stand, Mama June's experienced eye recognized the evenness of the stitches, the uniform rows of sweetgrass and the clever, subtle shift of color from the golden sweetgrass to the coffee-colored bull rush. To her mind, this weaver was a master.

One woman in a dull brown skirt and blue patterned blouse sat in the shade of a sprawling live oak. The woman's hands stilled and her face lifted in expectant welcome. She had short, steel-gray hair worn in tight curls around her head, a straight nose that flared wide, bold cheekbones and a jawline that could have been carved of granite. Her appearance was regal and might even have been regarded as rigid were it not for her eyes. They were wide, deep and full of expression, so that one would always know her opinion on a matter without her having to speak a single word.

"Nona!"

Nona's eyes widened in recognition and she raised her palms up. "Lord have mercy! Mary June! I haven't laid eyes on you in weeks!"

"I know. And what a spell I've been having!" Mama June replied as she stepped forward to take the strong brown hands into her own. The two women looked into each other's eyes as years of shared experiences flashed through both of their minds, tightening their clasped hands in unspoken acknowledgment.

"What brings you here today?" Nona asked, releasing her hold and folding her arms akimbo, eyes twinkling. Don't tell me you've come looking for a basket?"

"One can never have too many sweetgrass baskets," she replied, her gaze moving across the rows. "But actually," she said, fixing her gaze on Nona, "I've got some rather bad news. Is this a good time?"

Concern crept into Nona's eyes, though her smile remained fixed. "As good a time as any. I'm just sewing my baskets. I'd enjoy the company."

"I can't stay long. I'm on my way to the hospital. I don't know if you've heard, but Preston's had a stroke."

Nona brought a hand over her heart. "Goodness, no! I didn't hear a word about that! Now, that's a terrible sadness. How is he?"

"Very bad, I'm sorry to say. It left him paralyzed and he can't speak a word."

"Lord have mercy."

"He's as helpless as a baby. But he's been in intensive therapy. We have hope."

"You got to have hope."

"I honestly believe that the only hope he has of ever walking or speaking again lies in our getting him out of the hospital and back home. You know how much he loves Sweetgrass. I believe bringing him home will be his best tonic."

"He surely does love the place," Nona replied, nodding with affirmation. "Even so, *you* are his best tonic, Mary June. Always have been."

"Well, I don't know about that. But it is a big undertaking to bring him home." Mama June gave a brief account of the army of therapists she'd scheduled to work with Preston at home and the kind of therapy each would provide.

Listening, Nona was all amazement. "And they do all that

right there in your house?" When Mama June nodded, Nona shook her head. "It's like bringing the hospital home with you! I expect that'll cost you a bundle. All those professionals…"

"Insurance helps," Mama June replied. "Still, it's a worry. I've hired a live-in aide to see to Preston's medical needs. But the house is another thing altogether." She wrung her hands, unable to ask the question on the tip of her tongue, hoping Nona would read between the lines.

"What a time you've had."

"Oh, Nona, there's so much to be done. I expect to be busy as Preston's caretaker, you see. I'm also taking care of the business of the farm as well."

"*You* are?"

Nona's shocked tone might have been insulting from anyone else, but she knew Mama June better than anyone—and was well acquainted with Mama June's aversion to anything pertaining to money.

"Just until Preston is well."

Nona's brows rose. "That's a lot to take on all of a sudden."

"It surely is. Nona, I can tell you, I've been simply overwhelmed with all the decisions I have to make, and now with Preston due to come home…" She lifted her palms in a light shrug. "I probably should get some help."

Nona looked away, lowering her hands and reaching out to straighten a few baskets in a line on the long table. "Might be a good idea," she said in a slow voice. "Mary June, you might could get one of those cleaning crews. You know the ones I mean. A whole group of women come sweeping down on the house like locusts on a field and clean the house lickety-split."

Mama June couldn't speak for a moment. She felt a profound disappointment that Nona hadn't come to her aid, as she'd always done in the past. What she really needed was someone she could depend on, someone to help manage the house. What she needed was a friend to help her out. But she couldn't ask this without clouding the air between them.

"You're probably right," she replied, clutching her purse. "Well, I best be going. You take care." She started to leave, then suddenly turned back. Nona hadn't moved a muscle but stood, watching her. "I almost forgot. I wanted to buy a basket."

"Now, Mary June, you don't need to buy no basket."

"But I want to. I see your style has changed a bit. Look at that one with the popcorn along the edges," she said, pointing to a small capped basket. "That is a beauty. I'd like to have that one in my collection of your work or it wouldn't be complete. How much is it?"

Nona lifted the intricate basket and slowly ran her fingers around its edges, considering. "This one didn't take much time and there are some mistakes in it," she replied. "Eighty dollars."

Mama June took the basket in her hands and brought it close. "There's not a mistake on this basket and you know it. And it took a considerable amount of time to make. It's a bargain at a hundred."

She reached into her pocketbook and tugged out two fifty-dollar bills. Each dollar was measured these days. She'd intended to go to the market on the way home, but this stop just cleaned out her wallet. She handed the bills to Nona.

"Thank you," Nona said, pocketing the bills in her skirt without a glance.

"It was wonderful seeing you again. Morgan was asking after you."

Nona's brows rose high, creasing her broad forehead. "Morgan is back home?"

Mama June's face eased into a grin. "Yes! At last! You could have knocked me over with a feather." At the mention of Morgan, a child beloved by both women, the earlier tension fled as quickly as the traffic passing on the highway, and the words flowed more easily.

"What brought that rapscallion back home after all this time?"

"His father's illness, of course."

"Oh, Lord, of course. Well, he's a fine boy to come to his father's aid. I always said he was a fine boy."

"Yes, you did. And he is. I just wish *he* knew that. I don't know what I'd have done if he hadn't returned when he did. I've been quite beside myself with worry. Not only about Preston but about what to do with Sweetgrass."

"Come again? What do you mean about Sweetgrass?"

"There's a lot to be decided, now that Preston's taken sick. Adele has strong opinions on the matter, of course."

Nona grunted, crossing her arms akimbo. "That woman only has one kind of opinion and that's strong. What's she got to say about this? It's not her home no more."

Mama June shrugged lightly. "It will always be her home, in some way. It's where she grew up. It's her heritage. She'd argue it's more hers than mine. You know that better than anyone."

Adele and Nona had been raised together at Sweetgrass, where Nona's mother had been the housekeeper, as was her mother before her, and so on for generations. The two girls had always been oil and water, wise to each other's tricks and wiles. Both Nona and Adele were formidable women, neither the least cowed by the other.

"I know that Adele sees Sweetgrass not so much as her home but as her property, if you catch my meaning."

"That old chestnut..." Mama June shook her head. "Adele's a wealthy woman in her own right. Why would she have any designs on poor ol' Sweetgrass?"

Nona narrowed her eyes. "Money's only money. What Adele wants is something else besides that."

"She doesn't want Sweetgrass at all. In fact, she wants me to sell it."

"Sell it!" Nona's hand flew back to her chest. "You can't be meaning to up and sell Sweetgrass? Why, it's *family* land."

"I know!" Mama June echoed with feeling. "That's why I'm bringing Preston home. He's the one who ought to be making this decision. He's the one who took care of the land, not me."

Nona's brown eyes fixed upon her as she mulled this over. "That may be so," she said at length. "But seems to me, if Mr. Preston can't talk, then like it or no, it's going to be you making the decision."

A wave of anxiety washed through her, and Mama June could taste the salty rush in her throat as she choked back words. She clutched her pocketbook tighter to her chest.

As if she understood what she was feeling, Nona stepped forward and gently placed one of her strong hands on Mama June's shoulder. "We'll pray on it," she said. "God will not push you harder than you can bear. Jesus takes up for you when you need Him."

She knew Nona was trying to be supportive, but the weight of her dilemma weighed heavily on her shoulder.

"I best be off. I have more stops to make today than hours to make them. But I thank you for your prayers. I'll need them."

Sell Sweetgrass?

So many memories came flooding back to Nona at the mention of Sweetgrass. Lots of them good memories, some of them not so good, all of them springing from her life spent there. But good or bad, they made up a lot of years and she had to acknowledge them all, for pieced together, they made up the quilt of her life.

When she returned home a short while later, she found her

daughter, Maize, already at the house to pick up the children. Nona knew better than to mention Mary June's visit, but she couldn't help herself. She just couldn't keep the words in, having to tell someone. Now she'd have to suffer the consequences.

"You can tell her we don't work for her family anymore." Maize's face was flushed and she stood ramrod straight, her hands firmly planted on her slim hips.

Nona let out a long, ragged sigh. "She didn't ask me to come back to work."

"Good!"

Maize was just like a bantam rooster, pacing on the balls of her feet, shaking her head, eager for a fight. Anything at all to do with Sweetgrass or the Blakelys or her mother doing housework usually sent Maize off on a tirade that was more about Maize's raw feelings about race relations than anything else. Nona knew her daughter wrestled with the devil on these issues—always had. Edwin and Earl, her boys, had the same fire in their bellies, but they just up and left to join their uncles in the north. Maize was her baby, however, and the cord was strong between them. Maize had married a local boy, a teacher at a local high school, and settled here in Charleston, giving Nona two of the prettiest grandbabies she ever could have wanted. They were happy, but there'd been sharp, painful words about Sweetgrass between them.

Though she would never admit this to Maize, since it would be like pouring kerosene on an open fire, Nona had felt a stiffening of the spine when Mary June hinted at her coming back to work. She didn't know why, exactly. She was fond of Mary June, and working at Sweetgrass was just the way things had always been for her. She'd grown up into the job and was proud of the quality of her work.

Nona recollected how Preston's mother, old Margaret

Blakely, could make a statement sound cool and polite, but it was always understood that she was giving an order. *Nona, the shutters in the front room need dusting today.* It wasn't the order that rankled. After all, Mrs. Blakely was her employer. It was the way she said it, without a smile or without even looking her in the eye that had made Nona feel less about her work. Adele had been like her mother, even as a young girl.

Mary June Clark, though, was different. She was born to land, too, but never took on the airs. Courtesy for her was the same as kindness. She'd always asked Nona's opinions about what did and did not need doing, and she listened. The respect made the difference between them.

"You calm yourself down," Nona said to her daughter. "Mary June just found herself in a bind, is all. It's a shame about Preston Blakely. That poor family! Haven't they seen enough trouble? I don't know what they'll do now."

"It's no trouble for us."

Nona drew herself back. "Why, the Blakelys have been my friends for as long as I've been alive."

"You're *not* their friend, Mama," Maize said, giving her the narrowed eye. "You've got to get that into your head."

"Every Christmas, don't they send us a side of pork or beef from their livestock? And don't we have leave to take whatever we want from their land? Your daddy likes to hunt and gather wood, sure, but you tell me where *I'd* be without collecting the sweetgrass from my sacred spot. And whenever any one of us took sick, it was Mary June who came calling with food. If that's not a friend, I don't know what is."

"It's what they do. It's called noblesse oblige, Mama, not friendship. Rich white folks aren't friends with poor black folks like us."

"What do you know about any of that?" Nona asked, feeling her cheeks burn at being scolded by her own daughter. "You never worked in that house alongside them, you don't know about my relationship with Mary June. Or with Preston Blakely, either. Lots of things happen over seventy years, I can tell you."

"Answer me this. When was the last time she stopped by your basket stand to ask you to dinner? Or even out to a movie? That's what you do with a friend, Mama. Not ask them to come back to work for you."

Nona knew the difference between that kind of friendship and the friendship she shared with Mary June. "There are different kinds of friends at different levels. Don't I hear you calling those people you work with at that bank your friends? My friend this. My friend that. Yet, I never saw you go out to a movie with them, neither."

Maize's face pinched but she looked away.

"You think you know everything just because you got that college degree. Well, there's a lot to know about people and life that you can't learn in books."

"It's not just about the college degree, Mama. It's about getting educated, pursuing a career, competing in today's world. It's about being a player. That's the reality I want for my children. Not cleaning up some white folks' house, doing what they say, what they want, when they want it. This family's been in bondage long enough!"

Nona drew herself up to her full height, one hand steadying herself on the counter, the other clenching her hip. She glared at Maize, this child of her own womb who she loved with a mother's fierce pride, yet her eyes were dark with rage and she could feel herself trembling with the hurt and fury she was struggling to keep compressed inside.

"Just who do you think you're calling a slave, child?" Nona's voice was low and trembled with emotion. Maize's self-righteous expression faltered. From across the room, Nona's two grandchildren had stopped watching the television and were watching them with ashen faces and wide eyes. Nona's lip trembled at the shame of it, but she fought for control. When she could speak again, she said, "I'm sorry that you're so ashamed of your mother."

"Mama…"

She pushed Maize's arm away, sparing her dignity. "I'm proud of my work. It was good and honest and I was skilled at it. And it was my work that put you through your fancy schooling, young lady. Gracie!" she called out, turning to her granddaughter. The nine-year-old girl startled. "Go get me the family Bible."

Grace scrambled to her feet and retrieved a large, faded and worn black leather-bound Bible that rested in a place of honor on the bookshelf. She carried it to her grandmother with both hands as though she were in a church procession.

"Thank you, child. You're a good girl. Now, take a seat here at the table. You, too, Kwame," she called to her thirteen-year-old grandson. He groaned softly, dragging his feet to the table. "You're becoming a man and need to hear this most. This is your heritage."

"Mama, not again," said Maize, crossing her arms and leaning against the counter in passive protest. "They've heard this story a hundred times or more."

"And they're going to hear it one more time. These children can't hear it enough. And to my mind, you still haven't got the message in your head. Time was, the only way a family could pass on records was through the telling of them. But our family is one of the lucky ones. We've got the names written down. Right in here," she said reverently, passing her strong hand over the fragile, crackled leather.

"I might not recollect all the names," Nona continued, "but seven generations of our ancestors labored at Sweetgrass, and not all of them as slaves. After emancipation, we were free to choose to leave or stay. Most left. But your great-some-thing-grandmother chose to stay on as hired labor. They worked hard and saved smart and bought themselves a good piece of land from the Blakelys for fifty cents an acre. That's the land that we, and the other heirs, are living on even to this day. This land is where our roots are. This is *our* history." Her voice trembled with emotion.

Nona felt her family's ancestors gathering close about her as she grew old, closer now even than some of the living. Sometimes at night, especially when the moon was soft, the air close and a mist rolled in from the sea, she couldn't sleep for feeling them floating around her, comforting her, calling to her from across the divide.

She slowly sat in the kitchen chair and set the Bible on the wood table. The chair's worn blue floral cushion did little to ease her pains, but she gave them no mind as she opened up the Bible to reveal yellowed sheets of paper as thin as a moth's wing. Each page was crowded with faded black ink in an elab-orate script. She was proud of the fine handwriting of her kin. She often marveled at their courage to practice the skill, given the life-and-death orders against slaves reading and writing.

"Most of what I know about our distant kin was passed on orally in stories. I recollect just bits, mostly about a slave named Mathilde who came from Africa. And Ben, who escaped north never to be heard from again. You remember those stories?"

When the children nodded, she rewarded them with an approving smile. Maize hovered closer, joining the circle.

"Now, my great-grandmother was Delilah. That's her name right there. She was the last of our family enslaved at Sweetgrass, and it was Delilah who first began to write down our family history. She was the head housekeeper at Sweetgrass and a fine, intelligent woman. Taught herself how to read and write from the children's schoolbooks. Had to sneak them, of course, at great peril. It was only after the War Act that she felt safe to write openly. Must've been a fine day when Delilah wrote her first entry in this Bible. Look close!"

The children leaned forward to read the elaborate loops and the even shapes of Delilah's first entry on February 26, 1865. *Freedom Come!* The second entry was her marriage to John Foreman, and the third, the birth of her first child, a daughter named Delia.

"Her child—my grandmother—was the first freeborn in our line. After emancipation come, Delilah stayed on at Sweetgrass, working as a free woman, living in the kitchen house next to the main house with her husband and children until it fell to her daughter, Delia—your great-great-grand-mother—to note the date of her mother's death in this Bible. They buried Delilah in the graveyard on Sweetgrass where many of our kin were laid to rest.

"Now, Delia had a daughter named Florence. When she married, she didn't want to live in that kitchen house no more, so she moved here on Six Mile Road and built the house across the street. But she continued working for the Blakely family. Before long, she wrote in the Bible the name of her firstborn."

"Nona," read Gracie. "That's you."

"That's me. And I'm the last in our line to work for the Blakely family."

"There's my mama's name," Gracie said in rote, pointing to Maize's name. "And mine and Kwame's." It was a ritual, this pointing out of their names in the family Bible.

"You see the names, Kwame?"

"Yes'm."

Nona nodded her gray head. "Good." She firmly believed that with each recognition of their name in a long line of family, the roots of these young sprouts grew strong and fixed.

"Our family's been born and buried on Sweetgrass land near as long as the Blakelys have. This land is our history, too. And the sweetgrass that grows here is as dear to me as it was to my mother and her mother before her. Maybe more so, as the grass is fast disappearing from these parts. Our family's been pulling grass on this land since time was. Making sweetgrass baskets is part of our culture. I don't want my grandchildren to forget their heritage. That's why I'm teaching you how to make the baskets. It's part of who we come from. Even if your mama don't care to."

"Yes'm," the children replied, sitting straight in their chair.

Her face softened at the sight of them, her grandbabies. These were the beacons she was lighting to carry on into the future. And didn't they shine bright?

She reached out to place her wrinkled hands upon their heads, then gently offered them a pat. "Go on, now. It's time for you to get home and finish your homework. Kwame, don't forget to fix the spelling on that paper."

After kisses and quick orders, Maize gathered her children and sent them ahead to the car. She paused at the door, her smooth face creased with trouble.

Nona sat in her chair, waiting.

"Mama," Maize said at length, raising her eyes to meet Nona's steady gaze. "You're the strongest woman I know. You hold this family together, and I know I wouldn't be the woman I am without you. I don't mean to be so harsh about the Blakelys and Sweetgrass. I'm all churning inside with my feelings about them. You seem to have it all so settled in your mind. I envy that. I wish I could be so at peace with it. But I love you. And I'm proud of you." She laughed shortly and wiped away a tear. "And you're right. What do I know about you and Mrs. Mary June? Maybe she is your friend. Lord knows I have few enough of them myself."

Nona opened up her arms.

Maize hurried to her mother's side and hugged her, placing a kiss on her cheek.

Nona squeezed her youngest child close to her breast, relishing the smoothness of her cheek against her own. When Maize let her guard down and hugged her like this, all time vanished and it felt to Nona like her daughter was a small child again, seeking comfort in her mama's arms.

After they left, Nona remained sitting in the hardback chair, her hand resting on the treasured family Bible for a long while. She had to make sense out of her rambling feelings.

In retrospect, Maize wasn't totally wrong when she said the Blakelys weren't friends. Maybe *friendship* wasn't the right word for what she shared with Mary June Blakely. Maybe *bond* better described their relationship. Working in someone's home was more personal than working in an office. Maize couldn't understand that. She hadn't lived in that house all those years, hadn't shared the private moments or the secrets. Or the tragedies. Truth was, Nona couldn't explain to her daughter the complex feelings she harbored about the Blakelys. She couldn't explain them even to herself. She doubted Mary June could, either.

Nona placed her palms on the table and dragged herself to a stand. Lord, what a day, she thought, rubbing her back, feeling the ache travel straight down her legs. She carried the large book back to its resting place on the bookshelf. It wouldn't be too long before Maize would make the final notation about her mother in the Bible, she thought. Nona wasn't afraid of what was coming—no, she was not. She'd walked a straight path in her life, even if it seemed a bit narrow at times, and she would walk a straight path to the Lord when He called her home.

Sweetgrass

She gingerly nestled the fragile leather Bible between two sweetgrass baskets. One had been woven by her mother, Florence, and the other by her grandmother, Delia. She gently traced her fingers along the intricate stitches of the palmetto fronds that held together many strands of soft yellow sweetgrass. The baskets were old and dry, cracking at places, but the stitches held tight.

This treasured Bible and these precious woven baskets helped make her thoughts more clear. Looking at them, Nona realized that the histories of the Blakelys and the Bennetts were woven together just as tightly as the sweetgrass in these baskets. Like it or not, history could not be changed. It was what it was. Strong ties, the ones that are ironclad and bind souls, are forged in shared history, she thought. This was a bond, not bondage.

Nona readjusted the baskets on the shelf. Then she walked to a large cardboard box in the corner of the room, beside the sofa. In this box she stored the baskets she'd made to sell at her stand. Sorting through, she chose one she was particularly proud of. It was a deceptively simple design with the twisting handle she did so well. She held it up to the light, proud that the stitches were so tight, not a pinprick of light shone through. This basket would hold for generations to come.

Nona placed this basket on the kitchen table, then began to pull out flour, tins and her mixing bowls from the cabinets. All her earlier fatigue had vanished in the fervor of her new mission. She was clearheaded now and knew what she had to do.

5

The basket making tradition is a family affair. It was the custom for men and boys to gather the materials while women and girls sewed the baskets. Though this tradition continues, nowadays all members of the family gather materials and make the baskets.

SUNDAY DINNER HAD LONG been a tradition for the Blakely family, as it was for many Southern families. Nan recalled Sunday dinner beginning in the early afternoon, soon after their return from church. Nona used to cover the dining room's long mahogany table with the old damask tablecloth while Mama June set flowers from her garden in sparkling crystal vases. The Blakely silver would be set, polished to a burnished gleam, as well as the graceful candelabra that had come from the Clarks and had been promised to Nan.

She had taken for granted those days when the table was overflowing with uncles, aunts, cousins and friends. On those occasions when the extended family came, the children were sent, grumbling, to the kiddie table in the kitchen. But when it was just the immediate family, the children always sat at the dining room table and were expected to be on their best behavior. On Monday night, they ate on everyday china. On Tuesday night, Hamlin might slouch in his chair. On Wednesday, Morgan might rest an elbow on the table. On Thursday, Daddy might remain silent, engrossed in his thoughts. On Friday, Nan might stir her peas on her plate or laugh with her mouth full at something Hamlin said. On these nights, Mama June looked the other way.

But on Sunday in the dining room, Mama June's eyes were sharp and everyone was on their best behavior. Linen napkins were on the laps, no one left the table without being excused, Daddy was attentive to conversation, and each child was expected to know which fork to use.

The Sunday dinner tradition had fallen to the wayside after Hamlin's death, when Mama June couldn't summon the effort. It wasn't decided upon; the tradition just silently slipped away.

To Nan's mind, the end of Sunday dinners marked a sad turning point in the family's history. The sense of collective purpose, the ready conversation, dissipated as silent months turned into years. In time, Nan married and left home, followed by Morgan's angry departure to points west. Yet, even now, when she thought of her family, Nan thought of those precious years of joy when the family was strong and united together for Sunday dinner.

They arrived at Sweetgrass a little late. Chas and Harry had dragged their heels in a teenage sulk at having to get dressed up and spend a perfectly good day inside, bored to death. Hank seemed eager that they all attend the family dinner and had nagged at the boys to hurry. Nan looked into the rearview mirror. The boys sat sullen and resigned in the leather back seat of the sedan.

"Adele's already here," Hank said tersely as they pulled up to the house. Hank worked closely with Adele on development deals, thus Adele was not only a relative, but an employer.

Nan chewed her lip and checked her watch. "We're only a half hour late. I doubt we've even been missed. Boys," she called as her sons launched from the car. "Be on your best manners."

They climbed the stairs to the front veranda where Mama June's planters were filled with cheery yellow-and-purple pansies and all the brass was polished. Nan stood at the front door in her peach linen dress flanked by the tall, handsome men in her life. Beside her, Hank straightened his tie before ringing the bell. Nan picked a bit of lint from his shoulder and, alert to his tension, wondered why he seemed nervous about this gathering. Had he really been made to feel so much an outsider over the years? she wondered. She moved her hand to his arm and squeezed it reassuringly. He turned his head and looked at her with a quizzical expression.

The door swung wide. To her surprise, it was Aunt Adele who welcomed them in a sensational blouse of creamy raw silk, looking every bit the lady of the house.

"Here you are!" she exclaimed, her dark eyes brightening.

Preston's sister was a tall, proud woman, as fierce a competitor in golf and tennis as in the real estate development business she'd built. Her salt-and-pepper hair was neatly trimmed away from her face, accentuating her trim, athletic good looks.

Nan began her litany of excuses, but Adele blithely waved them aside.

"Oh, none of that matters. Come in, come in! And you two," she said, opening her arms to the boys. "Where have you been hiding? Come here this minute and give me a proper hug."

Shuffling their feet, they obliged, but Nan didn't miss the real affection between them. Adele was the godmother for both of her children. Never having married or had any children of her own, Adele doted on the boys and spoiled them with gifts. Mama June felt a little jealous that the boys spent more time at Adele's spacious home on Sullivan's Island, with her boats and pool and fridge filled with snacks, than at Sweetgrass. Adele was a wealthy woman who always had a spare dollar or three to hand out, while Mama June and Preston always had to pinch pennies.

Adele stood back to look at the boys. "My, my, don't you look handsome."

Chas rubbed his finger between his collar and neck. "Mama made us dress up."

"Dress up? Honey, in my day, you boys would be in a jacket and tie. Without air-conditioning, mind you. So count your blessings." She turned to Harry. "I thought you'd be out on the golf course this afternoon."

He grimaced. "I should be. I'm playing in a tournament next week."

"Your daddy told me. Say, I saw a new titanium putter at the club that's as light as a feather and sure to help your game."

"Yeah?" Harry exclaimed. "But I'll bet it costs an arm and a leg."

"Maybe not all that much." She winked. "Be good today and we'll talk."

"Now, Aunt Adele…" Nan interjected, not wanting the boys to always feel they needed a reward for good behavior.

"We'd better join the others before they wonder where we are," Adele interrupted, expertly steering the family into the living room.

The moment they stepped in, the room exploded with hoots and hollers. Morgan rushed out of his chair and wrapped Nan in a bear hug. The affection and banter flowed freely between brother and sister, spreading throughout the room.

Mama June wrapped her arms around herself, hearing the merriment as a string of firecrackers celebrating the family's reunion. Hank smoothly stepped forward to act as bartender, serving the ladies mimosas.

"Morgan, what's your poison?"

"Bourbon on the rocks, thanks."

"A man after my own heart."

"That sounds good to me, too, Dad," Harry called out.

"There're Cokes in the fridge," Mama June replied. "Help yourself. But first, come say hello to your uncle."

"I doubt they much remember you, Morgan," Adele said.

Mama June thought the comment unkind, but Morgan sauntered over, extending his hand with a lopsided grin.

"I'll bet you haven't forgotten that boar hunt, huh?" he asked.

Harry, who adored hunting, shook his head and readily took Morgan's hand. "No, sir!"

"What boar hunt?" Chas immediately wanted to know.

Harry launched into the tale, eliciting guffaws from Hank and Morgan. Mama June listened, attuned to the gift of storytelling that her grandson had inherited from his grandfather Blakely, along with Preston's throaty laugh. Seeing the genetic imprint carry on from generation to generation was, for her, a blessing of growing older. Her attention was distracted, however, by Adele. She meandered about the room perusing the colonial-era furniture with a proprietary air. She stopped before an empire bookcase that held several pieces of family silver.

"Well, I'll be...." She reached into the cabinet and lifted out a small engraved silver cup. "You found my porridge cup!"

Mama June came directly to her side. "Yes! After all these years we found it when we moved furniture in the dining room. It was wedged between the breakfront and the wall. Don't ask me how it got there."

"It was probably Press or Tripp that hid it there, just to rile me." Adele tenderly turned the burnished silver cup in her hands. "I never thought I'd see this again."

"Why don't you keep it? Take it home with you," Mama June offered.

Adele's gaze shot up. "How nice of you to offer me my own porridge cup," she said with sharp sarcasm that put Mama June's teeth on edge.

From the corner of her eye she caught Morgan's swift turn of head at the tone, his eyes searching.

Despite Mama June's protests, Adele put the porridge cup back on the shelf with a great show.

Mama June was sensitive to the fact that it was difficult for her sister-in-law to be a guest in the house she'd grown up in. Though she'd never said so openly, it was clearly understood by both women that even though Mama June *owned* Sweetgrass, she wasn't *from* Sweetgrass. And that fact was a major burr under Adele's seat.

Letting the comment slide, she smiled and announced it was time for dinner.

The large meal that Mama June had slaved over was consumed with relish and compliments. She beamed as she watched her grandsons help themselves to seconds of the chicken with Madeira sauce from an old family recipe. The cocktails had loosened their tongues and they talked amiably as they ate. For a while she felt transported in time to when such gatherings were commonplace at Sweetgrass. Morgan, never much of a talker, spoke openly about his life in Montana, and the boys ate up his stories and peppered him with questions. They liked him, she thought with delight. And the feeling was mutual. Too soon, it was time to clear the dishes, and Nan helped her serve the pecan pie and ice cream that was a universal favorite.

She was pouring coffee when a subtle mood shift indicated

they all sensed the chitchat was over and it was time to talk business. Their radars finely honed to such nuances, the boys asked to be excused from the table and dashed for the exit. Mama June sought Morgan's eyes and they shared a commiserating look.

He cleared his throat and all heads turned toward him. She had purposefully set him in Preston's seat at the head of the table, a gesture she knew had not gone unnoticed by Adele at his right. Nan sat to his left and Hank to Mama June's right at the table's other end.

"I wish my homecoming had been under happier circumstances," he began.

"Lord knows we all waited long enough, bless your heart," Adele said.

"Yes. A long time," he replied.

How extraordinary, Mama June thought. How coolly her son dealt with Adele's niggling.

"Well, you're home now," Nan said, springing to his defense. "That's what's important."

Mama June smiled gratefully at her daughter.

"Anyway," Morgan continued, "Mama June has asked me to stay on for a while. And I've agreed."

Adele's brows rose as she exchanged a quick glance with Hank, who frowned.

"That's wonderful," exclaimed Nan. "I'd hoped you would, what with Daddy in the hospital."

That was her opening. Mama June set her cup down in the saucer and straightened her shoulders. She looked around the table then settled on the supportive, bolstering stare of Morgan.

"I have good news. We are bringing Preston home!" she announced. "To Sweetgrass."

There was a sudden hush over the table, as though a bomb had been dropped.

"You can't be serious!" Adele blurted out.

"Why not?" Morgan asked. "It makes perfect sense to bring him home. It's even recommended by the doctors."

Hank threw his napkin on the table and leaned back in his chair in exasperation. "I should think it's obvious why not," he said. "The man can't speak. He can hardly move!"

"Hank!" interjected Nan, horrified.

Mama June's head swung toward him, speechless with disbelief.

"Why are you surprised?" Hank argued. "It may not be pretty, but it's the truth. We can't be romantic about this."

"But we can be civil," Mama June retorted.

"Mary June," Adele said. "I thought we'd talked about this."

"That doesn't mean it is what I decided," she replied. She could feel her back stiffening against the chair.

"This is ridiculous. I don't mean to offend," Adele said in that testy manner that informed she was about to do just that, "but everyone knows that Preston shielded you from financial decisions. You preferred it that way. Frankly, you can't afford to bring him home. There'll be medical costs, a decrease in family income and a rise in all of your fixed expenditures. You have to face the facts. You must consolidate and sell your assets."

"You mean," Morgan said flatly, "sell Sweetgrass."

Adele turned from Mama June to look at her nephew, her brow raised at the fact that he'd entered the fray. Their eyes met and held for a long moment.

"Yes," she replied succinctly. "Sweetgrass is your mother's greatest asset. And it's actually a very good time to sell."

"How lucky for us he decided to have his stroke now," Morgan replied.

Adele bristled.

"Adele," Mama June said in an appeal for understanding. "This isn't just about selling property. This is the family heritage. Preston has devoted his life to preserving it. Once Sweet-grass is gone, what will happen to us, to the *family?*"

Adele's face hardened. "The family will simply have to move on."

Mama June drew back. Her voice trembled with emotion. "I could never sell it out from under him. If the stroke didn't kill him, that surely would."

"Hank is right. You're being romantic. I'm very worried about you and Preston," Adele replied. "And disappointed in this decision." She turned again to her nephew. "I think it's plain irresponsible of Morgan to come home and interfere in what had already been decided by the family."

Morgan folded his hands on the table, but did not rise to the bait.

Adele's face tightened. "I hope you know what you're doing."

"Mama June, is it so horrible to consider selling?" Nan asked. Her soft voice broke the escalating tension. "You and Daddy have worked hard all your lives. You never spend a penny on yourselves and I can't remember when you've ever taken a vaca-tion. Every dime you earn you put right back into this place. If you sell Sweetgrass, you'll finally have a chance to take it easy. Really, Mama, won't you have enough to worry about now just with Daddy? Why do you want to worry about trying to hang on to all this land, too? Let it go. Enjoy life a little."

Mama June looked into her daughter's large blue eyes, so much like her own, and felt her resolve slip. The thought of letting go of the burdens of Sweetgrass, of simply moving on to someplace easier, of not pinching pennies and worrying about money, was seductive.

Yet the guilt of letting go of the family land that Preston loved more than anything else weighed heavily on her mind.

"Won't you miss Sweetgrass if it's sold?" Morgan asked Nan.

Nan's expression shifted as a soft smile reluctantly eased across her face. "Yes, sure," she conceded. "I guess I will."

"We all will," Adele interjected, casting an impatient glance at her niece. "That's not the point. We mustn't slip into nostalgia or we'll never be able to deal with what's on our plate today. Besides," she said as an aside to Morgan, "I thought you made your opinion perfectly clear years ago when you left. I believe it had something to do with dynamite and sending the whole place to hell."

"He was angry," Mama June quickly said. Making excuses for Morgan came readily to her.

"That was more about what was between me and my father than about the land," he replied, the first hint of steel entering in his voice. "And to that point, this decision is between my mother and my father."

He paused, meeting the challenge in Hank's glare. Then, spreading his palms against the table, he said in a controlled voice that brooked no further discussion, "Mama June has listened to all of our opinions and weighed them. She's made her decision." He looked directly at his aunt. "I'm sure if she wants you to know something more, she'll contact you."

Mama June felt a tightness in her stomach as Morgan's defense became offense. She glanced quickly at Adele. Her jaw worked at what she certainly viewed as impudence. Adele Blakely was not accustomed to such treatment and Mama June knew she'd hear no end of it.

"Well, I know when I've been asked to leave," Adele said, springing to her feet.

"Adele, don't go," implored Mama June. Adele often felt pique and walked off in a huff, expecting others to make amends.

"I can't say that I'm happy with this decision, but you obviously don't want my opinion." She shot a glance at Hank.

Hank rose and gave the *let's-go* look to Nan. She promptly followed suit. Adele walked swiftly out, followed closely by Hank. Nan shrugged helplessly then followed her husband from the room. Mama June heard her calling up the stairs for the boys to hurry up, they were leaving.

Mama June sighed and pulled herself from her chair.

"Let them go, Mama," Morgan said.

She was sorely tempted. She'd worked tirelessly for days to prepare this dinner and felt utterly spent. A mountain of dishes awaited her in the kitchen. She didn't care at that moment if Adele agreed with her decision or not, nor whether she stormed off, not to be heard from for months, as she'd done in the past. Nonetheless, her upbringing dragged her to her feet.

"It goes against my grain to let a guest, much less my sister-in-law, leave my home upset."

So she hurried after her, her heels clicking loudly on the polished hardwood floors. Nan was already at her car having a heated exchange with Hank. On the porch, Mama June placed her hand on Adele's sleeve, arresting her hasty departure.

"Let's not argue," she said to Adele.

"I'm very upset."

"I know. I'm sorry. But, dear, we need to come together now. For Preston's sake. He needs us all."

In a spontaneous rush, Adele stepped forward to hug her, tight and fierce. Mama June was swept back to long ago when they were best friends.

Adele pulled back and urged her with her dark eyes blazing, "Think again, Mary June. Before it's too late."

Then Adele released her and walked swiftly down the stairs to her car. Blackjack barked madly from his den beneath the porch.

Sweetgrass

Mama June heard the screen door slam behind her and felt her son's arm slide around her shoulder. She sighed and leaned into him, relishing his kiss upon the top of her head.

They watched until Adele's sleek Jaguar, followed by Nan's Lexus, disappeared down the drive, then stood side by side for several minutes longer. Each relished the peace of the family's departure. Each was going over in their mind the comments that had been made, dissecting the words and analyzing the intent.

"This storm will blow over," he said to her.

"Yes, I suppose so," she replied, though she didn't really feel so. Old scabs had been reopened that would take time to heal. "Perhaps I put too much store in all going well today. I so wanted their cooperation."

"And you'll have it. They just had to blow off steam."

"I'm not so certain. Adele can be rigid, and Nan's a dear but she follows Hank's lead."

"She's a sweet kid, but she has no backbone."

Mama June didn't respond, fearing that the same might have been said about herself over the years.

"Adele pinched the cup, you know," Morgan said with amusement in his voice.

"What? The porridge cup?"

He nodded, his lips twisted in disgust.

Mama June shook her head. "It was hers, anyway."

"You're not going to say anything?"

"No, let it go. I offered it to her, after all. Besides, it's not the first thing she's pinched, as you call it."

"You're kidding."

"It's never something of great value, at least monetarily. But over the years I've noticed a photograph missing, or a piece of family silver, or a painting from her old bedroom. All things that I'm sure she's rationalized belong to her. For whatever reasons, she needs them. I've found it best just not to say anything."

Movement caught her attention, and turning her head, she saw a thick-set woman in a blue floral dress and a purple slicker coming up the sidewalk from around back.

"Nona!" she called out with a quick wave.

Nona's face rose toward the stairs and broke into a quick grin. "'Afternoon, Mary June."

"Nona!" Morgan exclaimed, dashing down the stairs. He swooped Nona in his arms and they hugged warmly, instantly nanny and child again. Morgan held her at arm's length. "Let me look at you. I swear, you never change. Make a pact with the devil to look so good at your age? And it's no use lying. I know exactly how old you are."

"Just living the good life," Nona quipped. "More than I can say for you! What's all this long, shaggy hair? And buttons missing from your shirt? You used to be such a fine dresser. Remember those white bucks? Lord, you were like a peacock in those days. You need some caring after, that's for certain. Don't they have women where you been living? You can't find yourself a wife?"

"Come in, come in," Mama June exclaimed, gesturing with her hand toward the house.

"I can't stay long. I came along with Elmore. He's out yonder checking on the sweetgrass," she said, indicating the direction of the fields with a jerk of her chin. "The first pulling of the season will be here before we know it. Speaking of which…" She lifted her arms to Mama June to offer a beautiful sweetgrass basket with a curved handle.

"Elmore and I, we were sorry to hear Mr. Preston took sick and wanted to bring something. From our house to yours."

Mama June was more touched by the sentiment than she could express. She took hold of the intricately sewn bread basket made of coiled sweetgrass, rush and pine needles with the same reverence she would an olive branch. Inside the basket, tucked neatly in a blue-checked napkin, were Nona's homemade buttermilk biscuits.

She felt her heart shift and pump with age-old affection. "Nona, this is so kind of you. It's been a long time since I've tasted one of your biscuits. Morgan was saying how he longed for them. Please, won't you come in? We just had dinner, but I have pecan pie. And coffee." She grinned wide. Nona's love for coffee was well known.

"Maybe just for a coffee. It'll give me a chance to catch up with that wild boy of yours."

Later, after coffee and pie were finished and Morgan had gone off to tend to Blackjack, Mama June spoke in confidential tones to Nona about what had transpired that afternoon.

"Good riddance," Nona said, her lip curled in disgust. "That woman is a real pain in the you-know-where. Always has been."

"What have I done?" Mama June asked, staring out with dismay.

"You showed some backbone, that's what you've done. Praise Lord!"

Mary June placed her fingers to her brow. "A lot of good it did me. I've alienated my family. Now I'm alone."

Nona pursed her lips, then said, "No, you're not. You have me."

Mama June dropped her hand. "But…"

"I realized I was no kind of friend to let you go through this alone. Not after all we've been through together. Now, I can't do all I used to—and neither can you. But together we'll manage. I'll come by to make sure the house is running smoothly and make certain you're not starving while you tend to your husband. And I'll lend an ear when you need it. It's the least any friend could do."

Mama June's hands squeezed around Nona's. "I can't thank you enough. Just knowing you're here…"

"Let's not get all weepy. Lord knows, we've got our work cut out for us!"

6

Skill, craftsmanship and long hours of work are involved in making sweetgrass baskets. A simple design can take as long as twelve hours. A larger, more complex design can take as long as two to three months.

NONA SIGHED HEAVILY as she brought her van to a stop at Sweetgrass. She looked through the shaded windshield at the handsome white house. It sure was a picture, she thought, cloaked as it was in the pink light of early morning. She'd spent the better part of her life working in this old house and a part of her was happy to come back to it. Maize couldn't understand such feelings—and that was okay. Nona prided herself on the choices she'd made in her own life and didn't care to change her ways now. The wind did blow when Maize heard she'd decided to come back to work at Sweetgrass, but it was up to Maize to accept what was.

Nona pulled herself out from the shiny white van, stretching a bit after landing in the soft gravel. She'd bought the car after years of saving her basket money, and every time she looked at it, a ripple of pride coursed through her. Usually it was stuffed to the brim with her baskets, but she'd removed the treasures to store safely in her house until things were settled here at Sweetgrass. She pulled from the van a large canvas bag filled with grass, palmetto fronds and her tools. Every spare minute, her fingers sewed the baskets.

Blackjack greeted her in his usual manner, a grayed muzzle at her thigh and his tail waving behind like a tom-tom drum.

"Hello, you ol' hound dog," she exclaimed with affection, bending to pat the fur.

Morgan's voice caught her by surprise. "'Morning, Nona! You're here early. What? You can't stay away?"

His tall, lanky form came from around the side of the house. He was dressed in a faded old T-shirt that was torn at the neck, paint-splattered jeans and worn hiking boots caked with mud. His face was as yet unshaven, and his thick brown curls tumbled askew on his head. He looked like the eight-year-old boy she remembered running in from the field, blue eyes twinkling, to show her a robin's egg or a snake skin or some other treasure he'd unearthed.

Nona clucked her tongue. "What you got in your hands there?" she asked, indicating the towel he was carrying. "A frog?"

He lifted a paintbrush from the towel. "I'm fixing up the kitchen house. Mama June wants the new aide to stay there. I've patched up a few leaks in the roof, put in a window air conditioner in the bedroom, new screens on the windows and now I'm finishing up a fresh coat of paint. You know," he said, scratching his jaw, "it's looking pretty good. I'm thinking maybe I should move in, instead."

"Oh, no you don't. That girl's going to want her own space. So's your mama. You just be a good boy and finish fixing that place up for Miss…what's her name?"

"Kristina Hays."

She acknowledged this with a nod. "Well, I've got things to get done before Miss Hays arrives, too."

"I hope she works out."

"You and me both." She looked over to the house. "Seems quiet in there."

"Mama's sleeping now, or was last time I checked."

Her brows rose. "Your mama's still asleep?" She glanced quickly at her wristwatch. "She always rises with the sun. She's not sick, is she?"

He shook his head. "Just exhausted. I didn't bother her, and frankly, I'm glad she's catching up. She's been going non-stop."

"That's just her way. When she's got herself a project, she gives one hundred percent. And given that this project is your daddy, she's straining all her gears."

"Yeah, but she's sixty-six years old."

"I'm sixty-eight! What's your point?"

Morgan laughed. Nona was one of those people who was ageless. She seemed to him today to be the same woman she was when he was a boy. She still stood straight-backed and full-breasted, like some Wagnerian princess. Her hair still gleamed, too, though more like the black-and-white osprey's wing than a raven's. She wore it in much the same, short-curled style. Most of all, her spirit had not aged one whit.

One of his first memories of Nona was when he was three or four. Her finger was wagging and her eyes were flames as she scolded his older brother, Hamlin, within an inch of his life. Ham was much older, around thirteen. Yet there he was with his head bowed, filled with remorse. Up till that time, his big brother had seemed to him like a prince among men, a hero beyond reproach. Certainly his parents had never laid down the law like that. Morgan never figured out exactly what it was that Hamlin had done to rile Nona so, though he knew it had something to do with Hamlin taking Morgan out on the boat. Ham had taken him out lots of times without permission, but Morgan was too young to understand why Nona would be so upset about that. Only in retrospect did he see that it was an omen. Nonetheless, his earth had shifted that day as he witnessed her power over his brother.

Morgan put his hands up in mock surrender. "No point made."

Her dark eyes gleamed in amused triumph. "She'll get herself up before too long. You eat yet?" she asked him.

"Grabbed some orange juice and a Pop-Tart."

Nona wrinkled her nose in disgust. "It's no wonder you're looking like a scarecrow. I'm amazed you managed to live so long all alone."

"Who said I was alone?"

That caught her off guard and her face showed it. She quickly recouped, delivering a no-nonsense glare at his smirk. "Don't you just wish. What woman is gonna hitch her star to someone as dog-ugly as you? Come back inside in about half an hour. I'm fixing to roll out some biscuits and fry up some bacon. And coffee," she added, her body yearning for her beloved brew.

Morgan smiled as he watched Nona climb the stairs to the house. It wasn't often he could render Nona speechless.

Hours later, Morgan was applying the last coat of Charleston Green paint to the kitchen house front door when he heard a car pulling up to the house followed by Blackjack's gruff bark of alarm. The dog's arthritic legs strained under the effort of rising. Feeling like an old dog himself after a long morning of painting, he slowly straightened with one hand anchoring the small of his back. His gaze followed Blackjack's rush toward the sound of crunching gravel.

Sweetgrass

From around the house, a tall, lean woman dressed in bleached jean lowriders and a cuffed white shirt walked toward him with a straight-backed, confident, hip-swaying gait. Her oversize, scuffed brown leather purse banged against her slender hip in steady, seductive rhythm. Morgan watched her, squinting in the noonday sun. Against the glare, her long, wildly curly hair seemed an aura around her head that captured and held the golden light.

"Hi there," she called out as she approached. Her voice lilted at the end, like a song.

"Hello," he responded with more reserve as she breezily sauntered near. "Can I help you?"

Up close, the force of her personality dominated his first impression. The young woman vibrated with life. It sparked out from her bright blue eyes and shone from her very white, no-holds-barred smile.

"I hope so," she said, smiling straight into his eyes. "I'm looking for the Blakely residence."

"Well, you found it."

"Good! The directions said to turn in at the Sweetgrass gate and you're the only house I've found." She put out her hand. "I'm Kristina Hays. The agency sent me."

He blinked again. "*You're* the new aide?"

"Yes," she said, her smile faltering. "I hope you're expecting me."

Morgan quickly recouped. "Yes. Absolutely. I'm Morgan. Morgan Blakely."

She took his hand and he was impressed by the strength of her handshake.

"You seem surprised to see me," she said.

"It's just…well, you're different than I expected." He didn't quite know what he expected, exactly. "Younger," he added lamely.

"I don't believe in age. But don't worry, I'm old enough. And I've been doing this for years, though not in South Carolina. I only moved here a few months ago. From California," she added, as though this fact alone qualified her for the job.

Blackjack, who had been circling anxiously, finally could bear it no longer and nosed closer, boldly began sniffing her feet.

"Hey there, big fella!" she exclaimed warmly. "Are we ignoring you? What's your name?" She dropped her bag and bent to warmly pat his head and flop his ears.

Rather than be suspicious of the stranger, Blackjack whined happily at her attention, rudely pawing her legs.

"Blackjack!" Morgan called. "Back off!"

"I don't mind," she replied, still stroking the black fur. "Dogs like me. Blackjack, huh? Good name."

He lifted his chin toward the house. "Here comes my mother now."

He felt a boyish pride and affection at the sight of his mother striding along the path from the main house to the kitchen house. She was simply dressed in a dark skirt, floral blouse and sensible shoes. Her hair was a snowy-white mass twisted into a bun at the back of her head. Signs of the beauty she once was added charm to the graciousness and fresh, scrubbed appeal of her open, smiling face.

"Miss Hays? I'm Mary June Blakely. Welcome to Sweetgrass."

Kristina's warmth matched his mother's as she reached out to take her offered hand. The two women's eyes met and measured; Morgan could feel the tacit approval in the air.

"When does Mr. Blakely arrive home?" Kristina asked.

"Hopefully tomorrow. Possibly the following day. We've been anxious for your arrival to help us smooth his transition."

"Homecomings are always stressful, but if we're prepared, we'll sail through."

Morgan noted that his mother's shoulders relaxed at Kristina's use of the word *we*. Although she didn't voice it, he knew Mama June was worried what her new role would be once the aide arrived.

"How long have you been in this line of work?" Mama June asked.

"About eight years. I was trained originally as a therapeutic masseuse, but my dad had a stroke a few years back and I took care of him. I guess you could say I found my true calling."

"You *did* get formal training as a medical aide?" Morgan interjected with suspicion.

She cast him a sidelong glance, clueing into his worries about her qualifications. "It's all in here." She dug into her large leather bag and pulled out a crinkled white envelope. "I believe the agency sent you my résumé but I like to bring my own, just in case. All my formal training is listed, as well as my credentials as a massage therapist. But believe me, my real training came from taking care of my father."

Mama June's eyes softened with concern. "I'm sorry to learn your father was ill, too. Is he much improved?"

"He died last year."

"Oh, dear," Mama June responded. "I'm sorry to hear that."

"My father's stroke was quite massive," Morgan told her. "He's completely paralyzed on his right side and he can't speak at all. Are you familiar with cases like this?"

"Aphasics are my specialty," she replied.

"How wonderful," Mama June replied in a rush, obviously taken with Kristina. "We're lucky to have you, Miss Hays."

"Please, call me Kristina," she said with an all-encompassing smile.

"Morgan," Mama June said, turning to him. "Won't you

show Kristina where she'll be staying?" Then to Kristina, "Take a few minutes to freshen up and unpack. When you're ready, won't you join us for lunch? Say, twelve-thirty? You'll meet Nona. She's the other major link in our team."

He realized he was still standing there with a paintbrush in his hand. "Just give me a minute."

He walked back to the front of the kitchen house and dumped the brush in a plastic bag and covered the nearly empty paint can. Then he waved her over and began wiping his hand with a towel. "I've finished for the day. It would appear just in time, too." He indicated the kitchen house with a jerk of his chin. The brick was sparkling white with a fresh coat of paint. Morgan had also painted the shutters the same aquamarine color that was on the shutters of the main house.

"It's a nice place inside. There's lots of light. I think you'll like it."

Her generous mouth slipped open. "You're kidding, right? This place is for me?"

"For as long as you work here, anyway."

"I just assumed I'd be sleeping in some spare bedroom."

"You can do that, if you prefer," he said hopefully. "I can move out here."

"No! No, I love it!" She seemed genuinely pleased.

Morgan was torn between disappointment that she loved the kitchen house and pleasure that his hard work fixing it up was appreciated. "Come on in. I'll give you the cook's tour. Mind the paint."

It was a solidly built, one-story brick house that had both the charm and the disadvantages of antiquity. Morgan had to duck his head as he walked beneath the door's low lintel and led her into the small house. It was divided in two by an enormous brick fireplace. A second, smaller fireplace nestled in the northern wall, and on the southern, a small, angled greenhouse had been added. Behind the center fireplace was a second room of equal size with a third fireplace. This room was also white and spare, with only a black iron bed and a painted pine dresser against the brick walls.

"I haven't gotten around to putting the rest of the furniture back in yet," he said.

"I like my furnishings spare." Kristina's eyes scanned the room and her voice almost purred. "It's perfect."

The floor planks creaked as she walked around the room, her neck craning to study the dark wood crossbeams that dominated the ceiling. Her body was slim but taut, and he'd bet his last dollar she did yoga. If she liked things spare, like he did, then he knew she'd appreciate the simple charm of sunlight that filtered in through small, mullioned windows covered with crisp, fresh white lace.

"Was this the guest house?" she asked, taking interest.

He looked around the house dispassionately, having told the history countless times before. "Originally it was the kitchen house, which is what we still call it. Back in the 1800s when the main house was built, fire was a real threat, so kitchens were in a separate building. The servants would carry the food to and from the dining room. Sometime after the turn of the century, my grandfather added on to the main house, building a new kitchen. He added running water to this place, electricity and a septic tank."

"He made it a dwelling," she said.

"For the Bennetts, a family that's been connected to mine for generations. They moved in and lived here for a spell, but after they had a few children, they moved out to a house of their own. The next tenants were my parents. That brings us to the fifties. Daddy modernized it some more and brought his bride in right after they were married. They lived here till my grandparents died. At that point, my parents moved into the big house and it's been empty ever since. We kids used it as a playhouse, guests stayed in it occasionally, but as for tenants, you're the next."

"I'm honored," she quipped.

"I put in a new fridge and microwave. And an air conditioner in your bedroom. All the comforts of home."

"So I gather this place has been in your family for a long time?"

"You could say so," he said with a slow drawl. "Oliphant Blakely came over in 1769 with a land grant in hand. This started out as an indigo plantation. A house was built later that used to stand over there," he said, pointing out a window. Kristina moved closer to peer out. She was tall, but her head only reached the tip of his nose. He caught the scent of citrus and flowers, which was surprisingly fresh on this hot day. He reached over her shoulder to guide her line of vision.

"Over there, next to that big old live oak tree with the swing. See it? There's a plaque marking the spot. It was the oldest house in the parish."

"What happened to the original house?"

"The same thing that happens to a lot of the old houses. Earthquakes, fire, rot. Eventually a hurricane swept the foundation away."

She began moving back and bumped into his arm. Their eyes met briefly and the air between them was charged. They muttered quick apologies.

"So," she asked, walking away from him and looking around the room, "who built the new house?"

"Ah, that would be Beatrice. She was quite a character, our Beatrice. Oliphant's first wife died in childbirth and Beatrice was his second wife. She wasn't much more than eighteen when she married him and he was getting up there in age, but she bore him seven children, five of whom died before she did. After her husband died, Beatrice ran the plantation herself and took it upon herself to build the new house with an eye to future generations. She saw to every detail. That's a lot of doing for a woman back in the days when only a man could vote."

"She must've been a remarkable woman."

"From all the stories, I gather she was. Ran the plantation with an iron will." Then, because he couldn't help himself, he added, "But don't take my word for it. Ask her."

"I beg your pardon?"

He chuckled, pleased with her confused reaction. "Apparently, dear grandmother Beatrice haunts the house."

"Really? A ghost?" she asked, her interest peaked.

"So they say," he said, tucking his hands in his pockets and leaning against the wall. "Not that that's such a big deal in Charleston. Almost all the old houses boast a resident ghost."

She seemed intensely curious. "How do you know it's haunted?"

"People claim to have seen her walking the halls at night, or praying by her bedroom window, or rocking on the veranda overlooking the plantation. There've been dozens of sightings over the years, or reports of hearing her footfall, the creaking rocker, all sorts of things. Some say she worked so hard to build the place up, the old matriarch can't leave it. Nona won't sleep in the house. She swears she's seen Beatrice any number of times, as her mother did, and it creeps her out."

"Have you seen her?"

"Me?" He shook his head. "No. I wish I had. It might have made a believer out of me."

"I take it you're the skeptical type, then?"

"That's me. Doubting Thomas." He tilted his head as though inspecting her more closely. Her blue eyes sparkled with amusement. "And I think we can assume you're a hook-line-and-sinker type?"

"You've got me pegged," she replied with a light laugh. Their eyes met again and he could tell that she was enjoying herself, and that the attraction was mutual.

"Now, Hamlin," he continued, "absolutely believed Beatrice haunted the place. He used to try to make me stay up all night with him, waiting for her. But I was younger and fell asleep, got bored, whatever." He shrugged.

"Hamlin?"

Morgan brought his hands from his pockets and straightened. "My elder brother. Hamlin Blakely IV." His expression clouded. "He passed away years ago."

"Oh, I'm sorry." She paused, then adroitly returned to the subject of ghosts. "Well, who knows? If he saw the ghost, maybe I'll be lucky and see her, too."

"You're not afraid, then?"

"Me? Oh, no. Not at all. In fact, I think it's pretty cool. A haunted house…" She looked around the kitchen house and, chewing her lip, asked, "Say, this place isn't haunted, is it?"

"I thought you weren't scared!" He laughed and waved a hand at her instant objections. "Sure, sure," he teased. "Don't worry. I'm pretty sure no one's spotted a ghost in the kitchen house. You're pretty safe here."

Her cheeks flamed prettily. "I wasn't scared. Just curious."

"Right."

"Really!"

"Time will tell," he chided, liking her more. Kristina Hays had a self-possessed yet friendly demeanor which he found easy to be around. "But in the meantime, make yourself at home. When you're ready, follow the gravel path to the house and let yourself in. You can duel with the two women who've taken Beatrice's place at running this estate with iron fists. My mother and Nona. The dynamic duo. They're both pretty determined women and both extremely protective of my father."

"I like them already," she said, following him to the door, her eyes bright with anticipation.

A few days later, all was in order for Preston's arrival home. Mama June walked through the main floor of her house, clasping her hands tightly as she inspected every detail. Yellow light flowed from the lamps and the house smelled of floor wax, citrus polish and the abundant flowers that filled vases throughout. She felt a twinge of regret at seeing her lovely dining room converted into a makeshift hospital room. The doctors suggested it would be much easier for everyone if Preston stayed on the main floor to avoid stairs. Nan and her boys had helped move the dining room furniture into storage to make way for the hospital bed, the Hoyer lift and other medical paraphernalia.

Scanning the room, she couldn't help but smirk at the ornate crystal chandelier that hung directly above the rented hospital bed. It was the last hurrah of the room's grandeur and lent the sterile hospital-like room a certain *je ne sais quoi*.

All that was left was to wait. Restless, she moved on to the front porch. Great shafts of bright sunshine broke through dark clouds. Movement caught her attention, and turning her head, she saw Chas and Harry goofing around on the wooden swing, killing time.

Soon he'd be coming down that road, she thought, looking out at the avenue of oaks. She'd worked so hard to make this happen. Memories of the ambulance carrying Preston away to the hospital that terrible night sprang to mind. Her hand lowered to rest against her racing heart.

She'd never known such terror. She had been sitting in her room, reading her Bible for solace after the harsh words exchanged with Preston, when she'd heard an odd noise from outside her window. It sounded like the muffled cry of an animal, maybe the howl of a cat or an owl. She'd closed the Bible and cocked her ear, listening intently. What followed was a loud thump and crash, and shortly afterward, Blackjack's husky bark ringing with alarm.

Mama June had endured more than her share of death and sorrow in her lifetime, but to find *him* sprawled out on the floor, his face ghostly white under the harsh porch light...

She'd thought he was dead. She'd thought her own heart would stop at that very minute, too. But rather than panic, a strange calm came over her and she knew exactly what to do. Help had come quickly. She could still see in her mind's eye the small red taillights of the ambulance disappearing down the dark drive and Blackjack running after it, his bark mingling with the wail of sirens.

Her hand rose to her mouth, stilling the trembling of her lips. She shouldn't have argued with Preston! Such things she'd said to him, right here on this very porch. Words she'd muttered only to herself over the years. What had possessed her to say them aloud? She cringed with guilt at the memory of how his face had fallen with shock and some other, painful emotion...what? Defeat? Anguish?

"Oh, Lord, forgive me," she prayed, closing her eyes tight. The stroke had been her fault.

She thought a voice whispered her name in her ear. Mama June swung her head around to look out over the porch to the road, eyes searching.

Beyond the expanse of green grass the roadbed curved round from the front of the house down the avenue of oaks. Blackjack paced, sniffing the road, then jerked his head up, ears alert. Mama June's heart stilled. Her breath caught as the bright red hood of an ambulance broke through the green.

Sweetgrass

Blackjack's barking alerted the family. The boys' laughing stopped abruptly and their heads swung toward the road.

"He's home!" Mama June exclaimed in a choked whisper.

In a rush, Morgan and Nan rushed past to greet their father. Mama June remained frozen on the porch, clutching the back of a wicker chair. She closed her eyes, feeling an odd separateness.

"Mary June?"

She opened her eyes, grateful to see Nona's face near her own. Nona, who knew her so well. Nona, who had plucked her from her darkest moments. Nona's dark-brown eyes probed far beneath the veneer.

"What's the matter?" She moved closer and laid a hand on her arm.

Mama June knew that it was fear that held her back, fear of what his homecoming meant. "Oh, I'm just nervous, is all."

"Of what, honey?"

"Fear that I won't do right by him. What if Adele is right? I'm not skilled. What if I fail? The stakes are so high. He deserves better than me."

"You're the only one he wants, Mary June! You're the only one he's ever wanted. There's no one better than you. Now, go on out there. Your husband's home! What's he gonna think if you're not outside to greet him?"

She squeezed Nona's hand, nodded her affirmation, then took a deep breath and stepped forward to begin what she knew was the next phase of her life.

As the paramedics transported Preston up the front stairs, the family drew nearer in excitement, calling out his name in welcome while Blackjack's bark echoed joyously.

Welcome home! We missed you! Look who's found his way home!

The front door swung open as the group followed him in-doors, all save Blackjack, who commenced whimpering and pawing at the door. Ignored, he threw back his head and yelped pathetically, desperate to be near his master after such a long absence.

They placed Preston on the hospital bed in the middle of the room and settled him. The mood changed as the excitement of his arrival waned and the reality of his limitations became apparent. Nan and her boys hovered on the fringe. Chas and Harry's eyes were wide with shock at their grandfather's frailty, more obvious now that he was back in the familiarity of home. Morgan hung back near the door. He stood slump-shouldered with his hands deep in his pockets, his eyes unreadable.

Mama June's gaze swept the room then alighted on her husband. She saw immediately that he was confused. The family voices that she heard as music filled with joy and excitement, she knew he heard as a ferocious white noise he couldn't recognize.

Light blazed from the chandelier, flowing mercilessly down on Preston, pinning him like an insect under a micro-scope. Gone was the proud patriarch that sat at the head of the table with authority. This strange, thin man lay helpless with his right arm held crunched up against his chest and his fingers curled tight. Despite the tightness of muscle that held his body rigid, however, there was an uncontrollable shaking, and his eyes looked from left to right in panic. Mama June surveyed the scene with a profound sadness.

Then she saw Kristina approach him slowly and stand at the foot of the bed. There was a palpable power to Kristina's silence. She stood watching him for several minutes, biding her time, as everyone around them fell silent, too. Mama June could hear Nona rattling dishes in the kitchen, a mockingbird's song and the scraping and sniffing of Blackjack hunting a spider on the porch.

Preston's wandering gaze at last landed on Kristina. She seemed to grasp and hold his focus. Gradually, Mama June saw the wariness slip from his eyes. That must have been what Kristina was waiting for, because she walked around the bed to his side and, still without speaking, reached out to take his hand in hers and bring it to her chest. It seemed to Mama June to be a warm, even intimate, gesture. She could almost feel the connection between them herself. They remained looking at each other, his hand in hers, until slowly, gradually, his shaking subsided.

Only then, when he was calm, did she speak. "Hello, Preston. I'm Kristina," she said in her lilting voice. "And I'm here to help you."

Mama June released a long sigh of relief and thought to herself, *I am not alone.*

As if she'd heard, Kristina turned her head toward Mama June and, with her free hand, reached out and gestured for her to come near.

Mama June cleared her throat and stepped forward, surprised that her heart was pounding. Kristina took hold of her hand and placed Preston's hand in her own, connecting them.

"You need time alone with your husband," Kristina told her. "I'll be in the next room. Just let me know when you're done."

Mama June turned her attention to her husband and found him shaking again. She looked up in alarm, but Kristina was already herding the rest of the family out of the room. She brought his hand close to her chest, as she'd seen Kristina do.

"Preston," she called. His skin felt flushed and covered with a sheen of sweat. "Preston," she repeated with force, tightening her grip.

Preston's gaze stopped shifting to fix on her. Mama June

held his gaze, sensing with each second that she was his bea-
con to guide him through his confusion. Looking into his
bright blue eyes, she smiled reassuringly and, not releasing her
eye contact, leaned forward to place a gentle kiss on his
cheek.

"Welcome home," she told him in a soft tone.

She could tell that he knew it was her, yet he still seemed
not to register what she'd said.

"You're home," she repeated. "You've come home to
Sweetgrass."

She saw at last understanding and the first signal of peace
she'd seen in the blue waters of his eyes since this painful or-
deal had begun. His eyelids drooped with fatigue.

More comfortable now, she leaned against his mattress and
smoothed the thin cotton blanket over him. "It's been a hec-
tic morning, hasn't it? Why don't we both just sit here a spell
and catch our breath? We can pretend we're sitting on the veranda, watching a sunset. Shall we?"

He released a ragged sigh.

They sat together in silence while out on the veranda they
heard the creaking of the porch swing and the occasional laugh
punctuating the low murmurs of conversation. Gradually
Preston's shaking subsided and his breathing grew regular.

"Look at us," she said. "Holding hands like a couple of
kids." Her smile lingered and she said wistfully, "We haven't
done this in a long time, have we?"

She felt a faint squeezing of her hand. To her, it felt like
a bear hug.

"I know that we haven't been close in a long time. Too
long. But that doesn't matter now. I promise you, Preston, I'm
here by your side to stay. You've got me, for better or for
worse. I'll do my best to get you through this. And you *will*
get through this."

His eyes shone back at her and she wished she could comprehend what he was thinking.

"Well now, I just wanted you to know," she said, feeling awkward after the show of emotion. She kissed the back of his hand and tucked it under his blanket. "I'd best let Kristina do her job."

His expression changed.

"What?" she asked, peering closer. "You don't want me to go?"

His eyes blinked.

"Kristina is a lovely girl. Easy on the eye, too, as I'm sure you've noticed."

He blinked twice, with a deliberate slowness that caught her attention.

"I swanny, if I didn't know better I'd think you were trying to talk to me." She thought for a moment then asked, "You wouldn't be setting up some kind of…communication system?"

He blinked twice.

She leaned forward, eyes alert. "Is that two blinks for yes?"

He blinked twice.

"You are!" She brightened as a grin stretched across her face. "Dear, clever man," she said with a light laugh. "Why, I think we just might do all right after all."

7

———

"In coiled baskets, the shape is created by building the foundation, row upon row. The process is slow and deliberate and requires a remarkable continuity of precision."

—Row Upon Row

THE WEEKS PASSED. The Lowcountry bloomed as the days grew warmer, but no one paid much attention to the change going on outside the house. Inside, Preston's care dominated the passing days as everyone kept busy settling into new routines.

Kristina took over the supervision of Preston's daily care with an ease that Mama June found humbling. The therapists that came into the house had their specific goals and duties. From the moment Nona stepped back into the house, she managed its care with her usual formidable efficiency. As for Mama June, she helped out in the daily chores and made herself available to assist the therapists in any way she could.

It physically pained her to stand at the side of Preston's bed while the speech therapist worked with him. Her own mouth moved as she watched him struggle to form even a syllable, much less a word.

Sweetgrass

It was no different with the other therapists. As the physical therapist went through the body exercises, Mama June squeezed her hands together in sympathy when Preston couldn't move even one finger of his right hand. She nervously fumbled with the buttons of her blouse as the occupational therapist patiently helped Preston maneuver his clumsy left hand over a large button while training his left side to take up what the right used to do.

As she looked at him in the shadowy light, Preston appeared a mere silhouette of the man she once knew. She bent her head, closing her eyes in exhaustion. She felt so utterly depleted she could barely stand. Yet tired as she was, she knew her despair did not compare to his.

"Are you all right?"

Mama June swiftly turned her head to see Kristina standing beside her, her eyes soft with concern.

"Yes, dear, I'm fine," she replied, straightening her shoulders. She cleared her throat. "It's been a tiring day, that's all."

"Well, you don't look fine. You look worn out."

Her first inclination was to deny it, but Kristina had a way of getting past all pretenses. Mama June offered a weak smile and admitted, "Well, I am a little tired."

"Why don't you go to bed early tonight? I can bring you a tray."

"Heavens! The last thing you need is another patient. I'm fine and I'll eat with you in the kitchen." She covered a yawn. "But yes, I think I will turn in early tonight."

"I don't mean to pry, but is something else bothering you?"

She turned her head, feeling torn between keeping silent about her odd sense of displacement and voicing her concerns. "I don't mean to sound complaining or self-indulgent," she began hesitatingly. "It's just—" Mama June sighed. "I don't feel particularly useful."

Kristina's eyes widened. "How can you say that? You work from dawn to dusk. You do everything!"

"That's just it. I want to be his helpmate, but it sometimes seems that everybody has a role in my husband's care—except me. I'm sure you could all manage very well without me." She hated the petulance she heard in her own voice.

"We probably could," Kristina agreed. "But he could not."

Mama June looked up.

"You're thinking that taking care of Preston only has to do with organizing the schedules and bathing him, giving medicine, that sort of thing. Right?"

Mama June nodded.

"That kind of work is easy to measure. But there's another realm of caretaking that's more personal. It involves the mental well-being of the patient, his cooperation, his motivation, his desire to recover. Without it, we'd all fail. The responsibility for this part of caretaking falls squarely on your shoulders. You're a big part of his therapy."

Mama June cast a baleful look at Preston's bed. "Then I'm not doing a very good job of it. Every day he struggles to accomplish the smallest task, and every day he seems to sink deeper and deeper into depression. I thought he'd be fired up once he got home, but he seems more frustrated than ever. He's giving up."

Kristina nodded, her brow gathering with concern.

"That's not like him," Mama June told her.

"How do you mean?"

"He's not a self-pitying kind of man. You should have seen him before his stroke," she said wistfully. "He cut a fine figure. He was always so filled with life. And coordinated! Why, he could cast a fishing line into the water with the finesse of a master swordsman. Or let fly a net that would unfurl and spread so gracefully into the air, you'd swear you were watching a blossom unfold before your eyes. He could pluck any song on the guitar, too, just playing by ear. And he'd drive his car so fast, he was shifting gears more on instinct than anything else." She laughed lightly.

"So he was a redneck?" Kristina asked, teasingly.

Mama June's eyes softened with affection. "When it came to his car, he was just another good ol' boy in love with the open road. Some nights, we'd barely be on speaking terms by the time we got home, he'd get me so spooked with his driving. He drove fast just to rile me." She sighed and glanced back at the man lying on the bed. "Truth is, I wasn't ever really afraid. No matter what, he always made me feel safe."

"Men like that are rare," Kristina said softly.

Mama June nodded, her misting eyes betraying her composure. "That was the Preston Blakely I knew." She turned abruptly away. "I don't know who this man is."

"You can't give up now," Kristina urged. "He needs you."

She looked at the girl sharply, surprised that she'd think such a thing. "I'm not going anywhere!" she replied. "I didn't mean that. I'd never leave him. But frankly, I don't know if I'm being any good to him."

"Of course you are. What more do you think you can do?"

"I don't know. But there has to be something…." She tsked with frustration and crossed her arms, holding herself tight. "I knew his recovery wasn't going to be easy. That it would take a long time. The doctors drummed that into my head hard enough. But I was so confident I could do this." She shook her head. "The reality is another thing altogether, isn't it? I didn't plan on him being so discouraged, so frustrated. It's like he doesn't care! I don't seem able to cheer him up or inspire him in the least."

"He has to deal with his body not doing basic functions

that he used to take for granted. In a lot of ways, his body is like a baby's. He has to learn to do things over again. That can be very frustrating for him. But his mind is still sharp," she added as encouragement.

"That somehow makes it worse. He's trapped. Preston was a very independent, determined man."

"That hasn't changed with the stroke!" Kristina replied. "He has to use that determination. He has to work hard because he has a long way to go. But he *can* improve."

"He's always worked very hard. I can't remember when he spent a whole day in bed."

"That's the man you have to remember. The strong, determined man. You have to help him remember."

"How?"

"Talk to him."

"I've been doing that for weeks! I'm just babbling. It's getting so I hate the sound of my own voice."

"Don't talk *at* him. Talk *with* him," Kristina insisted.

"But that's impossible in his current state."

"Trust me, you can," she said quickly, dousing the frustration that sprang in Mama June's eyes.

Mama June didn't understand. "But how can you expect him to communicate if he can't speak?"

"Words are only one way to communicate. I've watched you with him. How do you know if he's happy?"

"His eyes," she replied with certainty. "I can tell what his feelings are by looking into his eyes."

"Exactly. And there are other ways you can reach him."

"You mean, without speaking?" Mama June thought for a moment, then shook her head in confusion.

"Well, he can smell," Kristina prompted. "A scent can trigger a memory in an instant, unexpected but powerful. And taste. What foods might bring back a special memory for him? Watermelon on a hot summer day? Hot cocoa when it rains? For me, it's cotton candy. Whenever I smell or taste it I'm immediately a little girl again at a carnival."

Mama June smiled, thinking that a huge cloud of pink cotton candy would elicit the same response from her.

"Think about using all the senses," Kristina continued. "There's one more, and it's the best one of all."

Mama June's mind raced through the possibilities: hearing, seeing, smelling, tasting…

"Touch," she replied.

"Bingo. You can communicate a lot just by laying your hands on someone. It takes you to a new level. A higher level. Think how powerful someone's touch can be. Or the lack of touch. Babies thrive when fondled and held, and fail to thrive when left untouched. Why would it be different for adults? Come on, Mrs. Blakely! You're his wife. Give him a massage."

"I don't know the first thing about massages," she replied in a dismissive tone. "I wouldn't know where to begin."

"It doesn't have to be a formal massage," Kristina hurried to explain. "You can begin by doing his exercises with him. Don't be afraid to touch him. You can't hurt him. It'll do him good, no matter what. What's important is that while you're touching him, you'll remember him. The real him. And as you remember, so will he."

Mama June brought her hand to her throat as a wave of anxiety surged through her. "I can't do that," she said.

"Why not? You've practiced his exercises."

"I can help him with his exercises, of course. But this massage. Remembering…I…I can't. It's too hard for me."

Kristina put her hand on Mama June's arm. It was surprisingly warm and comforting. "But we need to think about what's best for *him*."

Mama June had not thought of it from that point of view.

Remembering the past was something she'd always avoided. She needed to do that to survive. Whenever stressful memories arose, she pushed them back and forced herself to think of other things. Didn't her mother, her friends, everyone encourage her not to dwell on things? Could she really have been so intent on her own avoidance of grief all these years that she hadn't taken into consideration whether Preston might have needed to revisit the past?

"He's never asked to talk about the past before," she murmured.

"That was before. Now he needs to remember who he was in the past so he'll believe it's who he still is. And who knows, there might be something from the past that will inspire him to try harder."

Mama June chewed her lips and thought back to the sight of Preston's slumped shoulders the night of the stroke. She recalled the defeat she saw in his eyes, especially after she'd told him she didn't care about Sweetgrass. She still had nightmares about that.

"But...how would I begin?" she asked, faltering.

Kristina offered her a consoling smile. "It's not that complicated. Lay your hands on his body. Look him in the eyes. It's about connection. No one else can elicit the memories that you can."

Mama June shivered, and wrapping her arms around herself, she paced the floor. She was afraid to cross that threshold, to dig up all those hurtful memories again.

She peered into his makeshift hospital room. Her husband of forty-seven years lay on the hospital bed in the dark in what used to be their dining room, the room where he had sat at the head of the table. She could not leave him defenseless or alone against that kind of despair.

"All right," she said. "For Preston's sake, I'll try."

Sweetgrass

The darkness made his room cooler, but it was stuffy and smelled of antiseptics and medicine. She walked quietly on rubber-soled shoes to the double-hung window to yank the stubborn wood open. Though humid, the outside air was cooler than the room and a soft night wind was blowing. She and Preston had both grown up in the days before air-conditioning. The windows always used to be wide open. She knew he preferred a sultry breeze off the ocean to the steady coolness of a machine.

Heavily lined, yellow silk drapes festooned the window frame in starchy elegance, but the lace fluttered prettily in the breeze. Roused by the noise, Blackjack appeared at the window and he pressed his muzzle against the screen, denting it.

Mama June sighed in resignation and pushed back the lace. "You know he's in here, don't you?" she asked the dog.

Blackjack whined.

She heard a noise behind her and turned her head to see Preston's eyes open and shining. His left hand lurched out.

"You're awake," she exclaimed, and hurried to take his hand, holding it against her chest as she'd seen Kristina do.

He wriggled his hand free and impatiently flung his arm sideward to point toward the window.

"What?" she muttered, confused. "Oh, you see Blackjack? Yes, he's out there. He won't leave the porch now that he knows you're in here. I've given up trying to chase him off. He's made the settee his bed."

Hearing his name, Blackjack went up on his back legs and pawed at the screen.

"Stop that, now!" she scolded the dog. "Get down from there before you tear the screen, fool beast."

The dog dropped to his paws with a low, despondent grunt and disappeared from view.

"Well, he's gone off to settle somewhere." She looked back at Preston and her smile faltered. His arm was still out-stretched but his hand was limp with dejection, and he was looking at the window with a forlorn expression.

All her mustered enthusiasm fizzled in her heart. He didn't want her—he wanted the dog! Her cheeks flamed with embarrassment. How typical, she thought, hurt. He always put his dog or the land or something before her. She was an old fool. What was she doing here, anyway? There was noth-ing he wanted from her.

"Well," she said, clasping her useless hands together. "I'll just go see to your dinner." After a last, quick glance, she turned abruptly and left the room.

In the kitchen she found Kristina pulling a casserole from the refrigerator. Her expression spoke of her surprise at see-ing Mama June back from Preston's room so soon.

"It won't work," Mama June declared. She walked briskly to the teapot and busied herself filling it with water.

"What happened?" Kristina asked, closing the fridge.

"Frankly, he was only interested in the dog," she replied, lifting her chin to salvage her pride.

"The dog? What's the dog got to do with it?" she asked, not following.

"He saw Blackjack whining at the window and all he wanted was the dog."

Kristina's face softened and Mama June was ashamed to see the understanding and compassion she read there.

"So give him the dog!" Kristina replied.

"Blackjack is an outdoor dog," she explained.

Kristina put the casserole on the counter and walked closer to Mama June. "It might actually be a good idea to let Blackjack inside."

"Let him in? My house?"

"Yes."

"I love dogs, always have. But we've never allowed dogs in the house," she replied. "Humans have their place and dogs have theirs."

"Didn't you say that Preston and Blackjack used to do everything together?"

"Yes, surely, but always outdoors."

"But Preston can't go outdoors now."

Mama June didn't reply.

"Look," Kristina said gently. "Blackjack doesn't understand what's happened to his master. He's pretty desperate. And it sounds to me like Preston needs to be near his dog."

"Yes, yes, I understand all that, but what's to be done? It's a recovery room. It has to be sterile. Besides, he's dirty! He has fleas! And he slobbers!"

"Is that any way to talk about your husband?"

"What?" she sputtered.

Kristina laughed. "I'm joking!" Then her face grew thoughtful. "Seriously, though, I'm talking about this touching thing again. That's how Preston and Blackjack communicate. They're so lonely for each other, it's pitiful. Let's get those two together! What if I give Blackjack a good bath and brushing?" Kristina urged. "He'll be all clean as a whistle."

"But..."

"No mud on your floors."

"I don't know."

"It'll be great," Kristina called out as she waltzed out the door. "Trust me."

Mama June walked dazedly to a chair and, sitting down, slipped her chin into her palm. Well, she certainly had been outmaneuvered. Without a shot fired, she'd just lost the war. It was official. She was no longer in control of her home.

She shook her head. Dogs in the house...

★ ★ ★

The following morning, despite a brilliant blue May sky and balmy temperatures that had the birds outdoors singing, Mama June woke feeling a little down. She rose early, as was her custom, but dressed slowly. Her morning routine was uneventful. She was finishing the breakfast dishes when she heard the loud clunk of the outdoor water faucet turning on, followed by wild barking and Kristina's high-pitched shouts.

Mama June hurried to the side window, wiping her hands on her apron, in time to see Morgan running to join the fray. He grabbed Blackjack's collar and was trying to hold the big dog steady while Kristina squirted the dog with water from the hose, soaking Morgan in the process.

Mama June thought it looked more like a rodeo than a washing. Before too long Blackjack looked like a sleek otter and was just as slippery and squirming. Morgan was dripping wet and cursing at the dog. Kristina was laughing so hard as she soaped up the dog, she could hardly stand. By the time they were finished, the hose slunk along the gravel like a hissing snake, more soap was on Morgan than the dog, and they were both laughing in hysterics as Blackjack took off, dripping water, suds flying, down the road.

Mama June let the curtain slip and shook her head, laughing herself. That dumb beast was sure to find a nice smelly spot to roll around in before he came back, but she knew she'd let him in the house, anyway. No doubt Preston would get a whiff of Sweetgrass mud on wet dog and be in hog heaven.

She wrapped her arms around herself and looked at her immaculate kitchen. What the heck? she thought. So the house got a little dirty. So there was dog hair everywhere. How long had it been since she'd seen Morgan laugh like that, with his head thrown back and the wariness gone from his face? That alone was a small miracle.

The old adage was true, she thought, feeling a flutter in her chest that she thought might could be joy. Laughter was indeed the best medicine.

It was inevitable. Blackjack became a fixture at Preston's bedside. The family and therapists alike made do walking around the big snoring dog and he didn't seem to mind when a foot accidentally bumped him. Preston's good hand hung off the side of the bed to rest on the dog's head. Mama June had to admit it was a pleasant sight seeing the two of them resting beside each other again in such peace. It was as if order had been restored in the world.

Kristina was beaming as she worked and Morgan was whistling softly in the office. When Nona came into the house, however, she stopped short with a "Lord, have mercy!" Then, shaking her head, she proceeded into the kitchen.

The last person Morgan expected to see walk into the office that afternoon was Aunt Adele.

He'd heard the doorbell ring, Blackjack commence barking and a flurry of movement and voices. Then the door to his father's office swung open and Adele crossed the threshold as if the office were hers. Mama June followed her in, worry clouding her face.

"So," Adele began, setting her black purse onto a chair while her eyes scanned the disheveled room. "Mama June tells me that you've been plowing through Preston's files?"

Morgan glanced around the room. The tall black file cabinet was opened and files were stacked around the room amid books, coffee cups and ashtrays. He knew the office was a disheveled mess, and though it distressed his mother, he saw it as a work in progress. He lowered his feet from the top of the desk and straightened in his chair out of respect.

"Yes, ma'am. Such as they are."

Morgan smiled an unspoken thank-you to Nona for the tray of coffee she carried in. Nona rolled her eyes in commiseration as she set the tray down on the desk, then quickly exited the room.

Mama June followed her out. "I'll just leave you two alone to talk."

He glared at his mother for leaving, but she gave him an encouraging smile and waved before the door closed.

"What have you learned?" asked Adele, taking a seat.

"Well, there's a lot to go through," he began cautiously.

"Are you finding everything?"

"I'm still working on it. As you can see."

"Your father's filing system is nothing more than a series of tilting piles. He always claimed to know where everything was, but God help the one who has to find anything."

Morgan merely nodded his head.

"Do you need help? You must. It's a mind-boggling project."

"Nope. Not at this point. But thanks."

Adele paused, considering. "Morgan, I haven't seen you since the family dinner. It was awkward the way things ended, and I feel badly about that. You know my position. I still feel that this decision to delay the sale of Sweetgrass is serious and can have dangerous repercussions for your family. But since you seem hell-bent to pursue it, I'll help you. It's the least I can do. Time is of the essence and I can help speed this along. Meandering through those papers on your own will be like a tourist finding his way through the marshes. You need a guide. Your father and I have been involved in several business deals. I have all my records on those transactions and I'm familiar with the cast of characters. Let me help you make sense of it all."

Morgan hesitated but couldn't think of a rational argument against her request. His opposition was from the gut, and that, he reasoned, might only be attributed to his lifelong dislike of his aunt. Reluctantly he rose above it and nodded.

"All right. Thank you, Aunt Adele. When's a good time for you?"

She grinned widely. "There's no time like the present."

Later that afternoon, Nan made her way along the winding roads of the large housing development that her husband managed. The sale of her small portion of Sweetgrass land soon after their marriage had helped to launch the development. It was a lovely community, tastefully constructed, with lots of mature trees. Most of the houses were built in the southern tradition, painted pastel colors with wide, welcoming porches and surrounded by neatly manicured lawns, magnolias, crepe myrtle and oaks.

There was an orderliness to the well-maintained roads and a uniformity to the size of the plots and houses that was comforting in its familiarity. People rode bicycles on paths, green ponds glistened in the sunlight, the golf course stretched out as far as she could see, and if she followed the green-and-white arrow off the turnabout, she knew she would arrive at the beautiful clubhouse. Her children had practically lived there during summers, swimming, playing golf and tennis, and grabbing a burger. This summer the boys had jobs there.

The Leland family had one of the first houses built in the community. They'd raised their family there, made friends there, marked milestones in this neighborhood.

So…why did she only feel that quickening of excitement in her heart and a sense of pride and well-being when she passed through the gates of Sweetgrass? What was it about driving along the bumpy, rain-worn gravel roads under the heavy green of steepled trees that had her turning off the car's air-conditioning and opening her window, panting like old Blackjack at catching the scent of home?

Nan responded viscerally to Sweetgrass. It ran through her veins. Upon reaching the charming white house shaded by ancient oaks, her heart was at home. Whenever she left, she longed to return.

The gravel crunched as she circled the pond, and she was shocked to see Adele's sleek Jaguar coming out from the drive. She pulled over to the grass to allow her aunt room to pass. Adele slowed to a stop beside her car and rolled down the window.

"What are you doing here?" Adele asked.

Nonplussed by the question, Nan stammered, "I—I'm visiting my father."

"Of course," Adele replied. "I just saw him. It's so sad." Then with a change in tone, "Listen, dear, when you talk to your mother, don't encourage her in this fantasy of hers to hang on to this place. You're not being kind if you do." When Nan nodded, she smiled, pleased, and sang out, "Give my love to the boys. Tell them to come over and see the new boat. And have Hank give me a call. Bye, now," she said with a quick wave of her hand. The window slowly rolled up.

Nan felt a building pressure in her chest as she watched her aunt's car stir dust down the dirt road. *What are you doing here?* How could Adele ask that? She had every right to be here! Nan hated her own timidity for not firing back what she really felt. Like Morgan could. She thrilled at the memory of the battle lines drawn at the family dinner. She'd been so proud of her brother and her mother that day.

Hank and Aunt Adele had been furious. Nan knew that they viewed her visits to Sweetgrass as a defection.

The house was quiet when she entered. The doors to the dining room were closed, meaning her father was likely in a therapy session. She smelled something good emanating from the kitchen, where Mama June no doubt was preparing dinner. To her right, she spied Morgan through the half-opened door of her father's office, his head bent over stacks of papers on the desk. Behind him, file drawers were open and spilling their contents. She tiptoed to the foyer desk and tugged out a tissue from the box. Then, holding back a smile, she poked her head into the office, waving a white flag.

"I come in peace!"

The chair squeaked as he leaned back, grinning widely in welcome. "Come on in!"

Nan laughed and pushed open the door. "What happened here? Looks like a bomb hit."

"Feels like it, too. Aunt Adele was here."

"I know. I ran into her on the way in. I'm suffering from some shrapnel myself. What did she want?"

"To help."

Nan's eyes widened as she came closer to lean against the desk. "You're kidding? Both she and Hank seemed dead set against helping you."

"They still are. She knows our backs are up against the wall and figures if she helps us—how did she put it?—*get our ducks in a row,* we'd see right quick how we need to sell the place." He reached out to sift through the papers on his desk in a resigned manner. "And she might be right. I have to hand it to her, she can really plow through. She could have taught General Sherman a thing or two. We must've put in four hours straight today. But there's still more to go through."

Nan's attention shifted from the mess around the room to the half-empty bottle of bourbon on the desk beside a filled glass. She searched his face. He looked drawn with fatigue.

"Isn't it a little early for a cocktail?"

His slips twisted in a wry smile. "I felt the need of a little libation after the March to the Sea."

It was an innocuous enough excuse, except she'd noticed that whenever she came over in the afternoon, he had a drink poured while he was holed up in the office.

"Are you sleeping okay?"

He released a short laugh and reached for the glass. "Just fine."

"No nightmares?"

Morgan sipped the bourbon and set the glass down, then mopped his face with his hands.

"Are they still about Hamlin?"

He dropped his hands and nodded.

Ever since their brother's death, Morgan had suffered horrible nightmares. She remembered waking up, night after night, to his screams and the sound of Mama June running to his room.

"How often?" she asked gently.

"Not every night. But often enough. You know, the damn thing is, I haven't had one in years. Then I come back home and wham! They're back."

"Morgan, have you ever talked to anyone about them? Like a doctor?"

He shook his head and waved her off. "They're no big deal. I can live with them."

"But you obviously can't sleep with them. You look beat."

"It's not the nightmares, it's the bills. Talk about a nightmare. Things are really messed up. Adele dug up debts I hadn't even found yet. Money's really tight."

"Maybe you should sell. Hank doesn't think there's any other way."

He held up his hand. "Please, not you, too."

"Sorry. I don't have a position on this. I just want Mama and Daddy to be happy."

"Maybe you should take a position, sister."

"Oh, no, you don't! Don't you rope me into this," she said, shaking her head. "Hank is hard enough to live with, thank you very much. Frankly, he's pretty upset with you right now for stalling on the sale."

"I'm trembling with fear."

"Really, Morgan, why are you doing this? If the money is tight and you're losing sleep over it, maybe it's time to throw in the towel. After all, it's not like we'd be the only ones. Most folks can't hold on to large tracts of land anymore. Times are changing."

He sighed. "Right."

"It's not like you didn't try."

Morgan leaned back in the chair and laced his fingers on his belly. "It's been weird going through all this shit," he said, indicating the papers. "I never knew how hard Daddy tried to hang on to this place. He was...heroic. Talk about changing times. He must've tried everything he could think of to make this place earn money. Some of his schemes were pretty wild and woolly. Remember the fish farm?"

Nan burst out with a laugh. "Oh, Lord, I surely do. We lost a bundle on that one. And the tomatoes!"

"Then there were the cattle."

"Come on," she cajoled, trying not to laugh. "That one wasn't so crazy. Granddaddy had cattle. And sheep."

"They were dairy cows, by the way, but what's the difference? They both lost money." He laughed anew and asked, "Remember the solar-powered windmills?"

Nan recalled the rows of blades twirling in the breeze. "They were sure pretty to look at, though."

"But they didn't bring in one shiny dollar."

"Aw, be fair," Nan said. "All the funding dried up for alternative energy. That wasn't Daddy's fault, either."

"No, I know. But according to Aunt Adele, if it wasn't for her we'd be knee-deep in Angora goats right now!"

Nan burst out laughing, leaning against her brother's shoulder as they howled. They weren't making fun of their father so much as laughing at themselves. It felt good after so much tension.

"You know what's weird to me?" she asked him, drying her eyes.

"What?"

"Everyone being home again."

Their eyes met in understanding and she was pleased to see him nod.

"Even Nona. It's kind of like old times," she added.

"And not," he chided.

"No," Nan agreed on a long sigh. "It's hard to see Daddy the way he is."

Morgan rubbed his neck, then reached for the bottle. When he caught her staring, he paused with the bottle in the air. "Care for one?"

She frowned and said in a self-righteous manner, "No, thanks."

"Suit yourself." He was pouring his glass when Nona stepped into the room.

"I thought that was your car in the driveway!" she exclaimed to Nan.

Nan crossed the room and placed a kiss on Nona's cheek. She relished the scent of vanilla that always hung around Nona. When she pulled back she caught Nona glaring at Morgan.

"It's a little early in the day for drinking bourbon," Nona told him.

Nan looked over her shoulder with an I-told-you-so air.

"You put that poison down before you get so you aren't any use to me," Nona told him in a no-nonsense tone. "I need you. And *you*," she said to Nan, "to help me move some furniture into the attic. Kristina says that your daddy's going to be up and around in a wheelchair and we have to make room. In fact, why don't you give those two strapping boys of yours a call and tell them to hurry on over here? And when you're done with that, I've got some yard work that needs doing and windows that need washing. That hound has slobbered on every one of your daddy's windows so he can't see a thing. Hurry up now. That sun isn't going to wait for you!"

She gave them the what-for look they both remembered from their childhood that had always sent them running, then turned and headed out like a frigate at full sail.

Morgan set down the glass without touching a drop and pulled himself to his feet.

"Yeah, it sure seems like old times," he said as he rounded the desk.

"I can't wait to let her loose on my boys," Nan said, chuckling as she reached for the phone.

8

_____

The construction of the Cooper River Bridge in 1929 and the paving of Highway 17 made the route through Mount Pleasant a major north-south artery. Basket makers started marketing their wares from roadside basket stands to tourists and collectors. Today, sweetgrass baskets are treasured by collectors and museums.

A FEW NIGHTS LATER, after the house was quiet, Mama June slipped into her robe and slippers. The gray flickering light of a television shone behind Morgan's partially closed door. She crept soundlessly past and made her way down the stairs to Preston's room.

Moonlight dappled the walls. Blackjack raised his head when she stepped in and, when he recognized her, his tail thumped like a metronome on the floor. After a moment, he rested his pendulous jaws back on his front paws.

Preston's eyes were open and he waved her over to his side.

Mama June's heart fluttered as she approached his bed, knowing why she'd come. It was ridiculous for her to feel so nervous, she told herself. Preston was her husband of nearly forty-seven years, yet she could not recall the last time they'd shared a bed.

These were not the confidences a woman her age shared with a woman Kristina's age. So the young woman could not comprehend what she was asking when she told Mama June to *touch* her husband to communicate. Goodness, she and Preston hadn't communicated like that in years!

She did love him, however. And though there were times she did not even like him, her commitment and her love was unwavering. Keeping this in the forefront of her mind, she tightened the sash of her robe and moved forward.

"I couldn't sleep," she told him, drawing near. "You can't, either?"

He waved his hand to indicate no.

"Want some company?"

He blinked twice.

"If you don't mind, I'll sit right here," she said, sidling up to the bed. "Next to you."

His hand patted the mattress.

"Okay, scootch over," she said, nudging his thigh.

His hand stilled and his gaze sharpened.

She could have bitten her tongue. That was the phrase she'd always used when she crawled back into their bed after getting up to tend the children, or after a row between them had sent her to the kitchen for a cup of hot milk, or if she couldn't sleep. She sighed and gently placed a hand on his chest, then settled herself on the mattress beside him.

His gaze was fixed on her, questioning.

"I know what you're thinking," she said to him. "That it's been quite a while since we've shared a bed. Am I right?"

He merely looked on.

"I don't remember when we started sleeping in separate rooms. Or even why, exactly. It probably wasn't just one reason. More an accumulation of reasons, I suppose. They all seem insignificant now." She paused. "Morgan figured it out when he came home. He saw your things in Ham's room and asked me about it. I told him it was for comfort." She puffed out air in a short laugh. "I'm quite certain he didn't buy it."

The silence stretched between them accusingly. She took a deep breath, fighting the urge to give him a quick kiss good-night and retreat to the security of her bedroom. Instead, she once again took hold of his hand, as though to anchor her to the spot.

"You have nice hands," she told him, running a fingertip along his knuckles. "I've always thought so. Tapered nails like these are a sign of gentility, did you know that? Well, they are. So is the longer second toe. Jesus had that, too. Or so they say. You wonder how anyone would know that, don't you? I mean, you can't imagine *that* would be written down in the Bible somewhere." She laughed lightly at the notion.

Then, realizing she was running circles around what she'd come to say, she took a breath and started again.

"Your hands are strong, too. But you were never clumsy. That always amazed me. How you could maneuver these long, callused fingers like a surgeon to pin the tiny, paper-thin wings of a butterfly in your collection. Or on the boat, how you could tie knots so quickly. And when the wind was picking up, how you'd reach up and move a lock of hair from my eyes, just so." She shrugged slightly, blushing at the memory. "It was a sweet gesture. I never thought much about it before." She glanced shyly at him, hoping he'd read her feelings.

"I don't know why it took me so long to let Blackjack inside. I can tell it matters to you. It took a stranger to point it out to me. I'm...I'm sorry, Preston. I should have been more mindful."

His fingers patted her hand.

"It's nice for me to see you with Blackjack again. Like old

times." She paused to lick her lips. "I've been awash in old times today. Thinking of you. Of us."

Tentatively she brought her hands to the buttons of his pajama shirt. She felt unsure of herself and her stomach was tied up in knots.

"Are you still having difficulty doing up your buttons?" she asked, filling the silence. "Show me. Try undoing one."

He cast her a questioning glance but brought his left hand to his button. With only some difficulty, he undid it.

"Neatly done! How about a few more? For practice."

He did the task with only minor stumbling. His eyes watched her and she could sense his wonderment and curiosity as to what she was up to. She knew he was far too cunning to fall for her lame excuse.

Feeling a bit like a lady of the night, she reached over to delicately slip the thin blue cotton open, exposing his chest. His skin was paler than she was used to seeing and the fine hairs covering his chest were mostly gray. But the conformation of muscle and the curve of bone were as familiar to her touch as her own. Hesitatingly, she ran her hands through the hair, relishing the softness of it against her palms. His chest rose up and down in a steady rhythm.

"This feels real nice, doesn't it? It's been a long time since my hands have lain against your chest like this. I can't even remember the last time. Can you?"

He blinked once.

"Me, neither."

Then, with a deep breath, she gathered her courage and said, "But I can remember the first time…"

She was nineteen and a woman of leisure.

So Mary June Clark told Adele Blakely as they motored south down the highway from Converse College headed for sun, the beach and, hopefully, boys. College was out for the summer and the two roommates planned on spending the first two weeks of vacation doing nothing in the least bit productive.

Music roared from their open windows as they passed school buses and slow-moving pickups filled with crates of tomatoes. But whenever they passed a car with cute boys, Adele beeped the horn of her Mercury and they waved and called out hellos, giggling wildly when the boys honked and hollered back. The roommates made quite a pair, and they were well aware of the attention they attracted whenever they were together.

Mary June's beauty was delicate, like the wildflowers she loved. Her large, cornflower-blue eyes shone soft against pale skin. She was petite with a tiny waist and blond hair cut in waves that fell to her shoulders in the same fashion as the actress she was most often compared to, Sandra Dee. It was a comparison that her friends thought a great compliment but that Mary June always chafed under. She'd rather be compared to someone daring rather than doe-ish. Someone like Kate Hepburn.

As Adele was. Slender and tanned with glossy brown hair cut short in a bob, Adele had dark-brown eyes that shone with a confidence that was both attractive and intimidating. The two women were roommates by fate, friends by choice. This summer sojourn at the school year's end was seen by them as the culmination of a smashing freshman year.

They were done with boring lectures delivered in sweltering classrooms, greasy cafeteria food, endless late-night cramming for exams and early morning classes. Eisenhower was president of a nation at peace, the economy was looking up, the weather was glorious and they'd just finished exams. The world was their oyster, as someone they'd studied in English class once wrote!

As Adele's red Mercury chewed up miles of country road,

the girls nibbled Moon Pies, drank Coke and smoked cigarettes that Adele had smuggled in her purse. They were headed for summer and Sweetgrass.

Mary June was secretly apprehensive about her trip to Adele Blakely's home. Adele was from an established Charleston family. Her roots went way back—as did the memories of most old Charleston families. Mary June's own family went respectably far back, as well. Her ancestors had died in defense of the Confederacy. Her uncle William still donned the gray whenever there was a reenactment in the Sumter area. But though the Clark family currently owned and farmed more land than the Blakelys now did, the Clarks had never owned a true plantation nor had the rich history associated with their name that the Blakelys had. The Blakelys belonged to an exclusive order of Charleston society, and no amount of wealth or land could buy into that pedigree.

Adele had eased her mind, however, when she'd airily told Mary June that the Blakelys no longer walked in tall cotton. They both knew it was a sore reality to Adele that Mary June's allowance was considerably more generous than Adele's.

As the afternoon grew late, their excitement bubbled when they reached the small town of Mount Pleasant. Mary June spotted the rickety stands of the sweetgrass baskets alongside the road and remembered the time years before when she'd driven north to Myrtle Beach with her mother.

"Adele, stop!" she exclaimed, stretching her neck far out the window. Her blond hair whipped her shoulders as she leaned out, pointing to one wooden stand with dozens of baskets hanging from hooks. It nestled in the shade of a sprawling live oak and she recognized it as the one she'd stopped at before. Mary June still had that little basket her mama had bought her and had taken it to college with her.

"Why, that might could be the same woman. Stop the car, Adele! I want to buy another basket!"

"Sugar, we can stop for a basket any ol' time," Adele shouted back over the music. "Let's keep on going. We're not that far away from home. I'm hungry, thirsty and I'm just dying to pee."

Mary June fell back against her seat, scowling with disappointment. Adele could be so bossy sometimes. Casting her a sidelong glance, she felt the urge to prick her pride a bit.

"Mama says you shouldn't say that," she said, pushing her hair from her eyes. "It's not ladylike. Mama always says she has to powder her nose instead."

Adele flashed a wicked smile. "Well, my daddy says he has to piss like a racehorse."

Both girls burst out laughing and Adele pressed the accelerator a little more.

"There it is," Adele exclaimed a short while later, slowing the car and flicking on her blinker. "At last!" She squirmed on the seat. "If I can just hold it a little longer..."

Mary June's breath hitched as she leaned over and searched the seemingly impenetrable wall of tall, spindly pines that bordered the highway. She spotted a narrow break where a dirt road wound at an angle from the pines to the big road. It led to a large black wrought-iron gate, and over it, a word was fashioned in scrolled black ironwork.

Her heart beat loudly under her pink cotton blouse and pearls. She licked her lips as she read the word *Sweetgrass.*

"Blast," Adele cursed as she yanked the emergency brake. "The gate's closed."

"I'll get it."

"No, it's like a secret handshake. Blast," she swore again, yanking open the car door. "Just hold on a minute."

Her flats made prints in the soft dirt as she ran to the gate. As she fiddled with the lock, Adele hopped in a jig from foot to foot. Then she pushed open the gates and ran knock-kneed back to the car, slamming the door shut. Pushing back the sweaty hair from her face, she released the brake and roared forward.

"You'd think one of my lazy, good-for-nothin' brothers could have managed to open the gate for us. It's not like they didn't know we were coming. I don't know why it was closed. Tripp probably did it on purpose, just to rile me."

Mary June didn't reply. Adele was mostly muttering to herself, anyway, and she suspected the ill-fated brothers would soon be on the receiving end of a skin-searing verbal lashing.

Mary June looked out the window, captivated by what she spied just beyond the shaded drive. She was a farmer's daughter and appreciated the hours of labor involved in the maintenance of the orderly peach orchard they passed. Farther in the distance she spotted a dozen or so cattle grazing in the scrubby grass and beyond, the lush, mysterious swamp marsh.

When Adele turned onto the avenue of oaks, however, the farm girl's practical perusal slipped away. In the space of a gulped breath, she was just one more of the countless visitors entranced by the romantic and picturesque vision of a plantation house at the end of an alley of massive live oaks dripping with lacy Spanish moss.

The history and legends she'd read about at school or heard at her daddy's knee swirled in her mind, painting a rosy aura around the colonial house that sat prettily at the end of the lane. While her heart pounded in her chest, her mind was in the clouds, thrilled that she was so fortunate to be actually staying here, in this historical house.

And yet, as they made their way up along what was once an old carriage path, then circled around a small black pond in front of the house, she knew a moment's surprise and perhaps even a vague disappointment.

The house was much smaller than she'd expected. As a Southerner, she was well aware that not all plantation houses were the grand antebellum mansions made famous in photographs and movies. Many were charming, relatively modest dwellings, once the country houses of the landed gentry who spent most of their time in their grand city houses. Yet, even by those standards, Sweetgrass was small.

But beguiling. The white house had two fluted pillars under a curved portico and a narrow front porch that opened to a wide, welcoming staircase. On either side were one-story additions that added breadth and balance.

Adele rounded the circle then stopped the car in front of the house so abruptly, Mary June had to brace herself against the dash.

"Gotta dash or I'm going to have an embarrassing accident!" Adele called out as she pushed open her door and scrambled from the car. She rushed around the hood and made a beeline up the stairs of the house.

Mary June blinked when the front screen slammed. She sat for a moment, still feeling the rolling of the wheels in her veins. Within a few minutes, the close heat sweltered inside the car. She leaned against the door, and with one step she was enveloped in the scented air of the Lowcountry.

The early evening mist was soft on her skin and perfumed with the cloying scent of honeysuckle and confederate jasmine. She stood alone beside the car, aware of the intense quiet after hours of ear-blasting rock 'n' roll, laughs and shouted gossip. Her senses expanded and tingled as she breathed deep through her nostrils, almost tasting the salt from the tides. She felt the miles she'd driven slide slowly away like scales off a reptile.

She couldn't very well walk into the house uninvited, so

she stole these precious moments of peace before she had to meet the Blakely family to gather her wits. She walked a short way along the driveway, stretching her legs and getting better acquainted with the land. A rural girl, she was more at home out of doors than in and relished the chance to explore the sprawling camellia and azalea gardens, one on either side of the house. The azaleas were finishing their season and the camellias were budding.

Someone had been very clever in situating the house, she thought to herself as she walked. One side faced the glorious avenue of oaks. The other side faced the panoramic expanse of marsh, and just beyond, the dazzling blue-green Atlantic Ocean.

Reaching out, she placed her palm against the rough bark of an enormous live oak and leaned against the old tree. Her lazy gaze took in the vista of shadowy house and twisted oaks dripping in moss against the deepening pinks and blues of a Lowcountry sunset. The wind gusted, lifting the hair from her shoulders, cooling her damp neck like a caress.

Looking out, she had an intense sense that she knew this place, that she'd lived here by the marsh, beside these very trees, some time before. The past whispered to her in the rustle of the leaves, in the night song of the purple martins, in the soft, sandy earth beneath her feet. Was this what they called déjà vu? she wondered. But she'd never been here before, not in this lifetime.

She felt certain of only one thing. She loved this place called Sweetgrass, loved this house that sat enthroned by its surroundings like a dainty queen. She belonged here. Though it made no sense at all, she felt as if she'd come home.

She heard the front screen slam and a heavy footfall on the front stairs. The moment broken, her attention shot over to the porch to see a lanky young man with thick, light-brown hair coming down the stairs toward her. He was of average height, slim, and his tan shone against his crisply ironed yellow shirt. He walked with a confidence befitting a member of the household. Spotting her, he called out a hello. Embarrassed to be caught woolgathering, she waved shyly.

She pushed off from the tree and took a few steps nearer, her mind spinning on what she would say, when she tripped on a thick tree root that protruded from the ground. She went sprawling forward, a gasp caught in her throat.

Her hands landed on a chest as hard as wood and she felt herself being held firmly at the elbows.

"Whoa, we almost lost you there!"

She caught her breath and fumbled back to a stand, her cheeks flaming. Looking up, she saw a chiseled face that held many of the same striking features as Adele's. He had her straight nose and strong bone structure, and his wavy brown hair was cut short in the popular fashion of the day. But with a start she realized his eyes were not at all like Adele's deep-brown ones. His were an astonishing blue.

"I…I'm sorry to be so clumsy," she blurted out. "I guess I wasn't looking where I was going."

He stepped back to a polite distance, putting his hands on his hips. "Aw, don't worry about it. Those ornery old roots lie in wait for just that purpose. You've made their day."

He smiled then and it transformed his face from merely good-looking to one of exceptional charm. The smile made his eyes sparkle with such energy it was contagious, causing her to smile as well.

He stuck out his hand. "I'm Preston. Adele's brother. You must be Mary."

"Mary June," she corrected, taking his hand. She immediately recognized it as a farmer's hand, callused from hard work and chapped from frequent scrubbing. Somehow that made her feel a little less nervous with him and she visibly relaxed.

"You've been abandoned," he said. "Adele knows better than to leave a guest unattended. I've been sent to rescue you."

She laughed lightly at the notion, looking down and tucking her hair behind her ear. "Thanks," she said.

He reached his hand to scratch the back of his neck in an awkward pause while she clasped her hands tightly. Then, seemingly at a loss for words, he said simply, "Well, let's get your luggage."

As he was opening the Mercury's dusty trunk, the front door swung open and Adele returned, all relaxed and smiling, her arm linked with an attractive older woman in a blue shirt-waist dress. The woman's hair was neatly done up in a French twist and she wore pearls in her ears and around her neck.

Mary June quickly smoothed the wrinkles from her pastel pedal pushers and blouse, silently thanking the good Lord that she'd remembered her pearls. Then, remembering her manners, she lifted her chin to meet Mrs. Blakely's smile as introductions were made and courtesies exchanged. She smoothly replied to the gracious yet thorough interrogation as to her family, her church and her connections with Adele. Once the formalities were through, a distinguished Mr. Blakely appeared in jacket and tie and smelling of tobacco to guide them all into the house.

As Mary June followed Mrs. Blakely up the stairs, she looked over her shoulder at Preston, loaded down with luggage, behind her. She secretly smiled, for she realized he was looking at her again, this time with something more than admiration.

What a summer that was! The days quickly fell into a loose and lazy pattern. She'd thought Preston was an awfully good sport. Though he was older by two years and just graduated from college, he accompanied Adele and her out on expeditions. Her most favorite outing, however, was the fishing. Preston had risen before the sun and crept into Adele's pink bedroom to wake up the girls by wiggling their toes. Mary June woke at his first touch, but Adele mulishly kicked and whined.

"I hate getting up early and I hate fishing," Adele said, pulling the blankets over her head.

"Oh, come on, Adele!" Mary June said in a loud whisper at her ear. "You said you wanted to go."

"Y'all just go on without me."

Preston's low chuckle filled the dim room. "Come on, Mary June. It's no use. When she's in this mood, she won't budge. You can clean what we catch," he tossed back to his sister as he turned to leave.

She only grumbled under the covers.

As Mary June followed Preston single file down the stairs, she felt butterflies in her chest at the notion that she was going to spend the whole morning alone with him. They stopped in the kitchen to drink some cold milk and eat a few of Nona's biscuits. Then they packed apples and candy bars in a bag for later. The screen door squeaked when Preston pushed it open, rousing Mr. Blakely's two bird dogs to investigate.

Mary June stepped out into the dawn and paused, raising her face to the sky. She breathed deeply, relishing the tingle of cool morning air against her sleepy skin. The vision of piercing rays of dawn breaking through dark clouds was, for her, better than going to church. When she lowered her eyes, she saw Preston looking at her with a quizzical expression.

"I...I like being outdoors when the sun comes up," she said, looking down with a flush.

"I do, too," he replied with sincerity. "It's my favorite time of the day."

Mary June's gaze rose and she saw in his bright blue eyes that they'd reached some tacit understanding about each other.

He smiled crookedly. "Come on, early bird. We'll lose the tide."

They hurried across a lawn still damp with dew and reached the long wood dock just as dawn's brightening pink-and-yellow light began turning the dark waters glassy. In the hush of the early morning, marsh hens cackled and their rods and gear landed in the flat bottomed boat with seemingly great, echoing thuds.

Preston climbed in first, then reached out to offer his hand to Mary June.

The small motor bubbled in the water as they churned toward one of Preston's favorite fishing holes. He wouldn't tell her exactly where they were headed and she didn't really care. Her fingers skimmed the cool water and droplets of water splashed her face as she watched the birds come alive in the sun rising over the marsh. After a while he slowed their speed and searched the shoreline.

"Are we there yet?" she asked with a tease.

"Could be."

"What're you looking for?"

"I'm just reading the water. You have to think like a fish," he replied. "They like somewhere to hide and their eyes are sensitive to light. So I look for rocky spots or someplace in the shadows." He pointed to an area along the shore where a couple of live oaks bent over the water, shading it. "Over there looks like a good spot. See the rings on the water?" he asked, steering toward it. "That's fish taking a sip. They're in there, all right."

He brought the small boat to a stop in his chosen spot, then put a rod and reel together and spooled it with line. When he began baiting it, she protested.

"I bait my own line, thank you very much."

"Where'd you learn to fish?" he asked as he watched her hook a bait fish.

She shrugged with nonchalance as her fingers adroitly handled the rod and reel, but inside she was glowing at his admiration.

"My family farm in Sumter is surrounded with ponds, rivers, swamps and lakes. I learned to dig for earthworms before I could talk. My daddy always wanted plenty of worms. He'd give me a lard can filled with dirt and a drop of water. My job was to fill it to the brim." She chuckled as she added a weight to the end of her line. "One day I left the bait can in the sun. Never did that again."

Adele had told her that Preston was an ace fisherman, and as the day wore on, Mary June could see that for herself. He had smooth, quick acceleration in his casting and the release of line, an easy, unrushed way with the net, and the undeniable proof of several fish dropped into the cooler. Mary June desperately wanted to catch a fish, not to compete, but just so she could see again that look of admiration in his eyes. Today, it seemed she wouldn't catch anything but puny fish that were under the legal limit.

What impressed her most about him, however, was when he released not only the undersize, but any fish that he knew they wouldn't eat. He slipped an arm around her and taught her to hold the fish in the water by the tail and gently glide it back and forth while its gills flared open. She felt his warm cheek against her face and his hand over hers. When the fish stopped gasping, Preston said close to her ear, "Now let go." She opened her hand and Preston gave the fish a little shove toward freedom.

Mary June felt more euphoria at the release of that undersize fish than she ever had at the catching of one. Her cheeks felt flushed, and when she looked over at his face, mere inches from her own, and caught him smiling at her, she felt certain her own eyes held that glint of admiration she'd been searching for in his.

So many years had passed since that afternoon. Yet sitting on the side of his bed, Mama June wondered if she'd had many moments in her life as pure as that one in a flat-bottomed boat. She felt again the girlish rush she'd felt that day, and looking into her husband's eyes, she could tell that he was remembering it all, too. They'd fished together many more mornings, just the two of them, and though they didn't realize it at the time, Mama June knew now that it was those early mornings as the sun rose and the fish were biting that formed the bedrock of their relationship.

"You weren't much of a talker," Mama June told Preston, patting his hand. "Your son comes by it honestly. I had to work just as hard at fishing for words from you as I did for a bass or a bream. You must've thought I was a chatterbox, the way I kept going on and on. Sort of like I am now." She laughed lightly at herself.

"But you listened. And you laughed at the appropriate places, too. And you commented on this or that—giving me my line, I suppose." She paused in reflection.

"It just occurred to me. We're sort of back in the same boat again, aren't we?"

She sat silent for several more minutes, consumed with thoughts of all she'd just recalled about the early weeks of that fateful summer.

"There's something else I remembered," she said almost in a whisper. She licked her lips. "I know I told you that night you got sick how from the moment I stepped foot on Sweetgrass soil, I hated it."

She glanced at him. His eyes were trained on her.

"That wasn't true. I loved it, Preston. I truly did. Sweetgrass welcomed me from the first breath."

His hand reached up to clasp hers, holding it tightly against his chest.

Mama June was surprised by the sudden, heartfelt passion of the gesture and her heart tightened.

"Oh, you'll have me crying in a moment," she told him. She felt his fingers over hers, patting in an erratic beat. She leaned closer, enjoying the intimate connection that sharing memories with him elicited. In the dark, holding hands, it somehow felt as if they were ageless.

Later in her room, Mama June undressed, uncoiled her braid, then cracked the window to its widest point. Turning off the lights, she lay in the darkness in her cool, crisp sheets while outside her open window she heard the insects sing and the gentle rattle of the roller shade knocking against the wood.

What a wonderfully strange evening, she thought. She'd felt transported in time. Lying in the dark with the moist, Southern night breeze caressing her skin, Mama June could have been the nineteen-year-old girl she'd brought back to the forefront of her mind earlier that evening.

Who was that girl? she wondered. She brought her hands to her face to explore the contours like a blind woman. Looking at her hands, she recalled placing them on Preston's chest. Who was that boy?

She'd forgotten how enchanted she'd been at first meeting Preston. It seemed impossible she could have forgotten such a thing. His young face rose up in her mind's eye, chiseled yet thoughtful.

During those glorious two weeks at Sweetgrass, Preston had become the third musketeer. He drove the powerboat as

Sweetgrass

Mary June and Adele took turns water-skiing the Intracoastal Waterway. He commandeered their hiking expeditions through the murky woods, defending them against snakes and spiders. He accompanied them to the beach on Isle of Palms, where they slathered on baby oil and bodysurfed the waves. And on sultry, lazy nights when they were too tired or sunburned to go out for ice cream or a dance at Front Beach, they sat together on the screened porch and played endless hands of canasta, whist or hearts.

In some ways, he was the brother she'd always wanted. Preston was bighearted, protective and, at times, all knowing. At other times, especially on humid nights when she tossed in her bed, she thought he was anything but brotherly and wondered if she was falling in love with this quiet yet self-possessed boy.

Looking back now, Mama June knew herself to be a fool for not having realized that Preston wasn't being just a good sport. If she'd been older, more mature, more experienced, she would have realized that he'd been in love with her from the very start.

But she didn't realize that at the time. She was only nineteen, and to her it was simply a whirlwind of flirtation and fun that ended when she returned home to Sumter after the arranged two weeks.

Adele had begged and pleaded for her to come back or she'd just die of boredom. Preston, of course, lent his support to the argument, and Mary June didn't need to be asked twice. Perhaps if she'd stayed home in Sumter for the rest of the summer, Preston might have written or come to the college for a visit and their relationship might have followed a different course.

As it was, neither set of parents could say no to Adele when she had her mind set. So Mary June returned to

Sweetgrass after the Fourth of July to spend the rest of the summer. She'd expected to while away the time with Preston and Adele in much the same fashion as during the first two weeks of summer.

But on the afternoon of her first day back, Mary June Clark met Hamlin Blakely III—Tripp.

After that, everything changed.

9

───────

"It was a child's curiosity, watching my mother make them. It's like anything else. You watch a parent doing something, and after a while you just start doing it, too. That's how baskets are in a family. You just get involved."

—Joseph Foreman, basket maker

IT WAS MORGAN'S HABIT to rise early. He didn't need an alarm clock. The dawn song of the purple martins usually stirred him from his sleep before the sun rose.

He liked to rise before the others and go outdoors in the relative peace of dawn. He'd lived alone in Montana for so many years that he found the closeness of so many people again confining. In the isolation of his mountain home, he could loosen the noose of anger and resentment that he'd felt around his neck at the family home.

Since he'd returned, however, the nightmares had returned, too. Not even the usual dousing of the flames with Jim Beam or Johnnie Walker could stop them from ravaging his sleep. He intended to honor his commitment and stick it out at Sweetgrass for a while longer, but to keep his sanity, he avoided his father and the sickroom and sought refuge in the solitude of early morning runs across the property.

The land gave him room to breathe. As he crossed the untouched, natural beauty, he couldn't deny his connection to it. Like the migrating birds and butterflies, Blakelys had passed through these fields, generation after generation, each leaving his or her temporary mark before moving on. Always, however, the land remained—verdant, vibrant, as welcoming and fecund as a sweet-scented woman.

To him, the Lowcountry was a land of contrasts. Its inhabitants suffered devastating hurricane after hurricane, endured humidity so thick their lungs felt like they were blanketed by moss, and battled mosquitoes so hungry they'd feast through fur, feather or clothes.

The Lowcountry's landscape generously fed even the poorest of men a banquet from its waters, hosted a bountiful way station for a kaleidoscope of migrating birds, captured the magic of moonlight through the lacy fronds of moss and revealed God each evening in the unparalleled magnificence of its sunset.

The Lowcountry was a Garden of Eden, and once having bitten the apple, being ostracized from the garden was a living hell. Like him, most Lowcountry boys living elsewhere felt the tug of the tides drawing them home. The love of this sun-drenched land, the memories held in each blade of sweetgrass, was in his blood as sure as any gene that held eye color. Or predilection for disease.

So Morgan ran. Each morning his feet pounded the ground that his ancestors walked until sweat ran down his face in rivers. He ran to put some distance between himself and whatever it was that plagued his sleep at night. He ran hoping, irrationally, that it would somehow bring him peace. But no matter how long he ran or how far, it was never far enough.

Sweetgrass

Each path he took led to home.

Morgan saw Kristina working in the garden beside the kitchen house when he rounded the front circle. The ancient garden was a rambling, weedy, tumbledown affair, semi-enclosed with a low brick wall to the back and a picket fence along the house side. A narrow brick walkway in a herringbone pattern divided the garden into quadrants, and in the center of these was a copper sundial that had aged to a soft green patina.

Kristina was on her knees on the walkway, bent over the dirt and waging war with an enormous, tenacious weed. She wore jeans and an old white shirt rolled up at the elbows and tied up below her breasts. The enormous brim of her straw hat covered her shoulders like a tent. He walked along the path to her side, enjoying the sight of her well-proportioned form. Drawing near, he held back a chuckle at her low, breathy curses.

"Looks like you're losing that battle."

"Morgan!" She sat back on her heels and brought her gloved hand to her chest, spraying dirt across the bricks and her shirt. Her cheeks glowed from the battle, the blazing sun and the fine sheen of moisture on her skin. "You scared me half to death! I didn't hear you."

"I didn't mean to frighten you. I came up from the woods and spotted you here. From the looks of it, I'm not sure you're winning."

"Me, neither. Some of these roots go straight to China." She tugged her garden glove from her fingers and, once freed, reached her hand up to pull off her broad hat and fan herself with it. Her golden hair was pulled back in an elastic, and the curls, kinked from the humidity, formed cornrows along the side of her head.

"You've got some dirt…" he said, pointing to her shirt.

"Where?" Kristina looked down and saw the smudge over

her heart where she'd laid her hand. Brushing it off, she laughed and shrugged.

"Doesn't make much difference. I'm coated with dirt from head to toe. And by the time I'm finished today the sweat will turn it all to mud." She looked up at the sun and fanned her pinkened cheeks. "It sure is hot for May!"

"You're in the Lowcountry now. Hot comes early."

She narrowed her eyes, taking in his sweaty T-shirt, ragged-edged shorts and muddy running shoes. "You look pretty hot, too. What were you doing, running?"

"I'm getting familiar with the place again."

"Again? Have you been gone for a while?"

He nodded. "I moved to Montana years ago. I have a small place there."

"Ah, you're a western boy!"

He laughed but shook his head. "I might live in the West and work in the West, but I'll always be a Southerner. There's no escaping it. Trust me, I know. It's in the blood."

"Then why did you leave?" she asked lightly.

"Why do any of us leave home?"

She paused a moment before saying, "There's always a reason."

He wiped his brow with his sleeve. "For me, the leaving and the coming back both have to do with my father. Classic. Now, turnaround is fair play. How about you?"

She fanned her face with her hat. When she spoke again, her voice was flat. "I followed someone I thought I loved. Or perhaps I should say that I thought loved me. Another classic reason, isn't it?" She lowered the hat and gave it a light toss. It floated in the sky like a Frisbee before landing on a chair a short distance away.

The vulnerability he saw in her eyes disappeared so quickly that he couldn't be sure he'd even seen it.

"Well, I'm done for," she said with a quick smile. "Whew, it's hotter than Hades today. I could sure go for a swim."

"Why don't you?"

"Where?"

"How about the beach? It's a ways off but we could drive."

She frowned and shook her head. "I don't have enough time today for a beach outing. Duty calls."

"Well," he said with hesitation, "you could go to Blakely's Bluff. That's right close. I could tell you how to get there easily enough."

"Blakely's Bluff? Where's that?"

Morgan pointed off toward the rear of the house where the marsh became creek and, farther out, creek led to the ocean. "It's out there straight as the crow flies, on a spit of land that juts out into the ocean. It's a pretty place and there should be a small bit of sandy beach we try to keep up. There's a dock, too, though God knows what shape it's in. The family has a summerhouse there."

"Another house?"

"I wouldn't be too impressed. It's pretty rustic. There's no indoor plumbing or electricity. But it's got its own charm and you can change clothes there. You're welcome to use it as often as you like."

"Sounds wonderful. I'd love to go."

His eyes deadened. "It's just down the road. You won't need me to find it. If you follow that small back road around the house as far as it goes, it'll take you right to it. The house is smack at the end of the line."

"I'd love the company."

"I said no."

She acknowledged the cool tone with raised brows. "Maybe some other time."

"Yeah. Maybe. Now, if you'll excuse me, I've got to keep plowing through those financial records. Good luck with the garden."

Mama June stepped out onto the back porch and smiled to find Nona sitting there. Nona wore a scarf wrapped around her hair in her favorite color of sky-blue, which matched her slacks. Her head was bent over and her hands were tirelessly coiling strands of sweetgrass and sewing them up with long, thin strands of palmetto. Her traditional silver-spoon needle caught the sun as she worked.

Beside her sat a young girl of about nine years of age, her head also bent over a circle of sweetgrass about the size of a coaster. Her slim shoulders protruded from under her brightly colored tank top. The girl's hair was neatly plaited in braids and her skin was as smooth as coffee-colored cream. She looked up when Mama June approached, and her eyes were large and expressive. Mama June knew in a flash she had to be Nona's granddaughter.

"This can't be little Grace?" she asked.

Nona looked up and smiled in greeting. "It sure enough is. Grace, this is Mrs. Blakely."

Her eyes averted shyly, but Grace rose to her feet with coltish charm and extended a long, slim arm. "Pleased to meet you" came out in a breathy rush.

"Dear child, this is not the first time we've met," Mama June exclaimed, taking the child's small hand in both of hers. "I held you in my arms when you were no bigger than a mite. Your grandmother used to carry you everywhere she went in a Moses basket. Remember that basket?" she asked Nona, turning her head.

"I still have it!" Nona exclaimed.

Then facing Grace again, Mama June said, "You were a

regular visitor here at Sweetgrass. But it's been a long time, and now look at you. You've grown up! And what a pretty little thing you are, too."

"Thank you, Mrs. Blakely." Grace ventured a smile.

"Please, call me Mama June like everyone else."

Nona looked on with a pride that shone from her eyes and brightened her face.

"So your grandmother is teaching you how to make baskets, is she?" Mama June asked her as she made her way to the empty rocking chair beside Nona.

"This here's the one that's going to carry on my craft," Nona said. "She has a gift for it and she loves it, too. Don't you, honey?"

Grace nodded her head.

"Good for you," replied Mama June. "How about your mother? Did Maize ever pick it up?"

"No, ma'am," replied Grace. "My mama don't like making baskets. She thinks it's boring."

Mama June chuckled as she lowered herself into the rocker. "Yes, that sounds like the Maize I remember." She groaned. "My feet are so sore! The speech therapist is in with Preston and I've been looking forward to sitting down for hours." She looked over at Grace, who was picking up her handiwork.

"Come show me what you're working on today," she said, waving the child over.

"It's not much," Grace said as she handed over the three-inch coil of stitched sweetgrass. "I'm just making the bottoms. Same as always," she said with a theatrical sigh.

"It's a start," Nona said. "We all began in the same fashion—me, my mama, my grandmother and so on."

"But I want to make my own basket," she said with a pout. "I could, Granny. I know I could."

"You think so?"

"Honest, Granny, I really do."

Nona set her basket in her lap, then reached out her hand. "Let me see what you've got, child," she said, taking the child's circle of grass. She held the project up to the light. "I like to see if the stitches are tight and even. I might could see the sun peeking through, but I don't like to see too much. It has to be strong, too. Tough. Just like your fingers, eh?" she said with a laugh, reaching out to take hold of Grace's hand. She kissed the fingertips then handed the circle back to Grace.

"Is it good?" Grace asked, her eyes studying her own work.

Nona nodded. "That's a good one. Better than good." She peered up at the child, her dark eyes both teasing and specu-lative. Then she wrapped an arm around Grace, holding her close. "Maybe you are ready to build up a basket after all."

Grace stretched up on her toes in excitement. "Really?"

"Really. Now, gimme some sugar." She lifted her cheek, closing her eyes and beaming as Grace planted a noisy kiss. "That's sweet. Okay, go on in the kitchen and pour yourself some lemonade. I made it fresh from scratch. I knew it was going to be a hot, hot day today. You could bring us old folks a drink, too. How does that sound to you, Mary June?"

"Sounds delicious."

"Okay! I'll be back directly!" They watched the girl gam-bol to the kitchen, her joy visible.

"She's a great girl," Mama June said. "You must be proud."

"I am one lucky old woman to have a grandchild like her. She's never a moment of trouble. My Grace is a straight-A student. And she sings in the gospel choir. She's her grand-mother reincarnated. And her brother, he doesn't get into trouble, neither. Now, what he knows about is computers. I know nothing about computers! But my Kwame is making me a…what do you call it? That place on the Internet where I can show my baskets?"

"A Web site?"

"Yes, that's it! A Web site. He's making me one. Imagine that!" She laughed and shook her head as she rocked. "Thirteen years old and making his grandmother a Web site. How the world has changed. He's not much interested in making the baskets, though. Most kids his age aren't. They want to play with their computers or watch television. But he'll go out with his grandfather to our sacred spot to pull the sweetgrass and cut the bull rush. So I'm proud to say that Kwame does his part with the baskets, too."

"You're a lucky woman," Mary June said again, rocking and thinking of her own grandsons and how they hadn't come by to see their grandfather since his return home. She couldn't ask them to come, didn't want to beg. They were old enough to make that decision based on their own hearts.

Nona sighed and looked down in her lap at the circular basket she was building up. The stitches were tight and even, the basket getting taller and taller. She thought of all the mothers in her family that had taught their daughters this art form, and all the fathers who had taken their sons out to collect the grass.

"I'll teach Grace, and Grace will teach her daughters, and so it will continue," Nona said. "From one generation to the next. Mother to daughter. Father to son. God willing."

"God willing," Mama June concurred.

They rocked awhile in silence, each lost in her own train of thought.

"I'm worried," Nona said at length.

"About what?"

"Sweetgrass basket weaving has been passed on since the days of slavery, but after all these generations, I worry if my art is dying fast." She sighed. "I might be the end of the line."

"Why do you think that? You have Grace as an example of it being carried on."

"There's Grace, that's for true. If she keeps it up. Most young ones, they just don't care for making the baskets. Every generation, fewer and fewer want to sew. In my generation, most mothers tried to teach their daughters. There are some, like Maize, who just won't do it. And some that up and move away. Now, in some families—big families—it'll always be a part of them. But my family... We never had a lot of children so we're small now. And my two boys moved away. When the grandchildren come to visit, they just don't want to sit long enough to do it. My sister's got five girls and they all live here, but none of them know a thing about it."

"You can't make a child do what they aren't inclined to do," Mama June added, thinking of her own children.

"Not today, anyway. Back when I was coming up, it was different. Basket making was a part of our livelihood. We could earn a little extra money to put away. My mama didn't ask me if I wanted to make the baskets. Oh Lord, no! We children all used to gather in the shade and spend hours sewing the basket bottoms, just like my Grace is doing now. Today, though, the families can afford different things."

"Money was tight for all of us at times."

"Yes, it was. I put my basket money aside to save for college educations. Children like my Maize, they want to go to school and become professionals. That's where their interests lie. Not in the baskets. It takes an old geezer like me to try to keep it going."

Mama June laughed, then said, "Maybe the ones that stay might pick it up again."

"They might," Nona conceded, thinking of her own daughter. "It's like riding a bicycle, I guess. I only hope there's sweetgrass left for them."

Sweetgrass

"Why wouldn't there be?"

Nona looked at Mama June with eyes round with incredulousness. "Honey, take a look around at what's happening here. Where's the grass going to come from, eh? The grass is gone."

Mama June was taken aback by the finality of the statement. "Gone? How can that be? It used to be everywhere."

"It used to be we could go anywhere, too. Without some barrier. All over Christ Church Parish, we could walk back in the woods and just go get the palmetto and grass. Well, let me tell you, it's been many years since we could do that. That land is all gone for houses. You know the Mitchell piece?"

When Mama June nodded, she continued. "That's where lots of us used to go and gather. Now it's fenced off, just waiting to be turned into more houses."

"That piece of land had been marked for development for several years, but it's still untouched. Can't you go in just for the grass? Surely that wouldn't be a bother."

"No. They won't let anyone past the fence line. Same as with most places. Most all the fields are gone now. We have to go all the way to Georgia and Florida for our grass, paying an arm and a leg for it. A few of us have a secret spot, like me. But even there, it's in danger of disappearing."

Mama June sat back in her chair. "Why didn't I know this? You'd think it'd be common knowledge that the grass is disappearing. I'll bet most folks around here don't realize. Could it be replanted?"

"Sure. If the folks with the land would do it."

"I read about a piece of land planted especially for sweetgrass. What about that?"

"Up inland at Dill Plantation. Yes, they tried. It was kind of an experiment. But the grass, it wasn't right. See, the land was too fertile. There were lots of weeds and not enough hands to tend it. Here's the main thing, though. That grass, it come up too weak. Too flat. The grass that grows by the marsh and sea is curled. Take a look," she said, offering a blade of sweetgrass for Mama June to handle.

"The grass has to have lived a hard life to be right for the baskets."

Mama June felt the smoothness of the curled grass, grown tough and resilient through miserly bits of soil and water. She thought the same could be said of the people who made the baskets, as well. The triumphant endurance of centuries of hard living went into the creation of each work of art.

"So," she said thoughtfully, getting it straight in her mind, "it's the sweetgrass grown along the coast here that you need for the baskets."

Nona nodded, sensing where the topic was headed. "My family's been pulling grass from this place since time was. My family has a bond with this land, same as yours. It's our sacred place."

"It's a worry for you then. My selling Sweetgrass."

"I've been losing sleep over it." Nona sighed and laid her work down. "But there's nothing I can do about it."

"I'm worried that there's nothing I can do about it, either."

"It just don't seem right. Why do you want to sell? Well, not *you*," Nona hurried to amend. "I mean, the Blakelys? Morgan's back now. Doesn't he have an interest in the place? Or Nan? And what about Adele? Lord knows, she's got enough money to hold on to it."

"Adele's the one who most wants to sell. I don't know for certain, but Nan thinks Adele and Hank are cooking up some development plan using Sweetgrass as its cornerstone."

"They're no better than carpetbaggers," Nona said disparagingly.

"Oh, I don't know," Mama June said in a weary tone.

"Nan and Hank can't afford to keep this place up. Neither can Morgan. Not with the taxes and insurance the way they are. Preston and I are old now. *We're* the end of a line, I'm afraid. It's not much different than with your baskets. What can we do if our children don't want what we pass on? Or if they can't afford to maintain it? Or if they want to move on to somewhere else?"

"I don't know," Nona said with a sorry shake of her head. "But I do know we can't just give up on it. We're passing on tradition. Both of us. There's too much at stake for the future generations to just let it all go. There has to be a way to pass it down somehow. To keep the land safe, the sweetgrass safe. 'Cause once it's gone, it's gone forever."

Their conversation was interrupted by a shout of hello. Looking over the porch railing, Mama June saw Kristina at the bottom of the porch stairs. She was dressed in a gauzy shirt over a swimsuit and shorts.

"Where are you off to?" asked Mama June. "Looks like you're going swimming."

"I am. Morgan told me about Blakely's Bluff. I hope you don't mind if I take a stroll down there?"

Mama June darted a glance at Nona. Nona kept her eyes on her basket and rocked.

"Why, no," she replied. "Of course not. There's a fine place for swimming. But it's hardly a stroll. It's more a hike. You might try a bicycle. You're in luck, though. Morgan's checked all the tires. They should be fine."

"Really?" Her face bunched in thought. "He was a bit vague about Blakely's Bluff. Said if I just follow that back road there, it'll take me right to it."

"That's right, though that road goes a right far piece."

Kristina looked off at the road, considering, then back at

Mama June with a question in her eyes. She climbed up the stairs closer to them.

"Do you mind if I ask you something?"

Mama June glanced at Nona, who had stopped sewing her basket to look up with interest.

"I won't know till you ask me."

"Well, it's about Morgan. He seemed kind of upset when I asked him to come with me to Blakely's Bluff. I hope I didn't overstep my bounds."

Mama June glanced again at Nona, who muttered "Oh, Lord" and went back to her weaving.

"I'm sorry," Kristina blurted out. "I don't mean to pry."

"No, my dear," Mama June replied. "You aren't prying. It's no secret, but it's a painful topic. We don't discuss it much. Morgan never."

Her tongue stilled in her mouth at the prospect of the words it had to form. She knew it had to be said. Now was not the time for moral cowardice. She took a breath and said quickly, "You see, Morgan doesn't like to go the bluff." She took a deep breath.

Nona stopped rocking and filled in the silence. "Morgan's brother died in a boating accident off Blakely's Bluff."

Kristina's eyes widened and she appeared sincerely contrite. "I am so, so sorry."

"It was a long time ago," Mama June said in a distant voice.

"That's why Morgan won't go there," Nona told her. "It brings back too many memories. You see, Morgan was on the boat with Hamlin."

"Oh," Kristina replied, her face revealing that she understood all. "Poor Morgan."

"It was God's will," Mama June replied. It was a phrase she'd said so often it rolled off her tongue without thought or feeling.

After an awkward silence that indicated nothing more

would be said on the topic, Kristina mustered herself. "Well, thank you. I appreciate knowing the facts. I'll be on my way before it gets too late. A bicycle, huh? What a hoot. Haven't ridden one of those in a long time. But you know what they say. Once you learn… I won't be gone long. I'll be back in time for Preston's late-afternoon meds. See ya!"

The two women watched her lithe body hustle down the stairs and amble over toward the back shed with a vivacity and grace they could only envy. A few minutes later she was tugging a rusty red bicycle out and putting her towel and bag into an ancient wicker basket attached to the handlebars. She looked up at the ladies on the porch, smiled brightly and waved. Taking hold of the handlebars, she pushed off and pedaled down the dirt road, soon disappearing into the cluster of trees.

"That girl sure has a lot of energy," Nona said, rocking.

"It's part of her charm," Mama June replied.

"She sure has a way of looking under rocks, eh?"

"Yeah, I thought so, too."

"You know who she reminds me of?"

Mama June thought for a minute. "No. Who?"

Nona chuckled, low in her throat. "You, that's who."

Mary June stopped rocking. "Me? Why, you've lost your mind, Nona Bennett. Kristina Hays is nothing like me!"

"Oh, yes she is. Maybe not in her looks so much. And she's more forward than you ever were, but I put that down to her being a Yankee. What I'm talking about is that sweetness in the eyes, as if it shines straight from the heart. Same as you had when I first met you. You were a pretty thing and so eager to please. It was hard not to like you, same as her. And, Lord, you asked a lot of questions! Wanted to know every little thing about Sweetgrass. You were always there to lend a hand, too. And…she's riding your old bicycle."

Mama June scowled and resumed her rocking. "I wish I

knew why everyone likes to compare me to someone. Always did so."

Nona clucked her tongue. "It's more that people like to be compared to you."

"Nonsense," Mama June said in a fluster, her cheeks coloring. But inside, she was aglow. It was rare for Nona to offer a compliment, and when offered, it was sincere. Lately Mama June felt unsure of who she was, as if she was lost and trying to find herself again.

She looked at the gravel road that Kristina had just pedaled down. Nona was right. Kristina was riding her old bicycle. She remembered the many times she and Adele rode their bicycles to the bluff that summer.

"She's got a good heart. Anyone can see that," Mama June added.

"True enough."

"She is different from most girls around here, though."

Nona nodded.

"She rubbed my shoulders one afternoon and I swanny, I could feel the heat just pouring from her hands."

Nona's eyes narrowed in thought. "Might be she has the healing touch."

"Uh-huh. Just look at the progress she's made with Preston."

"I once knew a healer," Nona said. "He could put his hands over your troubled spot and it was like electricity come hot right off his hands. It even felt hot on the skin. I wonder if she has that, too."

"I do have to say, she's helped me with Preston," she told Nona. "Got me talking to him again about all sorts of things."

Nona went back to her sewing. "Interesting that she's got Morgan talking about Blakely's Bluff, too. I'd say that's a start. Like Grace's little coil of grass, she can build up from there."

They rocked in silence again as Mama June's gaze traveled its usual path across the water to the old weathered house on the bluff.

"Blakely's Bluff," she murmured, allowing the name to fall softly from her lips.

10

———

"All spring and summer, gatherers pull the sweetgrass, which slips out of its roots like knives from sheaths. Bundles of grass are then spread in the sun to dry."

—*Row Upon Row*

ANY TALK ABOUT BLAKELY'S BLUFF could send Mama June's thoughts spiraling to the past. When that happened, she read a book, studied the Bible or watched an old movie on television before sleep. More often than not, that would work as well as any hot toddy to help her avoid disturbing thoughts and drift off to dreamless sleep.

This night, however, she didn't seek the solace of a soporific. Her dreams had begun to take on a life of their own, and her recent chats with Preston had opened up a floodgate of memories. Rather than run from them, Mama June decided to heed Kristina's advice and revisit them. Then perhaps she could at last put them to rest.

For the memories were not buried. Not really. They were hiding under the surface, just waiting to rise at the mere mention of a word, like a critter in the marsh mud that feeds with the tides. Silence was no good for families, she thought. And the silence in her family had gone on for so long it was now the norm. She remembered the days when the family had been able to laugh and talk about most anything. The shroud that had been placed over Hamlin's death stemmed, she knew, from her own inability to so much as reference it.

Mama June turned from the window and walked aimlessly around her room. She was no better than the ghost, Beatrice, stuck in limbo between the past and the future. After Hamlin's death she had been beyond despair. She didn't care if she lived or died. Like many people raised in her time, she was offered advice like "just try not to think about it, honey," or "try to think about positive things." The more she turned away from painful thoughts and feelings, however, the less she seemed able to move on with her life.

This was true for Morgan, as well.

If she was truly honest, she'd admit how the memories tied to Blakely's Bluff went far deeper than Hamlin's death. Morgan could never know how far back the silence went. Preston knew. Preston had always known and had always protected her. He'd been her strength in the past. Now she had to face the past. She had to be strong for both of them. For their son's sake.

Mama June cracked the window open and let the night in, fragrant and balmy, not yet oppressive as it would be when summer pushed on. She untied her robe and laid it on the foot of the bed, then climbed under the welcoming covers. Laying her head on the pillow, she heard the bellowing song of crickets serenading her, filling her with a sweet lassitude.

Drifting off, she brought to mind once again Preston's young face, his reluctant smile—so much like his son's. Warmth flooded her at the vision and, relaxing, she closed her eyes and journeyed back. Back to her youth.

Back to Blakely's Bluff.

* * *

Bluff House perched on the edge of the earth like a dare.

It was originally built by Beatrice's grandson, the original Hamlin Blakely, an angry man scarred physically and emotionally by the horrors of the War Between the States. People said he'd wanted to go as far into the face of God as he could go.

The house faced the ocean squarely. Two straight, unembellished stories of cedar were weathered to a stormy gray. Black storm shutters framed each window. They were thick and unpretentious, built for purpose, not decoration. The house might have been foreboding were it not for the wide porch that wrapped around the front. This had been added by some later descendent with an eye for pleasure, not revenge. Its elaborate gingerbread was painted a bright white and welcomed the guests to sit for a spell in the offshore breezes.

Mary June Clark loved the house at first sight. She was thrilled by its contrasts, being both foreboding and inviting.

"Mary June!" called Adele from the dock. "What's taking you so long? Hurry up. We're ready to shove off!"

"Hold your horses, Adele!" she called from the Bluff House kitchen. "I've got to wrap up these sandwiches. One more minute."

She carefully sliced the three peanut butter and jelly sandwiches and wrapped them with waxed paper. These she added to the picnic basket along with cold apples and bottles of Nehi orange drink from the icebox. After tidying up, she grabbed a straw hat from a peg by the door and ran out toward the dock.

Preston was standing at the helm of the Boston Whaler. His light-brown hair was windblown and his body was lean and brown in ragged-edged shorts and a T-shirt. Adele's raven hair was bound in a red gingham scarf and her long, tanned legs stretched between dock and boat as she untied the ropes.

Sweetgrass

"Permission to come aboard, sir," Mary June called out as she reached them.

Preston grinned at the sight of her in her large floppy straw hat. He immediately came to the side of the boat to take hold of the picnic basket with one hand and lend his other to steady her as she climbed aboard.

Adele finished with the ropes and gave the boat a push from the dock. With a graceful leap, she hopped onto the boat, her teeth shining white against her dark tan as she grinned. Adele loved being out in the sun and was nearly as proficient on a boat as her brother. Mary June had gone out on the boat several times with Adele—just the girls. But whenever a male came aboard, there was an unspoken understanding that the women took a back seat.

It was Mary June's first day back at Sweetgrass. She'd brought many gifts of food and flowers from her parents to the Blakelys and, after sweet tea and friendly inquiries, the three friends packed their gear and headed straight for Blakely's Bluff.

The sun shone overhead in a cloudless sky. They took it slow. The engine bubbled as Preston carefully steered the boat through the tricky, narrow marsh creeks. The tide was high and the bright green grass waved from a sea of shimmering blue water as far as she could see. Mary June imagined this was the same landscape that the early settlers must have seen.

They left the creek and headed into what looked to Mary June like a wide-open arena of water as black as mud. Two creeks intersected into this bowl like two long, winding arms—one left, one right. The currents created an eddy that circled round and round, stirring up mud and creating the hole. It was a heady, wide-open space, all the more exhilarating to reach after traveling through a labyrinth of narrow creeks. Entering it, she felt the wind pick up and whip her hair back from her face.

"What is this place?" she asked Preston. They stood side by side at the helm, bumping shoulders.

He looked her way, his eyes impossibly blue against his dark tan. "We call this Shark Hole," he told her. "It's the deepest water in Charleston County, some ninety feet down."

She peered over the side to where it was deep and ominously dark.

"Are there really sharks down there?"

"Yeah, sure," he replied in a cavalier tone. "They're all over. You catch babies a lot, but I've caught some four-footers. There are some twenty-five species of sharks off our coast, just like there are in the salt marsh. Some of those beasts are big. It's deep here and when the tides change there's a strong current and a lot of bait fish. That's what they come for. There's silver perch, croaker, gray trout, mullet and spot, just to name a few." He offered a cocky grin. "Makes for some good fishing. I can take you, if you like."

She'd enjoyed fishing with him for different quarry, some more game than others. But she'd never tried for shark. "I might," she replied hesitatingly, unsure of how much action she really wanted.

Adele had been listening and leaned forward to shout over the roar of the engine, "Don't do it! Press lets all the sharks go. That means he has to get the hook out of its mouth. Think about it."

Mary June envisioned her fingers in a shark's mouth. "Sounds pretty tricky."

Adele rolled her eyes. "That's all you need, Mary June, to lose a finger. Wherever are you going to put that wedding ring then?"

"Aw, I'm careful," Preston countered. Then he winked. "Haven't lost a finger yet." When Mary June grimaced he said, "But if you don't want shark, all the fishing is pretty good here. Take a look over there. Those fishermen know where the good catch is."

He pointed out toward the water where she spied a sleek gray fin streaking through the waters like a bullet. Mary June's mouth opened in a gasp, thinking it was one of the sharks they'd just been discussing. Suddenly she heard a loud *whoosh,* and with an arcing dive, it disappeared under the water.

"Porpoises!" Mary June exclaimed.

"Dolphins," he corrected. "Atlantic bottlenosed dolphins."

"I made the fatal error at the tender age of eight and Preston has never let me live it down," Adele told her.

"How can you tell the difference?" Mary June asked. "They both look like Flipper to me."

"Honey, Flipper is a Southern boy," she replied with an exaggerated drawl. "He's bigger and brighter and a lot more fun than his Yankee cousin."

Preston gave his sister a gentle shove, then said to Mary June in his patient manner, "It's not hard to tell them apart. Bottlenosed dolphins have a long beak, like their name. And they're bigger. They're about seven to twelve feet long. A porpoise is snub-nosed, kinda like you," he teased, and pinched her nose.

She ducked back and quickly swatted his hand away, blushing.

"And a porpoise is smaller. Only about five feet." He snorted and his eyes traveled her length. "Again, sort of like you."

"Next you'll be telling her they're cuter. Sort of like you…" Adele teased.

Mary June smirked, but to her surprise, Preston colored and turned to check some gauge on the boat. Adele smugly caught her gaze and nodded. Adele had told Mary June that she thought her brother had a "thing" for her, which Mary June had hotly denied. Now, though still unconvinced, she wondered if it was true. Averting her eyes, she quickly looked back at the dolphins. She could only find one and it was streaking off to join his pod in another section of Shark Hole.

"We'd better get going, too, if we want to spend any time on the beach," Preston said, standing wide-legged at the wheel.

Preston pulled back on the throttle and they roared forward, the girls gripping their hats and grinning ear to ear as they cut through the choppy water. Mary June lifted her chin to the wind, feeling it pour over her like water. As far as she could see, there was only sea and sky. It was early afternoon and the sun was high overhead. They were headed for Capers Island. This was a favorite meeting spot of the local kids that Preston and Adele grew up with, and Adele was preening. Once they heaved anchor and came ashore, she targeted one boy in particular.

On any given day they'd just hang out for a while with whoever showed up, drinking Cokes and lying on the beach or swimming. It was the kind of lazy fun that was pure heaven after a tedious school year. The day, however, was regulated by the tides. After a few hours, Preston wanted to head back.

The girls groaned their complaints.

"Just a little while longer?" Mary June begged. She was lying on her back, soaking up the sun. "I've gotten so pale."

Preston was already on his feet, shaking out his towel. "Nope. It's already getting late. The tides are lowering. Come on. Adele!" he called. "Time's a wastin'."

Adele's face was mutinous, but she gracefully swallowed her complaints. She knew Preston wouldn't budge when it came to boat safety. At high tide, the seemingly smooth waters hid treacherous oyster beds that could rip the hull of a boat. During low tides, a boat could easily get stuck in the mud—and often did. Rescue missions were common along the creeks.

Mary June sat next to Adele and held on to the side of the boat with one hand, and with the other grabbed hold of her floppy hat. The tide was indeed going out. When they'd left Blakely's Bluff, the tide was high and water flooded the marsh from bank to bank. Now the water had lowered to the point where small islands of gray-green oyster beds emerged from under the water—pointed, razor sharp and dangerous.

Once back in the creek, one side of the boat was deep with the current; the other side was already in shallow water and revealed the high, scarred edges of marsh and streaks of muddy bottom, dotted with holes from fiddler crabs.

Preston's face grew taut and his eyes narrowed, alert. He slowed the engine to little more than a low growl as they snaked through the maze of marsh.

"Adele! Get the pole."

For once Adele did not return a flippant comment. She moved quickly to retrieve a long metal pole from the boat's bottom and this she put into the water on the shallow side of the boat. Where the water grew suspiciously shallow, she pushed with the pole away from the bank.

"Can we get stuck here?" Mary June asked, warily watching as Adele's pole repeatedly hit bottom.

"We can," he replied. "Folks get stuck in mud flats all the time. But we won't."

Even though at every turn another small creek opened to present them with yet another option, she knew Preston would pick the right one. She wondered how he could possibly know, there were so many it was confusing, but she felt sure he did. He'd told her he'd spent his youth in these marshes—swimming, in inner tubes and boats—as had his brother, his father and the forefathers before him.

She clutched the side of the boat and kept out of Preston and Adele's way as they navigated around narrow curves and walls of grass too high to see over. The sun overhead was high and relentless, coloring her exposed arms pink. She sighed with relief when she spied the angled roof of Blakely's Bluff over the line of grass. They could walk straight to it in minutes if they went as the crow flew. But by boat it took another twenty minutes of snaking through the grass before they rounded another bend in the creek and Bluff House and the long, welcoming dock was before them.

She lifted her hand to shield her view. Standing on the dock was a tall, dark-haired, handsome young man she'd not seen before. He was deeply tanned and had the lean, defined build of a swimmer. His arms were crossed at his chest in a defiant stance.

Mary June thought he looked rumpled, as if he'd just rolled out of bed. A cigarette dangled from his mouth, his shorts were ragged-edged, looking like they'd been cut with scissors, and his longish hair stuck out in disarray from his head. Behind him, two friends in similar shape sat idly on the pilings and drank beer from a cooler.

"Well, it's about time," the man called out as they approached. "Where the hell you been so long?"

"Hey, Tripp!" Adele called out, her face beaming with delight at seeing him. "You're back! Darlin', where the hell *you* been?"

"Never you mind," he said with a lazy drawl and a half smile that teased of unspeakable places. Then, shifting his dark-brown eyes on Preston, he said with a scowl, "Stop driving like a girl, Press. Just bring it on in."

Preston's face was stony as he brought the boat slowly, carefully into dock and cut the engine.

"Don't bother to tie it up," Tripp told him when Adele threw him the ropes. "I'm going right out."

"Like hell you are!" Preston shouted back. "That's crazy! The tide's near out. You'll run up on the mud and get stuck."

He tossed his cigarette into the water and offered Preston a patronizing pat on the back. "Don't you worry about me, *mother.*"

His two friends chortled as they stood, waiting to board.

Preston shook his brother's hand off and fired back. "You know better, but you don't give a damn."

"Sure I do," he said amiably. "Let's just call it a difference of opinion."

Tripp pulled the boat alongside the dock and tossed the ropes to a friend. His eyes, under thick brows, shone with an incredible magnetism.

"You know you're taking a big chance," Preston said. Mary June could tell he was simmering.

Tripp turned to face his brother, and though his smile remained on his face, his tone changed to reflect the insolence of age and experience. "What I *know* is this creek. Better than anybody. And that includes *you,* little brother."

Preston's eyes flashed with restrained fury. "Yeah, I've heard that story before. Well, I'll be damned if I'm going to go after you and get you out of trouble, big brother. *Again.* And if you rip up the bottom of *this* boat, like you did the last one, Daddy will have your hide on a platter."

"Yeah, yeah, yeah. Now, hurry it up, pal. If you didn't take all day getting back, I wouldn't have to worry about hittin' the bottom, would I? Shit, Press, you drive slower than—"

Preston climbed from the boat and stood face-to-face with his brother, shoulders back, glaring, daring him to finish.

Tripp was taller than Preston by a good three inches and had more muscle mass to his shoulders. There was a dangerous quality to his stance that was evident by his animal-like stillness. Yet Preston stood his ground.

Tripp let the sentence slide with a smirk and a shake of his head. He turned to look over his shoulder. "Come along, gentlemen. Climb aboard."

Mary June released a sigh of relief. She'd never met Adele's eldest brother, Hamlin, whom they called Tripp on account of him being a Hamlin with the triple III after his name. But she recognized immediately that Tripp was a bad boy.

And being a good girl, there was something intriguing about a bad boy.

Preston turned toward her to lend a hand as she climbed out from the boat. His hand was firm and strong, and with one swoop, she landed on the deck, almost crashing into Tripp. She looked abruptly into his face, inches from her own, and her breath caught in her throat.

She felt an immediate, almost animal attraction. Tripp had the same thick brows and straight nose that was a Blakely trademark and the same confident athleticism. But he had an unrestrained magnetism and charisma that were striking.

Mary June saw the same spark of interest ignite in Tripp's dark brown eyes.

"Who's this pretty girl?" he asked, looking directly at her.

Mary June averted her eyes.

"She's my friend, Mary June Clark," Adele answered him, stepping forward to grab hold of Mary June's arm. "Come on, sugar, let's head back."

Tripp released a smile. "We'll have to meet more proper a little later," he told her.

"Sure," she mumbled, flustered, before Adele led her away.

Preston stood by and watched the exchange in stony silence.

Tripp turned and his attention was captured by the boat.

He jumped in and, taking hold of the wheel, revved the engine, calling to his friends to hurry it on up.

"He's a damn fool," Preston said as he bent to pick up their gear.

"Aw, Press, he knows what he's doing," Adele countered. "You don't have to worry about Tripp."

"Yeah, right," Preston mumbled, then walked ahead with an angry stride.

"What was all that about?" Mary June asked.

Adele waved her hand and the two began walking toward their bikes. "Oh, don't give them no mind. It's always been that way between them. They fight about everything. Oil and water, that's them."

"I thought there was going to be a fight right there on the dock."

"Might've been. But Tripp tries not to rile Press too much."

"Really? I thought he did a pretty good job of it."

"No, that's just Tripp's style. He likes to tease. But he knows better than to tease Preston too much. That boy is slow to boil, but once he does, he's going to scald."

"Really?" she asked, curious about this side of Preston she'd not seen before. "Preston has a temper?"

"Oh, Lord…" She rolled her eyes. "Preston's got a wicked temper. He's careful not to lose it, but Tripp seems to know how to light his spark more than anybody else. Now, Tripp is another matter. He might like to tease, but he'll avoid a fight by being clever."

"It's sad that they fight so much. After all, they're brothers."

Adele sprang to their defense. "Don't get me wrong! They love each other something fierce. They can fight each other, but let anyone try to come between them and see what happens."

She was glad to hear it. "How come I didn't meet Tripp before? Doesn't he live here?"

"That's his house," she said, pointing to Bluff House.

Mary June was astonished. "He lives at Blakely's Bluff?"

"Daddy gave it to him when he got back from Korea. Along with a big parcel of land, him being the eldest son and all. I guess he figured Tripp needed a place of his own right now, after being in the war. Or he wants him to settle down." She lifted her shoulders as if to say, who knows? "Tripp's a hound dog and likes to roam, but he's loved Blakely's Bluff ever since he was little. Even though there isn't any electricity in Bluff House and you have to pee in an outhouse, Tripp used to sleep there all summer long, even alone when he was a kid. And Lord, when he grew up, he had some parties. Wild ones that I was never allowed to go to."

"Count your blessings. Your mama must've worried."

"Uh-uh, she didn't have to. Tripp's a big brother in every sense of the word. Real protective of me, if you know what I mean. He won't let any of his friends near me." She laughed. "I guess he's heard their stories. It's kind of a pain, though. But I like it, too. You know?"

Mary June nodded and wondered about those parties. "What about Press? Did he go to the parties?"

"Some. He likes to party, sure enough. But he's a different kind of guy. More like you, actually."

"What does that mean?" Mary June asked with a short laugh.

"Well," Adele began, choosing her words. "I mean, he's a decent guy. Strong, don't get me wrong. But good. I don't know if he was born that way or just turned out that way because Tripp was always such a wild card."

"How is he wild?"

Adele's eyes sparked and Mary June could see she was infatuated with her older brother. "Tripp likes to live life on the edge. He drives cars fast, drinks like a fish, and I swear that boy breaks a heart every month. Just look at the way he took the boat out as the tide's going down. Press is right, you know. I'd never take that chance. But that's Tripp. He'll take the chance just because he wants to."

"Sounds self-indulgent to me."

"I reckon. Some say he's reckless."

"I'd find that annoying to live with."

"That's what makes Press so mad. Over the July Fourth weekend, he had to go out and get Tripp and the boat after Tripp got stuck in the mud. Him and his drunk friends. Daddy was real mad that he was drinking on the boat and that the boat was damaged. But Tripp didn't care much. It's been a lot worse since he got back from the war. It used to be Tripp just liked to have a good time, but it was all harmless. He was just so hangdog contrite after, everyone had to forgive him. But ever since he got back from the war, the edge has been a lot sharper. And he doesn't care much about Sweetgrass anymore, not like Press does."

"Then why did your Daddy give him Blakely's Bluff?"

She shrugged. "He's a Blakely. And he's the eldest. He was going to get land sooner or later. Same as me and Press. Mama says I'm going to get the big house, seeing as how I'm the daughter and all." Her expression clouded as she picked at her nail. "But I've wondered about that, too. I mean, about why Daddy hasn't given Preston his part yet and why he gave Tripp Bluff House. Press figures it's on account of Tripp being a lot like the first Hamlin that built the house. They both came back torn up and disillusioned after war. Makes sense to me, anyway."

"Sounds to me like everyone is making excuses for him. Don't seem right to give something to someone just because they're in trouble or need help. People should be rewarded for doing well, like Preston."

"See?" Adele said with a devilish grin. "That's what I mean about you being more like Press. You both care about doing things right. You like the quieter things, like fishing and hiking in the woods and reading poetry and just sitting around talking and such. It's nice to watch you two together. Press is not shy, but he's kind of reserved. He had one girl-friend for a long while, almost all through college. Just when Mama started picking up wedding magazines, he broke it off. But I've seen the way he looks at you."

"He does not look at me!"

"Does too. Anyway, I think you're a good match."

"If I didn't know better, I'd swear you were setting us up."

"Worse things could happen."

Mary June linked arms with Adele and squeezed. "Let's not talk anymore about that, okay? It makes everything all confusing. I like things the way they are between Press and me right now. We're good friends."

"Okay. Time will tell," she added with a short laugh.

"Time will tell with you and Bobby Pearlman, too," Mary June said in a singsong voice.

Adele groaned dramatically and shook her head with a for-lorn expression. "Oh, I don't think so."

Bobby was an adorable boy whom Adele was mad for. She'd been angling for him since she got home for the sum-mer. He'd been the subject of numerous phone calls while Mary June was back in Sumter and Adele was planning her campaign to win him. One of the main reasons they'd headed straight for Capers today was because she'd heard Bobby would be there.

"Bobby's only got eyes for Cynthia," Adele said with a plaintive sigh. "I think that fish has been caught."

"Don't feel too bad, Adele. You know what they say. There are plenty more fish in the sea."

"I know, I know. And it's hard to be mad at Cynthia for too long. She's so sweet and we've been friends since the first grade."

They reached their bikes and loaded their bags and damp towels into the wicker baskets.

"Where's Preston?" Mary June asked, looking around.

"I don't know, probably still at Bluff House. Leave him be. He's always in a snit after he has words with Tripp. Let's go on home."

"You sure? I hate to just leave without telling him."

"He'll come along presently." Adele grabbed hold of the handlebars. "Besides, I'm starving. Florence's making lamb tonight and I swear I can smell the garlic clear from here."

Tripp never showed up for dinner that night. Nor did Preston show up early the next morning to wiggle her toes for a fishing expedition.

Mary June woke to the faint light of dawn. Rubbing her eyes, she rose on her elbow and peered at the bed next to hers. Adele was on her belly still deep asleep. She reached over to pull back the gingham curtain and peer out the window. Pale yellow-and-pink light flooded the marsh as dawn rose over the east. In these precious minutes before the sun shone high and bright, the air felt fresh and cool against her cheeks. Purple martins were dipping and diving across a brilliant azure sky in a glorious dawn dance. She thought she'd never tire of waking at Sweetgrass.

She pulled back her covers, climbed from the bed and, grabbing her robe, slipped her arms through the sleeves as she made her way down the hall to Preston's room. Holding her breath, she pushed the door open a crack, just enough to see that his bed was empty.

He'd been unusually quiet and preoccupied during dinner and didn't hang around afterward for cards or television. She scurried down the stairs, her bare feet quiet as she tiptoed from room to room. The house was quiet and still. Preston wasn't anywhere to be found.

Mary June went out to the back porch and settled into the big flowered cushions of the wicker settee, tucking her legs up under her nightgown, then wrapping her robe tight around, like a cocoon. She looked out over the creek and brooded, feeling very injured.

So Preston went fishing without her, she thought, hurt that he'd do such a thing. She couldn't imagine he'd be that put out just because she and Adele hadn't waited for him at Blakely's Bluff. That would be so childish, so unlike him.

Before too long had passed, she heard footfalls on the porch steps and turned, ready to present a proper pout to Preston.

Only it wasn't Preston. It was Tripp.

She couldn't stop herself before she brought her hand to her hair and smoothed it back from her face, then sat straighter in her chair. He'd already spotted her. His face, chalky from lack of sleep, slackened to a lazy grin. His dark hair was even shaggier than the day before, and he was wearing the same clothes, obviously having slept in them.

"Wait up for me, did you?" he asked, reaching the porch.

"No! I mean—" She blushed, realizing he was teasing her. "I was up."

"Early riser?"

"As a matter of fact, I am." Her voice sounded as prim as a martinet's.

"Well, I'm *not*," he said, and flopped into the adjacent chair, stretching out his long legs and settling in as if he was about to sleep right there. "Honey, I'm dog tired."

Sweetgrass

"Why don't you go to bed?"

He peeled open an eye and smiled. "That's the best invitation I've had today."

"Are you always so rude to girls you've barely met?"

"Especially to those I've barely met."

She was right about him, she told herself, prepared not to like him. He was self-indulgent and annoying.

"I've shocked you," he said. "I'm sorry. I'm tired, but that's no excuse. I can be just as insulting when I'm wide awake. Once you know me better, you'll learn to ignore me."

"Well, that's hardly complimentary to your character."

He shrugged. "I doubt you'll hear many compliments about me around here."

"As a matter of fact, I have. Adele sings your praises."

His insolent grin softened at her name. "Adele. Yeah, she would. She's a great girl." He focused on her. "And she picked you as her friend. That says a lot about you in my book. What's your name again? Mary something?"

"Mary June Clark."

"Clark... Who's your Daddy?"

"William Henry Clark. Our people have been near Sumter for forever." She could see he was trying to make a connection, so she interrupted. "I've already been through this with your mama and I don't think you know my kin."

"Hold on a minute." He scratched his unshaven jaw and closed his eyes, thinking. "You wouldn't be related to a Billy Clark from Spartanburg, now, would you?"

Her mouth slipped open, surprised that he really did know someone in her family. "Why, yes! Billy's my cousin. He was like a big brother and used to watch out for me when I was little. His family moved to Spartanburg when my uncle took a job there about ten years ago and I missed him something fierce." Her smile was bittersweet. "Well, what do you know? My mama always tells me to behave myself because you can't go anywhere in South Carolina without meeting someone who knows your kin. How do you know Billy?"

"We were in the boot camp together before we shipped off to Korea. He was good company, and man, Billy sure could shoot. There was talk he'd be made a sniper, he was so good. What's become of him?"

She shrugged, at a loss for words. "He was killed. At Pork Chop Hill."

The smile fell from his face. He muttered a curse under his breath as he ran a hand through his hair. His dark eyes emitted pulses of pain and a haunting guilt that she had to turn away from. In that fleeting glimpse she saw that though he'd come home, and though his scars weren't visible, this man was grievously wounded.

"I'm sorry," he said. "We lost a lot of good men there."

Mary June was surprised that she wanted to talk to him about Billy. She'd been nearly hysterical when told of his death and didn't talk about it with anyone.

"Billy was such a good ol' boy," she said, her eyes kindling. "He was always joking or telling a story. When I heard that he'd died, it seemed incomprehensible. I just couldn't believe it. He was the first person I'd ever really known that died, other than my great-grandmother who died when I was six. I was so young and she was so old. That didn't seem so unfair, like Billy's death. I had a very hard time getting past it. Sometimes I can still see his big toothy grin before falling asleep."

He listened to her and nodded with understanding. "He was a good man."

"It about tore my aunt Dottie apart." She sighed and looked off. "I'm grateful you made it back in one piece."

He pursed his lips, as though he might argue that, but decided against it.

"So what brings you to Sweetgrass?" he asked her.

She took a breath, forcing a smile. "Adele and I are room-mates at Converse. She invited me to stay a few weeks at the year's end. For a holiday. I came directly from school and we had such a good time, she campaigned for me to stay another few weeks. Naturally no one could refuse her."

"That sounds like the Adele I know and love."

They laughed together, easily and without any pretense. She relaxed, liking him more.

"So you'll be here for how much longer?" he asked.

"A month, I hope. If you don't kick me out first."

"Oh, I doubt that will happen. I've heard nothing but praise about you, too. Even from Nona. And let me tell you, if you pass her test, that's something."

"Really? I didn't think she liked me. She doesn't seem too friendly."

"It takes her a while to warm up to someone. But once she's on your side, she's there forever."

"Sounds like she's been on your side a few times."

He rubbed his jaw. "Yeah. She's covered for me a time or two."

She wondered if anyone could refuse this beautiful boy anything.

He gripped the sides of the chair. "Man, I'm beat. I need a shower, a shave and to crash."

"Would you like some coffee? And some breakfast? I could fix you some eggs."

He turned to look at her closely, his eyes narrowing in sur-prise at the offer. "Darlin', you'd be an angel of mercy."

She climbed from the settee, feeling as though she'd just sprouted wings, and led the way to the kitchen. There, she began making the coffee and scrambling up eggs, feeling strangely elated at the simple task of cooking this man his breakfast. She didn't eat, but sat across from him and sipped coffee while he did.

They talked about a lot of things, laughing and flirting. He could tell a story as well as Preston, except different. Both boys excelled in the Southern tradition. Preston spoke in an easy drawl, creating a world with words, playing each detail out till she could see it. Like the talented fisherman he was, he could reel you in and keep you dangling till he let you free.

Tripp's manner was witty and clever. He didn't dillydally but told a story plainly, adding choice bits of color. Best of all, he could deliver a punch line or observation so dead-on and fast, and with such a straight face, he had her rolling in laughter.

She was laughing when they heard the back door swing open. They both turned, eyes wide, like kids caught with their hands in the cookie jar.

"Well, well, well. What we got here?" Nona asked, stepping inside and dropping her packages on the wood countertop.

Nona was as slender as a reed and moved with a queenly grace. With her high cheekbones and full lips, Mary June thought she looked like a Nubian princess she'd read about in history books. Nona was about Preston's age. She was wearing a brown plaid flowing skirt and white blouse, neatly gathered at her trim waist with a wide leather belt. Her mother, Florence, worked for the family only part-time now, devoting more time to her family and the sweetgrass baskets she sewed. Nona chose to stay on at Sweetgrass and take over her mother's job. She was every bit as good a cook as Florence was, some argued even better. But her coffee was beyond compare.

"Is that coffee I smell?" Nona asked, her nose in the air.

"I made it myself," Mary June replied.

Casting a suspicious glance at Tripp, who remained smiling like a Cheshire cat, Nona reached for a cup and poured coffee into it. She took one taste and her mouth skewered.

"Aack. This ain't nothin' but black water!" she exclaimed, and poured the coffee into the sink.

Tripp barked out a laugh and shook his head. "I hate to tell you this, honey," he said to Mary June, "but you could learn a few things from Nona about cooking. Especially coffee. She's addicted to the brew. Same as me. And she prepares it with the reverence of a high priestess at an altar."

Mary June flushed, all her earlier elation crushed by embarrassment. "I—I didn't know your coffeepot," she stammered as an excuse.

Nona took the coffeepot to the sink, and after dumping the contents began rinsing it out. "What are you two doing up so early, anyway?" she asked them. Then to Tripp, "You smell like you slept in a still."

"I'm just coming home," Tripp replied easily, offering no information.

Nona didn't look up from the sink, only shook her head and clucked her tongue.

"I got up to go fishing with Preston, but he's already gone," said Mary June.

"Oh, he's been up for a long time. He called my daddy early. They're all down at the lower barn. They were looking for you, Mr. Tripp," she said with a roll of her eyes. "The lambs are coming in! Preston will be busy for days. You won't see much of him or Mr. Blakely."

"Does he need help?" asked Mary June. "I'd love to do something."

Tripp got up to clear his plate. "You'll probably be more in the way, honey. Best to stay clear. Why don't you and Adele go off for a swim?"

"I was raised on a farm," she replied sharply, niggled at

being treated like a child by this man. "We don't have sheep but we do have cows. I don't imagine the birthing process is a whole lot different."

Nona chuckled. "She got you there."

"Will *you* be helping?" she pointedly asked him. She didn't know what made her ask. Perhaps it was to test if what Adele had said about his interest in Sweetgrass was true.

He placed his dishes in the sink, then turned to face her. His eyelids drooped with fatigue. "Yeah, they'll rope me in. But it's going to be a long week. I'm going to shower and sleep some first. And then I'm going to have some of your coffee, Nona," he added with a wink. Turning back to Mary June, he said, "I thank you for making me breakfast. It's much appreciated. Maybe you'll let me buy you some dinner?"

It was the last thing she'd expected and she felt sure her face showed it. From behind her, she heard Nona's intake of air. Nonplussed, Mary June reacted on gut instinct.

"Yes, thank you. I'd like that."

His smile lit up his eyes. "Good. I'll see you later, then."

She watched him as he sauntered from the room, then turned just in time to catch Nona's raised brows and pursed lips before she returned to making her coffee.

For a minute, Mary June couldn't move. She felt shivery, scared and thrilled all at the same time. Sort of like she'd just jumped into the dark waters of Shark Hole.

11

————

"If I wake up in the middle of the night and can't get to sleep, I'll put a basket on the bed and get to work. I can really get lost in it."
—Mae Hall, basket maker

DOWNSTAIRS, NAN YAWNED like a cat in the uphol-stered chair that Mama June had put beside Preston's bed. Kristina was on a rare night out, Mama June was asleep upstairs, and it was Nan's night to sit with Preston until he settled. She was glad to take her turn, but it was getting late. Her lids were drooping and her voice was tired from reading aloud. She peeked over at her father. He looked as though he might be sleeping.

Uncurling her legs, she felt the blood rush as she stretched them. She wondered if her father missed being able to do such simple things. Ever since his stroke, she'd been aware of all the simple moves and gestures she'd taken for granted.

She stood and went to his bedside, surprised to see his eyes open when she approached.

"So, you weren't sleeping after all?" she said to him. "I thought that last chapter did the trick. But it seems to have worked on Blackjack. That old hound is out for the count. Listen to him snore!"

She saw her father's lips twitch and his eyes warmed in a smile.

"Well, you're going to outlast me tonight, I'm afraid. I'm off to bed. I can't keep the awnings up. I'll be back tomorrow and we'll finish the book, okay?"

She bent to offer his cheek a perfunctory kiss good-night. When she pulled back, his left hand lurched clumsily forward. Surprised, she looked down to see his larger hand holding fast to her smaller one.

Suddenly she felt once again like the little girl who used to climb on her father's lap for a story, or help steer "Mighty Mo," the tractor, as her daddy plowed the fields. He'd taught her how to wield a hammer and a nail when he built her the dollhouse that still sat in the upstairs bedroom. She remembered when she was eight years old how she'd peeked behind the curtains of the school auditorium when her daddy walked in. She'd thought he was the handsomest man in the room as he took his seat next to Mama June and the boys to watch her dance recital. He never missed one.

Best of all, she thrilled to those special days when he'd whistle for the whole family, cousins and all, to come to Blakely's Bluff for a rare overnight fishing trip on his old, converted shrimp boat. He called it The Project because he'd been working on that burned-out old hull for as long as anyone could remember. It was his pride and joy—and the butt of many family jokes. Preston outfitted the boat with bunks and rigged up a kitchen to make a seaworthy houseboat for family jaunts. It got so the Blakely clan couldn't imagine a family reunion without an outing on The Project.

What fun they'd had! All the young cousins hugged the railing and giggled with excitement as they waited for "The Captain" to ring the big brass bell and haul anchor. The aunts leaned over the porch railing at Bluff House, their skirts flapping in the wind like flowered flags, yoo-hooing and waving farewell. Her daddy was their Peter Pan and they sailed off to a Neverland of his making where—girl or boy—they didn't have to mind their manners, where they'd fish and swim all day, sleep like sardines in their bunks overnight and eat crab and fresh fish and crusty bread with their fingers till their tummies were ready to burst.

Sailing during the day, Nan saw her daddy standing straight-backed and wide-legged at the wheel and her heart nearly burst with love for him. And in the evenings when she was supposed to be sleeping below deck, she'd sneak upstairs to see her daddy wrap an arm around Mama June's shoulders under the moon. Her mama would look into his face and he'd kiss her. Nan's young heart fluttered to see it. She'd thought they were the happiest couple in the world.

Growing up, her daddy had been her hero.

When she married and became a Leland, however, her daddy had let go of her hand. She'd been grasping for it ever since.

She looked again at her smaller hand clasped in his larger one. The past few months had been a long journey for her. She'd had a hard time hurdling the change in the robust, indomitable man she'd known all her life. At first, she'd been afraid to care for him, to physically handle the mute, dependent man he'd become.

But it wasn't hard at all. As she helped her father eat his dinner, or guided him through his exercises, or read to him, Nan shared more with him than she had in many years. She thought of how hard he fought every day to recover, to regain something that he'd lost.

Tears filled her eyes as she held tight to his hand again after all these years.

"You're still my hero, Daddy."

★ ★ ★

Upstairs in her room, Mama June awoke from her dream chilled, despite the flush that formed a fine sheen of moisture over her body. The moonlight flowed into her room, filling it with pewter light. She gathered her blankets over her shoulders and lay still, listening to the sounds of the house. The only noises she heard were the muffled sounds from the television in Morgan's room. She wondered if he was drinking.

She turned on her side, restless. She was almost afraid to go back to sleep. She'd meant to dream about Preston, but it was Tripp who rose up to haunt her.

Why Tripp? Why now? she wondered. She hadn't thought of him in so many years. Sometimes she wondered if he were only a dream. Or some ghost that haunted the house. It was easier to think of him in that way.

But tonight she saw him as clearly and as alive as though it had happened yesterday. It was so hard to experience it all again. The tears on her face were fresh. When she'd started this journey she'd promised herself that she would tear away the veil and look at her life with open eyes. She would not shirk or hide again.

Mary June lifted her head and looked out at the landscape that was her home. In the shadows and shapes she could make out arching live oaks and pines, spikes of cordgrass and shimmering patches of the creek caught in the moonlight. Such a beautiful night. The air was soft and languid.

She closed her eyes, resigned, and remembered evenings just like this one spent in the arms of Tripp.

In the summer of 1957, Mary June Clark thought she knew who she was and what she wanted out of life.

Mary June was the only daughter of Will and Martha

Clark. She was a good student, a model of deportment and never caused her doting parents a moment of embarrassment. She went to a good Southern college and, like everyone else in her sorority, expected to find a husband and be married by the age of twenty-one.

Tripp Blakely was not someone her parents would have expected their daughter to bring home. Yes, he was handsome and he came from one of the finest families. But Tripp deliberately, even sexily, tested the well-honed Southern morals and traditions, daring to buck the lifestyle of the gentility he was born into. Mary June, however, saw Tripp as strong yet wounded, beautiful yet brutish.

For the first ten days of her second visit at Sweetgrass, Mary June helped in the barn with the sheep whenever they needed her. Preston was attentive and kind, always watching out for her. But he no longer took her fishing in the morning or went swimming in the afternoon or played cards with her in the evening. He was standing on the sidelines, like a polite young suitor whose shoulder had been tapped during a dance.

Mary June was oblivious to Preston's pain and Adele's disapproval. She was blind to Mrs. Blakely's curious looks and Nona's silent observations. During that summer, Mary June was swirling in the eddy of her romance with Tripp.

She was dizzy with his pace. Unlike Preston, staying home was not for him. He liked to go out every night. For the first few dates, Adele joined them. After a few nights, however, she opted to go out with Richard, her new heartthrob, and didn't disguise the fact that she was miffed Mary June didn't go with her group of friends, instead. For some reason Mary June didn't understand, Adele was irked that she was going out with Tripp.

Tripp and Mary June usually met up with a few of his friends and they'd caravan across the Cooper River Bridge to

downtown Charleston. Every night it was something different, but still somehow the same. They went where the mood
led them. Some days they'd hang out at Hampton Park and
feed Cracker Jacks to the ducks. Or they'd go to Shem Creek,
pile in someone's boat and sail across the harbor.

On sultry nights they'd cruise in Tripp's convertible, often
as far as the Grand Strand, to where the sweet soul music of
bands drifted through the night. They shuffled across the
dance floor, the boys in Converse sneakers, the girls in circle
skirts and loafers, to the seductive beat of beach music, with
drinks still dangling from their hands.

Or they'd go to the Battery to sit on a park bench in the
cool breeze and eat peanuts until the shells formed mounds at
their feet. If they were hungry they'd eat at a local restaurant
or buy snow cones from a street vendor and stroll down King
Street. She could still remember the feel of her circle skirt
skimming against her calves as they ambled aimlessly along.
At Woolworth or Kress department stores they made a game
of picking through the myriad toys and sundries set out in
trays and bins, making silly jokes and laughing like children.

But they were not children. Mary June was nineteen. Tripp
and his friends were twenty-four. They'd either dropped out
of college or, like Tripp, were sent to Korea after high school.
They had seen too much in the four years spent far from the
Lowcountry. Hot embers burned beneath their I-don't-give-
a-damn facades. When they'd sit at a restaurant or club, the
boys talked on and on, their hands moving from beer to cigarette like metronomes.

While the other girls clustered together and chatted, Mary
June silently watched them through the haze of smoke. She
thought that the boys laughed a little too hard, drank a bit too
much and didn't seem to know—or even care—what their
next step in life would be. Occasionally his friends teased her

Sweetgrass

for being trapped in college, telling her that she was wasting her time studying to be a member of the middle-class status quo. Tripp never joined them in the teasing, but he didn't stop them, either. What mattered, they told her, was to have fun, right now. To live today and let tomorrow take care of itself.

She was infuriated, insulted, and argued that they were completely wrong. Yet she was also intrigued. Their arguments were new, different and terribly confusing.

She voiced her feelings one night when Tripp took her to White Point Gardens. They were alone for a change, and went for a ride in Mr. Wagner's shiny, black, horse-driven carriage. The night was balmy and the breeze from the harbor caressed her skin. As the carriage rocked along at its easy pace, Tripp put his arm around her and she leaned against him, luxuriating in his warmth. Her fingers played with the buttons of his shirt. Gathering her thoughts, she asked him why he didn't seem to care about anything—not Sweetgrass, not his future, not even her.

Surprised by the question, he nonetheless took it seriously. He shifted in the carriage to face her, and even though the night was dark, she could see the fervor in his eyes as he tried, in halting sentences, to explain by quoting from some man she'd never heard of called Jack Kerouac.

Tripp spoke in rambling sentences. She didn't understand completely what he said, but it was something about how he was trying to break away from what was expected of him. He wanted to experience life, to travel and see the world. He said it was about a kind of freedom he was seeking that might lead him to a peace he hadn't yet found.

And then, looking into her eyes, he kissed her.

That, it turned out, was all the answer Mary June needed or wanted.

Only in retrospect did Mary June realize that he was being

completely honest with her. She didn't listen with her head because her heart didn't want to hear what he was really telling her. Instead, when he talked like that, Mary June felt very young and naive and completely infatuated. No one had ever said things like that to her.

When she talked with Preston, she felt more an equal partner in the discussion. They were coming from the same place and seldom argued. Talking with Preston was comfortable and safe. She could share her dreams with Press and they made sense.

With Tripp, she was unsure about everything. The words that spilled from his lips sounded thrilling and impossibly idealistic. She wanted to argue with him, but her position felt old and stodgy, despite her being younger.

Maybe it was because she was young and sheltered. Maybe it was because she'd always been an idealist at heart. But listening to Tripp, she was inflamed. She found him utterly beautiful. As the Carolina moon rose higher over the Battery, Mary June was over the moon in love.

"He's too old for you," Adele told her, dark eyes flashing.

They were sitting on the twin beds in Adele's bedroom, wearing baby doll pajamas and painting pink nail polish on their toes. The weather had turned fitful, raining on and off for two days and nights and turning tempers short. Tripp stayed out at Blakely's Bluff and Preston had traveled north to Columbia with his father on business. This threw the girls together to while away the hours for the first time since Mary June had started dating Tripp. There had been an undercurrent of objection brewing between them, but until that evening, it had not been openly voiced.

"What do you mean, too old?" Mary June replied, both

irked by Adele's assertion, yet curious to hear more. "He's only a year older than Preston, and you didn't think he was too old."

"He's two years older," Adele said crossly. "And I don't mean in just years, anyway. Tripp's older in other ways. Besides, he's not your type. Can't you see that?"

"No, I can't," she replied obstinately. Then, not wanting to argue, she said, "What's your problem, Adele? Can't we talk it out?"

"There's nothing to talk about! I plain don't like that you're going out with Tripp," Adele said. "And you're going out all the time! I don't even know why you bothered to come back to see me, since you never do." Her lips turned in a pout as she twisted the bottle cap.

"Are you upset that you're not coming along? You can come if you want."

"Oh. Thanks a lot," Adele replied, her voice dripping with sarcasm. "I don't need you to let me go somewhere with my own brother. Anyway, I don't want to go with you and those *old* guys. What do you do when they drink alcohol, anyway, huh? You're not twenty-one."

"The same thing I do when guys our age drink. I have a Coke."

Adele's chin stuck out as her mind veered to another line of attack. "Well, I don't think it's very nice what you're doing to Preston."

Mary June put the applicator back into her bottle of polish, exasperated. "*What* am I doing to Preston?"

"You know how he feels about you. And you just ditched him for Tripp."

"There is not, nor ever was, anything between Press and me!" Mary June cried, feeling suddenly wretched. She didn't want to think she could be hurting Preston. "So I couldn't have ditched him. Besides, we've invited him to join us, too."

"You don't think he'd go out with you and Tripp?" Adele demanded.

There was an awful silence while Mary June wiped a bit of paint from her toe.

"No," she replied, subdued. "Adele, I don't want to hurt Press, but I think I'm in love with Tripp. What should I do?"

"In love? Oh, come on, Mary June. You're nineteen. You aren't in love. You don't know what love is."

"Of course I do," she replied, feeling the insult. "I know it because it's what I feel. Why can't you be happy for me?"

Adele's face colored and she blurted out, "I just can't. It's not right. *You're* not right for Tripp.

Mary June's face paled as she began to understand the root of Adele's objections. Tripp was Adele's adored older brother. He could do no wrong in her eyes. Everyone expected great things of the eldest son who could outfish, outhunt, outtalk any boy in the county, who had fought valiantly in a foreign war and who could charm a snake from a basket with his smile.

"It's not about my being right for Tripp, is it?" she demanded. "It's about my being good enough for him."

"I didn't say that!" Adele fired back.

"You didn't have to."

The two women glared at each other, each holding their tongue. Then Adele looked at her feet and shifted her weight.

"Listen, Mary June," she said, looking up again. Her voice was conciliatory. "We've only got a week of vacation left. Then we'll be going back to Converse and Tripp will head to Europe. Let's not spoil our summer by arguing."

Mary June's breath hitched. She couldn't believe what she'd heard.

"Europe? Tripp didn't tell me he was going to Europe."

"See?" she said, with a hint of triumph. "That's what I'm talking about. He's been planning this trip to Europe for months. He's going backpacking from country to country. Solo. He'll be there for a year, at least. But who knows with him?"

The world shifted again for Mary June. She sat back against her headboard, feeling light-headed and speechless.

"I'm your friend," Adele said, moving closer. Victorious, she could afford to be magnanimous. "I don't want to see you get hurt."

Mary June startled Adele by jolting forward, climbing from the bed and marching with purpose to the closet. She pulled out a blue slicker that barely covered her thighs and put it on over her pajamas.

"What are you doing?" Adele asked, rising to her knees.

"I'm going to see Tripp."

"Like that? You can't. You're not decent! Besides, it's raining."

"I don't care."

"It's dark outside. You won't know where you're going. You don't want to go out there. Mary June, be reasonable!"

She slipped her feet into tennis shoes and bent to tie them, obstinately determined. She walked to the door and reached for the knob.

In a last effort, Adele cried out, "My mother will have a hissy fit!"

Mary June swung her head around, narrowing her eyes. "Who will tell her?"

The two girls glared at each other before Adele ground out, "I will."

"You do and you'll have to find yourself another roommate," Mary June challenged, then she turned and slipped out the door.

Mary June rode her bicycle through the steadily falling rain. It was stinging cold and woke her to the reality of what she was doing. She was being headstrong, foolish with her fury, and it felt great. Her heart pounded hard as she pedaled through thick mud and gravel, trying to follow the winding dirt road. The night was dark with low-lying clouds, and the road was bordered by high spindly pines and cragged oaks dripping moss like ghostly lace. She felt as if she was paddling again through the creek at low tide. All she could see was a wall of gray, with only a narrow muddy path to follow.

A path that led to Tripp.

Forward, forward, she told herself. She didn't think about the strange animal noises and rattles she heard in the shadows. She focused on the house that she knew sat at the end of the road, facing the sea. She pedaled toward an answer that she just had to have, that night, right away.

When she thought her lungs would burst from exertion, the road opened up to a clearing. Ahead lay the shadowy, wide vista of wetland and creek and ocean beyond. As she entered, the scent of salt and pungent pluff mud assailed her. She slowed her pedaling, and through the mist of rain Bluff House took shape. She rode directly to the porch, braking just as her tire bumped against the first step.

All was dark except for the faint flickering of yellow light from the upstairs bedroom. He was home and awake, probably reading by the light of a camp lamp. Feeling faint of heart for the first time since she'd started this mad escapade, she leaned her bike against the porch and scurried through the rain up the stairs to the front door just as lightning scarred the sky.

She felt breathless from the ride and from nervousness. Taking a calming breath, she knocked three times on the door. Thunder rumbled over the marsh, low and deafening. The storm was not yet over. Suddenly she didn't want to be standing out in the rain any longer. Making a fist, she pounded the door, her desperation and fear sounding loudly against the wood.

Thoughts of all the words he'd said to her in the past three weeks, all the emotions that they'd shared, all the kisses in clandestine places—his car, the boat, the beach, the moldy divan in the house—assailed her. All the scents as they'd clung together—mildew and salt, perfume and aftershave—engulfed her. Memories of trembling hands groping and fevered endearments whispered in the dark swirled in her mind as she kept knocking, unaware that she was crying.

The door swung open. Her breath caught in her throat as she saw his silhouette in the narrow slant of light from the flashlight in his hand. He was wearing a T-shirt and boxer shorts, his hair was disheveled and his face unshaven. He looked at her silently, his face creased with sleep and surprise.

Her hand, frozen mid-knock, moved to slick back the dripping hair from her brow. Suddenly she felt acutely embarrassed for showing up at this hour, crying, dripping wet in muddy tennis shoes and a slicker over baby doll pajamas.

"Mary June. What are you doing here?"

"You're going to Europe!" she released in an accusing cry.

"Yes." He paused, cocking his head. "But not tonight."

"When?" she demanded.

He seemed nonplussed. "I don't know! Maybe next month. Maybe not. I haven't figured it out yet. Soon."

"You didn't tell me. When were you going to tell me?"

Her eyes filled with tears, and though she fought for control, she knew she was too tired, too overwrought to stop them.

"Don't cry," he said, stepping forward.

"I'm not crying," she snapped, slapping back his hand. She hadn't come for his pity.

He looked at her oddly. "Okay."

She wiped her eyes and plowed on while she still could.

"It's just that, when Adele told me you were going, I thought that if it was true, then everything between us was a lie. Or it was all just some summer fling, the kind of thing you tell other girls about when they ask you how you spent your summer vacation. To giggle over. And I couldn't bear for that to be all it was." She looked up at him.

"You *changed* me." She flung this at him like an accusation. "I didn't ask for this to happen. Look at me, standing in the rain in my pajamas. I can't believe what I'm doing. But it feels good!" she exclaimed, her eyes lighting up.

"All my life, people have told me what was best for me. 'Mary June, you'll like this dress.' 'Mary June, you'll like this college.' 'Mary June, you'll like this boy.' And I went blithely along, never daring to question whether I really did or didn't, in fact, like them. Even your sister—especially your sister! 'Mary June, Tripp isn't right for you.'"

"She said that?"

"Yes! And the moment she did I knew you *were* right for me. Then when I heard that you were leaving, I knew I couldn't let it happen, not like that. I had to hear *you* tell me. I…I couldn't bear to let anyone tell me what was right for me any longer. So I grabbed my slicker. And I rode my bicycle. All the way here. By myself. In the rain," she choked out, giving up the struggle against the tears.

Tripp's face softened then, understanding it all.

"Mary June," he said again, tenderly now, stepping forward to reach an arm around her thin, shaking shoulders and pull her indoors.

His arm around her, sinewy and strong, felt right. It made her fractious self feel whole and her insane journey through the rain make sense. Stepping into the old, weather-beaten house that smelled of must and mildew, that was dark without electricity and chilled without heat, that stood out on a bluff challenging the gods, she was exactly where she wanted to be. As she heard the door click closed behind her, the storm seemed very far away.

The air thickened between them. He turned to wrap his

other arm around her and draw her close. She could feel his warm breath on her cheeks, laced with a trace of whisky. In his eyes she saw a question burning with the same intensity and singleness of focus as the beam of light in his hands.

It was an age-old question and she answered it in a timeless manner. This was not a moment for words. She could not reply with argument or discussion. No quote from a poet or author would do. Mary June was a woman and knew intuitively what to do.

Lifting her face, she pressed her small, frail body against his taut one, brought her arms around his neck, opened her lips and relinquished.

Mama June stirred from her reverie and paced her bedroom. Her mind was skipping as fast as her heart. The night breeze had fallen away. The outside air was still and pregnant with the scent of rain.

She walked to the window and clutched the wood pane, yanking it open. She felt stifled, unable to catch a good breath of air. A half moon shone brightly in a sky threatened with oncoming clouds. Her eyes were drawn, as they always were, to the familiar dark outline of marsh grass and sinuous creeks and beyond to the peaked roofline of Bluff House.

She couldn't force her way to the truth. It was elusive. She had to allow her memories to wash over her, like the incoming tide. To give in to them.

Her dreams brought the memory of a first night—and a last—to mind with the loamy verdancy and teeming mysteries of the marsh itself.

She remembered as if it were yesterday the smooth muscle of Tripp's chest against her cheek as she lay in the master bedroom at Bluff House. The great bed was positioned in the room so that they could see the moon through windows thrown open to the breeze. She remembered looking out at the endless sky, feeling the soft wind caress her nakedness and hearing the reassuring rhythm of Tripp's heartbeat against her ear, as steady as the sea.

"I never want the dawn to break," she told him.

He laughed, a soft rumble in his chest, and gently kissed the soft hairs on her head. She clutched him tightly then and told him that she wanted to stay on that defiant bit of land, in his arms, forever.

If he'd asked her to, she would have.

But he did not, and when the dawn broke the following morning with sun-searing clarity, she realized everything had changed. She hadn't expected the censure from Mrs. Blakely or Adele after she'd scurried through the damp grass, hoping to sneak back to her room unnoticed. Nor did she expect to be sent home immediately, neatly dispensed yet saving face because she was due to return home a few days later, anyway, to begin packing for the new college term. The formal goodbye at the front door of Sweetgrass strained all politeness. Mary June never expected to see it again. Mr. Blakely had stiffly insisted on driving her to the bus station. Adele had remained in her room.

When Tripp found out that she'd left, he'd come roaring into the bus station. He'd found her sitting primly on the wood bench staring at the wall in a daze, her suitcase touching her saddle shoes like a barrier wall before her. Her mouth slipped open in a gasp when she saw him rush into the small station. He beelined toward her like a hurricane, pulled her to him and kissed her right there in the open, not caring who saw them. He literally took her breath away.

"You came," she exclaimed, tearful with gratitude. She hadn't known what to think, what to hope for. He was her first. She'd heard stories. She'd been so ashamed.

He had a lump in his throat and spoke in a rush. He told

her how sorry he was that his parents had treated her the way they did, and how they'd had angry words, and how it didn't matter what they said, she could come home to Blakely's Bluff with him right that minute if she wanted to.

Tripp could be impetuous and defiant. She thrilled to this and was tempted, but of course she couldn't stay with him. Not like that. They both knew it. Though he could never know how much him telling her that meant to her.

Mama June closed her eyes tight and searched her memories, trying to recall if, in all that emotion, he'd ever told her that he loved her. She felt as if he had. He'd said lots of sweet things. But did he say those words? She simply could not remember.

She did remember that when the Greyhound bus pulled out of the small brick depot, the afternoon sun shone in her eyes so that she could only see the outline of his tall, lean form. She felt a moment's panic, feeling as though she were losing him. She struggled with the small window, pressing the tenacious metal levers until at last it opened. Then the bus turned and the sun was blocked by the heavy trunk of an old oak. And she saw his face, intensely searching for her. She reached out her hand and waved.

"Tripp! Tripp!"

His face lit up with a smile, a vision she'd keep in her mind for the rest of her life. His arm shot out as if he was reaching for her, then angled in a wave.

"Write to me!" she called out to him over the accelerating engine.

"I will!" he called back.

"Promise?"

"I promise."

The letters!

Mama June brought her hand to her throat as a chill shot

down her spine. Where were the letters? she wondered. What had she done with them? She hadn't thought of them for so many years. She was quite certain she'd never thrown them away, though. It wasn't like her to be careless with things of such importance.

She marshaled her thoughts, clearing the confusion with focus. She knew where to look. She hurried to grab her robe and slippers. From a chest on her bureau, she retrieved a black velvet pouch, which she put into her robe pocket. Then, with the forced march of purpose, she made her way to the end of the hall and opened the door that led to the attic.

She was immediately assailed by a waft of heavy heat and humidity cloaked in the scent of mold. Reaching into the darkness, she found a light switch. The narrow stream of light that flowed from the single bulb hanging from a wire was meager but enough to guide her way up the stairs into the large, pitched room.

She seldom went up there anymore, and in the summer the close heat was nearly suffocating. As she reached the top of the stairs, the attic felt foreign. Unwelcoming. She coughed lightly and her nose wrinkled at the thick coating of dust and grime that covered everything. Intricate spiderwebs cloaked the attic windows like tattered lace. Telltale signs of mice and the empty carcasses of palmetto bugs warned her that treasures had been damaged.

There was so much clutter! Why on earth did she keep all this? she asked herself.

She knew the answer. It was because she loathed to throw anything out that might have sentimental value. How ironic, she thought, to store the past but never tend to it.

She peeked in a few of the countless boxes but resisted the temptation to scrounge. There were so many and it was late. These were not what she'd come for.

Sweetgrass

She went instead to a far corner of the attic where several trunks lined the wall. The smallest of these was half hidden under several cardboard boxes. She pulled it from its hiding place and dragged it closer to the light, then lowered to her knees before it. She paused to catch her breath, swiping the sweat from her brow.

The black metal of the trunk shone eerily under the dim light. It was smaller than she'd remembered. The leather straps were coated with a film of mildew that came off on her hands. She reached into her pocket and pulled out the velvet pouch. A small brass key slipped from it into her palm. She put the key carefully into the lock and turned. Despite the years, the lock sprang open. Lifting the top of the trunk, she caught the pungent scent of cedar and must. But the contents were dry.

She gingerly picked through the layers of tissue paper, not quite remembering what she had packed inside so very long ago. These were her greatest treasures. She carefully removed three fragile, plaster prints of chubby hands. Her finger traced the three outlines: Morgan. Hamlin. Nan.

Under these lay an intricately embroidered christening gown that had been worn by her grandmother, her mother, herself and Nan. She made a mental note to pass it on to Nan to give her daughter-in-law someday. She sifted through assorted photographs, some bright with color, others darkened sepia. There were gifts from her young children—beaded jewelry, drawings in acrylics and watercolor, odd bits of clay resembling a horse, a duck, a flower, poems for Mother's Day and other emotional keepsakes that elicited sighs of wonder as she revisited the memories attached to them. Her breath hitched when she uncovered three silver boxes, each one containing a lock of hair—one dark brown, one blond, one a soft brown.

She reluctantly set these aside to sort through the cards and letters that littered the bottom of the trunk. These were the missives she'd received over the years that held some special meaning.

Then she saw them. In a searing flash she recalled how she'd painstakingly selected the petal-pink stationery with the creamy magnolias at the corner. The envelopes with torn edges were held together by the same strip of yellow ribbon she'd tied them with so many years earlier. Mama June picked them up, surprised at how light they were considering their weighty matter. Bringing them to her nose, she sniffed, but the perfume she'd girlishly spritzed on the paper had long ago faded away.

In a sudden rush she slipped off the ribbon and the letters spilled in her lap. Slowly, she sorted them according to post date, laying them in order on the floor before her. Then, taking the first, she opened the thin pages and began to read.

August 18, 1957

Dearest, darling Tripp,

Here I am, back at Converse, rooming with Adele. I think she's still a little mad at me, but whatever you said to her must have made a difference because we've made up and are friends again. Sort of. I'm still hurt, I can't lie. But she is my friend and I want her to be as happy as I am.

In truth, what I really want is to be back at Blakely's Bluff, at Bluff House, with you. I want to wake up again in your arms, even if I'm sleeping on that lumpy old mattress under your moth-hole-ridden cotton blanket and being bitten by a thousand mosquitoes that fly in through your windows to feast. It would all be worth it, just to be with you. Soon, I hope.

No, I haven't told Daddy yet about wanting to go to Europe. Don't be mad! I want to pick just the right time so he'll say yes. When I got home last week everything was so crazy. You can imagine. All my mother wanted to talk about was my getting ready to leave for college. My mama goes on and on about every detail. I wish she'd just go to college for me. I know they wouldn't have said yes if I'd asked then. But Mama has always been fired up about me going to Europe, too. Especially France. She thinks it will make me very chic. Secretly I know she wishes she could go. Anyway, she'll want to enroll me in a program or a school. I'm sure everything will work out fine. I'll be going home in a few weeks and I promise I'll ask them then. Be patient!

I have to go to English class now. We're studying American authors. I mean, how many times do I have to read the same old Nathanial Hawthorne stories?!! What do you think Dr. Durant will say when I suggest we read On the Road? Ha!

Write back soon. PLEASE. I miss you!

Hugs and kisses,
Mary June xoxoxoxoxo

August 24, 1957

Dear Mary June,

Things have finally settled down here. I never saw Mama so mad as she was when I brought you back home the next morning! I'm pretty sure she didn't believe that you were caught in the storm. Daddy just shakes his head. Preston won't speak of it. He won't speak to me at all, actually. It's pretty funny. They really can be so bourgeois.

I'm reading all about backpacking in France, Germany and Italy. We can go pretty cheap. Maybe we'll even make it to Spain, the land of Hemingway. I can run with the bulls at Pamplona and you can wear a mantilla. Cool. They say October is a good time to go.

I can't make it up next weekend. I've got a job. It's not much, just construction, but it's good money. We'll need it for the trip. I'm fixing up Bluff House, too. I really love this place. I think of you here. Makes me smile every time.

Love,

Tripp

September 1, 1957

Dear Tripp,

School is so incredibly boring. The kids are nice, but everything seems so pointless. I only think of you. I spend hours writing your name in my notebook and thinking about when I'm going to see you again.

When _am_ I going to see you again? I'm going to the sorority parties and the dean's teas, but only to be social. It's so lonely without you. I wish you could have come up last weekend. I'd love to introduce you to my friends. When can you come up?

Go to Europe in October? No way we can go in October! That's next month! My parents won't let me drop out of school midsemester. Didn't we talk about next semester? Or maybe even this summer? I'm sure whenever we go it will be great.

Lights are going out soon. Gotta go. Oh, how I wish I was falling asleep in Bluff House.

Love and kisses,

Mary June XXXXX

Sweetgrass

September 18, 1957

Dear Tripp,

I can't believe it's been a month since we've seen each other. I miss you, miss you, miss you! When are you coming up to see me? It's not such a long trip and we'll find a way to make it special. We always do.

Adele is going out with this boy from Aiken. He's very nice and very cute and his family raises horses. I think she likes him a lot. It makes me lonely when she talks about him because I think of you.

I know you don't have a phone at Bluff House, but couldn't you use a pay phone from town or even your parents' phone and call me? We said we would write every week, but we haven't. I love you. Please write soon.

Much love and many kisses,
Mary June

September 23, 1957

Dear Mary June,

Don't worry, I miss you, too. I've just been busy and I'm not much of a letter writer. Ask Adele. And you know I don't have a phone at Bluff House. So it's hard. I think of you all the time. And about our trip. It's going to be so cool. I'm looking into hostels. Can't wait to get out of here. Press has practically taken over the farm and he can have it.

Ask your parents! If they won't let you go, please let me know right away.

Honey, try to understand, but I really don't want to come up to your college and go to those frat parties. That's just not my scene. Any chance you can come here? Maybe take a bus to Charleston? I'll pick you up. It's beautiful at the bluff now. The fall wildflowers are coming up and birds are migrating through. Sometimes I just sit on the dock and stare out for hours. I'm writing a little, too. I'll miss Blakely's Bluff, that's for sure. It's a part of me. Part of my soul.

Come to Blakely's Bluff. It will be wonderful.

Love,

Tripp

September 28, 1957

Dear Tripp,

I guess I can understand about you not wanting to come up to the college. But I can't understand why you won't come up to see me.

We don't have to go to any parties. We could just spend time together. And with Adele, who misses you, too. (She's already dumped that boy from Aiken and moved on to another boy from Georgia.)

I can't come to see you at Blakely's Bluff because I'm going home next weekend. Remember? I'm going to ask if I can go to Europe. I've been planning what I'm going to say. Call me on Monday for the answer. (Fingers crossed.)

I really wish you'd make the effort to see me. It would mean so much.

Here's to Europe!

Mary June

October 7, 1957

Dear Tripp,

I know you tried to call and I'm sorry I didn't answer.

I have something I want need to tell you, but I just couldn't say it in the hall where other girls could overhear me.

I'm not going to Europe. I'm sorry. My parents won't let me go. They won't even discuss it. They're sure something horrible is going to happen to me. Ha, what a joke. Maybe next year, they said. When I'm a junior. Or maybe after I graduate. So that's that.

But it doesn't matter. Everything's changed. I hope you'll feel the same when I tell you.

I'm pregnant.

I had to stop writing and just stare at those words for a long time. I still can't believe that this is happening to me! I'm scared. I'm all mixed up and I feel sick all the time. But most of all, I want to be with you. I'm having your baby and I need you now more than ever.

Maybe I should come to Blakely's Bluff. We can be alone and decide what to do next. Please call me or write IMMEDIATELY. I haven't told Adele yet, though I think she suspects something. How can she not? I don't want anyone to know before I tell you. I hope you're happy about this. I know it's not what we'd planned, but we can make new plans together.

Love <u>always</u>,
Mary June

That was the final letter. Tripp had never written back. She'd never heard from him again. Mama June read each letter once, twice, three times.

Seeing his penmanship—bold and impatient like the man—brought him even more to life. She traced his signature with her finger, hoping to feel some connection, some tingling of sensation. There was none.

Her own penmanship looked impossibly young and naive. She had been so painfully young in so many ways. She was only nineteen! If she'd know then what she knew now, she might have made other choices. Why, she asked as poets had before her, was youth wasted on the young?

Mama June pulled herself up and walked to the attic window. She reached out to swipe away the cobweb from the window. The silken threads dissipated in the air like motes of dust.

As she stood in the debris of her memories, the past seemed more alive to her than the present. Reading these letters again, she could actually feel the pain prick her heart once more. She relived the heaviness of spirit and the desperate longing she'd felt as she waited for Tripp's reply.

She'd thought those long days that turned into weeks were the worst of her life. She couldn't know they were merely the beginning.

It was very late, yet Mama June knew the night was far from over. The attic was very stuffy and the humidity was unbearable. She put the letters back into the trunk, closed the lid and dragged herself to her feet. She felt light-headed with fatigue and she longed for sleep. Brushing the dust from her robe, she slowly journeyed down the stairs back to her room. The house was silent and dark. She heard Blackjack's nails clicking against the hardwood floors as he came to investigate the noise.

"It's me, Blackie. It's all right," she called in a stage whisper down the stairs.

The dog whimpered and she knew his tail was wagging. Then he turned and walked back to his master's room.

She peeked into Morgan's room as she passed and it was dark.

Back in her own room she washed the grime and dust

from her face, relishing the coolness of the washcloth against her brow. She reapplied cream to her face, and rubbing it in, she paused and stared at her reflection in the mirror. Her hand lowered and she leaned forward. She knew the contours of this face so well, each line and freckle gained through the years. Yet behind the facade of softening flesh she could still see the girl she'd always been staring back at her, all knowing.

"You fool," she murmured, looking deeper into her own eyes. "You poor old fool."

In the stifling attic, reading the words over and over, she'd broken through her girlish imaginings at long last and read what Tripp had truly told her between the lines. A simple truth she'd stubbornly refused to acknowledge.

Tripp had never really loved her.

12

———

"They'll come back to it. I wasn't into it, either. I didn't weave for about ten years, until I got old enough to appreciate the art."
—Annie Scott, basket maker

NONA PULLED THE DAMASK tablecloth from the ironing basket and fingered the fine linen. Age had rendered it soft as butter—and about as yellow. She couldn't count all the Sunday dinners this old fabric had seen, or the birthdays, anniversaries and graduations. A lifetime of milestones were recorded on this heirloom. She remembered old Mrs. Blakely crying like a baby in the kitchen when a guest spilled an entire glass of red wine on it. But Nona had worked with the fabric, day after day, gently, firmly, teasing the stain out. This tablecloth had been with the Blakely family for longer than she had. What stories this piece of linen could tell!

What stories she could tell.

She carefully spread the damask over her ironing board, smoothing out the wrinkles with her hands. Sixty-eight years she'd been connected to the Blakelys. Forty of those she'd been their housemaid. Four decades of caring for their house, meals, heirlooms…and the stains, she thought ruefully as she plucked away lint and a few black strands of dog hair from the linen. Her gaze caressed the fabric she knew better than anyone, even Mary June. So many stains she'd cleaned up over the years, each with a story of its own, and not a one could be seen. Her mother had taught her that part of a housemaid's duty was never to talk about the family, and Nona knew she'd done her job faithfully.

She licked her finger and tested the iron—it was plenty hot. Then, reaching over to switch on the radio to her favorite channel, she settled into the task. She loved to iron. The rhythmic motion was soothing and gave her time to reflect.

The kitchen windows were open to the sea and a fan whirred nearby, stirring the air. She knew in a few weeks— maybe even days—they'd be forced by humidity and mosquitoes to close up the windows and turn on the air-conditioning. So she relished these last few mornings of spring when she could stand before the open window with honeysuckle and jasmine in the air and a good baseball game on the radio.

She'd just touched the iron to the fabric when Morgan walked into the room. He was wearing frayed khakis and a faded navy polo. His brown hair was damp and slicked back, and he smelled of fresh soap. He'd probably just cleaned up from his run. She looked at his shabby appearance and wondered why she even bothered ironing his pants.

"Here comes trouble," she said in greeting.

He grinned with affection and swooped to kiss her cheek. "Good morning, gorgeous." He lifted his nose, sniffing. "Is that coffee I smell?"

"A fresh pot."

"That's my girl." He went for his quarry as straight and true as his granddaddy's bird dog. "Can I pour you a cup?"

Nona shook her head. "I've got mine. But you can top it off."

"Who's playing?" he asked, referring to the ball game on the radio.

"The Cubs."

"Chicago? You're still following them?"

She'd loved the Cubs ever since her brothers took her to a game when she visited them in Chicago soon after they'd moved there. She saw Ernie Banks hit two home runs and had been a fan ever since. Over the years she'd broken at least two irons with the whoopla she made whenever the Cubs hit a homer.

"Once a Cubbie, always a Cubbie. You can turn it off. They're losing."

He flicked off the radio and brought the coffeepot over to fill her cup. The tablecloth caught his attention.

"You know, I think some of my best memories were sitting in this kitchen watching you iron that tablecloth."

Nona's face softened with the memory. As she watched Morgan settle his long frame into a nearby chair, she recalled the young boy, thin as a rail with curls as tight as nap in the humidity, who came every day to her kitchen just to be with her. Sometimes she'd be ironing, or cooking, or baking—it was his job to lick the bowl. They'd talk about nothing in particular, but in between the lines Nona knew the boy needed a refuge where he could talk openly without worry or censure. After Hamlin's death, the kitchen was their sanctuary. Even as a teenager, a time when most boys would clam up tight, once Morgan crossed the threshold, he would loosen his tongue with her. She'd always chuckle to herself when folks remarked on how quiet Morgan was.

This boy was the reason she'd stayed as long as she did at Sweetgrass, and when he'd left, she left soon after.

"How long do you figure you've been ironing that table-cloth?" Morgan asked her.

"Funny you should ask. I was just wondering that myself. Too long to count, but somewhere around forty years."

"Sounds like a jail sentence to me."

"With time off for good behavior."

His smile turned serious. "It means a lot to me, to all of us, that you came back to help us out now. Even for a short while."

Nona pressed the iron to cloth. "I couldn't let anyone else tend to this tablecloth, now, could I?"

"You started working here as a girl, didn't you?"

"I used to come here with my mama, back when she worked here," Nona said, her arm pushing the iron back and forth in a steady rhythm. "Mostly I played with your daddy and Adele. We had some good times fishing in the creek and hunting lizards. I reckon I started working here part-time when I come of age, and by the time I was eighteen, I was full-time. A few years later your mother come here."

He grinned. "So you both started serving time together."

Nona cackled and shook her head.

"What was she like back then?"

Nona spritzed the linen. The droplets of water fell in a splay pattern.

"Your mother was a good woman," she answered truthfully. "Kindhearted. Maybe too softhearted for her own good. Anyone could see she was a real lady, and everyone who met her loved her."

"She seems so tired lately," he commented. "She's taking on too much."

Nona had seen the circles under Mary June's eyes, but didn't think it was the routine. Morgan had circles under his eyes, too. There was a lot going on under the surface in this family. She sighed. Same as always.

"She's not sleeping so well," she replied.

Morgan accepted that without comment. "What about Daddy? What was he like when he was young?"

Nona fixed her eyes on the man. So, he'd come with a purpose, she realized. He'd been gone a long while. And now that his daddy was sick, he was fishing for a few answers before it was too late. He knew that she was the only one who could give them.

"You've seen pictures," she answered, sidestepping.

His fingers tapped the cup in frustration. "I know what he looked like. But what was he *like?*"

She set down her iron. "Your daddy was a gentleman and the strongest man I've ever met. And I'm not talking about brute strength. He was as steady and firm as steel."

"And as inflexible."

"Sometimes," she agreed good-naturedly. "Sometimes he had to be. When his daddy died, he left him this property and a lot of debt. Those were lean times. Everyone thought his brother, Tripp, was the strong one. But he wasn't. It was your daddy that carried the weight of this family. This place." She paused. "Same as you."

Morgan's head shot up. "I'm not like him at all."

Nona scoffed and began ironing again. *You're a carbon copy,* she thought to herself.

"I'm not!" he stubbornly said to her silence.

"If you say so."

She continued ironing while Morgan brooded over his coffee.

"If you want to know who your daddy is," she said, "you might go visit with him and find out for yourself."

"I do visit him. Every morning," he muttered, not looking up from his cup.

"You go in to get the dog!"

"Hey, Blackjack needs his exercise. No one else will do it," he said defensively.

"I have no problem with you exercising the dog, Morgan. But don't go pretending that you're visiting with your father," she scolded. "You don't stop to talk to him, or spend any time with him at all. It's like you can't wait to leave the room."

Morgan lifted his chin to look at her with a haunted expression. "I'm doing my duty trying to keep this place afloat. Let's leave it at that."

"You could try, is all I'm saying."

"I have tried!" he exploded. "All my life! I'm done with that. Look, I love him. He's my father. It's taken me years to accept that we just don't get along, okay?"

She put down the iron and narrowed her eyes. "You have to let the past go, Morgan. You're not a boy any longer. You're a man."

"There are some things you can't let go of. Besides, there's no talking with him. He doesn't listen."

"You can't ever guarantee that what you say to anybody will be heard. But you've never had a better chance of having your father sit there and listen."

"Oh, boy, that's a sick joke."

"I'm not trying to be funny. He's eager for your company. I see it in his eyes. How can it hurt to just sit there with him for a while?"

"It's too late. It wouldn't change anything."

She threw up her hands, lest she wring his neck with them. "Everything's changed, fool! Think, Morgan. At last you can tell him what you really want to say and he can't stop you."

"That's making him a victim, isn't it? I mean, forcing him to sit there while I go on and on."

"I know you. It's not in you to be mean. What this is, Morgan, is a second chance, a chance to change how things are. Because your father will be forced to listen. And you'll be forced to speak. I'm old and I know, second chances don't come every day."

"I have nothing to say to him," he said, shifting uncomfortably in his chair.

"The hell you don't!"

"You sound like Kristina," he said, more to his coffee.

That caught her attention. She paused, her mind speculating. "She after you about this, too?"

"Yeah. Only she's nicer about it."

Nona chortled and thought, *good for her.* "She's a nice girl," she said, returning to her work so that she didn't seem too intent. But her eyes were peeled for any nuance on his face.

His shrug spoke volumes. "She's nice enough."

"You should take that girl out. She's been working hard and doesn't know anybody around here. Maybe take her to a movie. It's the decent thing to do."

"You think?" He stretched his legs out and crossed his ankles. "Maybe I will."

She hid her smile and reached over to turn the radio back on. To her surprise, the Cubs had pulled ahead. The announcer was shouting, and in the background the fans were cheering. Nona's grin blossomed and her blood raced in her veins. But in her heart she knew the excitement of victory she felt had nothing to do with the Cubs' double play.

It was late, but the summer sky was still blue. Morgan stood outside the Palmetto Grande staring up at the sharp, perpendicular lines of the art deco theater. The structure seemed to him as incongruous in the Lowcountry setting as the enormous neon globes did against the azure sky. The retro theater flared out to encompass a public square of chic shops and manicured walkways, all bordered with newly planted palms and tall nursery grasses that swayed in the evening breeze. Expensive cars were lined up to pick up moviegoers or drop off more, and farther back in the parking lot, more cars trolled for available spaces.

In his old jeans and a T-shirt, Morgan felt out of place among these folks dressed in trendy summer clothing. Young teens showing lots of skin called out like exotic plumed birds to one another. Older couples in island colors strolled leisurely by with time on their hands, some eating ice cream, some sipping coffee or wine at the outdoor café, and still others just stood in line for tickets. Most were here on vacation; the accents from the north and west sounded garbled in his ear. Time was, the only strange accents he heard around here were the mysterious cadence and rhythms of the Gullah.

Just beyond the theater, a new roadway with a steel guardrail barely restrained the wild, unruly landscape of the wetlands. Overgrown, spindly loblolly pines framed the jagged-edged border, and beneath them, a shadowed wilderness of dense yaupon, wax myrtle and magnolias competed for the sun's rays. The lizards, snakes and few birds of prey that survived in this area were compelled to fight fiercely for the scarce bits of habitat.

He'd been gone for too long, he thought. While he'd been carving out his own piece of the wilderness in the west, he'd turned his back on what was happening here at home. He'd thought the Lowcountry, with its slow pace and traditional ways, would never change. He'd thought wrong.

Morgan was struck, suddenly and fiercely, by what his father had been struggling to do all these years. Saving Sweetgrass was more than saving a family piece of land. Those three hundred acres between highway and marsh were an oasis of green space in this rolling desert of development.

Kristina came up behind him and monkeyed at his collar.

"Your label was out," she said. "Good movie, huh?"

He turned to face her, blinking with the interruption of his thoughts. "Uh, yeah. It was okay."

She searched his face. "You seem a million miles away."

"More like years away."

"What were you thinking?"

He shrugged, not able to put his thoughts neatly into words. "I can't get over how much this place has changed," he said simply. "I don't recognize it."

"Yeah? How so? It seems like your average upscale shopping center to me."

"You don't understand. When I lived here, we didn't even have a movie theater, much less a multiplex theater with a dozen or more choices. We didn't have a shopping center at all. We went downtown for movies. This used to be an open field full of sweetgrass. Now look around. There's not a blade of sweetgrass on the lot. But I noticed that didn't stop them from calling it Sweetgrass Center."

"At least they did a nice job of it," she said. "This is a pretty place and it's outdoors, not a mall. And they still have sweetgrass basket stands along the road. That's something."

"I guess," he conceded, feeling the tension in his chest ease a bit. He liked that she always tried to find the positive in any situation.

He turned to look at her, unable to stop the smile that spread across his face. He'd grown accustomed to seeing her blue eyes fringed with pale lashes, the smattering of freckles across her nose, especially after she'd been in the garden or swimming. Her wild blond hair hung loose around her shoulders, but during the day while she worked, she dramatically reined it in with an elastic and bobby pins. It was her choice of clothing, however, that, to his eyes, defined her style. Tonight she wore a flimsy top of crushed Indian cotton, low-cut shorts and sandals. A pearlescent abalone shell strung on a leather strip hung tantalizingly between her rounded breasts.

He looked away. They'd become friends in the past months, and it had been years since he'd had a friend. He didn't want to ruin a good thing.

"Come on. I'll buy you an ice cream."

She looped her arm in his. "You couldn't have walked me to an ice cream parlor back then, right?"

"Nope. But I could've bought you some shrimp or watermelon from a vendor. Maybe some pine straw."

They strolled through the crowded walkways to an ice cream parlor, where they waited in line and talked about the movie. He ordered a double coconut almond fudge cone, and after long deliberation, she decided on a raspberry sorbet in a cup. Rather than stay in the frigid air of the air-conditioned shop, they opted to sit outside on one of the benches and watch the parade of people pass them by. The sky was darkening, the weather was balmy and Morgan was enjoying himself.

"This used to all be a marsh," he told her, looking over the brick shops and windows filled with merchandise. "You couldn't even get to the Isle of Palms from here until after Hurricane Hugo. That's when they built the connector. The Sullivan's Island bridge was down and folks were hoppin' mad that they couldn't get back to their homes. Just over there a piece," he said, pointing toward the marsh, "Hamlin and I used to ride in our flat-bottomed boat looking for red drum."

"You don't talk much about what it was like when you were a kid," she said, scooping out the sorbet with a pink plastic spoon. "It's nice to hear."

"There's not much to tell."

"Oh, I'm sure that's not true. How could anyone live here and not have a million stories to tell? It must've been heaven for a boy here with the ocean and creeks for a playground. To go out on a boat—" She stopped, suddenly uncomfortable with the territory they both knew she was treading into.

He took a bite from his cone.

"Did you have any favorite places to hang out?'

He swallowed, relieved that she got the conversation rolling again in another direction.

"Actually, I did," he replied readily. "My brother and I discovered this good-size hummock that was fairly dry and not too buggy. She was a beauty. 'Course, we knew the Sewee Indians were there before on account of the shell ring, but we figured they were long gone and it was ours. Squatters' rights. We worked like the devil bringing in boatload after boatload of wood, any kind of old scrap we could lay hands on. Mostly from Daddy's storage house." He snorted. "He never figured out what happened to that heart pine."

He looked off, and in his mind's eye he could still see the rambling shack that he and Hamlin had built on that island they'd claimed as their own. They'd thought it was a castle. When they sat on the rickety porch surveying their kingdom of lush palmettos, cedar and shrubs overlooking a vast view of water, they'd felt like young princes among men.

"It was a fine-looking shack, with a metal roof and a porcelain sink and even an old icebox we found at some dump. It did the job for Cokes and sandwiches. We called it Bum's Camp. It was a special bond between us."

"It sounds like a pretty amazing place. Is it still around?"

"It burned down," he replied flatly.

"Oh. Gee, that's too bad."

"My father burned it."

She skipped a beat. "Oh."

"After Ham died, he found out that we were coming home from there when the accident happened. I don't know why he did it. Well, maybe I do. But he went straight there and torched it."

They sat awhile in an awkward silence while he wondered if she would pursue this. He hoped she wouldn't.

"Hamlin sounds like a dream big brother."

"Oh, yeah," Morgan said thickly. "He was that." A bitter-sweet smile shaped his face at the sudden memory of his older brother teaching him how to wield a hammer. "Hamlin could build anything. He taught me everything he knew."

"Hamlin was older than you by quite a few years, wasn't he?"

Morgan nodded. "Ten years. *A decade,* he used to say, 'cause it somehow made it sound like even more. He liked being the oldest one. I guess it made him feel in charge. Not that he needed anything to help him there. Ham was always the leader, no matter what the game. He made up all the rules."

"And you and Nan followed them?"

"You better believe it. Not because we had to, but because we wanted to. He was just so much *fun.* He knew how to do just about everything, and if he didn't, he tried it, anyway."

"Do you? Try everything, I mean?"

"Me? No. I tend to play it safe."

"I don't know about that. I heard about your exploits in Montana. Throwing yourself between bison and men with guns doesn't sound like playing it safe to me."

"Oh, that," he said with a self-deprecating shrug. "That wasn't dangerous, not if you know bison. The secret is in watching their tails. If they raise them, they're either going to charge or take a dump. In either case, your guard best be up."

She laughed and he liked the sound of it. It was open and hearty, as if she didn't worry if someone might look at her askance or tell her to hush. The sound of it made him laugh, too.

"What's wrong?" she asked, sensing the change in him.

"Nothing. Just the opposite. I was thinking, it's a new phe-nomenon for me to talk about Ham and laugh."

She smiled, relieved. "I'm glad. It sounds to me like you had some good times with your brother."

"I did," he said, and in a rush, images flooded his mind, all of his brother, all of them with him smiling. Hamlin fixing the rigging on the sailboat, laughing at the wind. At the wheel of Mighty Moe, giving the cousins a ride in the log-ging cart. Dipping Nan's pigtails in paint while she napped. Ham's face, serene yet focused, his tanned body arching for-ward, tossing a net over the water with the gracefulness of a dancer. Pulling the throttle of the boat's engine full back, his eyes shining with devil-may-care as they soared high then hit the water hard, laughing even when it hurt.

"I haven't thought of him in a long while. At least, not about the good times."

"Maybe you should."

Morgan stood up, ending the conversation. His ice cream cone was dripping like a volcano spewing lava. He held it at arm's length and extended his free hand to her.

"Are you done with yours?" he asked.

She gave him her garbage and he walked over to the metal trash bin and tossed it. He wiped the mess off his hands with the miserly napkin that came with the cone.

It gave him a minute to think. He had to admit, it hadn't been so bad talking about his brother. After Hamlin died, he'd shut down. He wouldn't go to his brother's funeral. He couldn't sleep, couldn't eat, couldn't so much as mention his brother's name. His parents had said he was in shock, that he needed some time, but it was more. He'd felt dead inside, as if he'd died beside his brother in that boat. He hated to go anywhere, because no matter where he went—school, church, shopping—everyone knew about the accident and everyone felt the need to come up and tell him how sorry they were, how bad they felt for him and, worst of all, how lucky he was to have survived. They wouldn't let it just go away. So he went away instead. He'd found it easier to survive if he avoided people and hid out.

Tonight, however, was different. He felt as though a window inside himself had been pried open after years of being tightly shut. He could breathe a little easier. Thinking about Ham, talking about him, hadn't been as painful as it used to be. Was it Kristina? Or maybe time was a healer, after all.

He looked over at Kristina sitting on the bench. Her profile revealed a softly rounded woman with strong bones. *Soft and strong.* He thought that an apt description. When he returned to her side, she stood and smiled easily into his face and he thought to himself, *I feel comfortable with her. I trust her.*

He wrapped an arm around her shoulder, an act that had her turn her gaze toward him, questioning. "Let's go."

They began walking, hip to hip, in the general direction of the car.

Nona put her hands on her ample hips and perused the kitchen garden. There were mounds of rosemary and parsley, purple spikes of lavender, flowery heads of dill, tall clumps of basil and row upon row of greens. And tomatoes, lots of tomato plants that promised sweet, warm fruit that would taste like heaven on a piece of crusty bread along with a leaf of that basil.

"That garden is making my mouth water," she said to Kristina as she walked through the black iron gate.

Kristina sat back on her heels and smiled in welcome. Next to her was an old apple basket filled with weeds. Nona thought her smile was as bright and cheery as the violas she was planting between the tomatoes.

"It's coming along," Kristina replied modestly, though her pleasure rang in her voice. "I don't know if I'll be here long enough to gather the harvest, but I love gardening. It's always been a hobby of mine. More of a passion, really."

"It shows," Nona said with admiration in her voice.

"I had a huge garden in California. The soil there is so rich! You could drop a seed in, spit on it and it would take off. The soil here is so different, though. It's sandy."

"Just give it lots of water," Nona advised. "That's the secret. Lots of water."

"It's such a pretty space, and someone obviously spent a great deal of time here once. It must have been incredible in its heyday."

"This has been the house's kitchen garden since time was. The main produce for the family was grown in the fields down the road a piece, back when this was a farm. At one time, we used to grow most everything we needed right here, aside from flour, sugar, coffee and such."

"Morgan told me Mama June used to keep the garden up."

Nona nodded and her eyes grew wistful in memory. "She surely did. I remember she planted herbs. And flowers. She always loved her flowers. Filled the house with them. Whenever she had a spare minute she'd be out here with a trowel."

"It's been a long time since this garden was tended."

Nona shrugged and looked off. "I reckon she lost interest after a while." Nona bent low to tug out a weed that was hidden beneath a leaf of mustard green. "It's good to see the garden taking shape again."

"And speaking of pretty spaces," Kristina said as she dug her trowel deeper into the soil. "I've been going out to Blakely's Bluff a lot."

Nona nodded, her gaze on the garden. "So you've said."

"It's a lovely place."

Sweetgrass

"It has the best view of the ocean anywhere."

"And the house! It's wonderful. Designers like to say a house has good bones. Bluff House has them in spades. Tall ceilings, big windows, a wide staircase and a view to die for. Whoever built that house knew what she was doing."

"He," Nona corrected. "The man who built it was a cantankerous old Confederate soldier."

"Says you. I say he was a wounded spirit, a visionary who needed nature to heal his wounds." She grinned widely and Nona could only chuckle in response. "It's kind of sad that no one goes there," she added.

Nona recalled that occasionally a cousin of the family came by to use it, and she imagined young Chas and Harry brought their buddies up for a weekend of no good. She didn't think any one of them did a darn thing to fix up the place as a thank-you, or even clean up after their sorry asses.

"It wasn't always like that," Nona replied. "The family used to go to Bluff House all the time. They had outings and reunions there, and big barbecues. Someone was always going out to the bluff. Mr. Preston, he had this old shrimp boat he loved to tinker on. Lord, he'd go down to work on that boat every spare minute. He called the boat The Project on account of that's what he always used to say whenever Mama June would ask him where he was headed. 'I'm going to work on my project,' he'd answer." Nona chuckled at the memory. "Those kids used to have good times there."

Kristina handed Nona a bottle of cold water from the cooler and paused to take a long sip of her own.

"I suppose things changed after the accident," Kristina said softly.

Nona drank from her water, gathering her thoughts, then reached out to pull on another weed. She wriggled it in her strong hands, easing it from its grip in the earth. "See this weed here?" she asked Kristina. "It's not so big when you look at it on the surface, but sometimes the roots go real deep. You have to be careful when you tug on them, so's they come up clean. Because if they break, they won't die and they'll come up again, stronger than ever.

"That's the way it is with the pain in this family. The roots go deep and the pain spreads to all of them. Everyone's afraid if they tug too hard something's going to break and the pain will grow all over again. So they just leave it be. But underneath, those roots just keep growing stronger and stronger."

She sighed heavily and looked at Kristina, deciding.

"Hamlin Blakely was a fine boy," she began. "Full of life and mischief, like a boy should be. He was the dickens, I tell you, and the apple of his mother's eye. He was but eighteen when he drowned. A terrible tragedy it was. I loved him and mourn him like a son, but my pain can't hold a candle to the fire Mama June endured. Lord, when she got the news I thought she would lose her mind. Ranting and raving and pulling at her hair. Even today I can't bear to think of it without a shudder. Hard times, they were.

"Mama June fell into a deep, deep despair. She wouldn't come out of her room. Wouldn't get out of her bed, not to clean herself or cook or care for her children that lived. They surely needed her, especially young Morgan. He was in the worst way. A lost lamb." Nona sighed heavily. "But I don't blame her. I don't think she cared about her own life, that's for true. There were days Elmore and I didn't think the family would make it through. We prayed on it. Lord, how we prayed!

"She stayed in her room for weeks and weeks. The doctors and the priest came, but nothing helped her snap out of it. In time, she came down on her own. She tried to do simple chores, but her heart wasn't in it. The slightest mention of young Hamlin's name or anything that even made her think of him would send her back to her room. After a while, the family used to call them her 'spells.' They kind of became a normal part of life around that house. *Mama June's spells…*"

"But she eventually came out of it," said Kristina. "I mean, she's fine now."

Nona looked out over the garden and wondered about that. "For a long time, she managed well enough, but she wasn't the same. You see, Mama June was the kind of woman who always saw the glass as half full. Know what I mean? But after the accident, well, the glass was empty. It was plumb dry. No one ever went back to Blakely's Bluff after the accident. They couldn't stand to. And those family reunions and such, they all stopped, too. The whole family kept to themselves and tried to make it through, day after day.

"Then the new parish priest came by to see Mama June. He was young and had all sorts of ideas and he somehow got Mama June to start volunteering at the church. She started off doing just this and that, real slow. But gradually she got more and more involved. In time she was like her old self, throwing herself into her work. That glass started filling up again. Praise the Lord."

Kristina listened, then nodded her head in understanding. "Thank you, Nona."

Nona slowly dragged herself to a stand, grunting with the effort. Kristina sprang to help her. Nona brushed the dirt from her skirt.

"But the roots," Kristina said. "They're still there, aren't they?"

She's a smart girl, Nona thought to herself, looking at her closely. The summer sun had darkened the freckles on her nose and pinkened her skin, but she was a pretty thing, and Nona wagered Morgan thought so, too.

"It's like I said," she replied, looking her in the eye. "You can't tug too hard. You've got to ease them up, wiggle them out bit by bit so they come out clean."

13

———

Basket makers use a sewing awl they call a "bone." Years earlier, this tool was made from an actual animal bone. In modern times, most sewers use the hammered-and-filed stem of a silver teaspoon. Many sewers grow attached to their bone and would be lost without it.

MAMA JUNE COULDN'T RECALL what day of the week it was. For the past several nights she'd had such dreams, so much tossing and turning, that during the day her mind was sluggish and preoccupied. Around her, the rest of the family was caught up in their routines and life marched along its normal path. She, however, felt as if she was walking in a fog, groping for landmarks.

One landmark was her husband, and she went straight to his room after dressing. Kristina smiled when Mama June entered and quickly rose from her chair opposite Preston, patting Mama June's arm in greeting as she passed. It was just a soft touch but one that had come to mean a great deal to Mama June.

Preston was dressed and looking quite well sitting by the window with a book. Blackjack lay at his feet in a deep sleep.

The dog pried open an eye when she drew near, thumped his tail on the floor twice, then went back to sleep.

Preston's blue eyes, however, were bright and he reached out his good arm toward her in greeting. She set the potted cyclamen she was carrying on the table beside his bed, then came close to sit in the chair across from his. Outside, dark clouds spread low across the horizon and gusts of wind rattled the wicker furniture on the veranda.

"Looks like rain," she said. "A good day to stay indoors."

He nodded his head, and she thought how much more muscle control he was gaining.

"Kristina is all smiles this morning, don't you think? Did you know Morgan took her to the movies the other night? Nona tells me they're going to the beach tomorrow. Could be we have a little romance going on right under our noses." His eyes brightened and she knew he was as amused as she.

"It's nice that he's enjoying himself some. He's been working so hard. He has some scheme for the property that he's excited about. No," she replied to his brows raised in question, "he won't tell me what it is yet. He says he wants to get his ducks in a row first." She made a face. "That's how he put it, ducks in a row. Adele uses that expression a lot. Do you think he's teasing?"

He chuckled and she joined him. Then her smile died as she felt the fog return.

"He's been talking about Hamlin lately, too," she said. She watched Preston's smile fade, and concern mixed with sorrow shadow his expression. "Nan tells me he's still having his nightmares. I think being home again is stirring up the mud, bringing up old haunts."

His brows furrowed.

"That's a good thing, isn't it? Going over things we've done or said in our mind, trying to get things straight. I mean, sometimes our memories are garbled and we have to…" She tightened her lips and looked out the window at the approaching storm. None of this made any sense to her. How could she explain it to him?

She felt his hand on her knee, and she swung her head back to meet his gaze. She saw understanding and infinite patience in them. She grasped his hand and held it, gaining courage.

"I've been having dreams, too," she confided. "Only they seem so much more vivid than any dreams I've had before. It's like I am reliving the past. No, that's not quite right, either," she said, shaking her head. "It's hard to explain. It's more like I am watching a film. I'm present but more detached, if that makes any sense. It started when I began talking to you about the first time we met. Remember? After that the dreams started. I've dreamed mostly of that first summer here, when I came with Adele. It's all coming back. All the details. We're all young again. I'm seeing you and Adele." She paused. "And Tripp." She glanced furtively at him. His expression had not changed.

"Oh, Preston, I found the letters!" she blurted out. "I went into the attic and found them and read them over and over." She shook her head. "What's hard for me to understand is how I could have so obstinately believed one thing, really and truly believed it, when the truth was there all along, staring me smack in the face."

She brought her palms to her face. "All these years I've let myself cling to the belief that, for all that happened, for all the pain and suffering, Tripp had loved me. Of course he didn't! I see that now." She dropped her hands and looked into his eyes, seeing again the compassion. "You knew that all along, didn't you?" Her sigh ended with a short, bitter laugh. "If only I'd accepted the truth early on. When I think of how I suffered, waiting for some word from Tripp…"

She settled back in the chair. "When I think of how so many people suffered." Her voice grew softer and she felt tired again. Across from her, Preston sat still, listening. She'd never really talked to him about what had transpired at college that fall, or how she'd learned of Tripp's death. They'd skimmed over the details, as they had once skimmed over the murky waters of the creek in a kayak.

Now, she told herself. It's time to tell him now.

"It was unusually cool that fall," she began. "I was back at Converse College and Adele was my roommate again. The first few days living together were difficult, as you can imagine after all that happened that summer, but we tried to mend things between us enough so we could get along. We scarcely saw each other. She was always energetic and busy. And frankly, I was so caught up in my own worries at the time, I didn't mind that we weren't as close as we once were. It might have even made things easier, considering I was secretly pregnant with her brother's child.

"I used to take long walks in the parks that surrounded the college. I remember the gold and scarlet leaves were especially bright that fall. I'd been at college for almost three months, and it had been at least ten days since I'd written Tripp about the baby. I waited by the phone in the dorm's hall every night, pacing, biting my nails. I tried to be patient and allow time for the mail to be delivered. Then after a few more days, I convinced myself that the letter sat on the table in the foyer of Sweetgrass, waiting for Tripp to stop by the house and pick up his mail. Or perhaps for you to be sent out to Bluff House to deliver it. But more days passed and still no phone call or letter came.

"Then one afternoon I came back to the dorm from my walk. I remember it was midafternoon and I'd gotten overheated and sweaty. The baby might've been no bigger than a pea in a pod, but he made his presence known. I climbed the stairs, and when I paused on the landing to catch my breath, I heard the muffled sound of crying. I suddenly became aware that the hall was unusually quiet. This was the busiest, noisiest time of the day, when the girls came rushing back from their classes and got ready for the evening. The silence was eerie. Wrong.

"I knew that something bad had happened, I sensed that somehow I was in danger. I was walking down the hall toward my room. Some of the other girls' rooms were open. I saw them huddled together, talking in hushed voices. They stopped talking and looked up when I passed by.

"My door was closed, but from behind it I could hear the sound of heart-wrenching sobs. I opened the door and there was Adele, lying facedown on her bed, sobbing piteously on her pillow. She had a telegram crumpled in her hand."

Mama June closed her eyes and brought to mind that afternoon in searing clarity.

"Adele," she said softly, approaching her with the same caution she might a wounded animal. "Adele, it's me. Mary June. Sugar, what's happened?"

Adele swiftly turned her head, her shoulders tense. Her eyes were swollen and smeared with mascara, forming a horrid mask of grief. She stared wildly at her for a moment, then focusing, she collapsed back on the bed.

"He's dead!" she cried out.

Mary June's mouth slipped open as she felt a rising sense of panic.

"Who?" she asked through dry lips, though in her heart she knew.

"Tripp. He's dead, Mary June! Here," she cried, thrusting the telegram at her.

Mary June stumbled back to her bed. Her mouth gasped for air that wouldn't fill her lungs as a roaring sound, like the ocean during a storm, filled her head.

Denial was immediate. "No, he's not!" she screamed back.

Adele choked back her tears. "Yes, he is. Read the telegram!"

Mary June looked at Adele with disbelieving eyes and then at the slip of paper she held crumpled in her hand. She did not want to touch it, to read it, to make it real.

Adele thrust the telegram toward her again, urging her to take it.

Reluctantly Mary June took hold of the crumpled yellow paper. She smoothed out the wrinkled telegram on her lap with trembling fingers and stared at it.

So few words for such an enormous message, she thought with an absurd calm. She read the words, then folded the paper, carefully pressing the creases as if by prolonging the process, she could cling longer to a thread of hope. When she could speak, she handed the telegram back to Adele.

"It doesn't say he's…he's dead."

Adele sniffed loudly and rose to sit. She grabbed a tissue from the desk and then released a great, shuddering sigh. She spoke in ragged sentences.

"I called home. I talked to Daddy. He told me."

He told me. He's dead.

Tripp was always so alive…. She felt suddenly cold and longed to climb under the covers of her bed and curl up, to bury her face in her pillow. Her mind darted to waking up at Bluff House in Tripp's bed, his arms around her as they lay like spoons. She'd felt so warm then.

"Mary June, do you hear me?" Adele shook her shoulders. "Mary June?"

She blinked, feeling as if she'd just been shaken awake. "I hear you."

"You scared me, sitting like that for so long."

Mary June shook her head, trying to clear it. She felt the storm still coming. "It can't be true," she told Adele with a stupor. "It's a mistake."

"It's no mistake! Mama can't talk to anyone," Adele went on, dabbing at her eyes. "Daddy says the doctor's given her something to calm down. And Preston…"

Mary June swung her head around, her chest tightening. "What about Preston?"

"Daddy says Preston and Tripp had a terrible fight over at Blakely's Bluff. It was a brawl like never before. They really tore the place up. Press came home bloodied. Mama about died on the spot. But when Daddy went to Blakely's Bluff to lay down the law, Tripp was good and drunk and wouldn't listen. He took the boat out. Daddy couldn't stop him. That's why he had the accident. He'd been drinking. And it was dark. Otherwise he never would have hit that oyster bed."

"Oh, God…" Mary June buried her face in her palms as a wave of despair swept over her. She was devastated yet, strangely, tears would not come. Perhaps because in her mind she'd already faced that he'd left her. Or perhaps she'd already cried so many tears, there just weren't any left. She wished she could cry, loudly and violently. It would be so much better than the cold numbness that spread through her veins as though she, herself, were dead as well.

Adele began shredding the tissue into little jagged strips. Gentle knocks on the door and the worried inquiries of the other girls went ignored. After a while the knocks ceased and the girls went to the dining hall.

Adele stilled her hands in her lap and fixed her gaze on Mary June.

"The only part I can't figure out," she said in a strained voice, "is what made Tripp and Press fight like that. Daddy said they were like to kill each other. Sure, they fought before, but never like that. Do you know why they'd fight like that?" Her tone was prodding, even accusing.

Mary June lay down on her bed, bringing her knees close to her chest, and knotted the end of her pillow in her fists. She knew, instinctively, that *she* had been the reason the brothers had fought so bitterly. She knew Adele had to suspect this as well. Yet neither of them could dare give it voice.

Hadn't Adele warned Mary June about Preston's feelings? She'd told Mary June not to date Tripp. She'd been dead set against it. They'd had words about it. But Preston had never declared himself, and despite his feelings for her, she knew that reason alone wouldn't have caused a fight like this. No, she thought with a shudder. She could only think of one thing that could. She turned her face into her pillow.

"The afternoon that we found out Tripp had died in the boating accident," Mama June told Preston, "we both cried and cried. It was so sad. Such a waste! Adele told me that you'd fought with Tripp and she'd wanted to know if I knew why. I suspected then that she knew about the baby. We were roommates, after all. She was sitting on the edge of her bed, watching me, waiting, I think, for me to tell her.

"I wanted to tell her. Oh, Preston, I wanted to tell someone about the baby! I was so afraid and lonely. I needed to vent with my friend, my roommate, Tripp's sister. My chest felt ready to burst with pain and secrets. But I thought, what good would it do to tell Adele about the baby now? Tripp was dead. I'd only just learned that and I needed time to figure things out. I was afraid Adele would be furious with me for being so stupid or for somehow besmirching her brother's memory with a scandal. I knew she'd end up making me feel worse. Adele's fury can be cruel. I couldn't handle a direct confrontation just then, and in the end I knew it would solve nothing.

"The shame was mine to bear alone. I'd brought it on myself. If I told Adele the truth about the baby and it became public, the shame and dishonor would carry over to Tripp and your whole family. I felt the least I could do was spare you that."

Preston squeezed her hand and she felt the power of his consolation.

"You know the rest." Mama June wiped away a tear that coursed a trail down her cheek. "What's done is done."

Mama June knew that with that decision made so many years ago, made with all good intentions, Mary June Clark had begun weaving the elaborate web of lies and silences that would bind her in the silken threads of deception for years to come.

That night, Mama June stood at her bedroom window and stared out at Blakely's Bluff. The clouds had rolled in, obscuring the moon and blanketing the sky in inky blackness.

She stood staring until her body grew heavy with fatigue and her lids drooped, eager to close. Reluctantly she climbed into her bed, turned off the light on her bedside bureau, then brought the sheets and thin summer coverlet over her shoulders. They were cool, as was the pillow. Laying her head down, she caught the refreshing scent of sage that Kristina had sprinkled on her linen to soothe her sleep.

Mama June lay on the cool sheets in the deep darkness and closed her eyes. She would sleep now, she knew. Her journey was nearing its end, but was not over yet.

Mary June Clark drove from college back to Mount Pleasant with Adele for Tripp's funeral. It was so unlike their first journey together the May before. Then the highways had been lined with the spring green of promise. Now the earth was dressed for sorrow in muted colors of gold, rust and the dying brown of fragile, crumbling leaves that littered the roadside. They spoke very little. Music blared mercifully from the speaker, allowing them consolation in their own private thoughts. The trip to the coast was the first leg of their separation, though neither of them realized it at the time.

Blame and guilt sat side by side, stoic and silent, each bound by a loyalty that, rather than unite them as it should have, divided the two as cleanly as the yellow line that coursed through the hard cement of the highway home.

Christ Church was filled with mourners that overflowed the small stone house of worship and onto the green grass that surrounded it. A tragedy, especially one to a family as beloved and respected as the Blakelys, is felt by a community. Yet when the victim is one as striking and young as Hamlin Blakely III, the outpouring of grief is like the bursting of a dam.

The Blakely family had ties that traveled back to the early days of historical Charleston, and to a one, the complex, extended branches of the family tree gathered at the family seat to mourn the loss of this favorite son. Several Episcopal priests presided over the mass, one of them an uncle. Even the bishop participated.

Mary June remained in the background, as was fitting the occasion and her position. She was neither Tripp's widow nor his fiancée. Indeed, no one outside the immediate family even knew of their whirlwind affair. It was better this way, she thought, sitting in the back pew between two strangers, one of whom wept piteously during the sermon. In contrast, Mary June sat erect and dry-eyed, with her hands clasped over her belly.

After the service, guests were invited back to Sweetgrass

for a grand luncheon in the Southern tradition. The comfort food of fried chicken, barbecue, slow-cooked greens, corn bread, biscuits and banana pudding helped to sustain the family and friends through their grief.

Mary June drifted away from the clusters of people toward the creek, to a wooden swing that hung from long, blackened ropes tied to an enormous, ancient live oak. The cragged branch arched over the glassy waters of the creek like an arthritic finger. During the past summer that seemed a lifetime ago, Mary June and Adele had sat squished together on the rough-hewn wooden seat like peas in a pod, their legs synchronized as they pumped, laughing and talking, one hand holding a side of the rope, the other wrapped around her friend's waist.

She sat alone on the seat now and rocked aimlessly. Her gaze followed the direction that the branch pointed to like some wizened old crone foretelling her future, for it directed her gaze to the creek that had claimed Tripp's life.

She stared out to sea while the family ate and reminisced. Some time later, she heard the crunch of a footfall behind her. Soon after, she felt the presence of someone at her side. Reluctantly she turned her head and lifted her gaze.

She hadn't spoken to Preston since she'd arrived the day before, though she'd seen him, of course. He was a pallbearer and spoke eloquently at the funeral. She thought he looked haggard though composed. Like most of the gentlemen, he'd removed his dark jacket and tie and rolled up his sleeves in the heat of the Indian summer day. He looked older, too, she thought, noting the crow's feet that cut into his deeply tanned face. There was something else changed that she couldn't put a word to. It was as if someone had snuffed out the incandescent spark of boyish innocence and youthful hope that once shone in his eyes. Death had stolen that from him, and she felt certain her own eyes were as smoky with grief.

"How are you?" he asked.

"Fine," she replied.

He looked at his polished black shoes as though he could read something in them, and asked, "I mean, really. How are you?"

Mary June looked at him more carefully, trying to read any innuendo in his tone.

"I'm fine," she replied, more emphatically.

Preston sighed and looked out into the creek. He had a strong profile, thinner, more defined than Tripp's had been. She saw a muscle twitch in his cheek and her hand tightened around the swing's rope.

"We have to talk," he said.

"About what?" Anxious, she kicked off from the ground, gaining some swing.

He reached out to still the swing. When she turned her head, they locked gazes.

"I know about the baby," he began.

Mary June's eyes widened. Her first reaction was to deny it. Then the shock of hearing the words *the baby* spoken reverberated through her, shaking her loose. The tears swelled in her eyes as she stared in disbelief. She'd held her emotions in check, yet she couldn't be strong a moment longer. She collapsed in his arms, weeping.

"Don't cry, Mary June. He loved you," he said earnestly, holding her tight. "I know he did. He loved you and would have married you. He'd have been a good husband to you and a good father to your baby. You have to believe me."

"He told you." It was more a confirmation than a question.

"Not outright. I found out on my own."

She hadn't thought of this. She felt an enormous relief to be able to talk to someone about the great secret she was holding inside of her. That it was Preston, someone she could trust, gave her strength.

"How?" she asked, needing to know.

"Your letter." When she startled, he went on quickly. "I went out to Blakely's Bluff for one reason or another, I can't even recall now. Tripp was out so I waited. The house was a mess. I mean, worse than usual. There were empty beer bottles everywhere and ashtrays filled with cigarette butts. The whole place reeked of a seedy bar. I was pretty damn disgusted with him, I can tell you. He was letting himself go. It was just such a waste."

He ran his hand through his hair, rubbing the back of his neck with an old man's weariness.

"So I started cleaning up," he said. "I just grabbed the trash can and commenced dumping garbage off from every surface. When I got to the table, there were all these papers spread across it. I was careful. I don't know if he told you, but he was writing a novel."

She realized it was just one more part of Tripp she was unaware of. "No."

"I just threw away those papers that were crumpled in a ball. I was sifting through the rest when I noticed some pink stationery. And I recognized your handwriting."

Mary June put her hand over her lips. "You read them?"

"No. Tripp came back and saw your letter in my hand. He was madder than hell and didn't believe me when I told him I hadn't read it. He started yelling and it just came out. Then I got mad that he got you…that he wasn't careful. I mean—" His face colored and he blurted out, "Hell, Mary June. Tripp was a lot older than you. He's had a lot of experience. He should've known better than to take advantage of a girl like you."

"Oh, Press, it wasn't like that. He didn't—"

"He did," he interrupted angrily. "There are things a guy can do—should do—to keep a girl from getting pregnant, Mary June."

She took a shuddering breath, exhaling slowly. It was too late to cast blame. *It takes two to tango,* as her mother would say.

He reached into his pocket and pulled out a packet of letters tied together with string. She recognized them as her own.

"I thought you'd want these back," he said, placing the letters in her hand. "I didn't want anyone else to see them and I couldn't just throw them out. They belong to you."

She gathered the letters in her hand and stared at the ragged edges where they'd been torn open with Tripp's finger. She wondered if he'd been excited to receive them, if he'd torn them open still standing. Or if he'd been amused by the gushing of a young girl so desperately in love and carelessly set the letters aside.

Looking at the petal-pink stationery festooned with magnolias and her swirling script, it all appeared so childish to her now. When she thought of Tripp's drinking, the wild despair…Tripp had told her he wanted freedom. How could she have been so blind?

Preston sensed her turmoil and took a step closer, grabbing hold of the swing rope. "Mary June… He loved you. He would have married you."

His face was crumpled with anguish and she sought to relieve him of the burden he'd obviously been carrying for days. He was the noble boy again who beat back snakes and spiders in the dark woods, and he was hell-bent to beat back this sad specter from her path as well.

She reached up to place her fingers over his lips. "Thank you for telling me that," she said. "Now you can tell me the truth."

He looked at her cautiously.

"Tripp was not going to marry me. That's what the fight was really about."

He searched her face for clues as to what she might know or suspect. Whatever he saw there tore away the final veil between them. Preston exhaled, resigned to the truth. He moved to sit on the ground and rested his elbows over his knees.

"The war changed him," Preston said, choosing his words. "It was like something was dead inside and he knew it. But he fought it. He traveled around the country when he first got back. That's where he was when you came to visit in May. I'd thought he seemed better when he came home. We all did. We didn't realize just how deep the hurt was, or that he could change so quickly. He was like the tides he loved so much.

"At times he'd seem swelled up with life, flooded from bank to bank—and man, we loved being with him then. At other times, though, the pain drained the life right out of him, leaving him dry and laid bare to the countless demons gnawing him to the bone." He paused, plucking the grass.

"I had to learn to read the tides, to look for the dark water and shallow shoals. When he came back to Bluff House that day, the minute I saw him I knew it was bad. It was like he'd already hit that oyster bed and was cut up and bleeding."

"Oh God," she uttered, bringing her hand to her mouth. "My letter."

Preston nodded. "He was torn up about it. He loved you, he told me that." He took a breath. "But he couldn't face getting married and settling down. I think he felt he wasn't fit. He knew what was the right thing to do. What was expected of him as a gentleman. As a Blakely. But somehow, he couldn't do it."

She felt humiliated. "So you told him to marry me."

Preston nodded.

Her cheeks burned with wounded pride yet she was grateful for his honesty.

He lowered his head and squeezed his eyes shut. "We fought about that."

They both knew that was a grave understatement of the bloody struggle they'd waged. Their last words had been in anger, and she knew then that after Tripp's death he'd run away in despair because he could not take them back.

"I'm sorry," she said.

"Why are you sorry?"

"I never meant to come between you two. I never meant for this to happen."

He paused, then said, "There's one more thing you should see."

He gave her one sheet of yellow lined paper. On it was Tripp's trailing scrawl.

"He wrote this on lots of the papers. Over and over. I saved this one for you. I think, well...I can only think it was what he wanted to say."

She brought the paper closer to read. Mary June recognized the words. On this paper, through the words of Jack Kerouac, Tripp had given her his answer.

This is the night, what It does to you.
I had nothing to offer anybody but my own confusion.

She pulled herself up from the swing to leave.

Preston rose to his knees to grab her hand.

"Mary June, wait. Marry me," he blurted out.

She swung her head around, unsure she'd heard right. "What?"

"Marry me," he repeated.

Her face crumpled in disbelief. "You don't mean that."

"I do. Please, wait. Hear me out. Have you given thought to what you're going to do now? With the baby?" When she shook her head he pressed on. "I have. And this is the only answer."

"I can't ask you to offer your future to me."

"You're not asking me! I'm asking you."

"No. I'm not letting you do this. You don't want to marry me. I don't want to ruin another person's life."

He shook her shoulders gently. "Mary June, don't you know that I've been in love with you since the day you tripped over that root and fell into my arms? Only when it was clear your affections lay elsewhere did I step aside. But things are different now and I don't have time to court you."

"I can't do this. It's too soon."

"Think, Mary June! This child's going to come without mind to when you're ready. You know what will happen if you have this baby out of wedlock. Even if the baby is recognized as having Blakely blood, it'll be labeled a bastard. I know that's a cold, hard word," he said when he heard her intake of breath. "But they'll say it. The secret of the baby's birth will be whispered behind raised palms every time that child enters a room. Not to mention your reputation. Simply put, it would be destroyed."

"They'll find out, anyway. They always do."

"No, they won't. We'll need to tell Mama and Daddy."

"No, Press. I'm so ashamed. They'll hate me all the more."

"No, they'll be comforted by knowing that a part of Tripp is still alive. Plus, they'll want to keep it hushed more than we will and they can help. No one will ever guess the baby isn't mine."

"Adele will."

His face tightened. "She'll wonder."

"She'll know."

"But we won't confirm it. Adele would never say anything to hurt us or the family name. Mary June, we can't breathe a word, not even in confession. If we do, people will find out. The truth will slip from a tongue without intention, but it will get out. We won't even think it."

"Do you really think that others won't figure it out?"

"You were here as a guest for the summer and dated Tripp in a whirlwind. No one really knew you were even a couple. We'll get married right away, and when the baby comes early, the worst they'll think is that you and I jumped the gun a little. Hell, Mary June, we won't be the first ones in this county to do that."

"But, Press..." She hesitated, struggling with how to say this. "I don't love you. Not in that way."

He grimaced, acknowledging this statement with a curt nod of his head.

"I know," he said, looking at her in a straightforward manner. "But that's not what's most important now. We have to think of your situation and what's best for the baby you're carrying. It's my brother's child. I will love it as my own. And in time, I hope you can learn to love me as I love y—"

She put her fingers against his lips. "Please, don't say it."

He took her hands in his. "Mary June, will you do me the honor of being my wife? I'll be a good husband to you, and I swear I'll be a good father to your baby." He smiled then, a boyish, hopeful smile. "Marry me, Mary June. We'll make a good life for each other and for this baby."

She thought for a long while before giving him her answer. This was the only course of action open to her; she knew he was right about that. She had to do what was best for the baby. She looked into his eyes, as bright a blue as the sky above, at his wavy curls that refused to be tamped down. Dear Preston...

"Mary June," he said again, leaning forward and pressing his lips against her forehead. His voice was husky with emotion. "Just say yes."

She closed her eyes and put her hands upon his chest, falling.

And once again, Preston was there to catch her.

"Yes," she replied.

While Mary June clung to the swing and rocked gently back

and forth, Preston sat and plucked the long, wild grass that grew in clumps in the sandy soil. He looked out at the sun shining on the surface of their beloved creek. The wind rose off the river, ruffling Mary June's blond hair from the collar of her dress.

If someone had looked up at that moment, they would have thought the two were sweethearts, stealing time together under the shade of the old live oak by the water. Months later, when the announcement of the marriage was made, guests of the luncheon would, in fact, recall having seen the two of them together that day and comment on how perfect a couple they'd seemed, right from the start.

Mama June slept late. When she awoke, the birds were singing in force and the piercing coastal sun had chased away all the evening's clouds. The scent of coffee and bacon was tantalizing in the air, and she could hear the rumbling noise of a vacuum cleaner downstairs.

She stretched lazily, fingers to toes, then relaxed again, languid in her bed. Glancing at the crystal clock on her bedside bureau, she smiled guiltily. Goodness, she couldn't recall the last time she'd slept so late. She felt boneless against her soft mattress, yet strangely refreshed.

Through her dreams she had revisited defining moments of her past. And now in the light of day she saw them clearly, without the clouds of deception.

Tripp had been a young girl's crush. As an old woman, she could see and accept with hard-earned wisdom that though he might have been in love with her, he did not truly love her.

Preston, her husband, however, *did* love her. With a deep, abiding kind of love. He always had. He may not have swept her off her feet or filled her mind with grand, airy philosophies. That was not his style. Preston was a man of the earth. He was rich and true and compassionate and steadfast.

And she loved him!

She brought her hands to her cheeks, flushed with amazement. When she began this journey, she'd hoped to help Preston remember who he once was. To help him. She didn't imagine that *she* would remember him.

Lowering her hands, she held them in the air, looking at them. They were small hands with fine bones, blue veins, oval nails and telltale age spots. To look at them, they were rather ordinary. Yet in the past few months, they had accomplished the extraordinary.

For years, hers had been a stale, tired marriage, one filled with disillusionment and disappointments. Her and Preston's conversations were perfunctory. They didn't share interests, nor did they even try any longer. They'd fallen into a routine of isolation. He often preferred to be alone than with her. He went for walks with his dog or spent time in his office with the door closed. This did not distress her, as she felt the same. They didn't argue; they were resolvedly civil. She and Preston had not been close in any intimate sense for years.

Yet, wonder of wonders, since his stroke she'd helped Preston with his range of movement exercises and given him massages. These hands had touched his body over and over in myriad ways. She'd had more tactile connection with her husband in these few months than she'd had in years. The touching had created a new intimacy between them.

Kristina had been right. Through touch, she'd remembered. She'd remembered all the good times they'd had in their long marriage. She'd remembered the tender moments, the kind gestures and the thoughtful words. And through remembering, she'd fallen in love with him all over again.

She'd endured her share of tragedy in her life, and it was serendipity that through this last tragedy she'd found joy. It was, she thought humbly, God's sweet mercy.

She rose and walked swiftly to the window, her long cotton gown catching the breeze. Leaning forward against the frame, she smiled. Yes! There was Blakely's Bluff, its steep pitched roof glinting in the bright sun. She didn't feel the usual uneasiness at seeing it. Tonight darkness would fall again and she would be ready for it. But right now the sky was cerulean and fresh salt air was blowing in from the ocean. It was going to be a beautiful day!

Preston was sitting up against his electric bed, already bathed, dressed and fed. Even his morning movement exercises were completed. Kristina was maneuvering the wheelchair into position near the bed to take Preston to the porch for his morning outing.

"Good morning," Mama June called out in a cheery voice as she entered the room. "And isn't it a lovely morning. You were very kind to let me play hooky."

"Not at all," Kristina replied. "It was long overdue. And you must've needed it." Her eyes brightened. "Aren't you chipper this morning?"

"I feel wonderful." She turned her head toward Preston. He, too, watched her with a glint of curiosity. "I feel happy."

"All this from a little extra shut-eye?" asked Kristina. "I'm definitely not getting enough sleep."

Mama June chuckled and reached out her hand for the gait belt. "It's your turn for a break. Why don't you take a few extra minutes for a cup of tea? I'll bring Press outside."

Kristina looked doubtful. "Are you sure you can handle his weight? It's not as easy as it looks. I don't want to come in here and find both of you in a heap on the floor. Then I'll have two patients to care for."

"How many times do I have to practice? I know what to do. And if I forget something, Preston can show me, right, darlin'?"

His eyes lit up and he blinked twice.

Kristina was reluctant, but she gave Mama June the two-inch cotton belt designed to help a stroke patient transfer his weight. "Remember to buckle it in front once you get it around his waist."

"I know."

"And be sure to make it tight enough, but not so tight that you can't get your fingers under it."

"Go," Mama June told her, nudging her forward. "I can handle it."

Kristina studied her for a moment. "He's all yours," she said with a teasing glint in her eye.

"Don't I know it?" Mama June replied in turn.

Once Kristina left, Mama June felt a sudden shyness. This man was her husband of forty-seven years; they were hardly strangers. And yet, they were. For so long they'd been more like roommates than husband and wife. Barely friends, much less lovers.

She looked at the man sitting in the hospital bed, his white hair gleaming, his eyes bright and alert. Once upon a time, this man had come to her rescue. He had stood by her. He was her knight in shining armor.

She went to his side, still smiling. "So, handsome. Are you ready to go for a stroll?"

At the sound of her voice, Blackjack rose up at the window and pawed at the screen. He was impatient for Preston to join him outdoors.

"He's getting pretty bossy for an old dog, don't you think?" she asked. She was glad to see a lopsided smile twitching at Preston's lips.

She reached for the lever, raising the bed's head and lowering the foot. She hesitated, licking her lips, a little nervous.

He reached out his good hand, resting it on her shoulder.

She looked up. His face was inches away from her own, and in his eyes she saw the gleam of confidence she'd depended on during their marriage. Bolstered, she shifted to sit on the bed beside him.

"Okay, then." She reached her arms around his waist, looping the woven belt around him. Her cheek pressed against the starchy fabric on his chest.

"You're enjoying this, aren't you?" she teased.

She stood again, taking a breath. Then, putting her hands around her husband, she took firm hold of the belt. It seemed such a feeble thing to help balance his weight. He was too weak to stand alone. She'd worked with Preston on a range of motion exercises, she'd massaged his muscles, she'd combed his hair and tended to countless other personal needs, but this would require both of their efforts. They needed to work together.

"We can do this," she said, centering her position on the floor. Once balanced, she looked again into his eyes, their best medium of communication.

They shone back with nervous concentration.

With her arms around him and holding tight to the belt, she offered him a seductive smile. "Shall we dance?"

His expression changed as understanding of the nuance slowly dawned. His corded muscles relaxed and he took a deep breath.

They began a waltz of coordination. Preston put his good hand on the nightstand. She bent at the knees. As he strained to push his body up, she pulled with her legs. Push and lift, rocking to a stand in choreographed cooperation. Her arms were around him, her head against his. The scent of sage and eucalyptus on his skin was clean and fresh.

Mama June heard an inner music in her ear as they moved, hip against hip, working together, shuffling across the floor, pivoting in a half circle, in each other's arms again, husband and wife, slow dancing.

Preston helped lower himself into the wheelchair. Their breathing came in short puffs of exertion. Once settled, Mama June's hands lingered at his waist as their strength returned. Her head stayed close to his. The intensity of his gaze drew her nearer. She leaned forward, naturally, closing her eyes as her lips touched his. It was a kiss as pure and sweet as a first one, familiar yet new, filled with longing and a hint of promise.

Mama June drew back, feeling her cheeks color. "Oh, my."

She thought he smiled as he held her gaze.

Her expression softened and she reached up to cup his chin in her palm. "I can't remember when I've enjoyed a dance more."

She remembered again the day he'd confessed his love to her, so many years before. She remembered how she'd refrained from declaring her own love.

"I love you," she told him.

She felt his hand tighten and his eyes filled with tears.

From the porch, Blackjack's piteous whine ended with a high-pitched yelp.

Mama June laughed and shook her head, glancing up to see the large black shadow at the screen. She smiled contentedly and bent to kiss Preston once more, lightly. Then she moved behind the chair and wheeled her husband out into the sunshine.

14

———

"South Carolina is rich in history, heritage and natural beauty. For us to continue to enjoy these gifts, we must accept our role as good stewards, and together, we will save the last great places."
—Mark L. Robertson, Executive Director,
The Nature Conservancy of South Carolina

SUMMER BLOOMED ALONG the coast of Sweetgrass. The grasses flourished between the dunes, grading into maritime shrubs and the brackish salt marsh. A profusion of wildflowers competed for attention along the horizon. Small, perfect yellow primroses ambled beside delicate oxeye daisies, the brilliant pink of swamp roses and the glorious pink, blue and white funnels of morning glories.

Morgan ran a path through the property. The landscape was familiar, but each day he saw something new. Each day he felt more keenly that his stewardship at this point in time could determine the property's fate for future generations. As he ran along the composted path, he knew that saving this piece of land went far beyond what was best for his father or his mother or even the Blakely family. These acres of wild open space lay unprotected, helpless against man's destruction. This land was as endangered as any bison or bald eagle, and as their habitat, even more crucial to save.

It was this realization that had brought him to his plan. He'd made a few investigative phone calls and thought the idea had promise. He looked at his watch. He had several appointments scheduled for today. He'd have to cut his run short if he wanted to be showered and ready on time.

Daniel Davis from The Nature Conservancy and Elizabeth Lowndes from the Coastal Conservation League arrived at Sweetgrass promptly at nine o'clock. Mama June welcomed her children's old friends at the front door with heartfelt hugs. Nona beamed at seeing folks she'd cared for as children all grown up and looking so prosperous. She'd made a fresh pitcher of sweet tea to serve with the cake and berries that she hoped would sweeten their visit.

Morgan stepped forward to shake the hand of the tall, tanned, broad-shouldered man he'd have recognized anywhere, even with his thinning hair. Dan was older by a good ten years, but he'd been a close pal of Hamlin's and a constant partner on fishing and hunting expeditions. Morgan often tagged along and had more stories about their antics than a farm dog did fleas. Dan came from an old family that was a strong force for environmental protection in the area. The Davis family had put thousands of their acres in the western section of the state into conservation easements.

Lizzy was as lithe now as she had been as a teenager, but her waist-long blond hair was now shoulder length and she'd traded in jeans and sandals for a stylish brown suit and heels. Yet her freshly scrubbed face beamed when she stepped closer, wrapped her arms around him and squeezed tight, same as always. She had a big heart and a generous spirit.

She'd been an on-again off-again girlfriend—someone Mama June had made no secret she'd like as a daughter-in-law—but mostly she was a friend. Lizzy was one of those girls that guys liked to hang out with because she was a good listener, could hold her beer and never said a mean-spirited thing about anybody. She was also a damn good sailor and a world-class fisherman. It didn't surprise him that she'd ended up with a degree in biology and a mission to protect the environment.

After tea and a visit with Preston and Mama June in the living room, Preston went to his scheduled physical therapy session while Morgan brought his guests to the privacy of the office to discuss the reason for the meeting.

"You know what I'd like to do," he began when they were seated. "I'm having the devil of a time trying to make ends meet. My father's been struggling to keep this place intact for years. Lord knows he's pulled about every rabbit out of his hat, but he can't change what's happening along the coast. Frankly, we can't afford to hang on to this place. I've been digging through my father's business papers and scratching my head looking for I don't know what. Bobby Pearlman suggested I look into a conservation easement, so I called you both for some advice."

"Bobby led you straight," Dan said with a grin. "There's no doubt that this is a plum property. I'd be lying if I said we weren't darn pleased when you called. The land along this corridor is disappearing faster than sand through our fingers. Developments are sprawling, and we're aiming to preserve as much as we can, while we still can."

"Especially because this is such an important migratory route," Lizzy added. "But Morgan—" She paused. "While the easement will protect the land's ecology and open space, you do realize that it also puts restrictions on the property, not just for you but for future generations?"

"That's part of what I need to better understand," Morgan replied.

"It's simple, really," said Dan. "As a landowner, you'll agree to sell or donate certain rights to the property, such as the right to develop it or subdivide." He offered a wry grin. "It would be our job to enforce your promise not to exercise those rights. Or your heirs."

"Well, actually, those rights no longer exist," Lizzy amended.

"Right," Dan agreed. "But the land remains in your ownership. Hey, we've all been struggling to keep our family property together. My family's estate was being eaten alive by taxes. We didn't want to sell it, though we had plenty of offers. We ended up selling some and putting most of it into easements. It's a compromise we could live with. Shoot, do you know what your land is worth now, with all that waterfront?"

"I have a pretty good idea," Morgan replied.

"Well, then." Dan continued rubbing his jaw. "My hat's off to you for considering an easement. A lot of folks are going for the money."

"My father is intent on keeping what's left of Sweetgrass intact."

Dan nodded his understanding. "The first thing to know is that the easement will remove the land's development potential. That in turn can qualify you for lower tax benefits. When all is said and done, the easement will protect the land for the future while your family can remain living on the land."

Lizzy nodded. "It's the most powerful tool you have at your disposal to keep your land, Morgan. At the same time, you'll be doing the public a service. Not to mention the environment. If we're thoughtful about it, we can make a difference. I know that matters to you. And to your daddy."

"Adele will be an obstacle."

"Of course she will," Lizzy replied with a smirk. "Your aunt is a voracious developer. She realizes the surging value of your land. Unfortunately, she doesn't recognize its important ecological value."

"Come on, Lizzy, his aunt's no villain," said Dan. "It's happening all over the country. To farms, ranches, timberlands, plantations and some choice hunting grounds, too. You know me, Morgan. That stings where it hurts."

"Easements are among the fastest-growing methods of land preservation today," added Lizzy. "They've protected more than two million acres in our country."

"The problem is, I still haven't figured out a way to maintain the land, even if the taxes are lowered," said Morgan. "We may have to sell in the end, anyway."

"If you're strapped for cash, you could sell the easement rights," Dan said. "We'd have to look into whether your property qualifies as a high-priority site, but I'd wager it would."

"Morgan," Lizzy said, "please consider this option seriously. The wetlands are being exploited, especially right here in our own backyard. When these swamps disappear, so do our buffers for flooding, for cleansing water of pollutants and for sheltering fowl and fish. We're seeing thousands of acres being bulldozed and it's breaking my heart."

"Mine, too, Lizzy. I'll consider all this carefully," he said, referring to the folders full of information both Dan and Lizzy had brought with them. "I can't make any promises. Like I said, we still have a lot to figure out, especially with Daddy's health now. And ultimately, it's not my decision." He smiled. "But I like what I hear."

When they rose to leave, Dan and Lizzy said again how great it was to see him, how happy they were he'd come back home and both elicited promises from him to call and come by for dinner and meet their kids. When he closed the door behind them, he clapped his hands together. Next he'd meet with Adele for their lunch appointment. He grinned widely. This just might work.

His appointment with Adele was at a restaurant along Shem Creek, a quaint section of Mount Pleasant known historically as a docking port for shrimpers. He used to hang out here with his buddies, grabbing a beer and a bucket of shrimp. Now there were several popular fish restaurants and pubs with a water view, a charming inn and a few office buildings built to scale. Tourists crowded the restaurants, and it took longer than he'd thought to find parking.

He glanced at his watch and hustled up the wood stairs of the restaurant. His aunt was always punctual. He was sweltering even in a cotton polo shirt and sighed with relief at the blast of cold air that welcomed him when he stepped inside the glass doors. The hum of voices and the clang of silverware and glass was a pleasant background as he quickly scanned the darkened room. Vickery's was a popular restaurant with both locals and tourists alike, but he'd thought it an odd choice for Adele, whom he would have guessed preferred a quieter, more upscale restaurant. Then he remembered that her office was located not far from here, and as usually was the case with his aunt, it made sense.

He spotted his aunt sitting at a choice table in the far corner of the dining room in front of a large plate-glass window. The view of the creek and marsh was spectacular. A few shrimp boats, encircled by gulls, lined the dock, and pelicans flew across the sky in formation.

"Aunt Adele, I'm sorry I'm late," he said, taking a seat. He did not kiss her.

"I should have warned you about the parking. It gets worse every year. But you're here now," she said, turning to signal her waiter.

She sounded absolutely cheery, and he thought that boded well. He relaxed a little, and when the waiter arrived at the table, he ordered a beer. Adele ordered a Bloody Mary.

He thought his aunt looked especially well. She had a glowing tan that made her dark eyes shine. Like coffee and cream, he thought. He ran his hand through his hair, grateful that Kristina had offered to trim it for him.

"How's your golf game?" he asked her.

"Oh, that," she said with a light laugh. "I seem to have hit a plateau. I play more for the exercise these days. But Harry! Now, there's a boy with something special. I wouldn't be surprised if he was offered a scholarship for golf. He might even go pro, he's that good."

Her pride rang in her voice, and Morgan wondered at her devotion to her grandnephews. "Really? I had no idea he was that good."

"Oh, yes," she affirmed. "What about you? Do you play?"

He shook his head. "I never got into the game. Fishing's more my thing."

She nodded politely, but he knew she wasn't much interested in his sports preferences.

"How's your dear father?"

"He gets better every day," he replied. It was the pat answer, though he was beginning to feel insincere. It seemed to him that his father, too, had hit a plateau.

"Are his therapists still coming in to see him?"

"Yes, ma'am. Like clockwork."

"Not for much longer, I should imagine."

"He has a while to go yet," he answered evasively. This would be a major hurdle to cross when the time came, but he didn't want to get into that with Adele now. He needed her support for his new venture. "You should come by and see him," he said, veering in another direction. "He'd like that."

"I should. I will." Adele twisted her face. "But to be honest, I find it very hard to see him the way he is now."

The waiter arrived to deliver their drinks.

"Do you know what you want to eat?" she asked him. "The oyster salad is very good. And the seared tuna is excellent."

"I'll have the tuna," he told the waiter. Adele ordered the salad.

"So, tell me," she said with all that out of the way. She folded her hands on the table. "What brings us together today? I'm assuming you got through all of your father's papers and have reached a decision?"

"Yes, actually I have."

"I'm glad to hear it." She leaned forward, all ears.

He knew what she was hoping to hear, but he persevered. "I've come up with a plan that I think just might give us a chance to hold on to Sweetgrass. I've already talked to representatives of The Nature Conservancy and The Coastal Conservation League and they've backed me up. I'd like to explore putting Sweetgrass under a conservation easement."

Adele's face went very still. "A conservation easement?"

"Yes," he said, troubled by her shocked expression. "In a nutshell, an easement will allow us to preserve the land and get tax benefits to help us keep it."

"I know what a conservation easement is!" Adele snapped. "What stuns me is that you're pursuing one. What do you hope to gain?"

His goodwill drained from his smile. "I don't hope to gain anything," he said stiffly. "What I hope to do is save Sweetgrass from being sold."

She blinked, as though trying to believe what she'd heard.

"If that doesn't take the cake," she said, leaning back in her chair. She had a hard smile on her face that was anything but cheery. "Here I thought you'd invited me to lunch so that you could tell me you'd finished going through all your father's papers and had discovered that the well had run dry and it was time to sell. I came in good cheer prepared to tell you all about the offer I've fielded from a very prominent investment firm. They're prepared to make a very handsome offer for Sweetgrass. Very profitable. You would all stand to make quite a bit of money."

Now it was Morgan's turn to be stunned. "I'm sorry to disappoint you."

"You have no idea," she said icily.

They were interrupted by the waiter delivering their food. They both remained silent as the plates were set on the table, their water glasses refreshed and a basket of rolls placed in the center of the table.

"I'd hoped you'd be pleased with the idea," Morgan told her, picking up his fork and stabbing at his tuna. "We could use your support now."

"No, Morgan," she replied, not moving toward her food. "You will not get my support on this. Nor on any plan to delay what ultimately must be done."

"I won't sell Sweetgrass," he ground out, setting his fork down.

"You won't have a choice," she countered. "You don't know all the facts, Morgan."

"What facts?" he asked, instantly alert.

"There's the matter of the loan."

He bridled. "What loan? There's no record of any loan. I've been through all the bank statements."

"This wasn't done through a bank. It was a private loan. From me."

"From you? For how much?"

"Five hundred thousand dollars."

His eyes bulged. "Five hundred *thousand?* When did this happen?"

"In 1989, after Hurricane Hugo. The farm was devastated, remember?" When he nodded, she continued. "Then you remember that your father lost his barns, most of his livestock and equipment, the crops… He was ruined. He couldn't re-build. He would have lost the place then."

Morgan rubbed his brow, recalling those hard times. "The whole area was hit bad, but I remember he said we were lucky. The house remained standing. And the avenue of oaks. He took it as a sign."

"Yes," she replied softly with a sad smile. "I remember him saying that. I couldn't agree with him, though. My house on Sullivan's Island was swept away, along with everything in it. I didn't feel like counting my blessings." She paused and looked off. "But it was Preston's style to do just that."

"Yes, it was."

"But we digress," she said, focusing on the current situa-tion. "He was in dire straits, so he came to me for help."

"And you lent him money."

"Under the most favorable of terms. He's my brother. I wanted to help him, but I couldn't afford to gift him the money. I dropped the annual rate to a lower rate. It was the best I could do and better than he could get anywhere else. He recognized that he might not get on his feet, and if such was the case, we set up a bailout, so if we had to sell, we'd split the profits at a sixty-forty split." She took a sip of her drink to give Morgan a chance to digest all that she'd just told him.

"Why did you wait to tell me?" he asked.

"I'd hoped it wouldn't come to this. I gave you every

chance to come to the decision to sell, which I still maintain is the only sensible thing to do. You must sell, Morgan."

"My father—your brother—loves that place. It means more to him than a home. It's his life's work. And you want to take it from him?"

"I understand he loves the property," she replied patiently. "I also understand that you love the property. But someone in this family has to be practical. Mama June needs to eat. Your father's nurse needs to be paid. And if the taxes aren't settled, the whole lot will be taken from him, anyway. Morgan, stop spinning your wheels. You really don't have a choice in this."

"Aunt Adele, just give us a little more time. I'll find a way to repay the money. I swear."

"I've waited fifteen years already, for my brother's sake. With Preston out of the picture—no offense, dear—I'm no longer confident I'll see the return of my sizable investment." She picked up her fork and began jabbing at her salad. "No. My mind is made up. I'm not waiting any longer. I have a buyer and the land will be sold."

Morgan stood up abruptly and pulled his wallet from his pocket. He took out several bills and laid them on the table. "This isn't over, Adele. No matter what you might think. I'll find a way to pay back that loan."

"You still aren't listening. There is no more time," she replied.

Morgan turned on his heel and marched from the restaurant, eager to get as much space between him and his aunt as possible. He slammed into a wall of heat and humidity when he stepped into the harsh, unforgiving sunlight. He stopped and stood squinting in the glare, dazed and wondering what the hell he would do next.

Five hundred thousand dollars. He'd been so stunned by the news that he didn't even ask how much was left to pay on the loan. But even if it was half as much, he knew they couldn't afford to repay it. They were limping by as it was. Even if he sold his ranch, he couldn't raise that much capital. And besides, there wasn't time. If he knew his darling aunt, she'd sic the lawyers on them immediately.

He went in search of a phone. He needed to call his lawyer, too.

Later that afternoon, Hank walked into Adele's office just as she was finishing a call to her lawyer. She lifted a finger in the air for him to wait. Her dark eyes watched him as he glanced around the room, his fingers fidgeting with impatience.

Hank was a handsome man, stocky yet fit in a crisp white cotton shirt and tie, even vain about his appearance. Good looks and amiability were an asset in the real estate business and Hank used these attributes as weapons. He was what she liked to call a back-slapper, a convivial fellow always ready with a clever quip or a joke. He was a fun guest at a party, but never too rowdy or too off-color, and never controversial. Most people were not aware of Hank's driving ambition. Beneath his easygoing facade he was hungry for power and wealth. Adele understood this hunger, even sympathized with it. She mentored Hank because he was both promising and loyal. And because he was the closest thing to a son she'd ever have.

She hung up the phone and indicated a chair with a turn of her hand. Hank sat down and crossed his legs.

"What's up?" he asked, eyes alert.

"I've just had lunch with my nephew."

"Morgan?" he asked, surprised.

She nodded. "He has a plan to save Sweetgrass," she said with exaggeration.

Hank frowned at the news. She reached into her purse and pulled out a package of cigarettes. Lighting one, she inhaled deeply, taking a moment to settle the pique that rose at the memory of the meeting.

"It was enough that I had to spend days with him going through every shred of paper in Preston's possession." She shook her head with disgust. "What a mess. I don't know how anyone can be so disorganized. I deserve an award for putting up with my nephew's attitude for so long without whittling him down to size. But this takes the cake. He has this idea of putting the land under a conservation easement. "

Hank shifted in his seat. "That's not a bad idea."

She scoffed. "It's not going to happen. We both know that. I'm at my wit's end, I tell you. When he called to schedule this meeting, I thought for sure he was going to tell me that they needed to sell. I was prepared to give him the good news about the buyers for the property and it would have been a happy ending." She took a long drag from her cigarette, then snuffed it out. "It's a shame it has to be this way," she said, exhaling.

"Are you sure?" Hank asked. "You don't want to be wrong about this."

Adele nodded. "I can say with assurance that they do not have a copy of my partnership agreement with Preston. I've just talked to my lawyers. They're starting the legal papers."

That evening, Nan drove home from Sweetgrass along the winding, tree-lined road. It was a dark night with no stars and heavy cloud cover. She took the curves slowly, wary of slow-moving possum or the sudden leap of a deer. When she pulled off Rifle Range Road into her development, she took a ragged breath and sighed, dog tired. She craved a hot bath, a chilled glass of wine and bed—in that order.

She'd volunteered to sit with Daddy so Mama June could go to bed early tonight. Morgan had taken Kristina into Charleston for dinner. He was fit to be tied when he came back from his lunch with Aunt Adele, but he wouldn't go into it. They were oil and water, those two, she thought, wishing it were different. It would make her home life easier.

As for Kristina, she and Morgan had been hanging out a lot lately. "We're just friends," Morgan had told her. She smiled. This *friendship* was a hot topic of conservation between Mama June and Nona on the back porch

The lights were burning in the living room as she pulled up to her own house. With a groan, she saw Aunt Adele's car parked in the driveway, carelessly blocking the entrance to the garage. Nan parked the car on the grass. She felt the humidity slam into her as she stepped from the air-conditioning of her SUV into the thick air of a Southern summer night. The crickets pierced the silence with swells of song, and frogs bellowed in the wetlands.

Nan slipped through the back door and made her way to the kitchen, careful not to make any noise so she could escape the heated discussion going on in the living room. She was about to tiptoe past when she heard Hank mention Sweetgrass. Nan paused, instantly alert, and leaned against the hall wall to listen.

"I don't know how much longer we can avoid giving them an answer," Hank said. "This group wants to move now. If we can't deliver Sweetgrass, they'll move on to another project."

"They're grandstanding," Adele replied. "There's very little out there with the same attractiveness or history of Sweetgrass."

"All true. But what good is that if the family won't sell?"

"They'll sell," she declared. Adele exhaled her frustration in a curse. "That boy's been a bother since he was in short pants. Morgan is family and he's had a hard time of it. But why doesn't he just go on back to Montana? Ever since he got here he's been interfering with business that's no concern of his."

"He can get pretty high-handed," Hank agreed. "When I offered to help, he just thanked me and smiled in that polite way of his that tells you to shove off."

"What did you expect? He knows you work for me."

"We should all be working on the same team."

"Agreed. But he doesn't see it that way. How can I get him to understand that selling right now is the best for all concerned? He stands to make a substantial sum of money. A deal like this one is hard to put together."

"You're preaching to the choir. Do you know how many man-hours I've put into this deal?" Hank asked disagreeably. "The dinners? The trips?"

"If all goes as planned, you'll be more than recompensed."

"I'm counting on it. So what do you want to do next? Time's a wastin'."

There was a long pause. Nan leaned closer to the door, straining to hear.

"Everything is in order. It's time to lay my cards on the table."

"When do you plan to do that?"

"I haven't been very good about making an appearance at Sunday dinner. I seem to make everyone uncomfortable lately. But I'll make the effort so Mama June will know my heart is in the right place. We want to minimize the stress and antagonism. They won't like what they hear."

"But they won't have a choice," he said in conclusion. "The buyout offer is ready and waiting for signatures."

"Good. Well," she said, "that should wrap things up. I'll head on home. I haven't fed my dogs yet and they'll be frantic."

Nan heard a chair scraping the floor. She didn't linger to hear the parting comments. She hurried up the stairs. In her room she changed into her nightclothes, then sat in the bed against the piled pillows with the blankets tucked around her waist. She waited for Hank to come up, her mind spinning with questions. At last he joined her in the bedroom, unbuttoning his shirt and yawning.

"What a day," he said, tugging the shirt off. "I'm beat."

"Why did Adele stop by so late?" she asked.

"Business, as usual." He sat on the cushioned bench at the foot of the bed and bent to untie his shoelaces. She heard the thud as each shoe hit the hardwood floor. When he straightened again, he turned toward her, mild surprise on his face. "When did you get home? I didn't hear you come in."

"Not too long ago," she replied.

"How's Preston?"

"A little better."

"Can he form words yet?"

She shook her head. "He's struggling, but he'll get there."

That seemed to end Hank's interest in her father's progress. He began removing his wristwatch.

"What's this about buyers for Sweetgrass?" she asked him point blank.

He swung his head around to glare at her, then with a frown, stood and set his watch on the dresser. She wondered if he viewed her as one of "the other side" now that she'd been volunteering with Daddy's care and spending so much time at Sweetgrass. If so, it was just one more chasm between them. She waited, hands folded on her legs.

"Remember that group from Maryland?" he asked. "The ones who came for dinner?"

"I made she-crab soup for them."

"Right. Well, they've decided to pursue the purchase of Sweetgrass."

"But Mama June doesn't want to sell it."

His shoulders slumped. "Honey, I don't mean no disre-spect, but your mother doesn't know what's best for her."

Nan's back stiffened. "And you do?"

"Yes," he replied, seemingly offended by her sarcasm. "I believe I do." He sighed with resignation and sat down on the mattress beside her. "Sweetheart, how many times must we have this conversation? You have to trust that I know the real estate business better than you do. And a helluva lot more than your brother." This apparently hit a sore point, for his temper flared. "He owns a few measly acres he calls a ranch. What does he know about tax law and maintaining a property like Sweetgrass?"

She thought of the many times she'd walked by Daddy's office to find Morgan nose deep in papers and books, or meeting with Bobby and their banker, huddled in conversa-tion. Or the times she'd leave late at night and wave at him as he burned the midnight oil bent over papers on the desk with a glass of bourbon.

She'd always known Morgan was real smart. He knew so much about a lot of different subjects. But he'd never done well in school, mostly because he often ditched classes. The teachers would call and talk to Mama June about how it was such a shame, him being so smart and all. The phrase they always used was "not working up to his potential."

But no matter who said what, Morgan plain hated going to school. He said he was bored, but even as a kid, Nan fig-ured out that he wasn't the same after Hamlin died. He stopped sports—even fishing, which he'd loved—and he never went back out to Blakely's Bluff. Instead, he'd always sneak off alone to the kitchen house or somewhere else with a book in his hand. He'd be mad when he caught her spying and angrily tell her to mind her own business. That was the main thing that was different after Hamlin died—Morgan got angry.

"I think he might know a lot," she replied.

Hank drew himself up, appearing wounded. "By that I assume you mean he knows more than me?"

"No," she replied, weary of the argument. "I mean there's a difference of opinion."

"Including your own, apparently." He looked at her with reproach. "It would have been polite to make your presence known instead of eavesdropping."

"Oh, cut it out, Hank." She was tired and had had enough of his false injury and superior tone. "This is my house and I can walk anywhere I want to in it. Not to mention, I'm not the one sneaking around," she added ominously. "If you and Adele are having secret meetings about my family, then you can have them outside our home."

"*My* home."

She skipped a beat. "I beg your pardon?"

He smiled urbanely, but it was cruel. "A brief lesson in business, my dear. Get your name on the deed."

Her mind stumbled over the implications. "What are you saying?"

"I'm simply stating a fact. This house is in my name."

"That was just a formality," she blurted out. "We talked about that. I was home with a newborn baby." She paused, registering what was being said. "The house was bought with my money," she reminded him.

"Nonetheless…"

She felt suddenly cold and wrapped her arms around her, blinking with agitation.

"Are you threatening me?"

"No, no, of course not!" He leaned closer, resting his weight against his hands on the mattress. "Honey, I love you.

I shouldn't have said that. I'm sorry. I must be more tired than I thought after going a few rounds with Adele. You know I don't mean it. I'm just trying to point out to you that sometimes women don't make the best business decisions."

She pushed back from his arms, physically repelled by his argument, unsure of what to say next. She'd heard this kind of statement all of her life, from her father and husband both. She wondered how many women had.

She drew a long breath, the weariness of the day weighing her down.

Hank frowned, and with an air of resignation, he straightened back from the mattress and placed his hands on his hips, studying her.

"So, that's how it is," he said with a tone of finality.

"Yes," she replied. "That's how it is."

She saw disappointment, then hurt, flicker in his eyes.

"Hank, let's not argue any more about this. It doesn't concern us."

"It doesn't concern us?" he exploded. "You know how hard I've worked on this. Nan, we need this deal to go through. I need it. Come on, honey, it's a good offer! And I'd be in line to manage the new development. We stand to make a big difference in our lifestyle. You're always talking about the past. About your heritage. Think about the future! Think what this will mean to our sons."

"I am thinking about my sons!" she exclaimed, her voice rising to match his. "And my family. The Blakely family. You've made it abundantly clear you want no part of them. But you're more than willing to make a profit off them." She regretted the words the moment she spat them out, but could not take them back.

He appeared blindsided. "Not for me. For *us.*"

She looked at her hands, torn by the emotion in his voice.

He reached out to touch her arm. "Nan…"

She shrank back from his hand. After an awkward silence, she said, "Even so."

He took a breath and straightened, increasing the distance.

Nan could think clearly now and found her voice. "For years you've belittled my family in front of our sons. In front of me. I didn't say anything, knowing how things were between you and Daddy. I was embarrassed for the treatment we both received. But, Hank, we have to see both sides. We did sell the land my father entrusted to me and it crushed him. My sons are the last in the Blakely line, yet we didn't give them a Blakely name. That hurt my father, you know it did. It's been tit for tat over the years and I want it to stop.

"Don't you see? Sweetgrass isn't just real estate. You can't measure its worth in dollars and cents. It's our home. It's who we are. It's where we're from. I'm afraid of what will happen to us if we lose it. That's what's at stake here, don't you see? That's what I want for my sons."

He looked at her long and hard, and she felt he'd really listened to her for the first time. She felt the stirrings of hope.

"I feel you've turned against me in this," he said.

Defeat washed over her. He'd offered opposition when she'd hoped for support. A profound sadness seeped into her bones, softening them, slumping her shoulders.

"Oh, Hank," she said wearily, "I'm not turning against anyone."

"Then support *me*."

There it was. The gauntlet was thrown on the ground between them. She knew they were talking about much more than the Sweetgrass deal. This was about him making all the decisions and her following them. This was about her continuing to give up her identity to absorb more of his. Rather than him supporting her during this stressful time, she was being asked to support him, regardless of her needs, or her desires, or even her happiness.

She looked up at him and held his gaze, loving him, yet at the same time feeling her backbone stiffen.

"I can't," she replied softly. Then, with more conviction, "I won't."

15

Basket makers are forced to travel outside the region in search of an increasingly scarce supply of sweetgrass, usually as far as Georgia and Florida. Many basket stands have been forced to move farther north or are displaced.

THE GRAVEL CRUNCHED as Nan circled the pond, then came to a stop in front of Mama June's house. Cutting the engine, she sat in the deep country silence. She wiped her eyes and leaned over to check her reflection in the rearview mirror. At least no one could tell she'd been crying. She glanced at her suitcase in the back seat.

Nan entered the house smiling. "Hi y'all, I'm home," she called out.

Blackjack immediately came trotting out from Preston's room, his hips wagging as hard as his tail, whining with excitement. She might only be gone for a day, but each time she returned, Blackjack cried as if she'd been gone for months.

"Take it easy, ol' boy," she crooned, stroking his black-and-gray head, which was pressed against her thigh. His muzzle was almost entirely gray now, she noted with a twinge of regret.

Sweetgrass

The dog was at her heels as she went first to her father. She thought his color looked better, and she was glad to see him sitting up in his wheelchair by the window. He'd lost so much weight that she still couldn't reconcile this frail man with the robust and ruddy father she'd grown up with. But his blue eyes shone when he saw her coming, and he reached his left arm out in a clumsy move toward her.

"Hey, handsome!" she exclaimed, leaning over to place a noisy kiss on his cheek. "Don't you look fit today? An ironed shirt, too! Mama June's got you all decked out for Sunday dinner."

She sniffed the air. "Something smells good, too. They're cooking up a storm. Lord, I'm so hungry I could eat a house. And you know what I brought?" Her eyes sparkled as she pulled out a package wrapped in brown waxed paper. "Some shrimp straight off the boat. I stopped at Shem Creek specially. And Vidalia onions! Your favorite. I've got a bunch of goodies to carry in from the car. I'll bring it on into the kitchen, then come back and visit, okay?"

Her spirits lifted. It felt so good to be able to walk into the house and hug her daddy again, freely and without reserve. The past weeks of helping her father with the simple tasks of daily living—eating, dressing, communicating— had reversed the role of parent and child. Disconcerting as it may have been at first, in time she'd come to feel his gratitude. And his love. A pat of his hand, the lighting up of his eyes when she entered the room—these gentle gestures, rather than grand ones, had served to stanch old wounds and help repair the bond between father and daughter.

Her arms were loaded with a box chock-full of fresh strawberries she'd picked up from the strawberry patch down the road. As she passed Preston's room into the kitchen, she hoped he'd be able to enjoy the meal. He'd been having difficulty lately with his swallowing.

"Look what I've brought!" she called out as she entered the kitchen. She stopped short at the door.

There were dozens of empty strawberry cartons stacked on the counters and the kitchen was redolent with their sweet scent. Nona and Mama June were both wearing aprons and stirring big pots at the stove. They looked up in unison when she walked in.

"Oh, brother. Talk about coals to Newcastle," Nan said, lifting her berries up with a laugh.

"We can never have too many berries," Mama June exclaimed with a light chuckle. "The more the merrier. Bring them on over to the sink and we'll wash them."

"We're gettin' up a head of steam now. Been putting up berries for days," Nona added. "These are the last of them. We can use your fresh berries for the ice cream."

"Just be sure to take some jam home with you tonight," Mama June added.

"I surely will."

"I hope you remembered to bring the shrimp."

"The shrimp?" Nan's face froze.

Mama June's head snapped up, her eyes blazing. "Don't even tell me…"

Nan laughed and hoisted the brown bag as evidence.

"You!" Mama June scolded, her cheeks coloring as she laughed. "You're worse than your boys, the way you act up."

Nan was buoyed by the banter. She carried the shrimp and berries to the sink, looking around for a spare inch of space. The table was covered with jars of cooling jam. Every few minutes she'd hear the cheery pop of a lid. Hearing the sound and seeing Nona and Mama June in aprons at the stove together brought to mind when she was little and the kitchen was her favorite place. She used to sit at the table like a cat and watch for the sucking in of the lid, laughing each time she heard the popping noise.

"The table is full up. Where are we eating tonight?" she asked.

"It's such a nice afternoon, I thought we'd eat out on the porch," Mama June replied. "We've already started setting up, but you might could see what we forgot. Morgan's out there churning the ice cream."

"Morgan? This I've got to see."

The porch was swept and a light breeze fluttered the corners of the pale pink tablecloth. Glass vases of gerbera daisies in brilliant shades of pink, small votive candles and stainless tableware anchored the fabric to the table. Soon enough, Mama June and Nona would carry out bowls of food, filling every available inch of space.

"Hey, sister," Morgan called out, a little breathless from the effort of hand-churning the ice cream. "What are you smiling about?"

"Hi, Morgan," she replied easily. "I was just thinking how, even when the table is casual, Mama June manages to make it festive."

"That's our mother."

Mama June came out, wiping her hands on her apron. "What about your mother?"

Nan's eyes softened at the sight of her. In all these years, her mother had changed surprisingly little. Despite her nagging Mama June to update her hair, her clothes, her shoes, there was something classic, even comforting, about seeing the timeless quality of her beauty. Her clothes were understated yet of enduring quality. Her face was smooth, lines crossing only at the brow and at the corners of her remarkable eyes. Mama June's white hair was neatly wound in the same style she'd worn for years. But tonight there was something else. Nan saw a new happiness glowing in her eyes.

"I was just complimenting your table."

"Why, thank you, Nan. I try."

"Honestly, Mama, I'm just going to give up trying. For years I've tried to keep up the tradition of family dinner at home, but it's just so hard. The boys groan when I try to make them."

"Can you blame them?" quipped Morgan.

"I'm serious," she replied to her brother with a mock scowl. "And these days, who has time to polish the silver or hand-wash the good china? How do you do it, Mama?"

"You forget I stopped," she replied wryly.

Nan remembered those sad days in a rush. The Sunday dinners had ceased suddenly and Mama hadn't come down from her room for the longest time. The whole household, which had been full of laughter, became as silent as a tomb. Her recollections must have shown on her face for her mother drew closer and wrapped an arm around her.

"You just wait till your boys are older and move out. You'll have lots more time on your hands then. And when the blessed day comes that you're a grandmother—" she squeezed Nan's shoulders "—*then* you'll have both time and the desire to fuss over such details, enjoying each one of them. Pack up your crystal and save your china for later, darlin'. Use paper plates if you have to. What's most important is bringing the family together. Family is everything."

Nan nodded, but the wobbly smile alerted Mama June that something was amiss. Her daughter's emotions were running too strong tonight. The cheeriness was a little too sunny, her voice a tad too high-pitched.

"Nan, is anything wrong?"

"No." Her lower lip trembled as she ventured a lopsided smile.

"I can see that. Come sit for a spell," she said, guiding Nan to a chair. She glanced questioningly at Morgan. He raised his shoulders in a confused shrug. They moved to the white wood rocking chairs in the corner and settled in. Nan looked at her hands.

"What's the matter?"

"It's nothing," Nan said. "I'm just overtired."

Mama June recognized the lie. "That's not true," she said gently.

Nan looked up. "This is my business, Mama."

Mama June looked at her daughter's rigid expression, even as her lips quaked with emotion. Nan had never been good at hiding her emotions. Unlike her brothers who excelled at the poker face, Nan was more like her and could no more hide her joy than her sadness. Her spontaneity was one of Nan's most endearing qualities. It made her a delightful hostess, a thoughtful friend and a zealous volunteer. But Lord, she could be stubborn, too. What standoffs they'd had while Nan was growing up, especially in the teen years! *That* quality Mama June thought she'd inherited from her father.

Mama June leaned back against the rocker. "It is your business, true enough," she replied. She tried another approach. "When will the boys be here?"

"They're not coming."

"No? I'm sorry to hear that. Hank, too?"

"He can't make it. It's just me."

"Are they ill?"

Her brow furrowed deeper. "I told the boys not to come."

Mama June stopped rocking and looked at Nan to explain.

"Mama, I'm fed up with their bellyaching about Sunday dinner. All they do is complain and whine till I can't stand it anymore. I've raised them to respect their elders, even if Daddy isn't easy to be around for them right now. Everything in life isn't fun, they might as well learn that right now." She frowned with sadness. "I…I let them know I was disappointed in them. What I really said was that they shouldn't come unless they wanted to. They're too old to force and I'm too old to keep yammering at them. They are who they are. It's their decision." She sighed and shook her head with defeat. "I wouldn't set places for them."

"Aw, hell, they're teenage boys," Morgan said in their defense. "They're being led by a different organ than their brain. The last thing they want to do is hang around a bunch of old farts on a porch every Sunday night. Trust me, they've other plans."

"That doesn't matter," Nan fired back. "They don't have respect for the family, for their grandparents, for tradition— and certainly not for me. You should hear them talk back! I never would have dared say those things to Mama June or Daddy. I don't know what I've done wrong."

"Where's their father?" Mama June asked with pique. "Seems to me he should have a strong hand in rearing those boys."

"Hank…" Nan said with a dismissive shake of the head. "He's a workaholic, and when he is around, he spoils them, trying to make up for having been gone so much. He buys them anything they want—a car, a boat, Xbox. He's the nice parent. The pal. I'm the mean parent. I do the day-to-day duty. I try to discipline them. But if they don't want to do what I tell them, Hank tells me to let up on them. He gives them that 'you know, she's a girl' roll-of-the-eye thing. The boys eat it up."

"But in the end, you back down," Morgan said.

Her eyes widened as she stared back at him.

The statement was not said with a cruel spirit. Mama June thought it summed things up honestly.

"It's three against one," Nan said in her defense.

Morgan shrugged again and lifted his palms.

Sweetgrass

There was an awkward silence as Nan stared down at her hands. A fat tear fell from her eyes and she nodded. "I back down," she conceded.

Mama June reached into her apron pocket, pulled out a tissue and handed it to Nan. She tapped at her eyes and sniffed.

Morgan set aside the ice cream churner and leaned forward, resting his elbows on his knees. "Look, Nan, you're a good mother, and I have to hand it to you, you laid down the law this time. Harry and Chas are good kids. They stay out of trouble, they're not on drugs, they're doing okay in school." His lips twitched. "And they know which fork to use. I know. I've watched."

Nan sniffled and laughed, grateful for the backhanded compliment.

"It doesn't give them permission to be rude," Mama June countered.

"That's right," Nan agreed. "Mama June never took back talk from you or Hamlin."

Mama June laughed lightly. "Oh, I wouldn't say that."

Morgan shook his head. "No, Nan's right. That's what I was getting at. There are limits. You and Daddy drew clear lines not to cross, and if we did, we got knuckled. Especially Daddy." His face darkened. "He drew his lines too strong, if you want to know the truth. He was a pain in the..." He caught himself and glanced at his mother. She was giving him a warning look. "He could really go off the deep end."

"Especially with Hamlin," added Nan.

Morgan swung his head up to glare at her. "Especially with Ham?" he exclaimed. "What, are you kidding? What house did you grow up in? He rode my tail like a hurricane. Nothing I did was ever right. Hamlin was the golden son."

Nan opened her mouth to argue, but Mama June raised her palm.

"Stop it, both of you," she said. She couldn't bear to hear Hamlin's name being brought up like this, as if he were still alive. With a lower voice she said, "We loved you all the same. Treated you all the same."

Morgan snorted, slumped back in his chair and crossed his arms, drawing Mama June's attention.

In contrast, Nan leaned forward to wrap her arms around her mother. As a woman, she knew instinctively that Mama June felt a sudden pang of longing for her dead son.

"Let's not make an issue of it. We know you did," Nan said. Pulling back, she added quietly, "And I love my boys equally, too. I love them both too much, that's my problem."

Mama June's smile was bittersweet. "What is it about sons?"

They heard a rumble of gravel in the driveway getting louder and closer. Then came Blackjack's rousing alert bark. Morgan crossed the porch and leaned forward over the railing, peering out at the front driveway. When he turned back, he had a crooked grin on his face.

"I'm glad you love them so much," he said, "because the two rascals just showed up."

The local shrimp was peeled and boiled in Old Bay spice. Red potatoes and bright green beans were slathered together in vinegar and oil and set beside a wooden bowl of freshly picked green salad. A plate of ripe tomatoes and Vidalia onions, homemade pickles, crusty bread, a cream cake and a pitcher of sweet tea that had been cooling on the porch all afternoon and was ready to be poured over ice rounded out the meal. The pièce de résistance of the night, however, would be the homemade ice cream served with fresh berries.

"Well, I guess that's that," Nona said, untying her apron. "All that's left is the eating." She moved slowly after a long day of canning and dinner preparations.

"Thank you so much for coming in today," said Mama June. "I've never seen so many strawberries."

"You say that every year. Wait till the peaches start."

"Lord help me, I can't wait. It looks like it will be a banner year." She sighed and put her hands on her hips. "Look at all this! Honestly, Nona, I couldn't have managed it this year without you. Are you sure you took enough jam? Do you need another box?"

"I'm all set," Nona replied, her eyes surveying the box of glass jars filled with bright red strawberry jam. This was a good batch, she thought. The strawberries were some of the sweetest she'd ever put up. As she counted the jars, in her mind she worked out that she'd give some to Maize, of course. And she'd keep some herself. The rest she'd set aside for gifts.

"Elmore should be along any minute to pick me up," she said. "He's out gathering more sweetgrass from the sacred spot. We've got a long line of folks that are waiting for grass. It's getting scarcer than hen's teeth. We can't keep up with the demand." She tilted her head as the front chimes rang out. "Speak of the devil."

"Don't run off," Mama June said as she untied her own apron. "Why don't you and Elmore stay?"

Nona paused, her apron in her hand. Slowly, she set it down on the kitchen counter. "Are you asking us for dinner?"

"Of course," Mama June replied readily. She gathered her apron, stained with jelly juice, into a ball and tossed it on a chair. When she looked up, her eyes were bright with welcome. "Do you think you can?"

The women's eyes connected. They both silently acknowledged that though they'd shared many meals in all the years, this was the first invitation extended for dinner as guests.

A slow smile spread across Nona's face. "That'd be real nice. I believe we can."

"Here he comes!"

Kristina maneuvered Preston's wheelchair out onto the back porch while the rest of the family stood to greet him, calling out hellos. The family was in high spirits. Mama June helped settle Preston into his place at the head of the table, the first time since his return home. His eyes were shining with pride and the bone-deep contentment she'd often seen on his face when he was looking out over his beloved plantation. This time, however, he was overlooking the smiling faces of his family and she felt her chest puff up so full, she thought she would burst.

She joined him in the survey of the table. To his right, Nona was seated beside her husband. Next to Elmore sat Nan whose eyes were as large as dinner plates as she beamed at her sons across the table. Harry and Chas, with the ignorance of youth, had no idea how happy they'd made their mother this evening, nor how proud their grandparents. It would be many more years before they'd come to realize that the gestures from the heart meant far more to parents than something purchased from a store. Kristina took a seat at the far end of the table, and Mama June didn't think it escaped anyone's notice that Morgan took the chair beside hers. Blackjack was content sitting a few feet away from the table with his bone.

After Mama June took her seat beside Preston, the family gathered hands and she led them in the blessing. As she said the words, she felt a strong connection with the people in the circle. Everyone she loved most in the world was gathered around her. Over the many years of her long life, she had met more people than she could remember, wonderful, charming people that she'd grown very fond of, as well as horrid, self-ish, egocentric adults she hoped never to meet again.

Yet in the twilight of her life, she'd come to realize that the people who truly mattered were the precious few who had stood by her through the worst times and the best. They were at her table tonight. She felt Preston squeeze her hand, and looking up, she knew that his thoughts were running in the same vein. With a resounding "Amen!" hands were released and as one they reached for the serving bowls. Laughter sang out from the porch as the feast was passed from person to person as quickly as the stories.

Later that night, Adele and Hank pulled up to the house. The sleek lines of the baby-blue Jaguar hugged the curves and came to a smooth stop. Adele cut the engine and looked out at the house she'd grown up in. The lights were shining on the back porch, and even with the car windows closed they could hear the quiet broken by high-pitched laughter. Curious, Adele drove the car farther around the circle for a better vantage point.

"Sounds like a party," Hank said.

Adele didn't reply. She pressed a button and the window rolled down with a smooth hum. It was a balmy night with a brisk breeze, perfect weather for sitting on a porch. Over the song of crickets and the bellowing call of frogs in the marsh, she heard the sweeter music of family talk amid the clinking glassware.

As her eyes grew accustomed to the dark, she could just make out the people sitting around the long table. She recognized the small frame of Mama June. Who was that beside her? Nona? Why, yes it was! Beside her...

"Is that Nan?" she asked Hank.

Hank leaned forward and squinted. "Yes," he said with an odd coolness.

"And Harry and Chas?"

He hesitated. "I didn't think they were coming."

She felt a small twinge of jealousy upon seeing the boys at Sweetgrass. "I thought you had your wife under control." She narrowed her eyes, trying to make out the person sitting at the head of the table. She gasped when she caught a glimpse of the thick shock of white hair.

"Why, Preston's sitting at the table! Did you know he was doing so much better?"

"He's been sitting up for a long time."

"Really?" Adele looked at Hank with a sharpness that belied her surprise. "I didn't know. You never told me. I just assumed he was lying in bed, rather like a vegetable."

"Oh, no. They had him up and out pretty quick. I have to hand it to Mama June. She's fierce as a lioness about him being part of family life."

"What a lucky man," she murmured.

"Preston?" Hank scoffed. "Yeah, right. The man's in a wheelchair, he can't walk or talk, and you call him lucky."

Adele studied the man beside her in the car. Hank looked younger than his forty years. He was a hard worker, had a good future, a great family. Anyone would think he was a fine specimen of health. But she knew that already he was on two different medications for high blood pressure.

"You never know," she told him. "In a few years, that could be you in that wheelchair. Oh, don't shake your head like that," she said with a wry smile. "Preston looked fit as a fiddle the day before his stroke. What you have to ask yourself is, if it happens to you and you are stuck in a wheelchair, will your kids care enough to be sitting at Sunday dinner with you?"

Sweetgrass

The smirk slipped from Hank's face. He didn't reply but turned to look out at the porch as a fresh round of laughter sounded in the breeze.

Adele's thoughts slipped back to nights just like this one when she was a young girl and this was her home. She'd forgotten what that kind of security felt like. Back then, no one in the parish had air-conditioning. Most summer evenings after the dinner dishes were cleaned, the family went out on the back porch for relief from the heat. The breeze blew in off the creek and the screens did their job keeping out the bugs. While the radio played, Daddy read his paper, Mama did needlework and she and Preston and Tripp might play a board game or cards and listen to the crickets sing. Nothing remarkable. She might have even complained about being bored.

"I almost hate to spoil their evening."

"That's not a good idea," he replied testily. "The papers are signed, dated and ready to deliver. And lest we forget, our clients are eager to move forward. There's nothing to be gained by waiting until tomorrow. We're here. We're ready. Let's get it done and deal with the aftermath tomorrow."

Adele knew what he said was true. She glanced again at the porch in indecision. There was movement and the scraping of chairs. The family seemed to be headed back indoors.

"All right," she said at length. "You deliver them to Morgan. I'll wait here."

Adele sat in her car smoking a cigarette while Hank delivered the papers. She was fully aware that she was sitting alone in the dark, on the outside, looking in at a home that would never be hers.

The thought brought a deep pain that still had the power to make her wince. She'd spent a fortune on psychiatrists, but the resentment was bigger than her. She couldn't get past it. The resentment was so old and deep, it had formed who she was today.

She had never married, never wanted to give up her independence to a man, never wanted children of her own. With her dark, glossy hair, her lean good looks and her sense of style—not to mention her pedigree—it wasn't because she didn't have offers. Adele never felt the need to get married. She never desired what she thought was the boring, limiting life of a wife and mother. She'd been totally absorbed by her career; it was the top priority in her life. While she was growing up, her family had been land rich but cash poor. She'd been determined to make lots of money on her own, and in her coastal real estate business she'd succeeded beyond her imagination.

But money had nothing to do with her deep-rooted anger against her parents, her brother and especially Mary June Clark for cutting her out of the family circle.

She looked at the charming house that seemed to glow in the soft light emanating from the mullioned windows. Seeing it made her blood congeal. She was raised in that house, too. This was *her* family home. Every time she drove away and saw Mary June standing at the door waving her goodbye, she wanted to scratch her eyes out.

The business should be completed quickly, she thought, and took another lazy puff from her cigarette. Suddenly the front door of the house slammed open and Morgan came marching out on a beeline for her. He walked with angry purpose, and in his hands he clutched the opened legal papers.

"Hell," she muttered, tamping down her cigarette. As he drew closer, she rolled her window farther down and raised her face in a starchy smile. "Morgan!" she exclaimed when he stopped at the window and bent to peer in. His face was dark with fury.

"What the hell is this?" he demanded, shaking the papers in his fist.

"You've read them?" she asked calmly.

"Of course I did. But they don't make a goddamn bit of sense."

"Watch your language if you wish to discuss this with me."

"I am watching my language! If you knew what I was thinking…"

Adele lifted her chin archly, but did not reply.

Morgan raked his free hand through his hair, reining in his fury, then took a deep breath. "Would you please come inside and discuss this in my father's office, Aunt Adele?" he asked in a strained, polite tone.

"I'd rather not," she replied. "It's late and I should think there's nothing left to discuss."

"You think—" he blurted, then stopped before he said something he couldn't retract. "You told me we owed you five hundred grand. But this says you're buying us out!"

"That's correct. The loan is in default, which you would have learned had you not stormed out of the restaurant. Your father failed to meet his interest payments."

Her calm was like kerosene on an open flame. He struggled to maintain his fury.

"He never told me about it."

Adele looked at him askance. "Should he have? Where do you come in here? Morgan, do you really think you've been privy to your father's business arrangements? You've hardly spoken to your father in the past ten years."

Morgan's gaze sharpened. "What is this agreement, exactly?"

"It's a loan with a partnership proviso activated upon default. Or if one partner dies or is incapacitated. In either case, I'm activating the buyout clause."

Morgan was thunderstruck. "So you're telling me you will own part of Sweetgrass?"

"No. I'll own all of it."

"I don't believe it!" he shouted. "Daddy would never deed away Sweetgrass for a loan. He'd put it up for collateral. That would make sense. But sell? No, never. Something's not right."

"It's all there," she said calmly, indicating the papers. She shifted in the car to face him more directly. "Now, listen to me clearly, Morgan. My partnership agreement is with your father, not you. And though this breaks my heart, your father is no longer capable as a partner. There is a buy-sell clause in that partnership that allows for me to buy out the ownership interest of this property—and I intend to do so. I have an attractive offer for this property. I'll allow you, because you're family, to sell to this buyer immediately. If you do, I'll agree to split the profits sixty-forty. It's a generous offer. You stand to walk away with a tidy profit. Everyone in your family does."

"And if we won't?"

"If you won't, I'll have no choice but to exercise my option to buy out the partnership according to the terms of the contract."

He looked away, his jaw working.

Adele's voice softened. "Morgan, dear, I appreciate what you're trying to do. But heroics now will get you and the family in trouble. We both love your father. However, I've faced the facts. I don't believe you have."

"You can stick your facts."

Her face grew hard and she threw up her hands. "Enough is enough. I'll have my lawyer send you a fair market price for the land in the morning."

"What's in it for you?"

She looked him in the eye. "What's in it for *you?*"

"I'm doing this for my mother."

"Ah, your mother. Well," she said with a bitter smile. "That's another story, isn't it? I wouldn't get involved with that if I were you. It goes too far back." She turned the key to start the car. The engine roared with power, then settled into a gravelly purr.

Morgan pressed his hand on the door, as though to physically stop her from leaving. "I'm going to fight you on this."

Suddenly the antenna snapped off in his hand. He looked at it dumbly; he wasn't aware he'd been holding it so tight.

Adele's face mottled and she said thinly, "I'll send you the bill." She pushed the button and the window rolled up.

Morgan yanked back his hand and was left staring helplessly at the darkened glass. He looked at the antenna in his hand with defeat. Muttering a curse, Morgan threw it on the ground and stomped back toward the house, his heels digging into the soft roadbed. As he climbed the first step, Hank came out from the house onto the porch. They both halted abruptly and stared at each other as the tension between them shot skyward. Morgan clenched his hands into fists. He felt the cursed papers crunching against his skin.

Hank paused a moment in indecision, fear pulsing in his eyes. He straightened his tie and hurried down the stairs past him, his heels pounding against the wood.

Morgan let him pass without incident. Hank was a small fish. His daddy had taught him to save his bait for the big ones.

16

———

"Young folks don't want to learn it anymore. I taught my son. I teach my kids at school. I taught a woman in Georgetown, anyone who wants to learn. I'll do whatever it takes to keep it going."

—Elizabeth Bennett, basket maker

INSIDE, THE HOUSE was dimly lit and quiet. His father's room was closed and a light shone beneath his door. He knew that Kristina would be settling his father for the night. He was glad of it. He didn't want his father present for what the rest of them had to discuss.

Light poured from the back porch and he followed the scent of freshly brewed coffee. He found Mama June, Nona and Nan serving coffee without any of the earlier laughter or chatter. Elmore, Harry and Chas sat in an uncomfortable silence around the table, glumly waiting. Morgan sighed at the threshold. All eyes turned toward him. He never felt their dependence more.

Mama June stepped forward to give him a soft kiss on his cheek. "Is she coming in?" she asked, referring to Adele.

Morgan shook his head. "She left. With Hank."

Mama June's face fell with disappointment. "Well, that's that."

"I tried to talk to that woman, but she's not budging. These are legal papers here. It's legit. The deal with Daddy was more than a handshake. Right now, Adele has a buyer for the property and she intends to sell it, with our cooperation or without it. It appears we've no choice. Adele's lawyer is coming with her buyout offer in the morning."

This was met with the expected round of angry denials and disbelief. Morgan watched his mother. She sat with her hands clasped on the table before her and said nothing.

"I hate that this is happening," Nan blurted out.

"Yeah, why is Dad doing this?" Harry asked. He was sulking and slouched in his chair. "What's wrong with him? Doesn't he care about us? I mean, isn't he part of the family, too?"

"It's because he's a jerk," Chas said, his chin jutting out.

"Children, don't talk about your father like that," Mama June reprimanded them. "Even though we don't agree with them, I'm sure both he and Adele are doing what they think is best."

"The best for whom?" Nan retorted. Her anger against her husband flared in her eyes. "Adele stands to make a fortune from this deal. She's already bought up the Mitchell piece."

Morgan's eyes widened with surprise. "That *whole* Mitchell piece?"

"Kit and caboodle. The plan is for another development to go in with I don't know how many houses."

"Lord, there goes my sweetgrass!" Nona exclaimed, raising her hands in dismay. "They'll be putting up their No Trespassing signs in no time!"

Elmore nodded, his eyes grave. "It'll be gone to us, that's for sure. Time was, sweetgrass used to be everywhere for the taking. Grew like a weed. Same with bull rush and pine needles. Now with all this building, I can't hardly find it nowhere. If we lose our sacred spot, I just don't know."

"I'm sorry," Morgan told them, head bent. "I wish I could have saved it for you."

"Child, it's not your fault," said Nona, patting his hand. She'd known this boy since he was born. He was a good boy and this wasn't his burden. "You came home to see your sick daddy. No one expected you to change the way the tide was flowing."

Nona quickly bent to pick up her large black purse from beside her chair. "We'd best be going now," she said, giving Elmore a pointed glance. "Thank you for inviting us for dinner."

Elmore's long, lean body rose with quiet dignity.

Morgan turned toward his sister. When Hank delivered the legal papers to Morgan, Nan had exploded with fury. Mama June, worried lest Preston be disturbed, had urged the two upstairs to talk privately. Obviously it hadn't gone well. Nan's eyes were red-rimmed, and her face pale and taut.

"Are you going home?" he asked her.

"No. Mama June said the boys and I could spend the night here."

He glanced at Harry and Chas. The boys slumped in their chairs and stared at their hands.

"I see," he said, thinking to himself that his sister finally hadn't backed down to Hank. That was something, at least.

"We'd best be off to bed, too," Nan said. "Boys…"

"I thought I could find a way out of this," he said to their retreating backs. "Bobby and I have been working on a plan, but with this loan, well…" He swallowed hard, feeling the crushing weight of their disappointment. He lowered his head and spoke softly, more to himself. "There's no way we can pay back that amount. There just isn't time. I'm sorry."

Sweetgrass

Later that same evening, Mama June came to Preston's office and peered in. She saw Morgan sitting at the large partner's desk that had been used by his father, his father's father, and his father before that. A modern touch was his laptop computer. Morgan was on the Internet again, no doubt researching legal terms, his fingers tapping across the keyboard.

She didn't want to disturb him. Adele had delivered a terrible blow to the plan he'd been working on with such hope. She could see his desperation in the tension of his face and the intensity of his tapping. But this couldn't wait. Reaching up, she knocked gently on the door.

He looked up quickly, startled by the interruption.

"Am I disturbing you?"

"Come in. Of course not," he said, rising to his feet.

"Sit back down, please."

He waited until she sat before returning to his chair. She looked around, not quite believing what a shambles the room had become since Morgan took possession. She'd thought Preston was disorganized, with all his tilting piles of books and papers. But this looked like a hurricane had hit. The room was stuffy and smelled of tobacco and old socks.

"I've come to talk to you about something important," she began.

Something in her tone alerted him because he promptly turned off his computer and gave her his full attention.

"First of all, I appreciate what you've done, son, to help me here at home. I know how hard you've worked. I couldn't have expected more. But as you said, our hand is forced. I don't want you to feel badly about how it's all turned out. Who knows?" she added with a slight lifting of her shoulders. "It may be for the best."

He opened his mouth to argue the point, but she pressed on.

"When you arrived, you asked me, rather persistently, what it was I wanted to do. Do you remember?"

Curious as to where this was headed, he nodded. "I remember it well."

"I asked that you help me bring Preston home to heal. We've succeeded in that and I believe it's done him a world of good. If that's all the time there is, then that's the Lord's will. I can't thank you enough for all you've done."

"I appreciate that, Mama."

She took a breath. "You might also recall that I wanted your daddy to be well enough to make whatever decision had to be made concerning Sweetgrass. Morgan, your father must be told."

"What?" he asked with astonishment. "No, not yet. If you tell him this, he might relapse from the strain."

"No, Morgan. He's my husband. And he's still the head of this family."

"Mama…"

"I won't be dissuaded," she replied, raising her hand to halt his argument. "From the start I said the final decision must be his. That's what all this was for." She rose slowly to a stand, feeling every one of her years. "I'll tell him."

"Wait," Morgan said. He stood. "Please, let me tell him. This was my job. I owe him that much."

Morgan stood outside his father's room, looking in. The narrow beam of light from the hall formed a cone, revealing Preston lying on the bed in the center of the room, sleeping soundly. He thought back to when he first saw his father in the hospital and how he'd been so shocked to see his vibrant father trapped in his paralyzed body, unable to communicate. He'd made progress since then, but not nearly enough.

Sweetgrass

This was a sad, pitiful time, he thought. He couldn't stand seeing his father like this. It shook him to his core. Even when Morgan was a young buck, his father could still kick him in the butt to get him out of bed and do his chores. Now the tables had turned. His father was helpless and weak. No one really knew what was going to happen to him.

He pulled the door slowly, the cone of light narrowing. His father slipped back into darkness, and with a soft click, the door between them was again closed.

Morgan left the confines of the house and started walking. He didn't care where he was headed, he just had to move and put some space between himself and the people in the house.

Out on the porch, Blackjack was dreaming the dreams of wolves in the open night air. Yet at the sound of Morgan's footfall he raised his head, then dragged himself to a stand, his rear legs shaking with the effort. His black tail wagged in welcome, and without a word needing to be spoken, the old dog followed Morgan down the stairs to pace at his side.

The gravel crunched beneath his feet as he walked, and he felt a slow unwinding of the coil of tension in his chest. Lifting his nose to the wind, he breathed deeply. The breeze often picked up late in the evening, carrying with it the sweet-scented moist air that was, to his mind, a signature of islands. He loved his ranch in Montana. He enjoyed falling asleep in the crisp chill of the mountains and closing his eyes while outside his window he heard the serenade of owls, the eerie cries of a mountain lion and the skittering of unknowns in the dark.

Yet he couldn't deny that the balmy breezes off the ocean that tasted of salt softened his bones and brought him to his knees.

It was why he'd had to stay away. It was too hard to come home. Sweetgrass ran in his blood along with the genes of all the generations that had gone before him. Hate it as he might, he loved this place.

And his father would shake his head and say it was typical that Morgan would only realize this when he was about to lose it.

Morgan felt dog weary and empty of spirit. He was a war-torn soldier who faced his losing battle. On this night before the surrender, he felt for the first time a connection with his long-dead ancestors who had once fought and died for a lost cause. His father had always told him that there was nobility to failure. That fighting for something one believed in, even if the battle was ultimately lost, was heroic.

Morgan wished to God he could feel one small shred of heroism. Where was the sense of self-worth and confidence of character that his father had declared shone in the brave knight's heart? Where was the unshakable belief in one's righteous purpose that gave the samurai the courage to plunge the knife?

His greatest agony was not that he'd been unable to hold on to this land. To have achieved that would have been pure magic and luck. The history and pageantry of the once-proud plantation known as Sweetgrass would persevere, even if in another's care. The dead would take care of themselves.

No, he saw his failure reflected in the eyes of the living who clung to the promise that the land would always, some-how, hold them together. That this great old house and avenue of ancient oaks and cragged bluff over water and wav-ing sweetgrass by winding creeks were, intrinsically, vitally, essentially *who they were*. When they looked at him, they believed that he could save the place, and thus, save them.

Well, he couldn't. He was no one's savior. He couldn't even save himself.

Sweetgrass

He walked the avenue, thinking how he'd spent the better part of his life seeking isolation. Yet tonight, under a sliver of moon along this singular, narrow road, with an old dog at his heels, he'd never felt the oppression of his loneliness more.

"Go on back to sleep," he told Blackjack when they returned to the house.

Blackjack looked up at him with indecision in his dark eyes, sensing that something was not right.

"Go on, old friend," he said, patting the dog's broad head. "I'll be all right."

Blackjack shuffled off, climbing the stairs in his slow, arthritic gait.

Morgan turned to walk a short distance farther, measuring each step, ending up at the small, white brick house with a Charleston green door. Raising his hand, he knocked.

After a few moments a light turned on, shining through the windows to pierce the darkness. The door swung open.

Kristina stood before him with one hand on the door frame, wearing what looked to him like boxer shorts and a camisole. He'd remember later that it was stretchy and lavender-colored, with tiny pink flowers along the neckline. At that moment, however, all he saw was her incredible hair, an aurora borealis framing a sleep-worn face, and large, expressive eyes that seemed to understand the depths of everything he felt without a word being spoken.

She opened her arms to him. And bowing his head, he entered.

The hour was late. Mama June had just finished her evening Bible reading when her bedroom door swung open and Nan rushed in, her eyes wide. She clutched her long, white cotton nightgown in fists and the fabric rustled the air as she ran to her mother's bed.

"What! Are you all right?" Mama June asked, taking off her glasses and setting them aside with her Bible.

Nan climbed up on the bed, tucking her toes under her nightgown and leaning against her mother. Her face was pale but her blue eyes were bright.

"You're shivering. Here, put this throw over your shoulders. What on earth happened?"

Nan blinked hard, as if she was trying to make sense of it all. "I…I just saw a ghost!"

Mama June fell back against her plump pillows. "No!"

"I did!" Nan said breathlessly. "I can't believe it!"

"I can. Tell me what happened."

"I…I was crying in bed, boo-hooing like a baby, when I got this weird sort of feeling, like I wasn't alone." She spoke quickly with excitement. "I looked over and there at the foot of my bed I saw this… I don't know how to explain it. It was kind of like a blurry white figure."

"Wearing an old-fashioned dress?"

"Yes!" she exclaimed, surprised that her mother would know this. "And a cap. Mama, do you think it was Beatrice?"

"I do. Darlin', you just saw your great-great-something grandmother."

Nan stared back at her in disbelief. "I can't believe it," she murmured.

"You wouldn't be the first one."

"I know. I've heard the stories all my life. But I never believed them." She cracked a smile. "I sure do now!"

Mama June chuckled, wondering what Beatrice was up to, appearing to both her and Nan. "I'm a believer, too. I saw her myself. Not too long ago."

"You did?" Nan asked, sounding a little betrayed. "Why didn't you tell me?"

"I didn't want you to think your dear old mother was losing her marbles."

"Well, what did she look like when you saw her?"

"Just as you described her. Only she wasn't standing by my bed. She was right over there," she said, pointing toward the window. "Just standing there looking at me."

Nan looked over her shoulder at the window, eyes speculative. "It's kind of spooky, isn't it? Seeing a ghost, I mean. Were you scared?"

"Scared? Heavens, no. Unnerved, maybe, especially those first few nights afterward. I confess it was hard to turn off the light. But I haven't seen her since. Beatrice has been in this house for three hundred years. Seems to me if she meant us any harm, she would have done it by now. No," she said, her gaze wandering the room. "I think she watches over us somehow. Maybe she's trying to tell us something."

Nan's brow furrowed and she wrapped the coverlet closer around her shoulders.

"You know Nona won't spend the night under this roof," Mama June told her. "She's seen Beatrice a couple of times. And so did her mother."

Nan looked up, her eyes sparking with tease. "But did they get gifts?"

Mama June tilted her head. "Gifts?"

Nan nodded and spread open her hand on the mattress. In her palm lay an antique brooch. The rich red-gold of the pin shone coppery against her skin.

"Where did you find this?"

"At the foot of my bed. When I turned on the light the ghost was gone. But I found this right where she was standing. I swear, Mama, it wasn't there before."

Mama June gingerly picked up the pin and examined both

sides carefully. It was as delightful as it could be, clearly a fine piece of nineteenth-century craftsmanship. The pin was centered with a glass-encased miniature of painted ivory depicting the house of Sweetgrass in a rural countryside scene. On the back, the initials BB were delicately etched into the gold.

"I've never seen this piece of jewelry before, never even heard it spoken of. And I would have." She gave it back to Nan, somewhat awed by it all. "It's very special. She must have meant for you to have it."

Nan's face grew thoughtful and she brought her hand close to her chest to study the pin. "Why me?" she asked softly.

Mama June wondered the same thing. "That's a question you'll have to ask Beatrice. But I should think it was because she felt you deserved it. Or perhaps that you need it. Why do you think?"

Nan closed her hands over the pin and brought it to her chin. She shook her head with such fervency that Mama June's focus sharpened.

"Mama, I feel lost," she said in a despairing voice.

"Nan!"

"I'm almost forty years old and I don't know who I am. I don't think I have for a long time." Nan's face crumpled.

"What's the matter, precious?" she asked, leaning forward to rest a consoling hand on her knee.

Nan wiped her eyes with the sheet and leaned farther back against the pillows, her knees bent. "I've been so busy being Hank's wife and the boys' mother, driving and cooking and cleaning and arranging this or that for *them,* I've never stopped to consider what *I* needed. Now I'm just…so empty."

"That's normal at this point in your life," Mama June replied, trying to be consoling. "Your children are grown and they're not so dependent on you any longer. They want to branch out on their own. It's a transition phase."

"It's not just the boys... I don't know if I can explain."

"Try. I'll listen."

Nan took a bolstering breath. "You see, when Daddy got sick, it was a wake-up call. For the past few months, coming home to help with Daddy, I've remembered who I used to be, back when I lived in this house. How it used to be between us. Part of it was just being here at home again. We've gotten closer as a family. That's important to me. And I saw you with Daddy, how every day you come to sit with him and talk with him. After all these years, you still share something special and I...I don't share that with Hank."

"But you always seemed to have such a good marriage. A picture-perfect home."

"I know it seemed like that, because that's all I've worked for. I had this vision of what our family life was like before Hamlin's death. In my memories, everything was perfect. *You* were perfect. But after Ham died, all that died with him. Everything just fell apart. I missed our life. I missed *our family.* So I thought—I tried—to bring that perfection back in my own family with Hank. I wanted to be the perfect mother and wife. Not just for me, but for you."

"Oh, Nan..."

"But I couldn't," she blurted out. "I've failed in everything."

"Nan, you couldn't have succeeded because perfection doesn't exist! There's no such thing in real life. We weren't perfect, not by any stretch of the imagination. Least of all me. Oh, Nan, there's so much you don't know. We were just a happy family in a normal, everyday way. Then we were devastated. When we looked back on the good days, they became golden in our memories. I know, I did it myself. They shone brighter than they really were. Maybe we needed them to shine, to help us through the dark times. But, Nan, you can't live my life for me. You have to live your own."

Nan swiped the tear from her cheek and sat straighter, intent on telling her mother what she meant. "But that's part of it, too. Being home again, I remember how *I* used to be, before I was married. I was popular. I was a leader. I was involved in everything at school. I had such dreams. I believed I could be anything I wanted to be. Mama, I don't know what happened to that girl. Did she just disappear as I grew up? Is that what happens to that dreamer inside of us when we get older? Or does she just get pushed further down? When I'm here, I catch glimpses of her again and I wonder—did I leave that girl here at home?"

Mama June remembered that ambitious, joyful girl, too. She looked into Nan's eyes, shining bright with intent. "I believe she's still inside of you."

"I think so, too," Nan replied, hope entering her voice. "I like that girl. And I mean to get in touch with her again."

Mama June's lips eased into a smile as she took the pin from Nan's hand. "Lift your chin," she told her daughter, then pinned the brooch on Nan's nightgown.

"It suits you," she said, admiring it. "It belonged to a strong, pioneering woman. And now it belongs to you."

Nan's eyes glistened.

"Nan, it's wonderful that you're exploring who you are, but why must you leave Hank to do this?"

"Because I can't do it with him. He's not there to support me, Mama. He only wants me to support him. It's like he considers it my job description. As long as I ran a nice home, raised his children and was a willing partner in bed, all was right with the world. We set up a pattern early in our marriage where I gave in to him on everything that mattered. He got stronger and I got weaker. It didn't just happen, Mama. I let it happen, helped it happen, because I somehow got it into my head that that's what a woman did if she wanted to be a good wife and have a good marriage."

"Helping your husband *is* good," Mama June said. "You want a strong husband."

"Being a doormat is not good," Nan countered. "Morgan was right when he told me to get some backbone!"

"But, precious, can't you have a backbone in your marriage?"

"Of course I could, if I'd started earlier. But for me, it's too late to change. The pattern is too fundamental in our marriage. And after what he did tonight—" She shook her head. "I don't want to go back to him. I've made up my mind." She paused. "I'm leaving him."

Mama June did not move a muscle. She couldn't quite believe she'd heard correctly. "You're leaving Hank for good?"

Nan nodded. "I was going to ask you after dinner, but then all hell broke loose. I was hoping... Mama, can I come back home?"

"Of course," she instantly replied, but regretted them the moment the words slipped out. She didn't want to be instrumental in a rash action that might destroy a marriage. "But, Nan, are you sure? Let's think about this a minute. This is an awfully big step. You should go to counseling or talk to a priest first. You don't want to act rashly." She hesitated, thinking the worst. "He didn't hit you or anything...?"

"No, no, nothing like that. And it isn't so rash, really. It's been more a long, slow slide."

"I didn't see it," said Mama June, deeply concerned now.

"You weren't meant to." Nan lifted her slim shoulders. "So here I am."

Mama June looked at this daughter who was so very much like her. And it occurred to her that perhaps this was the first time she'd really seen her daughter since she'd been married.

"So here you are," Mama June said. She wrapped her arms around her daughter and they leaned back against the pile of pillows. "And here you'll stay until you and Hank work this through, one way or the other."

"You and Daddy have been married for such a long time. I suppose you're disappointed in me."

"No," she replied gently. "Oh, dear child, you can't ever know what goes on between a husband and a wife, not even when they are your own parents. Don't compare your marriage to mine. Each marriage is as different as the people in them."

Nan took comfort in her mother's words and cuddled next to her. "Can I sleep in here tonight? With you?"

Mama June chuckled, thinking it had been a very long time since one of her children had crawled into bed with her. "Of course," she said, and moved over on the mattress, tossing down the covers for her.

Nan crawled under the covers and fluffed up the pillows, feeling very much like she was eight years old again and coming to her mama's bed after a bad dream.

Mama June reached over to turn off her bedside lamp. Immediately the room plunged into darkness, but soon after their eyes grew accustomed to the dim light.

"If you're hiding out from ghosts," said Mama June wryly, "this room is Beatrice's favorite haunt."

"Oh, I'm not afraid of her," Nan said.

"Oh, no?"

"Really, I'm not. She spooked me. I'll be honest about that. But—promise not to laugh—I got the feeling she was smiling at me. As if she was proud of me. Maybe even was glad I'm here. Does that sound crazy?"

Mama June smiled to herself and glanced over at the window. A slant of moonlight filtered through the panes. "No, precious, it doesn't sound crazy to me in the least."

17

———

"Basket styles tend to follow familial bloodlines just like a dim-pled smile or a special talent for singing. Still, each one is as dif-ferent as a fingerprint or helix of DNA."

—J. Michael McLaughlin

THE NEXT MORNING the sun was mockingly bright. Morgan rose early to sneak from Kristina's house up to his room like a randy teenager afraid of getting caught. She'd kissed him soundly before he left and, looking clearly into his eyes, gave him not a single word of advice.

For that kindness, he'd be forever grateful.

He showered, shaved, put on a clean, ironed shirt and pressed khakis, and smoothed his damp hair back from his brow. Leaning his palms against the bureau, he stared at his reflection in the rectangular wood-framed mirror. It was the same mirror he'd stared into as a boy. The shape and bones of his face were different, but the eyes were the same. So, too, he thought, was the anxiety behind them. He straightened, adjusted his belt, then went downstairs.

His mother was waiting for him in the kitchen. Her eyes

brightened at seeing him, shining with nervousness. Nona lingered over her coffee, her dark eyes watching him. She knew what was happening, as usual.

Mama June offered him a cup of steaming coffee. He took a few gulps but refused the bacon and biscuits. He couldn't eat.

"Your father should just be finishing his breakfast," Mama June told him, wiping her hands on her apron. She glanced up at him then, her meaning pulsing. "Now would be a good time for a visit."

Preston was sitting upright in his bed watching the morning news. Beside him was a tray with his mother's favorite Blue Willow pattern china half filled with the remains of his breakfast. He was shaved and dressed in a soft blue cotton shirt that was a near match to his eyes. These lit up when Morgan stepped into the room.

"Hey, Daddy," he responded.

Kristina swung her head up from her task at the sound of his voice. She came from around the bed to turn off the television. She moved briskly and with purpose, casting him a loaded glance as she passed on her way out of the room. Only Blackjack remained, his tail thumping on the floor beside Preston's bed.

His father's eyes fixed on his face.

Morgan looked around for a chair, and finding his father's favorite wingback near the window, he went to drag it over closer to the bed. Sitting, he crossed one leg over his knee and leaned back, each moment as labored and artificial as though he were on a stage.

"Nice day," he began lamely.

The business of a one-way conversation was excruciating. He'd spoken only two lines and already he felt exhausted, frustrated and ready to bolt. Where was his voice? Sitting beside his father, he felt again like the frightened kid he saw staring in the mirror this morning.

Morgan closed his eyes and took a deep breath. He wanted his father to see him not as the boy he remembered, but as the man he'd become. What could he say? What could he tell him that would convey that image?

"I'm sorry I haven't been in to visit much," he began. He looked at his hands and gave off a short, bitter laugh. "I always seem to be apologizing to you for one thing or another, don't I?"

He brought his leg down and leaned forward, closer to his father, intent on being heard. "I suppose you might be curious just what I've been up to these past years. Where I've been living, that kind of thing. Where do I start?" His fingers tapped his boot.

"Well, Montana is a nice-enough place. I have fifty acres, which is a spit in the bucket up there, but it's all mine. I've got a couple of horses," he went on, knowing his father would be interested in the livestock. "Tried goats for milk, but they were too much work." He chuckled, pleased to see a quiver of a commiserating smile on his father's face.

"There's a cabin that I built myself. It's not big," he added modestly. "Only two bedrooms, but the well water is sweet and I've got a beautiful view that can sometimes take my breath away. Remember how you always talked about seeing the breath of God as it blew across His earth? I could feel that there, Daddy. When the wind whistles through the pines I swear I can hear the angels sing."

He chuckled, a little embarrassed at his emotion. "Everything is so big there. The land stretches out forever, and the only thing bigger than it is the sky. A man can lose himself in a sky like that." He paused, getting to the heart of it. "It's a lot different from here, where there's not a blade of grass that doesn't connect me to some memory. I reckon that's part of Montana's appeal for me. There's not a lot in the landscape to remind me of home."

He cleared his throat, reining in his emotion. "I manage a herd of bison for a big ranch. They're some rich movie folk who come by from time to time. They're nice enough and leave me alone to do what I'm hired to do, which suits me. I don't have many friends, but then again, I never felt I needed more than a few true ones. I wish I could tell you there was some fine lady back home waiting for me. I know Mama June wishes there were. But there isn't. I've had my share of lady friends. But it never seems to work out very long. I reckon it's my fault. To a one they tell me there's something missing inside of me, something that keeps me from being able to commit."

He closed his eyes. "I don't know, Daddy, but they may be right."

Opening them again, he saw his father looking at him intently, without criticism. Morgan knew without doubt that he was being heard. It was a far cry from the one-sided conversations they used to have. It was, in fact, a new experience in their relationship, and he felt the coil inside himself loosen more, freeing his tongue.

It was ironic, he thought to himself. All that time spent alone on a mountaintop trying to look inside himself and he saw nothing. And here he was peeling away the layers under the silent gaze of his father. He wondered if this was how the sinner felt in a confessional.

"I don't blame them for things not working out. I blame myself. It's hard to love a good woman the way she deserves when I can't see beyond just getting through each day," he continued. "I'm good at my job. I don't cheat my employer of a dime I know they can afford to lose. I pay my taxes even though I believe it's highway robbery. I go through the motions of living, day in and day out, year after year. But I don't feel a lot of joy in it. I can't remember the last time I did."

He paused, knowing that wasn't entirely true. He could mark the day—eighteen years earlier—when the joy in living ended, but he didn't want to go into that with his father now.

"I'm not a mean man, Daddy. I care about people and animals and the earth we live on. You taught me that. But I am an angry one. I struggle to keep that blackness from roaring out. Trouble is, I'm not always strong enough. After a time, the anger always wins out. It begins with a sinking low for no specific reason, then the hurt starts howling. The only way I know how to douse the pain is through drink.

"I thought that if I stayed away from home it would be easier on everyone. I always seemed to fail you somehow, and I just had to stop trying. I don't like living angry. It makes me feel small. And I sure as hell didn't want to fight with you any more. So I stayed away.

"But then you called me on the phone." He lowered his head and shook it. "That threw me for a loop. I never did find out what you wanted to tell me that night. I keep wondering what could have been so important that you'd pick up the phone after all those years to tell me." He felt his throat thicken. "That night you called...I know it was the night of your stroke. I looked at the phone bill and it was right about the time you had it." He felt his voice waver and struggled to maintain composure. "I got to wonder, Daddy, what the hell did I do that time to cause this?"

His father's left hand lurched out toward him, grasping his shoulder and holding the fabric tight. His strength surprised Morgan as he drew him closer. Their eyes met and it startled him to see Preston's eyes glisten with tears. Morgan surrendered to the pull and leaned forward, putting his head against his father's chest. His father's hand moved to his head, shaky with emotion.

Morgan squeezed his eyes tight. He felt his father's forgiveness. In that moment the final layer peeled away and he laid himself bare, vulnerable, his underbelly exposed.

"Daddy, I'm sorry I wasn't here for you when you needed me. I know how hard it's been for you to keep this place going. I know what it took. I should have been a better son."

For a while his father's hand rested on Morgan's head. Then he leaned back in his chair, and Preston's hand slid to the mattress. Morgan reached up with both hands to smooth back his hair, then mop his face with his palms.

"There's more. I wasn't sure I should tell you this but Mama June insisted." He cleared his throat and rubbed his palms together.

"When I came home after you got sick, Mama June asked me to stay and help her bring you back here from the hospital. She's a tough little lady under that delicate shell. We both know that."

Preston blinked his red-rimmed eyes twice.

"Well, sir, my job was to work out the financial situation while she took care of you. That was the deal. I like to think we were making progress. You're looking better. We're all happy about that. You'll be walking around giving orders again in no time."

They both knew that a long series of battles had yet to be fought by Preston, but it felt good to sound the battle cry.

"As for me, I've been digging around best I could, making ends meet. And I've been working on a plan to get a conservation easement on the property. There are lots of benefits that I believe you'd like. Most important being the tax breaks that would allow us to hang on, awhile longer, anyway."

Sweetgrass

His father jerked his head in a nod of approval.

Morgan rubbed his jaw, groping for the right words to tell him the rest. "But things have suddenly changed."

His father's brows lowered in caution as Morgan reached down beside the chair where he'd placed a manila envelope. Bringing it up, he pulled out the papers that bore the heading of the legal firm employed by Adele Blakely.

"Last night," he began, "Adele delivered these papers. They outline a loan you got from her in 1989 after Hurricane Hugo. Do you remember?"

He saw Preston's eyes searching, as though he was trying to remember.

"It was for five hundred thousand dollars. The expiration date for the loan has passed. She won't even discuss further terms. See, what I don't understand is her claim that there's some kind of a partnership agreement that she entered into with you. According to the partnership terms, if the loan defaulted, or if you died or were incapacitated, it would trigger a buyout clause. Does this ring a bell?"

His father appeared confused and didn't make any response. Morgan had a feeling of dread, but he pushed on, thinking it was better to get it all out in one fell swoop.

"The bottom line is Adele is preparing an offer to buy us out even as we speak, and we have no option but to sell." Morgan began to lose heart. "She's acting on this, Daddy, and it looks binding. Mama... We thought you should know what was happening."

Preston's gaze suddenly sharpened and his shoulders tightened. He began making strange noises, working his mouth as though trying to say something.

Morgan drew back, confused by the force of his father's reaction. Beside the bed, Blackjack began whining.

"What, Daddy? What?"

Preston's eyes pleaded with him as he held eye contact. Shaking with the effort, he raised his left hand high. Then, with a swift slash in the air, he slammed it down upon the tray, scattering the china.

Morgan leapt to his feet. His mouth was dry, but he pushed out the words as guilt cut deep in his gut.

"I'm sorry, Daddy. I know I failed you again."

In what looked like fury, Preston kept bringing his hand down again and again on the china, breaking a cup, drawing blood.

"I'm sorry," he cried again. Morgan's heart beat hard and perspiration beaded on his forehead. He tasted salt, not knowing if it was sweat or tears. "I'm sorry."

Mama June felt sure her knees wouldn't hold her as she ran. Her heart was beating wildly. She didn't know what she'd find as she followed the sound of Preston's eerie screams. Was he having another stroke?

Entering the room, she saw Preston's arm flailing and his face colored beet-red, as if he was having a fit. She'd been taught that outbursts could occur, usually because of anger or frustration, but she'd never expected this.

"Hush, Blackjack!" she ordered sharply. The dog stopped barking but panted and whimpered as he ran from person to person then back to Preston's bed.

Kristina ran into the room and hurried around her to go directly to Preston's side. She put her hands gently on the corded muscles of his shoulders and softly urged him to relax.

Mama June looked sharply at her son. "Morgan, I think you should go."

Morgan swung his head toward Kristina. She didn't interfere with the family dynamics, but in her eyes he saw her opinion shining bright and clear. *Stay!*

"No," he told his mother. "I'm staying."

Mama June looked at his face, surprised by his decision. "Then hold on to that dog," she told him. "He's not making things better."

Mama June locked gazes with her husband and slowly approached him.

"Preston, it's me, Mary June," she said, trying to quiet him. "Hush, now. It's all right. You have to stop this. Stop it right this minute. You'll hurt yourself. And you're breaking my china!"

Preston began to quiet. Even though his breathing remained ragged and his hands still trembled with agitation, she could see that he was working hard for control. He was bathed in sweat.

"Are you all right?" Kristina asked him. She was massaging his shoulders and spoke calmly. "Are you in pain?"

He jerked his head no, but all the while he stared fiercely at Mama June. While looking directly at her, he raised his hand and slowly, painstakingly, brought it over the tray, then let it fall, crashing onto the china. The bowl clattered against the plate, chipping the rim.

"Have you lost your mind?" she exclaimed. "That's my mother's china!"

He lurched forward, reaching out to hit the china again.

"Whatever is the matter? Is this something to do with my mother?"

When he hit the china again, she moved closer, eyeing him sharply even as his eyes bore into her with an alarming urgency.

"Preston, are you trying to tell me something?"

His whole body seemed to shiver with relief. He blinked twice.

"Lord, help us, I'm sorry! Morgan, he's trying to tell us something! What can we do?"

"Play twenty questions," said Kristina. "He can respond yes or no. Preston," she told him, "we know you're tired. But try."

Preston took several bolstering breaths.

"Go ahead," Kristina said.

Mama June looked at the tray, wondering where to begin. There was nothing there but leftover breakfast. She put her hand out and began, speaking clearly. "Is it the tray?"

He blinked once.

"No. The breakfast? Is it food?"

He shook his head.

She searched the tray. "The china?" she said with exaggeration.

He nodded.

"What?" she asked, surprised. "The china?"

His eyes shone as he blinked twice.

Mama June was bewildered. "Morgan, what were you telling him when he had this outburst?"

Morgan stroked the dog's head as he held on to his collar. "I'd just told him about Adele's buyout offer."

Preston's hand jerked upward in agitation.

"He's excited about that," Kristina said. "You're on the right trail."

"So you're not angry with Morgan?" Mama June asked Preston.

His face grew sad and he shook his head no.

"Oh, thank the Lord," she said with a tremendous relief.

"It sounds to me like he got angry about Adele," said Kristina.

Mama June drew closer. "And that's when you broke the china, right?"

When he nodded, Mama June felt a stirring of hope. She walked around the room, muttering the word *china,* her finger tapping her chin, fumbling with the pieces of the puzzle. "There's something there. It's niggling in the back of my brain. I just can't quite grasp it."

Morgan stood and placed his hands on his hips. "What the hell does a Chinese plate have to do with a partnership agreement?"

Mama June stopped abruptly and looked up, eyes bright. "That's it!"

She walked to where the papers were scattered beside the bed and picked them up.

"What is *it?*" Morgan asked, coming closer.

"It's something about a Chinese Partnership! When you said it, something clicked in my brain. Is that right, darlin'?" she asked Preston.

Preston's eyes shone with triumph.

Morgan felt the thrill of the hunt in his veins. "I don't get it. Bring me up to speed."

"Chinese Partnership. Your daddy told me something about it years ago. I remembered it because I'd thought it was a funny name for a partnership. You were unhappy about it," she said to Preston. "I remember that clearly. He had a hissy fit because his sister wouldn't loan the money using the farm as collateral."

"Which would've been standard," Morgan said.

"That's what he'd asked her for. But Adele came up with this partnership idea."

"I'm still lost," said Kristina. "What's a Chinese Partnership?"

"I have absolutely no idea," Mama June replied. "But I know whatever it is, it's got to do with whatever scheme Adele is cooking up."

"I don't know, either," Morgan said. "I just wish to God I knew if Daddy still had his copy of the agreement floating around."

"I'm sure he does," she said, relief shining in her eyes. "Your father never threw anything out, especially not a legal document."

"Then I'd like to know where it is. I've prowled through every sheet of paper in his office. There's no record, not even a memo of any such agreement."

"Did you go through the boxes stored up in the attic?"

"The what?" he exclaimed. "Why didn't you tell me about them?"

"Because they're all old papers. Anything still viable your father kept in his office. But maybe it got mixed up with something else? It was a long time ago, after all."

Morgan's eyes gleamed as he looked at his father. "If you can go through all that to tell us about the Chinese Partnership, you can bet the farm I'm going to find that damned agreement."

Mama June hurried to Preston's side. She cupped his cheeks in her hands and bent to kiss him soundly on the mouth. "You really are an incredibly clever man!"

Any attic in the month of July is hot, but an attic in the southern United States at any time in the summer is a living hell.

Morgan breathed in air so thick and humid he imagined the mildew growing on his lungs. He prowled through cardboard boxes so moist they were mushy to the touch. His father's leather briefcase was coated with a layer of mold, and cartons of file boxes were filled with yellowed papers polka-dotted with mildew. The black dust coated his fingers like moss, and the sweat poured from his brow and down his back faster than he could replenish with the sweet tea Nona kept bringing him.

Despite the punishing heat, however, Morgan didn't rush. He charily scrutinized every paper that passed his hand.

Sweetgrass

Hours crawled by, yet he was surprised when he was called down for lunch. The morning had passed, but he'd only dug his way through half the attic. Mama June, worried he'd pass out in the heat, insisted he take a cool shower and change his clothes, which he did gratefully. She prepared him a cool lunch of gazpacho soup, cold salmon, salad niçoise and ice cream for dessert. Thus fortified, he returned to Hades.

Several more hours passed in his deliberate slowness. He finished plowing through another stack of boxes and moved them to the back of the attic. Coughing in the stirred dust that floated in the relentless rays of sun from the windows, he faced another stack of sealed boxes. He was wiping his brow with his sleeve and considering whether to just call it quits for the day when his gaze fell upon a box with the black magic marker numbers *1989*.

He dropped his arm and his heart skipped faster. With a wild swipe he tore off the tape and dug into the contents. Slow down, he ordered himself, and his fingers slowed to a painstaking pace as he flipped through the files.

He found the post-Hurricane Hugo damage report that his father had filed with the insurance company. It was painstakingly thorough and portrayed an accurate picture of the devastating loss of his dairy house, the smoke house, a herd of cows, outbuildings and barns, the peach orchard and the harvest of his crops. Morgan found old tax bills—almost laughable compared to today's bill—the mortgage payments, health insurance, life insurance...all of the usual records of bills and payments made. Then his hands stilled. He saw it. A manila file marked *Adele*.

The sweat made the dust on his fingers muddy, so he paused to rub his hands against his pants. He took a deep breath. Then he reached out to pick up the folder. Like all the others, this one was spotted with mildew and soft to the touch from all the humidity. He opened it. Several legal papers slipped out into his lap. He licked his dry lips and began to read, scanning the papers quickly. Then he went back and read them again, more slowly this time, making sure he didn't omit anything important while his adrenaline had the best of him.

When he finished, Morgan leaned back against the stack of dusty boxes and stretched his long legs out in front of him. His mind wandered as his gaze traveled down his dirty T-shirt to his khaki shorts. He'd cut them from old trousers and the hem was raggedy and frayed. Motes of dust clung to the soft hairs on his legs.

He looked at the papers in his hands again. Slowly, a grin creased the dust coating his face, spreading across his cheeks, stretching from ear to ear. He felt absolutely giddy. A small giggle escaped from his lips. He looked around, making sure no one could hear him. Then from his gut a laugh burst forth.

Oh, dear Aunt Adele. We have you now.

He laughed again, and with a jubilant whoop he reached over to grab hold of his sweet tea. His hand was so sweaty he knocked over the glass and the tea spilled all over the small chest it rested upon. Muttering a short curse, he put the contract papers carefully back into the file and set it out of harm's way. Grabbing the towel he'd been using to wipe his face, he began mopping up the tea. The dark tannin colored the leather strips of the old chest and he worried if some of the liquid had somehow spilled between the cracks of wood into the contents of the chest.

It was unlocked. He lifted the lid and immediately caught a whiff of the scent of mothballs and cedar. It was a dainty trunk, a girl's chest, lined with a feminine floral fabric. Someone had taken steps to preserve this chest. It seemed to

Sweetgrass

be filled with mementos of the past. Looking closer, he recognized the plaster cast of his hand that he'd made for his
mother as a little boy. Enchanted, he took it out to study it.
Was he ever that small? he wondered. He also found his sister's print, and choking up a bit, his brother's. He placed his
hand beside Hamlin's chubby print, dwarfing it.

Curious now, he began to browse through this collection
of odds and ends, most of them about him and his siblings.
He hadn't known his mother had saved all this stuff. He knew
she was tenderhearted and nostalgic, but discovering the three
silver boxes that held locks of each of their hair gave him new
insight into the depths of her devotion.

He chuckled when he read some of the cards they'd made
her for Mother's Day and birthdays. It amazed him that he actually remembered them!

There weren't many photographs, just the few select set
into this treasure box by choice. The first was a photograph
of him, Hamlin and Nan hanging in the big oak tree like
monkeys and Mama June sitting on the circular bench
beneath. Her feet were tucked under her skirt, a scarf was at
her neck and she was radiant. Morgan remembered that she
smiled a lot in those days.

There were more photographs—the kids in school or in
costume or with Santa. There was one of Mama June and
Daddy. His father looked so young with his smooth, tanned
skin and can-do smile. His wavy hair—so much like
Morgan's—refused to be slicked back in the style of the day;
a wayward curl hung over his forehead. His arm was tight
around Mama June in a possessive grip, and both of them
were smiling at the camera.

He recognized a photograph of his Blakely grandparents,
even though they'd died before he was born. There was one
of Granddad and Grandmama Clark, too. Aunt Adele smiled

327

up from another. She was young, windswept and, Morgan thought, a real looker.

One photograph caught his attention. Bringing it closer, he studied the black-and-white photograph of a handsome young man in jeans and a T-shirt rolled up at his biceps. He had dark hair and a wide, engaging smile. At first glance, Morgan had thought it was his brother, Hamlin. But the man was older and the clothes were all wrong. Checking the back of the photograph, he saw the words *Tripp, Blakely's Bluff,* written in his mother's script, and the date *1957*. He'd seen photographs of his uncle Tripp before, but not many. There was this mystique about the man and something very secretive about his death. He remembered people talking about it in hushed voices after Hamlin died. His uncle had died in a boating accident, too, and it had angered him that people were making comparisons.

He put the photograph back in the box. It was just a lousy coincidence, he thought now as he'd thought then. A cruel twist of fate.

Growing weary, he poked around a few more things and began to lose interest in the oppressive heat. He glanced through the papers quickly now. There were some scattered papers of pink stationery, probably from Nan when she was a teenager. He chuckled softly, remembering how religiously she'd written home from college. He casually read a few lines.

My dearest Tripp,
I can't believe it's been a month since we've seen each other. I miss you, miss you, miss you! When are you coming up to see me? It's not such a long trip and we'll find a way to make it special. We always do.

Morgan froze. What the hell? This wasn't from Nan. It couldn't be. Picking it up, he recognized his mother's handwriting, only younger, not as defined, with lots of flourishes. *Dearest Tripp?* Not Preston? He looked at the date—1957. The year his parents were married.

His mouth went dry and he could hear his blood roar in his ears. He shouldn't read it. After all, it was personal. He hesitated. Hadn't his mother given him carte blanche to go through everything in the attic? He looked over his shoulder, his gaze crafty, feeling it was wrong. But something was tugging at him. What was going on? What else didn't he know?

He lowered his head and began to read.

Morgan drew his knees close to his chest, his arms dangling lifelessly over them. The letters lay scattered on the floor beside him. He didn't feel the heat intensely any longer. He didn't feel anything at all. It was as if he was some meaningless, dim-witted bug that had haplessly flown head straight into a gossamer web of lies and deceit. He felt unable to move while the spider's venom spread throughout his limbs, numbing them.

Yet even in the numbness he felt a thrumming of pain that told him even though he felt dead, wished he were dead, he was still alive. He knew this feeling. It was how he'd felt after his brother's drowning.

He used to go to remote places like the barn or the attic to curl up, close his eyes and wait for sleep to finally come. When the nightmares began, however, they were worse— much worse. That's when he'd started reading. He read anything he could get his hands on and he read all the time. In books he'd found a place to escape.

But he was too old to hide out in attics and forts. The truth was the truth, like it or not. He knew what he was getting himself into when he'd decided to read those letters. No one put a gun to his head. It was his choice.

He rose quickly and immediately felt light-headed. Bursts

of white light and black dots clouded his vision. Putting his fingers up to pinch the bridge of his nose, he breathed deeply and waited to get his equilibrium back. Then, feeling as old and gimp-legged as Blackjack, he made his way from the sizzling heat of the attic down into the cooler air of his mother's house.

He found her in her room, reading by the window. Her head darted up like a small bird's when he walked in, and over the rims of her reading glasses her blue eyes brightened at seeing him. Then, registering his dirty state, the seriousness of his expression and the way his hands hung low at his sides, her smile grew shaky.

"You didn't find it?" she asked.

He walked closer. "I found it."

Her brows knit in puzzlement. "Oh? It wasn't what you'd hoped?"

"I guess. I don't know," he replied dispassionately. "I'll have to show it to the lawyers and let them tear it apart, but I think we've got something. We have a chance."

She looked at him, her eyes clouded with confusion. "That's what you wanted, right? Then why the sorry face?" Her eyes narrowed in speculation as she reached out toward the mattress. "Come sit down. Tell me about it."

Morgan took a deep breath and looked around the room, aware of the ticking of the clock. It was a tidy room, bright and airy with windows overlooking the marsh. Her slippers were set beneath a porcelain hook that held her chenille robe. A large armoire adorned with hand-painted flowers stood against the far wall. Her small writing desk was tucked beneath a dormer and on this was a silver-framed photograph of the family, taken years ago, shortly before Hamlin's death. He looked to be about eighteen. Morgan thought back. His brother was born in April 1958. The date of the letter was September 1957. He clenched his hands.

She looked different to him now. The halo he'd always placed around her head had tarnished. He felt betrayed. It was like he didn't know her anymore.

He sat stonily on the edge of the mattress, directly across from his mother.

"Morgan, something's wrong."

Morgan lifted his right hand and held it out to his mother.

Her gaze lowered to his hand. Clutched in his fingers were several sheets of pale pink stationery. Mama June's eyes widened in recognition. Her mouth opened in a soft, wounded gasp.

For a moment, neither of them spoke. In his mother's pale eyes he saw shock, then horror, then sorrow flicker as she stared at the innocuous-looking sheets of paper that they both knew held her deepest, most private secret.

"You read them." It was more a confirmation than a question.

"Yes."

Her eyes were round and she wrapped her arms tightly around herself.

Morgan drummed his fingers against the paper. His nails were rimmed with dirt from the attic. Mama June held her breath as she watched a small tic work in his cheek.

"Was Uncle Tripp Hamlin's father?" he asked abruptly.

"Oh, God," escaped her lips. This was the one question she'd steeled herself against for forty-seven years. She physically brought her shoulders in, making herself smaller, turning away from his relentless stare.

Her mind scrambled for choices. She could simply reply no. But Morgan wasn't stupid. He had the evidence in his hands and he could figure out by counting that she was lying. Or she could choose not to answer him at all. She could tell him it was none of his business, berate him for sneaking through her personal things and ask him to leave. Her mind veered from this choice. Hadn't she walked down that path of silence too often already? Lord, don't let me be a coward now, she prayed.

Turning back to face him, she nodded almost imperceptibly. Forty-seven years of pain streamed down her cheeks.

Morgan looked stunned, as if he'd just taken a bullet but hadn't yet fallen.

"When were you going to tell me?"

Her shoulders slumped at hearing the hurt in his voice. "I don't know."

"You might never have!" he said accusingly.

"If it were up to me, no! I don't think I ever would have. What's in those letters is private. You weren't meant to read them. No one was," she said, her voice rising in self-defense.

"I'm not sorry I read them! It's the only way I ever would have known. God! I can't believe it." His laugh was bitter, even desperate. "It explains a lot about you and Daddy."

"You don't know anything about the two of us!" she cried. "How dare you speak of that? You weren't even born then."

"Is he even my father?"

She sucked in her breath and looked into her son's eyes. They were the exact same shade of blue as his father's.

"How can you even ask that?"

His eyes grew icy, mocking. "How can I ask that?" He lifted the letters. "I'm not the one who was tramping around like some—"

Mama June's hand shot out to crack against his cheek.

Morgan's head jerked back and his eyes filled as they stared at each other, both stunned at how far they'd gone. She felt the ice between them—a glacier of silence—explode and splinter into a million shards around them.

"Morgan…" She reached out to him, her palm still tingling. She'd never raised her hand to him before.

Morgan's eyes brimmed with disbelief and hurt. He brought his hand to his cheek.

"Preston is your father," she said in a voice that allowed no doubt. "Yours and Nan's."

Morgan slumped and dropped his forehead into his palm. He seemed to grind flesh against flesh. His tears were flowing freely now.

"Then why did he love Hamlin more than me?"

Mama June's heart cracked at seeing her son's agony.

"He didn't!"

"Yes, he did!" he exclaimed, rearing back and raising his tear-filled eyes at her accusingly. He seemed angry that he was crying, ashamed. He was like an injured animal, snarling and lashing out. "Don't lie to me! It won't work anymore. Everything Hamlin did was the best. Everything I did was shit. It was hard enough to live in the favored son's shadow." He took a labored breath. "But it was impossible to live up to the *potential* of Hamlin after he died."

"Morgan…"

"After Hamlin died, every time Daddy looked at me, I saw disappointment. I could see…" He swallowed thickly and brought his voice under control. "He was sorry it was Hamlin that died out there instead of me."

"Stop it! Stop it right now!" she cried out, not fully comprehending the depths of what she'd heard but rejecting it all.

"I won't," he said with wounded belligerence. "It's the truth. Hamlin could do no wrong. But Daddy found something wrong with everything I did. He pushed me, pushed me till I couldn't take it anymore. I hated him for it! Hated him for making me feel worthless." His voice cracked but he forced out, "I hated him for not loving me."

Mama June grew frightened as she watched her son break up. This was something bigger than she knew how to heal. It bordered on dangerous.

"Morgan, please try to understand," she said, wringing her hands. "Yes, your father loved Hamlin very much. No one can ever doubt that. But *you!* Don't you see? It's not that he didn't love you enough. It's that he loved you *too much*."

Morgan stepped away, shaking his head. "I don't believe you."

"You are his son. He loves you."

He laughed bitterly, then turned and fled the room.

18

———

"Sharing the knowledge is like giving something back."
—Harriett Bailem Brown, basket maker

NONA STEPPED OUT ONTO the back porch to find Mama June sitting in her rocker, her shoulders quaking. She came directly to her side and placed a hand reddened from dishwater on her shoulder.

"I saw Morgan dash out of here like a bat out of hell," she told Mama June. "And here you are crying. Someone's got a story to tell."

Mama June brought her hand to her mouth to muffle her crying and shook her head, indicating that she didn't want to talk about it.

"Mmm-hmm," Nona hummed through pursed lips. She came around to her customary rocker beside Mama June's and settled noisily in it.

"It's been a long day...and it's only three o'clock," she said. When Mama June didn't reply, Nona added, "I can sit here for the rest of the day. I'm in no hurry, and Lord knows I deserve it."

The two women sat in their usual rockers and didn't speak. The quiet of the vast outdoors buffered them against the noise of all the family issues and problems that had blared resoundingly all day. Mama June ceased crying and let the peace settle in her. With a true friend, there was no need to fill the void.

Mama June turned her head and looked at her friend. The strong angles of Nona's face revealed the character of the woman. Mama June knew she could tell Nona anything and it wouldn't leave this room. She was, other than Preston, the only living soul who knew all of Mary June's secrets.

"Morgan knows," Mama June told her.

It took a moment for Nona to piece together the meaning in her mind. She knew that Morgan was digging around in the attic, but there were so many secrets in this family, she wasn't sure which one he'd unearthed. But when she saw the gravity in Mama June's expression, she knew it had to be the big secret.

"Maybe it's time," she replied.

Mama June's face crumpled. "When is it a good time to break your son's heart?"

"What happened?"

With a steady cadence, Mama June filled Nona in on all the day's details. It had been a morning of revelations and an afternoon of upsets. A day of extraordinary highs and lows. Nona's expressive eyes shone as she nodded her head and dotted the conversation with exclamations of surprise and support.

"I've never felt so old," she said to Nona.

"You *are* old," Nona countered.

"Look who's talking!"

"I know I'm old," Nona replied with a wry grin. "But I'm not complaining about it." She leaned back and studied the marsh. In their unspoken dialogue, they shared an exclusive shorthand. "He had a fire lit under him, that's for sure," she said, knowing that they were both wondering where Morgan was. "Hope he knows what he's doing."

"There are days when I don't think I know who my own son is," Mama June said. "Of all my children, he was always the question mark." She rocked back and forth, mulling the mystery over in her mind. "I always knew who Nan was."

"She's the easy one. Nan was the princess," Nona said wryly.

"That she was. But she had a good heart and always tried to make everyone happy. And she's bright as a new penny. Problem is, she likes pretty things and made some bad choices to get them."

"That child made her bed."

"Yes, but she's not sleeping in it."

Nona shook her head, frowning. "That's not good. She needs to finish what she started. Hiding out here at her mama's house isn't going to solve anything."

Mama June rocked a little faster, annoyed at the prospect of sending Nan home to her husband. "She needs a little time away from him," she argued. "Besides, this is her home. Where else can she go?"

"Not under her mama's skirts."

"She's not hiding. She's thinking things through. Nan's leaving Hank."

"Oh, Lord…"

"It'll be tough on her, not to mention the boys. She'll need us."

Nona rocked but didn't reply. A line of worry creased her brow.

"Now, Hamlin," Mama June continued. "He was easy to figure out. He was full of do and dare. But impulsive, too.

Reckless. Like his father," she added softly. Her face clouded and she lowered her eyes. "I'll never know if either one of them might have outgrown that and matured into something quite special. But Morgan…"

"Morgan's special," Nona said in a defensive tone.

"Yes, of course. It's just, I don't know who he is. That's an odd thing for a mother to say about her own child. He was always such a quiet boy. He never told me how he felt or what he thought about anything. I'd ask him a question and he'd answer with one word. Yes or no." She shrugged. "I love him, of course. He's the apple of my eye, you know that. But I worry about him. He never talks to me or to his father, either. He always shuts us out."

"He shuts *you* out?" Nona asked incredulously, her eyes protruding.

Mama June heard the sharp tone in Nona's voice and turned to look at her. Nona had stopped rocking and was sitting straight, the sharp bones of her face catching the shadows.

"Yes," Mama June replied hesitatingly. "Why are you look-ing at me like that? You've got something to say to me?"

"Lord help me, woman, but I do. I can't sit here anymore and listen to you go on about how that child shut you out. Mary June, the God's truth is that you shut that boy out the day your other boy died! There's no use you trying to deny it."

"Nona!" She began to rise.

"You sit down, Mary June, and hear me out!"

Mama June made a point of standing.

Nona leaned forward. "You're saying you don't know who he is. Harrumph. That's true enough. Saying he's quiet and all. Morgan's been right there under your nose all along. It's time you took off those rosy glasses and saw your son for who he really is."

Mama June did not hear anger in Nona's voice. That

would have sent her walking. Instead she heard the unshakable veracity of a friend about to deliver a "come to Jesus." Gripping the edge of the rocker, Mama June reluctantly lowered herself back into the chair. She had to stay. She had to listen. She couldn't turn away. Nona had known Morgan since the day he was born and loved him as she did. If Mama June trusted anyone's opinion, it was Nona's. Still, she swallowed thickly. From the look in Nona's eye, this was going to be hard to hear.

"All right. I'm listening."

Nona shifted in her chair, settling in. "You wonder why he never talked to you?" She paused, giving Mama June the eye. "It's because you never *let* him talk to you! I saw early on what was happening. When he was little, you and Mr. Preston were too wrapped up in your own grief to pay your boy mind. Preston, all the time he was out working in the fields or doing something with Sweetgrass. Only time he spoke to that boy was to give him orders."

"I know he could be hard on him."

"Don't you start blaming him. You weren't there for him, neither!"

"How can you say that?"

"Don't go shaking your head at me. I was here! I'm the one who held that boy in my arms while he cried himself to sleep during one of your spells. I cleaned him and fed him when his mama couldn't do the same for herself. I talked him through some mean moments when I thought my heart would break. Mary June, that boy hated himself!"

"No, he didn't!" It wasn't a denial but more an exclamation of pain.

"Yes, he did. Maybe still does. He blamed himself for his brother dying and him living. That's too big a thing for a boy of eight to carry all on his own."

"Why didn't I know?" Mama June cried, clutching the arms of the chair. "Why didn't he tell me?"

"You wouldn't let him tell you!" Nona reached out and put her hand over the back of Mama June's. "Honey, you were in a darkness so deep you couldn't lift your head high enough to see what was happening in your own house. Those were sad times, Mary June. The saddest any mother can bear. We were all grieving, but none of us like you. I pray to Jesus every day I never have to know the grief you knew."

Mama June slipped her hand away to reach for the tissue in her apron. She swiped at her eyes and sniffed.

Nona sighed and took a steadying breath. There was more that had to be said. "If you're strong enough, if you love your boy enough, you'll see that the plain hard truth is, in grieving the son you lost, you neglected the boy that lived. I'm not saying you meant to hurt him, but that's the way it is, the way it worked out."

"How? I always loved him. I never blamed him! It was an accident."

"You didn't blame him in words. That's part of the problem, don't you see? You couldn't let him or anyone else even mention Hamlin's name in this house. And Preston was no better. He shut tight like a clam in icy water whenever Hamlin's name was mentioned. That silence festered and stank and made everyone in this family sick. You never let him deal with it. He kept all of it inside, tearing him up like a cyclone."

Mama June put her hands to her face as tears streamed down.

"I'll tell you who your son is," Nona said in a low, steady cadence. "Morgan has a kind heart. You see that in a child that is kind to animals. It's in the way he pets them, or brings an injured bird home, or takes a dog out for a walk when no one else will."

Mama June nodded, remembering. Her face lost its tightness.

"He looked out for this family, too," Nona went on, more gently now. "He knows his family duty. He knows what's important. You say he's quiet? That's because he's watching. I've seen him watch the faces of you all while you're talking or eating dinner. His eyes don't miss a thing. He knows who's hurting and he worries. He's careful not to get anyone upset."

Mama June stopped rocking. "He was careful not to get *me* upset."

"Especially you. But Preston, too. And Nan. Morgan took for himself the burden for Hamlin's death. He carried it for the whole family. It's no wonder he had to leave. If he'd stayed, he'd have died under that weight. If I were that boy, I'd have run, too."

"Oh, my poor boy…"

"He's no boy!" Nona exclaimed, tossing up her palms. "He's a man. You and Preston both have to face that. And the fact that this man is your last hope for salvation."

Nona rose slowly, feeling as ancient as the marsh. She put her hand to her back as she straightened, an old pain flaring.

"Well, that's all I've got to say about that."

Mama June couldn't reply.

Nona stood with her arms crossed, looking out at a squadron of pelicans flying low over the marsh. Mama June's forehead was cupped in her palm.

"Do you want some coffee?" she asked. "Maybe some ice water?"

"No," Mama June replied tonelessly. "Thank you. I'll just sit out here for a while."

Nona looked searchingly at her face and found nothing there to alarm her. She looked again at the sky. The sun was full overhead. It reflected in the water in shimmering rays.

★ ★ ★

An hour later, Nona went to the porch again to check on her friend. She found Mama June still sitting in the rocker, but she'd stopped crying. She was looking out again at Blakely's Bluff.

"Mind if I join you?"

Mama June startled, and when she looked her way, her eyes were red-rimmed, lifeless. She sighed with resignation. "Of course not."

Nona lowered into her chair, then reached into the canvas bag beside her rocker. In it were her supplies and the basket she was working on. She pulled out a big coiled flower basket with a lovely wide handle. She was nearly done with it. She looked at the tight, even stitches of palmetto and the dark strips of rush interspersed, its thick blades giving the basket strength. She especially liked the big pieces. They showed up so nice and attracted the eye on the highway.

Setting this one aside, Nona dug farther into the bag to pull out a skein of silky grass, strips of palmetto leaves, then some darker bull rush and pine needles. She turned toward her friend.

"Mama June, I've given this a lot of thought."

Mama June stopped rocking and turned her way. "Oh?"

"It's time for you to begin a basket."

Mama June looked confused. "Me? Sew a basket?"

"You heard me. You've been watching me all these weeks and asking all your questions. I was waiting on you to ask if you could sew one."

"I wanted to. But I just never thought I should ask. I mean, this is part of your culture. I didn't think…"

"Oh, I teach folks if they're white or black, if that's what you're getting at," Nona told her. "Don't matter to me as long as I keep the art alive—and as long as you keep the rows straight," she said with a light laugh. "It helps folks appreciate all the work and time that goes into making a basket. So, are you going to let me teach you?"

"You don't have to do this. I know you didn't mean to hurt me."

Nona pursed her lips. "I don't have to do anything! And who says I'm hurting you?" She smiled craftily. "Your fingers haven't played with this grass yet."

When a smile reluctantly escaped Mama June's lips, Nona continued more seriously.

"Seems to me we're coming to a fork in the road. There's lots going on and I worry if we don't do this now, we won't have the chance later. What we put aside today are tomorrow's treasures. And I think right now you need to make a basket, Mary June. Weaving these grasses together will do you good." She paused. "Work through that nasty arthritis."

"I don't have arth—"

"See? I can still get you going."

A tremulous smile crossed her face, and hesitatingly, Mama June nodded. "All right. Where do we begin?"

Nona grinned in satisfaction. "First we have to knot it," she replied, gathering her materials together.

Mary June leaned forward to watch Nona's fingers work more closely. They sat shoulder to shoulder, their heads bent close. Nona twisted a bundle of pine needles, soft and pliable in her strong hands, holding the ends of grass in her teeth. She tied a rounded knot and began the coil.

"You make it look easy," said Mama June.

"Been doing this a long time," Nona readily replied. She lifted it for Mama June to see. "The knot is the very beginning of what's to come," she said. "It has to be strong to hold the basket together."

Next she reached over to take a handful of sweetgrass. The separate strands were slender, and even with her experienced grip some spilled out from the bundle to the floor.

"You can't help but lose some," she commented when Mama June bent to pick them up.

"Used to be we only used sweetgrass to work up the basket. I do love the look of it and the feel of it in my hands." She sighed and her smile was bittersweet. "When I hold this grass in my hands, sometimes I imagine that I'm sitting with my mother and my grandmother, and all the women who sewed with this same grass from this same field. All of us sewing in the old way taught at our mother's knee. My kin—generation after generation—are buried in that field of sweetgrass and their spirits flow into these blades of grass in my hand. It's my blessing to weave us all together, to bind us tight with these strips of palmetto."

She paused to look Mary June in the eye. "It's all a woman can do," she said. "We take hold of all these blades of grass in our hand. Some are soft and sweet like sweetgrass. Some are strong and tough, like the rush. And some are pliable but weak, like pine needles. Each blade is special. Each of them is needed for the basket.

"We women are the weavers. We take them all in our hands, then bind them together best we can, hoping to build up something beautiful." She sighed. "It's all we can do."

Their eyes met and held.

Nona smiled again and pulled out a small leather pouch from her bag. It was creamy-colored and soft with age. Inside was the hammered and filed handle of a teaspoon. Its patina was burnished with age. She held it in her hand as if it was spun glass.

"This was my mama's 'bone.' That's the old word we use for the tool we sew with on account of the old-time sewers made a tool from real bone, like a rib of a cow. Nowadays, though, most like a teaspoon handle. I couldn't sew without this one," she said, holding it fondly between her fingers. "Don't know what I'd do if I lost it. I make all my baskets with it. Hope to pass it on to Grace someday."

"And this," she said, handing over another teaspoon handle with baroque filigree, "is your bone. Elmore hammered it smooth just for you from an old silver spoon he found lying in the sweetgrass field. Don't know how it got there. Coulda been left on a grave. Coulda been a hurricane." She cackled mischievously. "Maybe ol' Beatrice left it there."

"It wouldn't surprise me if that old ghost was throwing the silver around," Mama June said, venturing a laugh. The smile quickly disappeared. "Thank you, Nona," she said more seriously, taking the spoon in hand. "This means a lot to me. More than I can say."

"You're welcome." Nona handed her one of the small coils begun by Grace. "This will be a good start."

Mama June took the sweetgrass coil and fingered it, thinking of the young girl who'd sewn it, remembering her as a baby in her arms, and now a vivacious, bright adolescent filled with the dreams Nan was talking about just the night before.

"How come we've never done this before?" asked Mama June.

"Time wasn't right before," Nona replied readily. She handed her a skein of grass. "Now, take a small bundle of grass. That's right. Now, feed it into the coil, like I do."

Mama June watched as Nona expertly fed strands of grass into the coil as she wrapped it with the thin strip of palmetto.

"You're sewing it like thread," Mama June interjected.

"That's right. Now, you try it." She watched as Mama June struggled with the thin grass.

Mama June's fingers felt clumsy and the grass slid between her fingers. "You make it look so easy."

Nona chuckled. "Don't let it slip. You be the boss of that basket!"

She leaned over to closely watch Mama June's progress, stopping to guide her hands as she darted her tool into the grass to make a space for the binding strip to pass through, pulling it back through, feeding more grass and then wrapping the bundle tight before the next stitch.

Time passed as the two old women sat weaving side by side. Row upon row, the circle expanded, growing wider and wider, the stitches radiating outward like the spokes of a wheel.

19

"Footfalls echo in the memory
Down the passage which we did not take
Towards the door we never opened."

—T. S. Eliot

MORGAN DROVE AIMLESSLY all afternoon. He drove
north up Highway 17 to Bulls Bay, passing lines of blue sewer
pipes being laid and bulldozers that lay still, like great beasts in
the field, waiting to devour still more sections of precious wetlands. He cruised through his old haunts in the Old Village and
then Shem Creek, where he saw college kids and young exec-
utives carouse at the bars that littered the docks beside the few
remaining shrimp boats. Finally he crossed the old, rusted Grace
Bridge that spanned the Cooper River toward Charleston.

The sun was just lowering, setting the sky afire over the
water. Against this backdrop, he felt a thrill of awe at seeing
the progress of the new bridge being built practically on top
of the two older ones. The enormous steel structure seemed
to grow at an amazing pace, faster and higher toward the
clouds, like Jack's fabled beanstalk. And like Jack in the fairy

tale, he felt certain the structure would change the lives of all Charlestonians forever.

The enormity of the new diamond-shaped bridge dwarfed the delicate truss bridge he'd come to love over his lifetime. So many milestones were marked by crossing that narrow two-lane bridge to and from the coast and the city. It was difficult to imagine the Charleston horizon without it.

He sighed, confused with the warring emotions that always came when he tried to reconcile the fast pace of change along the Southern coastline. His parents and their friends were like the old Grace Bridge, he thought, looking dispassionately out the window. They spanned the same years, they were old and rusty, and they were part of a Lowcountry that was fast disappearing.

He reached the high point of the old bridge and looked out over the Cooper River. The port was overflowing with containers piled high, waiting to be loaded onto the enormous ships that would carry goods across the ocean. All healthy signs of growth, expansion and progress. Beneath the bridge, the waters teemed.

He remembered the submarines that used to slide under this bridge back during the Cold War. Some of those babies were nuclear subs with enough warheads to ignite Armageddon. You could bet that put Charleston high on the enemy list for bombing, he thought. Of course, it was all hush-hush. They weren't supposed to know they were even here. His brother used to tease him when a sub rolled under them as they drove over this bridge. It was damn scary for a young kid to see. Those things were enormous and they slunk under the bridge like deadly monster sharks. Hamlin wasn't scared of them, though. Ham wasn't afraid of much.

He reached for the bottle of bourbon in the brown paper bag and took a gulp. His brother's ghost was riding shotgun in his truck. He could feel his presence all afternoon, breathing down his neck. Ham was making up the rules again, same as always.

So when the sun set and darkness fell, it didn't surprise him when he found himself driving down the dirt road that led to Blakely's Bluff. Cypress, tupelo, live oak and countless shaggy pines and palmettos loomed high around him like a jungle. He could barely see ten feet ahead of him in the starless, moon-deprived blackness, and he cursed out loud to his brother as he gripped the wheel and leaned forward, squinting hard. The road twisted like a snake through the swamps. A couple of times he almost landed in a ditch, food for the alligators.

He was already food for the mosquitoes. The windows were rolled down to fend off the sweltering heat and the mosquitoes were feasting. The sound of frogs swelled around him, bellowing with a chorus of crickets, cicadas and katydids.

A breeze carrying the scent of the sea warned him that he was nearing the bluff. Then, suddenly, he broke through the tunnel of foliage into a clearing. A sliver of moon cut through the velvety blackness allowing him the miserly silhouette of a large, bold house against an eerie vista of dark, swiftly moving clouds.

Bluff House. He felt a shudder rack his body. The house loomed against the horizon, its secrets clinging close in the shadows, daring him to approach. So many conflicting memories assailed him at the sight.

He stopped the truck and stared, his heart pounding in his chest. The old engine rocked the truck while countless, nameless bugs, attracted by the headlights, slammed suicidally against the windshield. Morgan cut the engine and instantly all was still. The only sounds he heard were the steady, rhythmic rolling of the surf and the soft wing beats of insects.

Morgan knew he had come, literally, to the end of the road. He had a choice to make. He could stay here for the night and face the ghost of his brother, or he could turn the truck around and leave Blakely's Bluff forever.

He leaned against the steering wheel and lowered his head against his arms. He couldn't fight this any longer. It wasn't the drink talking, or the fatigue, or the malaise that was settling into his bloodstream as thick and brackish as silt-laden water in a swamp ditch. He heard his brother howling, calling his name in the wind.

"All right, you son of a bitch," he muttered. "I'm coming."

That night, Morgan screamed.

He was in the boat again. In Shark Hole. The sky was threatening and the clouds were boiling. From somewhere in the miasma, thunder rumbled. Morgan was afraid. He didn't feel safe. He wanted to go home.

"We've got to go home!" he kept saying in a panic, over and over. "We've got to go home!"

Hamlin was in the boat with him. He was bigger and powerful and he was laughing. "We're okay," he kept answering. "Don't worry."

The thunder grew louder, deafening, and the wind picked up, causing whitecaps to form on the open water. Morgan felt his body seize, knew that they should've gone home before the skies got ugly. He'd said so!

But Hamlin only laughed. "We're okay. Don't worry."

The wind hadn't been so bad at first, but then, suddenly, it freshened and began to blow a little harder, and a little harder still. It felt like they'd sailed right into a black wall of cold. Whitecapping was bad news for a flat-bottomed boat. They had to pass through open water before they reached the relative protection of the tall marsh grass.

The sides of the boat were low. As he clutched them, Morgan's knuckles turned white. The boat took a beating. The engine started losing power and water began coming in over the rim.

Hamlin stopped laughing then. "Put this on!" he called out, and tossed Morgan the life preserver. There was only one.

"You take it!" Morgan screamed.

"I'm okay!" he called back. "Put it on, squirt!"

Morgan did as his older brother ordered. He always did what Hamlin told him to do.

Hamlin clutched the motor with a strange gleam in his eye and turned into the wind. The waves took his measure. They were bullies, broad-shouldered and granite-jawed as they rammed against the boat. Hamlin gritted his teeth and guided them across the whitecaps in the moaning flat-bottomed boat. They bucked high and hit the waves hard, heading toward the marsh in a zigzag pattern. But the motor was weak and began to sputter. They just didn't have enough power to ride the top.

The boat kept getting smaller and smaller and the waves bigger and bigger, until they appeared to Morgan as a primeval beast ready to devour them. Over the howling wind he heard a horrible crack as one of the boat's braces, worn from the pummeling, broke clean in half. Water gushed in, spewing high, victorious. Morgan felt the cold water as pure terror and cried for his big brother.

"Ham! Ham!"

Time altered. With a sudden thrust Morgan felt himself somersaulting in the air in slow motion. He saw feet and legs and hands and wood and darkness, then suddenly—bam—he was underwater. All was quiet, peaceful. For a split second, he wanted to stay. But he bobbed to the surface, gasping for air, his arms and legs suspended in the cold water. But there was nothing to hold on to.

Where was Hamlin? He saw his brother's head not too far away. He opened his mouth to call but the wind whipped a spray of salt water across his face. The droplets stung like pellets and he coughed. He closed his eyes just for a moment. Just long enough to stop the stinging. When he opened them again, his brother was gone. Panic's aim was true. Morgan thrashed and cried and screamed. "Ham! Ham!"

He felt himself being pulled under. His mouth was filling with water, he couldn't breathe, but he told himself he couldn't go under. Would not go under. He had to keep his head above water. He had to find his brother. He clawed at the waves, desperate, angry, crying, reaching, screaming.

Morgan jolted forward, gasping for air, his eyes wide with terror. He was bathed in sweat. He looked around the room, ready to bolt at any strange noise. It took a few minutes for him to awaken from the nightmare enough to recognize where he was. The moonlight seeped into the room like a stain, giving his skin a surreal pewter sheen.

He collapsed back against the bed and raised his arm to cover his eyes. He'd had this same nightmare many times before, though not so vividly in years. When he was a kid, he'd had it over and over again. He'd always wake up screaming and crying. It got so he hated to fall asleep.

He ran his hands through his hair, waking up a little. Though his mind was hazy with fatigue and drink, he compelled himself to bring the details of the accident to mind again, this time while he was awake. He had to come to terms with what had happened that day. He sensed his brother lurking, demanding that he face it. He heard his voice in his head.

He rubbed his eyes and stared out. Enough of this crap!

He was done with this. "Come on!" he called to his brother. "I know you're out there. Let's get this over with once and for all!"

Think, squirt! What were you doing when the storm hit?

He dragged his thoughts back to that fateful day. It didn't start out as anything special. It was just a summer day like so many others. They were at Bum's Camp, as usual. He'd seen the bad weather coming and he'd told Hamlin that he thought they should go home. But his brother was working on something and didn't want to. He'd teased him, calling him a worrywart and a baby—stuff like that. When the thunder began rumbling, though, Hamlin checked the sky and figured it was time to head back. But by then, even though Morgan was only eight, he knew it was already too late. They had to cross open water in a small boat. It was Hamlin who'd taught him not to take chances with the weather.

You were scared.

"Damn straight I was scared." He'd clung to the sides of the boat like a baby. When he looked into his brother's face, however, he saw the dare that could spark in his eyes without warning. Hamlin held tight to the engine, his coarse, sun-kissed hair slicked back by the wind and the golden, chiseled muscles of his athletic body angled forward, as hard and unrelenting as the mast of a ship. He was laughing.

Hamlin was ten years older than Morgan, a snot-nosed, know-nothing kid. To him, his brother was a god. Hamlin was more of a father to him than his own father was. He'd taught him most everything he knew. But he had a wild streak and took a lot of risks. He laughed at danger. He'd laughed in the dream. Morgan heard him laughing now.

His laughing had made Morgan feel angry. But when it had stopped, he was scared. He didn't believe Hamlin when he said they'd be okay.

Did you think I made a mistake?

Morgan could sense his brother's presence very near.

"You did the best you could. It wasn't your fault the engine gave out."

But then I gave you the life preserver.

Morgan nodded, tightening his lips. "You should have put it on yourself!"

So you think it was my fault that I gave you the life preserver?

"Not your fault. But if you'd been wearing the life preserver, you wouldn't have died."

But you would have.

"No," he ground out. "I would have held on to you. I wouldn't have let go."

He heard Hamlin laughing again. *Oh, yeah, sure, squirt.*

"I would have!"

The laughing stopped and the voice grew gentle. *You did try to reach me.*

"I knew it was bad. I kept trying to grab hold of you. To save you."

I was your older brother. I should have been looking out for you.

"You did. You were."

You're right, pal. I gave you the life preserver.

"I kept reaching for you! I couldn't find you." Morgan's eyes filled with tears and he began weeping openly. "I couldn't do anything. I was just floating there, getting farther and farther away. The waves kept hitting me and I was choking. I couldn't do anything."

You survived.

After a few moments he calmed and could answer. "Yes. I must've swum. I can't remember. I just know I ended up in the creek. The tide was lowering and I hugged the grass line for all I was worth. I got cut up pretty bad by the oysters, but I hung on until someone came."

Sweetgrass

Who came? Who rescued you?

Morgan paused and it was as if the fog rolled back. He saw a boat coming. Hearing his name being called he'd cried out, "I'm here! I'm here!" He clawed through the fog, trying to see who was calling his name. Suddenly the mist cleared and he saw a man's hand reach out to grab him and haul him close, calling his name over and over, "Morgan! Morgan!

Not Hamlin. Morgan.

"It was my father who came for me. He pulled me out of the water."

That's right, brother. Never forget that.

Morgan choked up. He couldn't reply.

Never forget me.

Outside the window, the wind rattled the marsh grasses and brought the long, drooping fronds of the palmettos scratching against the house. Morgan closed his eyes tight, reached out to the empty darkness and wept.

Mama June was awake before her husband. She'd come to Preston's room the night before to climb into his bed. She'd craved his warmth and needed his strength, both of which he'd freely offered, wrapping his good arm around her and holding her close against his body. They lay like spoons while she wept and told him all that had transpired.

She was terribly worried when Morgan didn't return home. She'd wanted to rouse the family to go out searching for him. But Nona's words had held her back. *He's not a boy. He's a man! You and Preston both have to face that.*

So she waited for the dawn in her husband's arms, gathering strength. When the first pink rays tinted the walls, Mama June crept from Preston's bed, careful not to disturb him, and went stealthily to her room. She dressed in the dark, putting on whatever she grabbed first, and slipped her bare feet into tennis shoes. She knew in her heart where she was going. There was only place Morgan could be.

The morning air was cool when she stepped outside, and she lifted her face to the dawn. She felt her resolve crystallize as she crossed the damp lawn to the old woodshed. She pulled out her old red bicycle. The paint was rusted and the old wicker basket was ratty, but the tires were full. She didn't want to wake the family with the roar of a car engine, so she hopped on her trusty Schwinn and began pedaling down the dirt road that led to Blakely's Bluff.

Her legs pumped as her tires skimmed along the edge of the marsh. Dragonflies, as brilliant a green as the marsh, darted among the tangles of vines and shrubs devouring mosquitoes. She recalled another time she'd pedaled with the same sense of urgency toward Bluff House. History repeated itself—she personally experienced this—and it struck fear in her heart.

"Please God, let me find him safe. And when I do, help me to find the courage to speak."

As she pedaled, her mind carried her back to the days she'd spent at Blakely's Bluff, not with Tripp, but with his son, Hamlin, and Morgan and Nan, and most of all, with Preston. She could think back on those happier times now and not shrink back. She and Preston had created a good family. From the ashes, they had forged a strong marriage. How happy they'd been! They couldn't know tragedy would strike twice.

She'd been stuck in a sorrowful pattern for too long. Not that she'd ever forget or expect the pain to be gone completely. But she wasn't afraid of the pain anymore. She supposed that meant she was healing. And getting old. Perhaps with age you didn't get all the pleasures you had when you were young, she reasoned, but at least you understood them better.

Her legs were tiring and her heart pumping hard as the road curved and she broke through the tunnel of heavy foliage. Straight ahead the blue-gray waters of the ocean stretched far out to where the deep water become cobalt and boldly met the sky at the horizon. It was a cloudless sky and the sun was still rising. Already light dazzled like diamonds on the water.

She'd forgotten how beautiful it was at the bluff. Or how much she loved it.

Mama June pushed back a lock of sweat-laden hair from her forehead, then heaved her weight against the pedal to ride the final yards to the house. As she approached, she saw that the weather had done a fair job of splintering the house's gray wood and peeling back the white paint from the front porch. It would have looked more dilapidated were it not for the house's strong, uncompromising lines and the cheery hanging pots dripping with blooms of geraniums and petunias on the front porch. She rested the bicycle against the porch railing and stepped foot on the stairs of Bluff House for the first time in more years than she could remember.

Inside, the airy, sparsely furnished rooms of the house were surprisingly tidy. The floors and cobwebs had been swept clean, and new candles were ensconced in shining hurricane lamps. Stepping into the kitchen, she saw that the old, chipped porcelain sink had been scrubbed. Small clay pots of herbs lined the windowsill. It had to be Kristina, she thought, and felt a gush of tenderness toward the woman for her thoughtfulness.

"Morgan!" she called out. "Morgan, are you here?" There was no answer. She couldn't believe he wasn't here. She'd been so sure. The windows were wide open. Unnerved, she went to the window and called out again, louder, "Morgan!"

"Out here!"

Her heart pumped with relief as she followed the sound of his voice back outdoors. A motion caught in the corner of her eye and she turned her head toward the long, weathered dock that extended far out over the marsh to deep water. She spied the unmistakable shape of her son standing at the end of the dock, barefoot, his shirttails flapping in the breeze and his pants rolled up above his calves. She waved. He didn't wave back.

The dock seemed to stretch forever as she made her way along the splintered wood toward her son. He turned his head to look out to the sea, a gesture of pique, but she pressed on. She'd always thought he looked so much like Preston, but in profile, she saw her own outline in the narrowness of his jawline.

She had to stop making comparisons, she told herself. Morgan was not like anyone else. He was himself. Today she would begin seeing him for who he was.

She reached his side, and though she longed to reach out and hold him, his rigid stance held her at bay. "I thought you might be here."

He turned to face her, and she was shocked by the deep circles under his bloodshot eyes, accentuated by his dark stubble. He smelled of hard liquor and a hard night.

"Are you all right?"

He nodded. "Yeah," he replied in a husky voice.

"Morgan," she began haltingly. "I'm sorry you had to find out like that."

He swung his head back toward the sea.

She clenched her fists, unsure of what to say next.

"I was wrong not to let you talk about Hamlin and his death and what you went through that day out on the water. I see that now."

He shied away. "I don't want to talk about it."

"You have to. It colors everything you see, everything you do! And I have to let you talk about it. You and I, we've always turned away from even thinking about that day. The minute we

358

felt sad or someone brought it up, we'd shut down. We wouldn't go there. Just like we wouldn't come here to Blakely's Bluff because it was a painful reminder of what had happened."

He remained silent.

"Maybe it won't bring Hamlin back to life, but it will bring his memory back so that we can openly remember him. Talk about him. So we can remember the good times. Morgan, there were so many good memories."

Tears flooded his eyes and he looked away. "I miss him."

"I do, too. And I've missed you. Oh, Morgan. Sometimes I feel I lost both my sons that day."

Morgan lowered his head and his shoulders shook.

Her throat constricted but she pushed out the words. "I'm your mother and I failed you. I let go of your hand. I'm sorry. Please, let me have a second chance."

"It wasn't your fault, Mama," he choked out. "It was mine. I'm no good."

"It wasn't your fault, Morgan! It wasn't my fault. It wasn't even Hamlin's fault. It was an accident. It happened. And if we try to blame it on anyone, even ourselves, we'll never get past it. We'll remain among the walking wounded and never get on with our lives."

She wiped her eyes and took a steadying breath, determined now to save her son.

"We won't drown in these tears, Morgan," she said, grabbing hold of his shoulders, forcing him to look at her. "I'm glad you found those letters. Do you hear me? I'm glad! There've been enough secrets between us. No more! We need to talk to each other honestly, even if the truth hurts." She laughed self-consciously. "Even if your cheek hurts."

He hiccuped a laugh and shook his head. "I crossed a line there. I'm sorry."

"Oh, Morgan," she said, feeling a tremendous relief. "We've

all made mistakes we're sorry about. But we're good people. I'll tell you everything so that you can understand what happened. Why we made the choices we did. We love each other. We care about each other. That's what family is all about."

"I do love you, Mama." His voice shook with emotion.

Her heart opened so wide she thought she could envelop him in it. She saw his blue eyes, vulnerable and daring to trust, his brown curls, matted, and the planes of his face coursed by tracks of tears. She thought of the boy, then quickly stopped herself.

He wiped his eyes and sat down on the edge of the dock, then surprised her by tapping the wood beside him in invitation. She felt enormously grateful for this small offering and lowered herself to the warm wood.

He didn't talk for a while and she allowed him his peace. She sensed he wanted to tell her something more and bided her time.

"I dreamed of Ham last night," he said at last. He kept his eyes on the water, but she saw a muscle twitch in his cheek. "He was here."

She swallowed hard, believing him. "Do you want to tell me about it?"

The tension fled from Morgan's face and revealed his surprise that she'd ask him to speak openly about his brother.

He began to talk then. Mama June dangled her feet over the edge of the dock and listened, relishing every word. When he was done, he was spent. She took her son's hand and led him up to Bluff House, to the big bed that stood before the open window and the ocean's breeze. She tucked him in and smoothed his hair from his brow.

"Shh… You can sleep now. Close your eyes," she told him, her voice calm and soothing. "I'm going to tell you a bedtime story."

He closed his eyes. Immediately his jaw slackened.

She sat in the old ladder-back chair near the bed and took a deep breath. It was, she thought to herself, never too late to tell one's child a bedtime story.

"Once upon a time," she began, "there was a castle deep in the forest in a place very hard to find. The land around the castle was depleted and the people troubled because of the poor health of the king."

Morgan pried open an eye. "Is this Parsifal?"

"You've heard it?

"You told it to me a million years ago."

"Now, hush and let me tell it to you again."

He closed his eye.

"Let's see, where was I?" She thought a moment, then began in a fairy-tale cadence.

"Parsifal was raised by his mother in the isolation of the woods. She didn't want Parsifal to leave her, but Parsifal was true of heart, like his father, and wanted to be a knight. So, against his mother's wishes, he left home without so much as a goodbye. He spent many years wandering in the forest. But, being pure of spirit, one day he was allowed to see the hidden castle of the wounded king, who was known as the Fisher King because he was a first-rate angler. Now, the Fisher King was also the custodian of the Holy Grail. The great king was dying, however, and had cruelly been struck dumb."

Morgan shifted, listening.

"On entering the castle, Parsifal approached the Fisher King. But he was so overwhelmed by a strange vision that he failed to ask the king the one crucial question."

"What was the question?"

"*What ails you?* Because of his failure to ask about the king's suffering, when Parsifal woke up the following morning, the castle had disappeared. After many more years of wanderings, during which our hero suffered and endured many trials, Parsifal gained wisdom. Through his own merits, he was allowed to enter the castle again."

"What happened then?"

"There are different endings to this story."

"Don't give me that 'you have to write your own ending' stuff. I'll never fall asleep thinking about it. Just tell me the ending you like best."

She chuckled lightly. "Well, I think Parsifal figured out that suffering was a part of life. When he was given a second chance, Parsifal followed his noble heart. He returned to the castle and asked the king the right question out of love and compassion. In doing so, he restored the king's health and saved the castle's fate." Her shoulders lifted in a light shrug. "No matter who tells the story, ultimately Parsifal succeeds as king."

"Not a bad ending."

"I thought you might enjoy it." She rose and drew nearer to place a kiss on his forehead. "Now, go to sleep, son. Rest. When you wake up, we'll go home. Your father is waiting for us."

20

———

"If we don't change the way we grow, we will simply sprawl into the last remaining things we love about the coast. There aren't just alternatives to sprawl—there are great alternatives to sprawl."

—Dana Beach, South Carolina Coastal
Conservation League

WHEN MORGAN RETURNED home, he went first to his father's room.

Preston was sitting in his wheelchair gazing out the window. One hand rested on Blackjack's broad head, the whiteness of his skin a sharp contrast to the black fur. His face was pale and one side slackened unnaturally to the right. Morgan saw his father as an ailing king, surrounded by the accoutrement of illness.

When he entered, his father's blue eyes brightened, matching the brilliance of the azure sky outside the window. His lips moved slightly and his left hand rose subtly in a faint gesture of greeting.

Morgan drew near to his father and bent on one knee beside his chair so that they were face-to-face. His father reached out, placing his good hand upon his shoulder. The gesture was clumsy, but his grip felt like a metal clamp.

Morgan looked into his father's eyes and saw himself—a man, a son—in the reflection. Taking a breath, he asked the question that he'd rehearsed in his mind as he traveled along the lonely dirt road on his long journey from Blakely's Bluff to home.

The house smelled of boiled greens while outside the savory scent of barbecue had mouths watering. Nona and Mama June were cooking up a feast for family dinner—perhaps the last one they'd share at Sweetgrass. Chas took a real interest in the pig slow-roasting over the open-pit fire and was getting pointers on the fine art of making red sauce from Elmore. Meanwhile, Morgan and Harry shucked corn and kept wood on the fire. Nan and Kristina were giggling in the kitchen, making a trifle with the first batch of peaches.

"Sounds like you girls are nipping a little too much of the brandy!" Nona called to them.

The two women sang back for everyone to mind their own business and prepare to experience a little heaven on earth.

Mama June heard that and smiled as she placed bowls of artichoke relish and watermelon rinds on the table. She felt she was already experiencing a little heaven on earth.

The wind swept through the palmettos as her gaze captured her family. She tucked the image in her heart to bring out later, like a treasured photograph. She never thought she'd see the family laugh together again as they were now. Though it was hard to believe they might really be losing this place. Yet, if losing the land was what it cost to get her family back, then she thought it was well worth it.

She looked up at the house, half expecting to see the ghost of Beatrice standing at the window, watching them as always.

She felt a bond with the founding ancestor. Beatrice's son, the first Hamlin, had returned from the war a broken shell, but she'd helped him heal by helping him to build Bluff House. When he died, she persevered, moving the family forward.

"We've done all right in the end, haven't we?" she said to her spirit. "We both raised our babies straight and true, and we both buried our young and had to carry on. Look at them," she said, her gaze moving back to the lawn where her children and their children were gathering at the table. "They love one another and will watch out for one another. I guess we can't ask for much more from life than that, can we?"

"Mama June! Dinnertime!"

The dinner was a finger-licking success, the trifle memorable. After the last of it was devoured and the coffee was poured, the family sat on the porch. Their blessings that day included a sea breeze that kept the mosquitoes at bay. When all were sated, Morgan at last brought up the topic that lay in the back of all their minds.

"Here's the deal," Morgan began, leaning back in the wide wicker chair. "In a nutshell, the Chinese Partnership provides a means by which one partner can buy out the other, but the terms preclude her lowballing him. The partner entering the buyout bid has to make the terms fair enough that she would find them acceptable if the tables were turned."

"I don't get it," Chas said, scratching his head.

Morgan held back his smile and took the question seriously. "Okay, let's say you and Harry were partners and you wanted to buy out Harry's half of the business. If you make an offer to buy him out, then he is forced to act. Harry can either sell his half or—and this is the good part—he can turn around and offer you the exact same amount of money you offered him. If he does that, then you would have to sell it to him."

"So my offer would have to be sweet in case I had to eat it, right?" he asked.

"Exactly."

Harry spoke up. "Is that what Aunt Adele did?" When Morgan nodded he asked, "Then why don't we just buy her half?"

Everyone chuckled while Morgan rubbed the back of his neck. "See, that's the problem. It takes time to raise that kind of cash. We might know what Adele is up to, but even knowing, I don't know what we can do."

Nan looked at her father with worry, but his expression was unreadable. "Are you saying we're going to have to sell? After all this?"

He didn't reply.

Nona looked up, alarmed. "But what about the cemetery? We can't be having nobody disturbing that."

"Don't worry. The cemetery is well marked," Morgan replied. "Even if the place is sold, they can't move it."

"I'm not talking about the Blakely cemetery," Nona replied, drawing back.

Morgan was perplexed. "Then, what cemetery?"

Nona glanced at Elmore. He nodded for her to go ahead.

"See, there's another cemetery. One out by the marsh, where the sweetgrass grows. It's far, far back where no one hardly ever goes anymore. My mother told me about it, on account of her uncle ran a funeral home. She remembered walking in funeral processions there when she was little, usually at night. She took me there so I would remember where it was, too. And I take my children, and my children's children."

"Who is buried there?" Mama June asked, stunned.

"Why, the slaves, of course," Nona replied. "And all sorts of black folks for a while after." She paused. "My ancestors are buried there."

Sweetgrass

"My heavens, I had no idea," Mama June said, her hand at her chest. "All this time and we did nothing to mark the grounds?"

"It wasn't meant to be found," Nona said somberly. "Long ago, most slave cemeteries were in faraway spots where the land was poor and the plantation owners didn't care about it. Most likely in swampy areas or among trees and thick shrubs in the middle of fields where the value of the land was low."

"I've heard about slave cemeteries being found around these parts," Nan said.

"Child, there are old slave graves hidden all over the South. Over time, that land by the coast shot way up in value. It's been bought up and the graveyards were closed, same as the sweet-grass fields. Families weren't allowed to bury there no more or ever visit them again. I can't see letting that happen here."

Morgan leaned forward on the table. "Are you sure there's one here?"

"'Course I'm sure!" she said, looking at him as if he was a fool. "Not only *on* Sweetgrass, but *in* the sweetgrass. It's right where we do our pulling. Only a handful of us know about it. It's not written down nowhere. We know about it mostly through the stories. I'm not sure even Elmore is clear on where all of it is, exactly, and he knows that piece of land better than anybody. See, graveyards like these were used for generations by tradition. You won't find them in deeds or in other legal papers."

"How big are we talking about?" asked Morgan.

Nona looked questioningly to Elmore for an answer.

Elmore's long face had deep lines that coursed down the bones and planes of his face like dried rivers through canyons. He scratched his jaw with his slender, gnarled hands. "Oh, I couldn't say, exactly. A few acres, maybe. I seen pottery and mirrors here and there scattered all through the sweetgrass fields. And shells, like the Gullah use. Snakes, too. Lord help me, there's plenty snakes in there."

"Elmore's afraid of snakes," Nona confided.

"I am," he said loudly and without apology. "I hate them critters. Especially the rattlers. They shake that ol' tail." He shook his head, frowning.

"What do the mirrors and shells have to do with it? I don't understand," asked Mama June.

Nona spoke up first. "Those are grave markers. These people came from Africa. They weren't Christian. They didn't have the same beliefs or religious practices. And the plantation owners didn't care one whit where the slaves were buried as long as it wasn't in good land. They sure didn't offer them fancy headstones, neither. Tombstones are rare. Back in Africa, when somebody was buried, their kin put some of their favorite items on the grave and let nature carry on. So that's what our people did."

"If there's a cemetery out there, then that's sacred ground," Mama June said. "It has to be preserved. No matter what happens to the rest of the property."

"Could a cemetery be enough to stop Adele?" asked Nan, rising up in excitement.

Morgan tapped his lips, wondering what he could do with this information. "Let's not get ahead of ourselves. Now, I've heard of land development projects being stalled by claims of burial grounds in place. But often it's only a stall. Usually they work out some sort of legal compromise, like moving the bodies or partitioning off the area. South Carolina has laws protecting cemeteries, but they're unevenly enforced. I'll check on it tomorrow but I doubt it will do much good in the long run. A few graves won't stop Adele."

"A few?" Nona asked, eyes rounding. "There're a whole lot more than a few in there. Son, we're talking about generations of slaves. Time was, this was a big working plantation. I reckon there are a couple a hundred graves in there!"

Everyone looked at her in hushed shock. Morgan couldn't comprehend that many graves on the property without anyone having recorded it. But even through his shock, he knew it could very well be true. From grade school on, Morgan knew that slaves died by the thousands in the Carolinas and Georgia. Especially children. He figured that there had to be many unmarked, unprotected slave cemeteries all along the coast.

"Can you take me there?" he asked, trying to tamp down his burgeoning excitement.

Elmore put his big hand on the table and spoke solemnly. "I can. I'll do whatever we can to ensure our ancestors rest in peace."

The following day, Morgan marched into the kitchen carrying a suitcase and moving with the swift, forward movements of a man on a mission. His trip to the cemetery earlier that morning had renewed his hope. The suitcase hit the floor with a thump, and in a swoosh he opened his arms and scooped Nona up into them.

"Give me a kiss, sweetheart. This old boy is heading north!"

When he bent to kiss her, he was enveloped in her familiar scent of vanilla. Nona clucked her tongue with surprise as he gave her a sound kiss on the cheek. "Just where're you going?"

"I'm off to Columbia to try to convince a bunch of bureaucrats to start an official investigation of that cemetery right away."

Maize, who had come by to visit her mother, looked at him skeptically. "Why would you do that?" she asked suspiciously.

He looked her way, grinning. "Hey, Maize. Well, first off,

it's the right thing to do. Second, we're about to lose the right to have any say in the matter. An offer to buy this place is on its way even as we speak."

"You think it's just some graveyard," Maize replied. "Well, think again. There are organizations we can call that preserve old cemeteries. I'm going to form a committee to take legal action to return this cemetery to the community. Nobody is going to bulldoze our ancestors' graves!"

Mama June walked in carrying Preston's tray. Her eyes were round as she glanced uncomprehendingly from face to face.

"Hold on there," Nona said to Maize. "Nobody here is talking about bulldozing graves!"

"Actually, she's right. It *is* a threat," Morgan said honestly. "There are cases where houses have been built right over gravesites. I'm hoping they'll send some archeologists out here."

"So you figure that the cemetery will act as a stall?" asked Maize.

"At the very least," he replied unapologetically. "When I was in Montana, we managed to hold off a major development project because an old Indian burial ground was discovered on the land. If it turns out that there are as many graves here as your father thinks there are, the state will likely designate that part of the land as historical property. That will mean you and others who have family buried there will be able to pay your respects without worry about someone building over them."

"You don't care about the cemetery," Maize countered. "All you care about is saving your land."

"That cemetery is important to us, too," Mama June interjected.

"Maize, your family and mine have been entwined together for hundreds of years," Morgan said to her. "I'm not proud of all that's transpired in that history, but I'll tell you this. Fate is having the last laugh, because all these years later, both of our families are about to lose this land for the same reasons—taxes and family members wanting to sell. We're all about to get screwed."

"He's right," Nona said. "Our family bought our piece way back for fifty cents an acre. We're worried about hanging on, too, and wonder what's going to happen if family members want to sell."

"This property is a linchpin," said Morgan. "If it goes to development, so will other big pieces like it. Then the threat will turn to all the smaller communities like Hamlin, Six Mile and Seven Mile till there's nothing of the old Lowcountry left. It'll disappear from the landscape, just as the sweetgrass did."

"I'm talking about saving a graveyard," Maize said. "You're talking about saving a community. How can we fight that kind of change? Developers are powerful people."

"That's the beauty of the American system. We've got to get folks fired up. Sitting back feeling helpless is what they're counting on us to do. They won't expect us to fight back."

Maize's expression changed from one of doubt and suspicion to reflect a spark of interest.

"Come with me to Columbia," he told her. "You're a banker. You know the system. We need your voice to represent your cause. Speak for your family, Maize."

"All right, I'll come. For my children's sake," she declared. "But so help me, Morgan Blakely, if you don't keep your word on this, I'll come after you so hard you'll wish you were buried in that cemetery."

He barked out a laugh and put out his hand to shake hers. "Damn, that doesn't sound too good for me. I'd better work hard."

"Give me half an hour to pack up and I'll be ready," Maize said.

"Great. I'll pick you up."

Mama June and Nona exchanged glances over raised brows while their children walked out the back door together, making plans.

"Did you ever…" said Mama June with amazement.

Nona shook her head. "I've been trying for years to get my Maize involved with her history and her ancestors, but she's always turned a deaf ear."

"She surely didn't turn a deaf ear today."

"No, she did not!" Nona laughed loudly. "Heaven help Morgan. The Lord works in mysterious ways."

"Those two have been ornery and cantankerous with each other since they were in diapers."

"I don't know about you," Nona said, "but I need a cup of coffee."

"There's some made," Mama June said. "I'll heat it up."

"You know I'm not going to be drinking that burnt coffee!" Nona replied, wrinkling her nose. "This calls for a fresh pot."

Morgan was a man on fire.

After he returned from Columbia he gathered together the family and his closest advisers in his father's office. Then he wheeled his father into the room with ceremony. As he progressed toward the imposing desk where he intended his father to sit, Preston jerked out his hand, stopping the wheel. Preston moved his hand to indicate to his son that it was Morgan's place to sit behind the desk now. Morgan locked eyes with his father. He raised his brows in question. Preston nodded, his eyes gleaming with pride.

Leaning against the desk, Morgan brought everyone up to

speed on the events of the past several days. His mind was working fast so he began to pace as he talked.

"Well, we've got a little time, thanks to Maize's amazing efforts upstate. I swear, Maize, you were born to politics. We've just been informed that the State of South Carolina has put a moratorium on all real estate transaction concerning Sweetgrass until the fate of the old slave cemetery is determined."

It was a solemn moment. Nona looked up to praise God.

"This gives us a reprieve. Here's where we are. Adele officially placed this offer to buy on the table," he said, lifting the papers in his hand. "By doing so, she formally initiated the terms of the Chinese Partnership." His eyes gleamed and his smile grew crafty. "Adele doesn't know, however, that we understand the terms of this unique agreement. Or that we have our copy. Thanks to Daddy."

He smiled at his father as everyone in the room applauded Preston's heroic effort.

"Adele has underestimated us all. Sold us short in more ways than one. She led us to believe that her contract with Preston was a standard buy-sell agreement," Morgan continued. "And that due to the default loan and Daddy's stroke, she could use that as leverage to force the sale. She felt so confident in our blind ignorance that she boldly put forth this paltry offer for the land and then had the nerve to call it fair. She expected us to gobble it up and be grateful for the crumbs.

"But the paltry offer works in our favor. We came up with a plan that has met with Daddy's approval. It just might work, providing we can act fast." He walked briskly to the desk to retrieve sheets of paper outlining the plan. Nan took them and passed them around.

"Bobby has spearheaded a proposal that calls for mixed-use

commercial development of Sweetgrass. We have to raise capital to meet Adele's purchase offer and we have to raise it fast. To accomplish that, we're immediately putting on the market a fifty-acre portion of the land that borders a stretch of the highway for retail development. It's a compromise we can live with. Thanks to Bobby's connections, we have a lead on a buyer. How's that for fast?

"Whatever land that is deemed part of the burial ground by the archeologists will be offered by the family to the town of Mount Pleasant for a cemetery, along with an additional three surrounding acres with the idea that the town would build a historical park in honor of those laid to rest. Finally, all the remaining acres of Sweetgrass will be placed into a conservation easement so that it will remain as green space in perpetuity."

While the people in the room nodded their approval of the plan, Morgan saw Preston's eyes fill with tears. Mama June placed her hands on his shoulder and he reached up to take her hand.

"We'll need to push this proposal through zoning, of course," he said. Everyone laughed, knowing this was likely their toughest battle.

"It's a great offer for the city," Dan said. "How can they not love it?"

"I'm glad you think so, pal," Morgan said in a jocular mood. "This is where you come in. You too, Lizzy."

He'd called his old friends in for this emergency meeting and privately let them know in no uncertain terms the urgency of the situation.

"We're here," Lizzy replied, her voice clear. She couldn't wait to secure this choice piece of Lowcountry as green space.

Morgan acknowledged her support with a grateful nod.

"As soon as we have our ducks in a row—" he paused to wink at Mama June at using Adele's favorite expression "—we will step forward and present our buyout offer to Adele. That amount will equal to the penny what she offered to us." He paused, savoring the moment. "The beauty of the deal is that by the terms of the Chinese Partnership, which she invoked the moment she put her offer on the table, Adele has no choice but to accept." He smiled wryly. "We're literally making her an offer she can't refuse."

"It's positively Confucian," Bobby said, his lips turning into a satisfied grin.

"We all need one another now, perhaps more than we ever have. It's times like these when it's good to have good friends," Morgan said, his eyes traveling from one face to another: Preston, Mama June, Nan, Nona, Elmore, Maize, Bobby, Lizzy, Dan and, standing quietly in the corner, her eyes shining, Kristina.

His voice shook and his heart expanded. "We few, we happy few, we band of brothers."

Maize shook her head. "You couldn't leave it alone, college boy. You had to end with Shakespeare."

A few weeks later, Morgan hurried to his office to answer the phone, which rang insistently. Whoever it was would not leave a message but kept calling over and over. He lurched for the phone just before the answering machine clicked on for the third time.

"Hello?" he barked into the receiver.

"Do you really think you'll get away with this?"

Morgan released his breath and leaned against the desk. "Aunt Adele."

"You have a nerve, turning the tables on me. By what right do you think you can do this? My partnership is with Preston, not you, and any court will find him incapacitated."

He almost laughed at her audacity. "The partnership agreement that you presented to us was a fraud."

"You have to prove that."

It was an empty threat. "We both know my copy is original. If you'd prefer, we can go through forensic analysis, the costs of a court case and let the newspapers have a field day with the family's reputation."

"That could drag on for years. Do you think you can last that long?"

"I know we can. But that won't happen, Aunt Adele."

"And why not?"

"Because if this goes to court, you *will* go to jail."

There was no response. Morgan pressed on.

"Let's not belabor this. You will accept the offer, which is a very handsome return on your investment. I didn't want to do this, considering how you lied and cheated with your bogus contract. I thought keeping you out of jail was repayment enough, but my father insisted we abide by the terms of the contract. He's honest and noble and wouldn't cheat you of a dime. That's the difference between you two. You will accept the offer and the matter will be sealed. The partnership is dissolved. It's over, Adele."

There was a long silence and he wondered if she'd hung up. Then she spoke.

"I want to talk to my brother."

"No," he replied. "You just don't get it. We don't want to see you. None of us."

This time he did hear the soft click as the phone was disconnected.

Mama June sat on the porch of Blakely's Bluff. She often came to the bluff lately, to tidy the house, to have family dinners or sometimes just to sit alone, as she did now. So much had happened in the past months. She sensed she was standing on a precipice about to step over into a new era.

She'd telephoned Adele the night before and asked to meet with her. The business of the contract had ended badly. The two of them went far back, and there were issues Mama June felt they needed to air. She'd been prepared to argue the point, but to her surprise and relief, Adele readily agreed. She should be arriving any minute, she thought.

She'd chosen Blakely's Bluff to meet because it was away from the main house and would afford them privacy. It was also the site of what Mama June believed was at the root of the family's problems with Adele. The history between them started here.

It was early fall and uncomfortably hot. All eyes were on the Caribbean where a tropical depression was forming. Mama June fanned herself with a folded piece of paper that did little more than stir the air. The old porch chair was hard, and not a single breeze came in from the sea to cut the thick miasma of humidity that seemed to hang over the coast like fog. From far off she heard a faint rumbling of thunder. A good storm would be just the thing to break this heat, she thought to herself.

She didn't have to wait long. She heard the whine of a car engine, and a minute later, saw the pale blue Jaguar emerge from the trees into the clearing. Mama June's hand darted to her hair to smooth it.

Adele emerged from the car and stood for a moment, one foot on the car's ledge. Through heavy, dark sunglasses, she looked out over the dock and the water beyond for a moment.

"I still expect to see The Project out there," Adele said.

Mama June didn't reply but stood to greet her.

Adele turned and the two women faced each other. Mama

June could feel the vitriolic mixture of stale affection and fresh animosity flow between them. Adele closed the car door and walked to the porch, her eyes taking in the house as she approached.

"This place never changes," Adele said.

"I wish I could say the same for us."

Adele's brows rose at that as she came up the porch stairs.

"Won't you sit down?" asked Mama June, indicating a chair with her hand.

This was not a social meeting; they both knew that.

Adele took her seat and set her stylish black purse beside the chair. "What's all this about?" she asked.

It was typical of Adele to take the offensive. Mama June looked at her hands, saw the wedding band there, then, reassured, looked into Adele's face. Her eyes were hidden by the dark sunglasses, but they had never given many clues to what Adele was thinking, anyway.

"Was it worth it?" Mama June asked plainly.

A short laugh escaped Adele's lips. She pressed her palms together, thinking, then set them down on the arms of the chair. Her fingers tightened and she replied through thin lips, "Sweetgrass should have been mine. You know that."

"Yours?"

Adele's face paled and her voice shook, betraying her straight-backed composure. "Don't act so surprised. It was all set, long before *you* ever came to Sweetgrass," she said, her tone meant to diminish Mary June's position.

Adele looked out at the sea and spoke in recitation. "My father told me what he'd planned to do. Tripp was to get Blakely's Bluff and the land around it. Preston was to receive another chunk of land with the outbuildings and orchard. And I, their only daughter, was to receive the house and the furniture." Her tone changed. "I remember polishing the stair railing as my mother told me, 'Take good care of it, darling. Someday this house will be yours.'"

There was an uncomfortable pause during which Mama June wondered how long Adele could hold in her simmering rage.

Adele turned back to Mama June. "But then Tripp died. And when our parents passed on, they left all of Sweetgrass to Preston. Not even a small plot was left to me so that I could feel a part of the family—*my* family! The great Blakely heritage, as I've heard so often in my life.

"It was hard to believe that even in these modern times, the boys got it all. I found that cruel and belittling. And infuriating! What about me?" she cried, her voice rising as she leaned forward and pounded her chest. "I was made to feel a guest in my own home! I was an outsider in my own family."

The wind gusted and thunder rolled, closer now.

Adele visibly pulled herself together, straightening her sunglasses. "I can't ever forgive my parents for that. Or Preston. Or you. And you have the nerve to ask me, was it worth it?"

Despite all, Mama June couldn't help but feel pity for Adele. It was wrong for her to be excluded from the family property.

"Why didn't you tell us? If you had come to me and told me how you felt, things might have turned out differently. Why didn't you ask for the house as repayment of the loan? If you had, I would have given it to you!"

Adele drew herself up and whipped off her sunglasses, revealing dark eyes that were flames of fury. "Ask you?" she said with her voice trembling. "You would have given it to me? It was *my* house! Who are you to give me what is rightfully *mine!*"

Mama June sat unmoving in her chair and slowly understood all. There was no possible way she could make this right with Adele. In Adele's mind she'd been dreadfully, unforgivably wronged. In some ways, Mama June agreed that she had. Yet if she'd learned one thing this summer it was that the past was over and one had to live in the present. Adele would never understand that Preston wasn't hoarding the land as much as struggling to keep what little was left of the property intact for future generations. He'd never meant to hurt her.

"So all this was your way of getting even?" she asked without rancor. "Tell me, what would you have done if you'd won and Sweetgrass was yours?"

"I would have sold it," Adele replied, her tone flat and without emotion.

Mama June shivered and looked up at the darkening sky. The storm was moving in fast. "You know what's really sad?" she said in way of conclusion. "You say that you wanted to belong to the family. So you tried to belong through owner- ship of a house." She shook her head. "Adele, a family is not a house. Nor a piece of land. Preston tried to hold on to the family by holding on to the land and it didn't work. The Blakelys are not just this land. That's our history, yes, but it's not us. You belong to a family through relationships. That's what a family is. And that, I'm afraid, is what you've lost."

Adele turned on her. "I regret that I ever brought you home to Sweetgrass."

Mama June felt the words deeply. "There were days I regretted it, too," she replied honestly. "But I believe my des- tiny was here, for better or worse."

Adele rose, grabbed her purse and started down the stairs without a goodbye. This time, Mama June did not go after her. At the car, Adele turned once more to look at Mama June.

"Tell my brother goodbye for me," she called out. "Tell him not to wait, I won't be back. Tell him…" Her eyes flashed with tears. "I don't give a damn about his forgiveness. I don't forgive him!"

Without another word, she drove off.

Mama June watched the sleek car disappear into the foliage just as the first raindrops began to fall.

21

—

"As long as there is an ocean, there will be sweetgrass."
—Ruth Singleton Middleton, basket maker

AS WAS THEIR CUSTOM, Mama June and Preston sat side by side on the front porch watching the sun lower in its predictable, fiery path into the horizon. Another day was done. Mama June reached to place her hand over his, a familiar-enough gesture but bittersweet nonetheless. In years past, it had always been his hand that covered hers. Not that it mattered, she told herself. All that mattered in this sunset of their lives was that their hands were still united.

The house was blissfully quiet. Morgan and Kristina had gone to spend the night at Blakely's Bluff, and Nan had returned home to set her own house in order. Divorce was never easy and this one would be no exception.

"We're empty nesters," she told him. "Again."

She heard his chuckle rumble in his chest.

"I kind of like it, us being alone. I can't believe I'm saying this, but all that excitement is just too much for me. I've found I miss the peace. How about you?"

She didn't need to look to see if he was blinking twice. The gentle pat of his hand was answer enough.

She sighed. She was thinking about how to phrase her next question.

"Our children have grown up at last," she began. "I'm proud of who they've become. We're very lucky."

She paused, unknowingly stroking his hand.

"I know it's hard for you to see the land broken up, but I know, too, that you're proud of the way Morgan's found a way to save Sweetgrass for the family. Your son came through for you. That has always been your dream. You thought I didn't know that, did you?" She turned to look at his face. "I know about that phone call you made to Morgan the night of your stroke."

Preston turned in surprise and looked at her.

"He doesn't know why you phoned him. He thinks it was a call to duty—and I let him think that. It's your place to tell him the truth. He'll want to know it someday, and you'll know when the time is right.

"But I know the truth. I know why you called him. He was your prodigal son. You loved him and you wanted him to know it. And I love you for having the lionhearted courage to pick up that phone and make the first call."

His chest filled with air and he exhaled a ragged breath.

"We've lived through a lot, you and I. It's been a good life. It's been a hard life. It's been," she added with a soft chuckle, "the life that was handed to us. We've made our choices the best we could." She rubbed his hand, choosing her words.

"We have one more to make. I'm afraid to ask you what I'm about to ask." She cleared her throat and faced him. "I'm wondering, Preston… Can we…I believe we should leave Sweetgrass."

His eyes widened as he stared at her.

"You need more help than we can provide for you here! Your progress, as good as it's been, can be better. I've talked to your doctors and they agree. I hate to think you're being held back. Besides, the in-home services will be ending soon, and darlin', I'm just too old to carry this by myself. We both agreed, we don't want to be a burden to our children."

Preston continued to stare at her with unflinching attention.

She persevered. "The details of Morgan's plan will work out, Morgan will see to that. He's doing a fine job and I do believe Kristina will stand by his side." She licked her lips. "I thought we could give Blakely's Bluff to Morgan. He's always preferred Bluff House to this one. It suits him."

She looked around at the stately house she'd come to as a bride nearly half a century earlier. It never appeared more beautiful to her eyes than it was at this moment in the brilliant hues of the Lowcountry sunset. She thought of Beatrice. She'd been a strong, pioneering woman. She'd built this house, and Mama June thought the matriarch had signaled her choice of standard bearers. Beatrice's legacy of strong, independent women would continue with her daughter.

"I'd like Nan to have this house. Your parents did not do right by Adele. And I'm ashamed that we persevered in that sorry tradition by giving Nan but a paltry few acres of wetland. She's earned better by right of birth and by loyalty."

His mouth worked uselessly, and she could see frustration building in his eyes.

Tears filled her own eyes, believing she was destroying his lifelong dream by asking him to leave Sweetgrass now.

"I know you love this place. Sweetgrass has been your whole life. You've worked every day from dawn to dusk giving it your all—your sweat, your blood, your tears. I daresay even your heart. Who am I to ask you to leave? You took pity on me forty-seven years ago. You've given me a home, your name, your honor, and I hold those gifts most dear to my heart. But I believe this is the right thing for us to do. Forgive me, Preston, for asking this," she said, her voice trembling. "Forgive me."

Preston rose up straighter. His chair shook with his effort and with a great show of strength.

Mama June drew back, choking back her tears, stunned into silence. She looked at his face. A fine sheen of sweat formed on his upper lip as he worked his mouth.

Mama June leaned forward, holding her breath.

He closed his eyes and took a breath. Then, opening them, he tried again.

"All."

His lungs filled, and with great concentration he moved his lips.

"For."

Weary now, but with fiery determination, his mouth worked to form one more word.

"You."

He collapsed back against his chair.

Mama June gasped and her hand flew to cover her trembling mouth.

All for you.

Forty-seven years of misunderstanding were swept clear with those three words. *All for you.* Was it true? Could he have loved her that much? She lowered her hands, noticing that they were shaking. Then, lifting her searching gaze into her husband's eyes, she understood what he was telling her.

It was never for Sweetgrass. It was never for Tripp. It was never for the children. Least of all, it was never for me. Everything I did. All I ever worked for. It was all for you.

Mama June was humbled. She was exultant. She felt free from the past at long last.

Preston's face grew solemn and his eyes glistened as he nodded his head in confirmation.

Mary June Blakely leaned far over to wrap her arms around her husband and rest her weary head upon his shoulder. She breathed in the scents of sage and eucalyptus, ones she'd forever more associate with him, and watched the sun slip soundlessly into the horizon.

Autumn creeps into the Lowcountry. After the dog days of August wind down and the children are dragged from the beaches, September seems to slide by. Lowcountry folks stay close to home and keep their eyes on the sky and their ears tuned to reports of storms swirling in the Atlantic Ocean. Only by October, when the hurricane threats settle down a bit, do the people start to relax their guard and take notice of the subtle shift in nature occurring under their very noses.

The tourists were migrating with the birds, heading northward to begin another year of school and work, packing up their memories of days swimming in the surf, golfing, fishing in the creeks and sightseeing the historic buildings and plantations.

Mama June loved the fall. Summer schedules were always bustling and everyone was dashing off somewhere. In the fall, however, the days were shorter and the lovely crispness in the air encouraged folks to take a walk in the woods.

The Blakely and Bennett families had gathered together at Sweetgrass to meet the state-authorized archeologist for a hike to the sacred spot. They drove in cars and trucks down the road to where Elmore told them to pull over and park. They'd have to go the rest of the way on foot. The vehicle path through the fields was well worn and wide, so Morgan could push Preston's wheelchair over the crisp leaves and compost for the remaining several hundred yards. When the path ended, Elmore led the way, beating a rough trail through the woods and wildflowers with a large stick. Harry and Chas flanked the wheelchair, pushing hard when they came across a rut or root. But the day was dry, the air cool, and Preston laughed for the pure joy of being out of doors in the wild again.

Mama June smiled, witnessing his happiness. It was a glorious day. The ground was blanketed in the vibrant purples and gold of wildflowers. Flitting over them was a cornucopia of bright orange Monarchs and fritillaries, yellow-and-black swallowtails and the sweet, common yellow sulphur butterflies that she adored.

As much as she thrilled to all these things, however, nothing prepared her for the wondrous sight that awaited her at Nona's sacred spot.

For most of the trek the group chatted and laughed in a companionable manner. Elmore led them through the dense woods toward the light of a clearing. As they drew nearer to the sweetgrass field, however, a reverential hush fell upon the group. The crunch of their footfall sounded noisily against the woodland quiet. Mama June felt as though they were entering a great temple filled with light. In her mind, the souls of the departed rose up to greet them. They were entering sacred ground.

Leaving the dark woods, she stepped out onto a low ridge overlooking the sun-kissed clearing. Mama June's breath was swept away in a gasp. There, in the breadth of land between marsh and forest, the low, undulating coastline was aflame with a sea of brilliant pink sweetgrass in full bloom. The whistling wind rippled the grass, cutting across the acres like waves across a rosy ocean.

Interspersed among clumps of sweetgrass, she could see a few dozen broken white headstones. She had never seen a more heavenly eternal resting place.

Nona came closer to link arms with Mama June. They looked into each other's eyes and felt the bond resonate between them. Nona knew of her and Preston's decision to leave Sweetgrass for a care facility. She knew, too, how hard this leave-taking would be for everyone.

"I know you've a lot on your mind. But I always say it's best to make major decisions in a cemetery," Nona told her. "Puts everything in perspective."

Nona smiled and squeezed her arm, then moved on to join the archeologist and other family members.

Mama June stayed back with Preston. Together, they watched the ragtag army march through the field to investigate the secrets of the gravesite. Elmore, Nona, Maize, Grace and Kwame led the group. Morgan, Kristina, Nan, Harry and Chas followed. And with a jaunty step, Blackjack brought up the rear. His black tail wagged in the air like a metronome through cotton candy.

Yes, Mama June thought, our children *will* weep when we are gone.

She moved to stand behind Preston's wheelchair and placed her hands on his shoulders. He reached up to grasp hold of one and held tight.

This was a bittersweet moment for them. Mama June's gaze swept across the fields, and she thought their leaving in the autumn was an appropriate metaphor for their lives spent together at Sweetgrass. Together, she and Preston had shared the impulsive passion of spring and the lush, halcyon days of summer, with all its storms. And now, looking at their children and friends gathered at this sacred spot, they celebrated the harvest of their life together. Mama June sighed, knowing that the season that followed was the quiet serenity of winter. This season, too, would have its own sparkling moments.

She looked at the man with whom she'd spent most of her life. Preston's eyes were as bright a blue as the sky, and his hair as white as the cumulus clouds overhead. His chin was upright and noble as he looked out over his beloved land, land that he'd cared for for so many years, just as his father and grandfathers had before him. Now his son would act as its steward.

Likewise, Maize would carry on to protect this sacred spot that held her ancestors and all the precious sweetgrass that bloomed across it for generations to come.

She patted his shoulder. Preston turned his head, his gaze searching hers.

"Let's not be sad. Someday we can come back to Sweetgrass, you know. The kitchen house will be perfect for us. After all, it's where we began our life together. It's only fitting that it be where we end it. But for now, my dear, it's time to carve out a little peace for ourselves, just for you and me. Someplace where you will grow strong again, with me right by your side."

Mama June leaned close to press her cheek against Preston's and fervently whispered, "All for *us*."

AUTHOR'S NOTE

There are countless, wonderful sources of information concerning sweetgrass and the art of basket making. I've listed only those few that I have directly quoted from in my chapter headings and recommend them to anyone interested in learning more about this ancient art form.

Dufault, Robert J., Mary Jackson, Stephen K. Salvo. *Sweetgrass: History, Basketry, and Constraints to Industry Growth.* p. 442-445. In: J. Janick and J.E. Simon (eds), *New York, New Crops,* 1993.

McLaughlin, J. Michael. "Sweetgrass Baskets, the Quintessential Lowcountry Souvenir." and "Island Memories." *Wild Dunes Island Resort,* pp.28-32.

Raven, Margot Theis and E. B. Lewis. *Circle Unbroken: the Story of a Basket and Its People.* New York: Farrar, Strauss and Giroux, 2004.

Rosengarten, Dale. *Row Upon Row: Sea Grass Baskets of the South Carolina Lowcountry.* Columbia: McKissick Museum, University of South Carolina, c. 1986.

Weir, Carol. "Weavers Continue Decorative Tradition." *The Island Packet.*

ACKNOWLEDGMENTS

The author is grateful to Daisy Porcher and Joseph Stoudenmire, Gabriele G. Gregorie, Shay Gregorie, Elizabeth Gregorie, Phillip and Georgia Ann Porcher, and John J. Mahoney for sharing knowledge, history and favorite haunts along Porcher's Creek and Porcher's Bluff. Thanks also to sweetgrass basket sewers Elizabeth Bennett, Florence Coakley, Vera M. Manigault and her mother, Ethel J. Manigault, Harriett Bailem Brown, Joseph Foreman, Mae Hall, Ruth Singleton Middleton and Annie Scott.

For assisting with my research, thanks to Karl Ohlandt, Dale Rosengarten and her book *Row upon Row*, Dr. Noreen Herring, Eleanor Jones, Dr. Judy Stoewe, Charlotte and Ken Tarr. Thanks also to Angela May, Marjory Wentworth, Nathalie Dupree, Barbara Hagerty, Mary Edna Fraser, Mary Scholtens, Brucie and Low Harry, Catherine Sippell, Julie Beard, Cynthia and Bobby Pearlman, Paula and David Skinner, Leah Greenberg.

Thanks to my superb agents Kim Whalen and Robert Gottlieb. Also thanks to Eileen Hutton and Brilliance Audio for the marvelous audio book. And great love to Martha Keenan for her sensitive editing.

This is a novel about family, and I'm I thankful to all the many immediate and extended members of my family for the deep well of memories that I draw upon as I write.

A little girl, all alone, with a note that reads 'Please look after me'. What would you do?

Four years ago, nineteen-year-old Travis Brown made a choice: to raise his newborn daughter on his own. So far he's kept her safe, but now he's lost his job, his home and the money in his wallet is all he has.

As things spiral out of control Travis is offered a lifeline. A one-time offer to commit a crime for his daughter's sake. Even if it means leaving her behind. Even if it means losing her.

What would a good father do?

www.mirabooks.co.uk

M262_TGF

'What was so extraordinary about her? What did she have that I'm so horribly deficient in?'

As your husband grieves his mistress,
you find yourself falling for the family she left behind,
but they don't really know you.

You can go back to the husband who loves you
second best or be content to live as a pale
imitation of another woman.

Two paths, two lies.
Which way would you turn?

www.mirabooks.co.uk

Best friends. Two worlds.
One second chance.

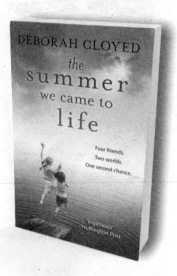

Every summer, Samantha Wheland joins her
childhood friends on a holiday. But this year
one of the gang is missing.

Since Sam's best friend Mina lost her battle against
cancer six months ago, she's been struggling to
find her way forward without her. Lost and left
behind, Sam finds herself relying on the diary
Mina gave her before she died.

www.mirabooks.co.uk

I suppose in the beginning it was a love story...

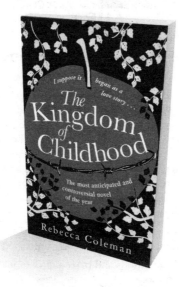

You've fallen for your son's best friend.
You are a teacher.
You are abusing your power, your responsibility...
your student.
You know it's wrong. But you cannot stop.
A love story. A horror story.
Innocence, forbidden, obsession.

Controversial, unsettling and fascinating—
you won't be able to stop talking about
The Kingdom of Childhood.

www.mirabooks.co.uk

M263_TKOC

MIRA

The mark of a good book

At MIRA we're proud of the books we publish, that's why whenever you see the MIRA star on one of our books, you can be assured of its quality and our dedication to bringing you the best books. From romance to crime to those that ask, "What would you do?" Whatever you're in the mood for and however you want to read it, we've got the book for you!

Visit **www.mirabooks.co.uk** and let us help you choose your next book.

★ **Read** extracts from our recently published titles

★ **Enter** competitions and prize draws to win signed books and more

★ **Watch** video clips of interviews and readings with our authors

★ **Download** our reading guides for your book group

★ **Sign up** to our newsletter to get helpful recommendations and **exclusive discounts** on books you might like to read next

www.mirabooks.co.uk